For (

THE SACRIFICIAL
WOOD

The story very intriguing.. The meaning, more so.

8-18-24

OTHER TITLES IN THE FAITHWALKER SERIES
BY DARRYL S. MARKOWITZ

Call of the Tree: Book One
The Dead Forest: Book Three
Succession: Book Four
Unnatural Disaster: Book Five

THE SACRIFICIAL
WOOD

THE FAITHWALKER SERIES BOOK TWO

DARRYL MARKOWITZ

FaithWalker Publishing

The Faithwalker Series:
Book II: The Sacrificial Wood

Copyright © 2008 by Darryl Markowitz.

Third Edition 2021

All rights reserved. No part of this book may be reproduced or transmitted in any form or by any means, electronic or mechanical, including photocopying, recording or storing information in a retrieval system, without prior written permission from the publisher.

This is a work of fiction. Names, characters, places, and incidents either are the product of the author's imagination or are used fictitiously, and any resemblance to actual persons, living or dead, businesses, companies, events or locales is entirely coincidental.

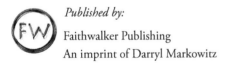

Published by:
Faithwalker Publishing
An imprint of Darryl Markowitz

Cover and Interior Design: Creative Publishing Book Design
Cover Art: Bogdan Maksimovic

ISBN Paperback: 978-0-9818469-8-9
ISBN eBook: 978-0-9818469-9-6

Printed in the United States of America

Acknowledgements

My deep appreciation to my dear wife who is an integral part of my life, who knows the pain of keeping faith, but keeps it anyway.

About the author

Since fourteen-years-old responsibility came to this author's understanding that to understand WHAT is Life, Love, Wisdom, Understanding, Justice, Truth, and Peace is more than a calling, it is the reason for our Being. It needs to be pursued with all one's heart, mind, soul, and strength. Darryl Markowitz's books fulfill that purpose. Nothing else is more relevant than the sincere search.

The characters and events in The Faithwalker Series books are fictitious. Any similarities to real persons, living or dead, are coincidental and not intended by the author.

CHAPTER ONE

Into Every Life A Little Rain Must Fall

"Father, I am eighteen now. What does it mean that I am a man?" The Prince had grown taller and more muscular than the King.

"My son, what do you want it to mean?"

Surprised, he looked the King in the eye, "Is it about what I want, or about what truly defines a man?"

"That is an excellent question, but I thought that is what I said!"

His son nodded. "It is also true for a woman."

King Mafferan reached out his right hand and his son respectfully, firmly took hold. Once again his father leveled his eyes into his son's. "Which hand is holding the other?"

Fred's home was the best Stephanie had ever seen, with modern working appliances, immaculate furniture, and a cleanliness that bordered on sterility. Stephanie had now become a major component of that cleanliness, having been assigned many upkeep chores. "It's not fair to everyone else that you bring your filth into the house. You must help keep it clean," her father had told her. There seemed to be more implications than could be put into words as to what that filth actually was. But practically, it translated into her being a twenty-four-hour maid service. Her father had fired the hired help upon her arrival. Her chores began that hour.

At first, she told herself it was the same meaning as when Vaughn encouraged her to keep her self-respect by washing up and brushing her teeth. After her mother's funeral, she hadn't felt like doing either. Then she said to herself, *I've been struggling very hard to be a clean woman inside. It's hard work to be a truly right woman in thoughts and feelings. Scrubbing the floors, the walls, and dusting and such, is sorta like the hard work inside myself.*

While she cleaned, she prayed to be a pure woman, to understand more deeply how she had been tricked into the evils of her past, and what words she might one day be able to use to help others be free. But her memories still brought her profound shame. It made her scrub the floors even harder. It seemed her memories troubled her more now, than they had in the place that had generated them.

But cleanliness is supposed to bring happiness . . . why then, the more I live in this house, do I feel emptiness? I never had such a beautiful bed. It's better than Tracy's bed. I never ate better, but . . .

In one way, Stephanie's previous life never existed. There was zero conversation relating to her past. Yet, every time she

SACRIFICIAL WOOD

passed by her father, her past is all that wordlessly shouted from him – a continual punishment for ever having existed. It was in the immediate flashes of anger and disgust in his eyes, how he stiffened every time Stephanie passed by him as if a bad odor had just wafted in. For Fred, she was someone who must be kept busy. There had to be a reason to justify her presence, her very existence on this planet.

What's the meaning of all these luxuries? I used to cry for even a single doll. Lana has plenty of dolls . . . but Oh God, what is happening to her? What's happening to me? I feel so empty. What am I?

After three weeks, Stephanie finally got a chance for time to herself. She needed privacy, but her father had planned out every second of her days and nights. Yet, from working extra hard to please him, he finally relented, showing slight surprise that she was so compliant. It took every ounce of her strength to effectively maintain the facade. But she knew it wasn't working. It was just a matter of time.

Every night she wept silently. In the darkness her terrible past and present twisted together into grotesqueness. They seemed to feed off each other. Yes, she now understood more and more the feelings that had driven her into degradation. *Too much so, perhaps,* she whispered out loud to herself.

She didn't dare let anyone hear her crying. But now, her father had taken every one else out to dinner, so she finally retrieved Vaughn's envelope she had hidden away. *The secret to his strength and the reason he loves me,* she remembered. *Oh God, I need it now.*

3

She held the envelope sacredly in her hands before opening it. Finally, she delicately separated the sealed flap and pulled out a single sheet of paper. Immediately, she wept at the sight of the title and it took some time to regain herself.

The Helpless Finds Help
*What twisted forsaking
has caused such a disease?
That I should be reared
in ignorance and misery?*

*Where those I looked
even way up to,
have given me emptiness,
raised me to be so too?*

*What terrible canker
has eaten away the root?
Those who were given to sustain,
have disdained to bring forth fruit.*

*Yet, in spite of it all
I found within myself
that which had no place
on the tree that brought me forth.*

*And when they found
this fruit might be good to eat,
they chopped off the branch,
and tried to trample it under their feet.*

❖ SACRIFICIAL WOOD ❖

*I thank God for being merciful,
for blessing me with love.
To be disowned for this sake
is my deliverance from this hell.*

From Vaughn to Stephanie with all my love
*(We can't have all things to please us,
no matter how hard we try)*

Stephanie wailed for a long time. She could hear Vaughn singing that mournful tune from some long forgotten person named Jillian from a country called Wales that no longer existed. *We can't have all things to please us* . . . and she ached for his comfort now. She remembered asking later, *But what if there are* no *things to please us?* But for Vaughn, there was always goodness to be had, no matter what. *No matter what,* kept echoing in her mind.

Pictures upon feeling pictures flooded her. There were also pictures of goodness, of grasping hope and desire for real life. But these words from his poem burned within her. *In spite of it all* . . .

As she held the sheet of paper sacredly in both hands, she felt the love, Vaughn's presence, and all the growth she accomplished before she was forced to live with her father, before her mother was murdered, before she was sent away to the other side of the country, thousands of miles from her only true love. All of it came rushing back into her.

But the profoundness of that growth of true love, true goodness, and that understanding, and her desire to feel it again, now, mysteriously vanquished her present miseries. *In spite of it all,* she whispered, as she could feel impending doom clawing around the edges of her tentatively newborn solace.

This poem addresses exactly what I need to do. She bowed her head and thanked God for all His blessings. *Whatever fate I have to meet, I will meet it with this knowledge, this feeling. We can't have all things to please us, no matter how hard we try. So I'll just appreciate what I do have.* She whispered through her prayers, *Thank you Vaughn for your secret. Love transforms us within and delivers us from the hideous fate of being the loveless. To love is a treasure not to be compared to any suffering! Even when you're not here Vaughn, you are with me.* She knew it was just a matter of time before her father sent her away. She didn't know how she knew, or how she could be so sure, but she knew. She wondered what it would be like to be locked away on the State Work Farm.

☙

Stephanie finally enrolled in school and she had to make up all the work she missed, as she started three weeks late. There were rumors amongst the other high school students that before the Second Civil War that successfully split the United States, before the Great Religious World War that caused the Second Civil War a hundred years ago, well, these were just rumors, but it was said that the children in schools were out of control. She shook her head, *That's hard to believe! Anyway, what good does it do to think about it?*

Somehow, Stephanie didn't know how, but she did all her school work and still maintained most of her chores. Jean,

Fred's wife, had pleaded with Fred to be allowed to do some of Stephanie's housework, seeing as how she was in school. She also gave Stephanie a weekend day to go to the library to study. Fred didn't like it one bit, but when Jean pointed out that libraries were the greatest accomplishments of *man*, and that he always wants them to appreciate more deeply the greatness of *men*, he relented.

Stephanie, in her blue flowery, long dress with short sleeves, sat at a shiny brown table with books strewn in front of her. The library had stacks upon stacks upon tall stacks of books and ancient card catalogues and computers that sometimes worked. But the task was daunting. Still, she was out of the house, and it kept Vaughn in her heart as she searched to fulfill her promise to him. *King Metran, where are you?* As she thumbed through yet another index, a sweet voice interrupted her concentration.

"Hi, what ya doin'?" she said with a soft smile while she set her school books down, sitting at the table next to Stephanie's. She didn't look like anyone Stephanie had ever seen before, inside or out. Her long, thick, straight black hair shined with a vibrancy that accentuated the same quality in her face, but she wasn't oriental. She had large, rich brown eyes, the same strange brown as Stephanie's, and a golden tan complexion. She wore a black, sleeveless top and a long black skirt, but her modesty tempered her extreme beauty. To match her physical presence, kindness seemed to radiate from her and something more that Stephanie couldn't even begin to understand.

Stephanie smiled with instant appreciation. "Oh, hi, I'm trying to find some information for a friend."

"Well, I guess this is the right place to find it, huh?" she giggled and Stephanie giggled back.

"Yea, I suppose. The problem is that there are so many books here, I don't know where to start." She waved her hand around.

The young woman got up and stood next to her, sticking out her hand. "Well, let's start with, Hi, my name is Arlupo. What's yours?"

Stephanie took her hand and shook it warmly as they stared at each other. "Hi, thank you for being so kind. I'm Stephanie. You have the prettiest hair I've ever seen, so long, so straight, so black, so shiny."

Arlupo smiled shyly a half smile. She could sense that Stephanie was not only paying a compliment but asking a question with her statement about her hair. "Thank you. I'm native to this land. The Appendaho are my people, a very ancient people. The last of us live in the hills to the East a few miles from here. My father is very wise and doesn't want our people to die out completely. So he sent me and others to public school to learn your people's ways, so we can help our people survive."

Stephanie sat back in wonder, feeling an instant bond to this mysterious stranger. "Wow, I don't know anything like that. Thank you for telling me."

Arlupo looked her straight in the eye. "You have a sweet face, true eyes. Not like many I see. And, you're also very pretty, and have the most beautiful red hair I've ever seen."

Stephanie hung her head and smiled. "Thank you. Will you join me?"

The young woman pulled up the chair next to Stephanie and sat down, squaring herself around to face her. When they made eye contact again, Arlupo queried, "So, what are you looking for?"

Stephanie shuffled through some of the books and pulled out the paper Vaughn had given her. "This is the paper my friend gave me before I had to leave."

Arlupo's eyebrows rose. "Leave?"

Stephanie's head immediately dropped, staring at Vaughn's list but not really focusing on it. "Yes, I used to live way on the East side of the country with my Mother. But when she . . . died, I had to come here to live with my father." Stephanie was rubbing her thumb over Vaughn's paper as she held it. Arlupo noticed.

Her eyes focused deeply on Stephanie as she spoke softly. "I'm so sorry about your Mother. I see your pain. But I also see that your friend isn't a girl."

Stephanie picked her head up again wondering was her love for Vaughn that obvious, even this far away from him. "No."

Arlupo continued to stare deeply into Stephanie. Stephanie could feel her sweet presence enter into her soul. Arlupo continued her assessment, "And though you're young, you have a woman's love for him!"

Stephanie's eyes widened in wonder and goose bumps spread over her arms. "How do you see such things, so quickly?"

"Is it true?" They held each other's gazes. Stephanie recognized something deeply familiar in her, but she couldn't find the words to understand it. This young woman had something powerful in her eyes.

"Yes, it's true."

Arlupo spoke light-heartedly, almost a tease, "I'm not of your people. We're not raised blind. So life is easy for us to see."

※

As they hovered before the dirty blue orb, its vision of unfolding events caused spasms in their serpentine rippling and shimmering. Scraback distinctly noticed his Master's tail-tip twitch twice, nervously, but he knew better than to let GrrraGagag know he knew. Nausea spread into their great, glistening black Eyes that occupied most of their bulbous heads. It was through the precious Great Eye that they consumed. It was through the Eye that they could vomit. The worst thing in the ether would be for an Alpha to throw up. Scraback turned to his Master for understanding, but his Master seemed perplexed.

"What? Who are these people? Where are their trees? Scraback . . ."

"I'm looking, Master, but . . ."

Scraback waved his arm that protruded just below his head from the center of his serpentine body causing the orb to do a fast search for the Appendaho's ethereal trees. For every human being there also had to be an ethereal tree spiritually connected to them in the Dead Forest. How else could the Alpha tend their human crop? The trees made it far easier to prune the humans properly. Yet, there are those rare instances in time when one feels the meaning of a powerless moment sucking one into the dreaded unknown, until . . .

SACRIFICIAL WOOD

"Oh, I remember now. You won't find them in our Forest! This goes way, way back. Some kind of mystery . . . around the time of Lockula. But we were told not to worry about these people because they always secluded themselves and never mixed with outsiders. So, the High Council just decided they didn't need our attention. They have been, for the longest anyone can remember, non-people." GrrraGagag narrowed his Great Eye at the orb vision. "But now, it seems they've come out of seclusion. *Now*, we have to plant trees for them!"

Scraback's brow twisted and his ripples rippled in astonishment. "Master? How do we do *that*? I thought every one born came with a tree?"

"There are always exceptions, underling! The orb gives us the ability to deal with them. The truth of these people only the Father really knows. The files have been locked away by the Father, and even the High Council knows but a bit of them."

"Then, Master, shall we inform the . . ."

Master GrrraGagag's answer almost seemed rehearsed. "Not necessary. The rules are clearly stated. Anything in our vision belongs to us. We have a *right* to them. As long as those people stayed out of our vision, they belonged to the Council. Now they belong to me . . . ahhh . . . us."

"How do we create trees for them if they weren't born with them?"

"That's easy. We can extend our Eye through our trees to touch the treeless. Then, once they are touched, their tree will appear in our Forest and the Council can't say anything about it. Then, because more and more belong to our Forest, they also come in contact with more that need trees, and in almost no time at all they will *all* belong to our Forest. Perfection achieved. I have to say, Scraback, we owe a lot to that red-headed slut. If it wasn't for her, we wouldn't have gained such treasure. That makes destroying her all the more pleasing." The Master poked Scraback with a serious tail, emphasizing each word, "We never want to owe anyone!" It was rule six in the *Alpha Code of Ethics and Bylaws of Behavior*—A true Alpha must have no sense of obligation to another. Only then may they further our Great Purpose to purify reality. Only then does every Alpha achieve its true rank.

Scraback doubted, "Master, are we able to use Stephanie to touch them? She has all that *glow* now."

GrrraGagag growled under his breath. He never used Earth names to refer to his food, but there was no rule against it so he couldn't rebuke Scraback. "Hmm, we shall see, won't we?" The Master's Eye twinkled, its blackness turning even more vibrant. "We should first review what's been happening to her. I believe after we're done with her review, by the time we catch up to her present again, we should be able to use her. She must be temporarily avoiding her father's full influence. As soon as she finds out what's happened to her *loved one*, we'll manage her just fine. But first, let me show you where those strange people come from. It will serve as an invaluable lesson for what we must *not* do."

Scraback *hated* when his Master put his arm around his neck but didn't dare say anything about it as they both leaned closely together toward the dirty blue orb. The stench of his

SACRIFICIAL WOOD

Master's Great Eye grew worse by the moment. *It's unheard of for an Alpha not to wash his Great Eye,* Scraback secretly complained. Worse, the blue glow began to sting but Master GrrraGagag held him fast. He remembered how his Master cruelly, joyfully forced him into the orb and held him while he writhed in pain. He knew his Master would regret it. He just had to figure out how to make it come to pass. *A true Alpha would . . .*

"Look way back into the Forest, about fifteen rows from the very back, Scraback."

As soon as Scraback focused, it was as if he himself raced through endless dead trees of various maladies, all glorious, in spite of their diversity. All of them were perfectly ordered, having breaks, gashes, twists or turns in just the right spots to ensure the chaos of life didn't exist. Suddenly, the Forest came to rest in his vision through the dirty-blue of the orb at the fifteenth row. Just a little further back, and they would have seen the beginning of time itself . . . well, the beginning of their Forest anyway.

"Wow, the trees were so much bigger back then."

"They lived a lot longer," his Master taught him.

"What do those gaps in the Forest mean?"

"One was caused by a natural disaster, a great flood. Don't worry about those, now. Focus on *that* tree, there." Master GrrraGagag's tail pointed into the orb with disgust. It was one of the most magnificent trees Scraback had seen with its trunk wider than any other. Sprawling dead branches reached so far out that they hovered over many trees. Each branch twisted in perfectly ordered twists. None were broken, so that meant pruning away life wasn't even necessary. Then, mysteriously, the top was chopped off and there was a gaping split in its perfectly dead trunk. The split looked out of place and ugly and made Scraback shudder.

"Master, is that split supposed to be there?"

"Mmm, it is hideous, isn't it? That's because it's the wrong kind of death to be in that tree!"

Bewildered, Scraback protested, "Huh?"

GrrraGagag's grip tightened even more as he nudged his underling a bit more into the orb. "All will be made clear if you just do as you're *told*." Scraback well understood his Master's inflected frustration and focused on Lockula's tree. The tree turned into a vision of his past. Scraback noticed his Master seemed to be calmer, lately. *I wonder why?*

On top of a green hill, between marble pillars, Lockula sat on his throne. His golden hair, muscles to the full, light brown eyes and a will like steel seemed to dominate everything, everywhere. He gazed over the mountains in the distance and seeing a hawk flying higher than he thought right, he called to it. Racing toward him, it plunked at his feet, quivering in its death throws.

"Mafferan, do you see that I don't allow anything to think itself higher than me?"

"Yes, Lord Lockula." The boy would not raise his eyes, thankful that his curly, dark brown hair hid them when his head was bowed. He tried not to think or feel anything about the hawk. He was only twelve years old and had been serving for three years. Why he was chosen, he could not fathom. All he knew was that he had a burning desire to live, which he hid as best he could from the all-knowing *lord*.

"You *will* forever serve me, and one day, if you keep bringing me beautiful women, I may let you share one, for an hour." He laughed, pleased with himself.

"Yes, Lord Lockula. Thank you for your kindness," came his soft, emotionless words as he realized he was staring too long at the dead bird.

Lockula stretched out his bare, muscular arm and pointed behind the boy. "Go over there and bring me that big rock."

Mafferan did not turn around, but spoke instead. "Lord? How am I to bring such a huge thing?"

"Like this . . ." He reached out his arm with his hand open, then closed it partway as if to pick up something. Then, as his arm lifted, so did the boulder. He brought his arm inward, and the boulder raced to him, almost knocking Mafferan in the head had he not ducked reflexively. He knew all of Lockula's games. But Lockula squeezed his hand tightly. The boulder crumbled to dust above the boy, covering him in grit and powder, choking his breath.

He praised the king as he hacked up the dust. "That is very powerful, Lord. I cannot even think how one could do such a thing."

"I know. Your minds are so weak. I don't think you can think at all. At least this hawk could soar as I can." Then he looked more plaintively at the boy. "Mafferan, I'm bored with my people. What can I do with them so I'll not be bored?"

Such questions, such a tone always began some new twisted torture. Mafferan tried his best to copy the tone in his reply.

"Lord, they feed you, pleasure you, give you their honor and respect, you are their god, what more could you want?"

Lockula threw out his hand and Mafferan went flying, then Lockula caught him in midair and suspended him there. "*Idiot*, do you think I don't understand every puny little thought you have. When you call me a god, make sure it's with a capital G, *God*."

"Forgive me, LORD Lockula."

Overwhelmed, Scraback's arm grabbed his Master, not thinking of the disrespect. "Amazing! There were men like that? Why are they no longer around? Lockula was so much like us. He…" Scraback lost control of himself. A dangerous thing to do, but for some reason, GrrraGagag ignored him.

"*Idiot*, he was only a shadow of us. We showed him that part of his mind to do those things. He was supposed to rule the Earth forever."

Bewildered again, Scraback forced the question, "What happened?"

"The young man killed him."

Scraback's indignation twisted himself around to put his Eye into his Master's, shouting, "*What?*"

For some reason, Master GrrraGagag actually seemed to be enjoying himself. "That's right, even we underestimated him, otherwise we would have warned *Lord* Lockula. It took us days to figure it out. Every contingency was guarded against. Even the food he ate wasn't able to be poisoned."

SACRIFICIAL WOOD

Scraback intensely immersed himself into the orb, ignoring its stinging blue glow. He hated his Master bating him. "But I see the people brought him his food."

"Oh *that*, he burnt that up as a sacrifice to himself. He only ate directly from special trees from which he picked fresh for himself every day."

"How was he killed?"

"Poisoned."

In pain, Scraback reflexively tightened his coils up against his head and whispered, "What?"

Enjoying the various twistings and turnings of his student's Eye, GrrraGagag pointed his tail. "Look and see if you can figure it out. There's a special tree file right here." He flipped his tail sideways, its tip darting across the orb's control center, which consisted of various off-blue colors, every much as ethereal as the rest of the orb. "This is a compilation of all observations on the boy's activities." Tap, tap, tap went the Master's tail. Every tap added to his delight.

Scraback reviewed the days Lockula went about ruling his people, of him being pampered, being sadistic, being bored. He had decided to sacrifice a human being once a week from a random drawing. Of course, with his power, it was never really random, and people began to suspect as much, more so when the people who always got selected had, in some small way, offended his Highness. Of course, *Lord* Lockula knew their thoughts, which made it all the more effective and fun. The terror fascinated him. The depth of control was simply intoxicating. And then one day he clutched his belly, curled up into a ball like an infant in the womb, shrieked a miserable cry, turned red, and died.

Scraback was confident he would be able to figure it out. But Ethereal sweat began to drip off his bulbous head near the end of his fifth time through and he was getting Eye strain, and unfortunately unable to hide his disappointment.

"I'm sorry Master GrrraGagag, but I don't see how."

"Details, Underling, details. Look there, what is the boy doing?" GrrraGagag pointed deep into the orb shaking the very tip of his tail for fine detail.

Mafferan had a shovel and was loosening and heaping dirt around one of his lord's apple trees.

"He's cultivating the tree."

"Now watch closely . . . closely, right *there*." The tail whipped with frightening speed, pointing, the very tip vibrating. But Scraback didn't see anything interesting.

"Where?"

GrrraGagag grabbed him tighter with his arm and shook him, jabbing his tail at the scene. "There, right there, watch his left leg." *This is so much fun. When I shake him, his head bounces all around. It's a wonder he can see anything.*

"Ahhhh, huh? I think I saw a rock drop from inside the bottom of his pant leg. So?"

"Now watch the next day, and the next, and the next…"

Scraback did a quick orb review and in minutes gave his summation. "Hmmmm, every day he did the same thing for, for, for…five years! But I still…"

"Arsenic or something. The rocks carried a poison. It took five years for the concentration to build enough in the soil to where the fruit would absorb a lethal dose. Or at least that's our best guess. But no one can figure out why he died so suddenly, why he didn't get sick before. We think it was a poison that has an all or none effect. It doesn't show any signs of harm until it reaches a concentration to kill you! But no one's really sure since we couldn't actually go and investigate."

"But how did the boy know of such a thing."

"Details, he paid attention to *details*. The villagers had long ago discovered the waters from the one hillside were poisoned. Animals that drank them died. They collected some of the rocks and mixed them with food scraps to control rats. But the boy knew Lockula was bigger than a rat, so he brought a lot of rocks."

"How did he know that the poison would enter the food?"
"Ahhh, details. Trees that grew near the poisoned water bore poison fruit. That's one of the reasons Lockula never ate the villagers' food."

"But then wouldn't he suspect they would try to poison his land?"

"Nope, it never occurred to his pompous mind. He knew they could bring poisoned food, but only *he* had the power to move mountains, so he figured without moving the poisoned mountain to him, he was safe eating directly from his own trees. Detailsss…*small* details. It never occurred to him that through tiny deeds of rebellion, a tiny rock here, there, there, that *that* could bring down one such as him. That's why I chose him as your example, so you will always pay attention to *details*." The tapping stopped and GrrraGagag set himself directly in front of his student to evaluate him.

Scraback continued to ask questions, "But he knew all his thoughts. Why didn't he discover his plan?

"Even though he had the ability to read them all, I don't think he ever checked. And even if he did, I don't think he would have believed it. The first thought he would have seen was that the young man wanted to poison him. He would have dismissed it as impossible and not looked any deeper. Or, say he found the thought that he would poison him by putting a small rock under his tree. It sounds absurd. A small rock is not a mountain."

"But surely, the boy must have been afraid and doubted whether his plan would even work, so why even attempt it when…let me find his tree." But out of the corner of Scraback's Great Eye he saw his Master flinch.

"You can't do that." GrrraGagag said, looking away.

Scraback sensed this was something he should really understand. "Why?"

"Because his tree isn't there!"

"What? But that's impossible. I saw him."

"You saw him through *Lockula's* tree and others in the file!" GrrraGagag's tail pointed, "Right there is where the young man's tree *used* to be, that *gap* right there!"

"What happened to it?"

◈ SACRIFICIAL WOOD ◈

Master GrrraGagag curled his tail around his own neck, scratching his head with its tip. "It's a matter of great debate, as are the others who are missing. Some say that the Father was so angry that he simply annihilated his existence. Others say the people were so upset that Mafferan killed their Lord that they tore him limb from limb, and begged their god to take away his very existence. But others say....never mind." The Master flung his tail down in deep disgust which made Scraback all the more persistent.

"What? What do others say?"

With a lowered Eye and an ephemeral scowl GrrraGagag whispered, "That Mafferan was born with a glowing trunk, and since it was so early in time, we didn't know very well how to deal with such a one. We thought that having him serve Lockula would be sufficient. Some say, that one day, after some years of Mafferan's rule..."

Scraback turned sickly gray all over. "His rule?"

"Of course he took over. Those were *glowing* times for us, before we learned better. Some say, after years of his rule, his tree caught fire and burned up! These Appendaho are his offspring. We know they're his offspring because they're all treeless."

With puckering ripples, Scraback shivered all over, barely whispering, "What does it mean?"

His Master seemed to imperceptibly shudder, but there was no other trace of reaction to his question. "No one knows."

"Oh Master, please, let us continue, my Eye is longing to taste them."

They picked up with Stephanie's immediate past right where they left off earlier.

"I'm not of your people. We're not raised blind. So life is easy for us to see."

"Wow, that sounds so mysterious. I don't quite understand, but somehow I do." Stephanie's eyes went distant. "To not be raised blind, Oh God, how wonderful that must be."

Arlupo returned to the original subject. "What is it you're searching for?"

"Oh, here's the paper Vaughn gave me. I've been trying to find out about an ancient book some wise king is supposed to have written." She handed Arlupo the paper.

"Why does he want to know?" Arlupo wondered whether he had seen the news story on TV where she told of her people's ancient history. She thought to herself, *Strange, that such a story should be broadcast at all, but stranger yet, that it went national.* When the interviewer showed up on Arlupo's doorstep, she knew her father would also want her do it.

Stephanie's eyes traveled to the beyond as she thought of her only love. "I don't know why he wants to know. But Vaughn," she took a deep breath and sighed, "there is no one like him. At least, I've never met anyone at all like him. He's a thinker, and he sees and understands things that others don't."

Arlupo seemed to focus more intently on Stephanie. "And you? Does he make sense to you?"

Stephanie's eyes softened even more, "*Oh, yes*, more than anyone. That's why I love him so, besides saving me from… well…terrible things." Stephanie refocused on the young woman. "But, I don't think I've ever met anyone like you, either." It was as much a question as a statement. But Stephanie's pause was only answered by peaceful silence. "Well, does anything on that paper look familiar?"

Arlupo casually scanned it. "May I take this and show it to our elders? Perhaps they know something I don't."

Stephanie scrunched up her shoulders. "I suppose. I memorized everything on it, but it's one of the only things I have from Vaughn, so I would like it back when you're done." She felt a pain in her heart when she agreed to let Arlupo take the paper. She wondered just why she would hand over such a valuable possession. She cherished it more than anything else except the poem. But, for some reason, she couldn't resist Arlupo's request. She was so kind.

"I understand. So, where and with whom do you live?"

Stephanie looked away, hesitating. "I live with my father, his new second wife, and her daughter."

Arlupo was cheery. "Well, that's good. At least..."

But Stephanie cut her off, "*No*, it's not. But Jean's very nice, but she reminds me of my mother."

Arlupo tried again with a little extra added cheer. "Oh, well, that's good. At least..." But was cut off again.

"*No*, it's actually *not*. She reminds me of my mother when she used to be terrible."

Arlupo eased back in her chair. "Oh, but you said she's very nice."

"Yes, but she doesn't know how to value her life! She becomes whatever my father tells her to be."

Every word Stephanie spoke became more strained than the previous and Arlupo noted it. In fact, she had never been so drawn in by another's focus. All of a sudden Arlupo felt a strange feeling.

Sadness! Only ancient tales told of such feelings. She noted that, too, but moved on.

"What about your sister?"

Stephanie's answer was in reverse of the last. It became less strained as it proceeded. "She's not my sister. She's her daughter but not my father's. She's five years old and I like her very much. We play together…but…I'm worried about her."

"Why?"

Stephanie hung her head while she spoke, forcing down a lump in her throat. "Because I see my father doing the same thing to her as he did to me."

Arlupo's expression deepened as she sensed…felt her meaning. "What did he do to you?" she asked softly, trying to hide the gravity of her own feelings for her new friend. Arlupo let out a slow, hidden sigh.

"He…confused me terribly, made me hate what I am, and made me think I could never be…anything."

Arlupo summoned her will to hold back any tear trying to push outward. Her father had warned her she would come in contact with many things that didn't exist in their secluded life. She took Stephanie's hand. "Oh…I'm so sorry…but what about now? You seem to understand something about these things now."

SACRIFICIAL WOOD

Stephanie picked up her head, looking straight into Arlupo's eye with all the strength and determination she could muster. "He's still trying to do that, but I know better. I try to agree with him as much as possible. I try to find some truth to what he says or does, but mostly, I just try to make him *think* I agree. But I'm scared, because..."

Stephanie looked away again, biting her lip. Arlupo placed her hand on her shoulder. New thoughts were instantly generated within Stephanie.

Her hand on my shoulder feels so comforting. I can feel her goodness through her hand. No one has ever made me feel comforted before except for Vaughn. But this is different... like......like...her eyes are so dear, warm, loving...like a sister.

"Stephanie, right?" Arlupo broke Stephanie's private interlude.

"Yea, sorry. I got lost in thought."

The young woman leveled her eyes into Stephanie's and squeezed her shoulder tighter. She spoke with a touch of force, "Stephanie, why are you so scared?"

Damn, Stephanie thought, *I don't want to cry.* She turned away again but couldn't keep from sniffing. "Because I don't want what happened to me to happen to Lana ...and I think my father will soon send me away!"

Arlupo had determined to keep her poise. *One thing at a time,* she told herself. "Lana? Your sister?"

"Yeah, I suppose you could call her my sister."

"Stephanie, it seems that you already love her. I think you can call her that. I think, especially at her age, she would see you as that."

Stephanie shook her head in disagreement. Arlupo folded her hands again as she listened. "Oh no, I don't think so… or at least not when she gets older. My father is always saying how I don't really belong to his family, but he was obligated to take me in by the government, and how I had to earn the right to stay. So, I'm to always help Jean take care of the home and things. But *she* has me take care of Lana, which, actually, I really love to do."

"Maybe you can help Lana to understand."

Stephanie leaned forward, placing her hand atop Arlupo's. "That's just what I'm afraid of. To do that, eventually, maybe soon, I'll be saying and doing things that my father will *hate*."

I can feel her heart through her hand! Oh Light, her pain… Arlupo looked away, which was surprising to her. She had never ever looked away from anyone. But then again, she didn't know many outsiders, nor was she familiar with the particular feelings now flooding her. "I see."

Stephanie continued, "My father doesn't want any *woman* or *girl* to feel they're equal to a man. He constantly puts us down because we're female. He leaves no room for thinking or feeling any differently."

Arlupo could only listen at this point. Listen and feel. These things were more than just strange to her.

Stephanie tried to describe to her new friend what she felt. "I'm scared because I feel the truth pushing inside of me to speak. But if I do, I don't think I can survive the consequences. And I'm really not very good at keeping my mouth shut. Things have a way of just speaking for themselves in me." Despair clearly overwhelmed Stephanie. She couldn't hide her tears, so she just let them roll softly from her hung head. "I'm sorry for troubling you with all this…I shouldn't have dumped on you. It's my problem."

Stephanie went to withdraw her hand from Arlupo, but Arlupo grasped it, holding it firmly. Arlupo's young heart was near to bursting. Stephanie's explanation also helped her to understand the feelings that Arlupo absorbed through Stephanie's touch. Arlupo's thoughts had never been deeper, her secret prayers never louder. Stephanie's life flashed in Arlupo's mind and she could almost see her father, too. Stephanie could feel the presence of goodness around her. Arlupo made the invitation.

"Maybe…maybe you need some good friends, first. Would you like to meet my family? See where I come from? Meet my people?"

Stephanie felt like it just rained on her desert.

"Oh God, *really*? Oh, I would love that. But I would have to get permission first…and…I don't think they'll allow me to go." She hung her head again.

"Why doesn't Jean tell your father…?"

Stephanie vehemently shook her head, "Like I said, she's like my mother used to be. She's afraid of being without him. Now that she has a daughter, she's even more afraid. But sadly, she thinks she's helping her daughter by being with him. But she's really destroying her."

Arlupo tried again. "You know, why don't you invite me to your house? Then, I can invite you and your sister to spend time with me."

But Stephanie had an answer to that, also. "I don't know. I'm not supposed to bring anyone home. I would have to ask. But I don't think they'd allow me to bring you. I suppose we could just meet here."

But that wasn't good enough for what Arlupo had in mind. She tried again. "Do you ever have to go shopping for them?"

"Oh yes, all the time. They give me a big list."

"And how do you get it all home?"

"Well, the store is only a few blocks away, so I walk. But I usually have to make more than one trip."

Arlupo squeezed her hand tightly in affirmation. She had a look of determination. "*Good*. I'll help you carry your groceries home."

"I don't know. My father will think I was at fault for not…"

"When do you go shopping next?"

"Tomorrow."

"Good. It's supposed to rain. I'll help you carry them home so that you won't have to make extra trips in the rain. Even your father knows he would look like a complete *idiot* if he were to try to deny you help in such a situation. Even if he would say something to you alone, he wouldn't dare say it in front of a stranger. He knows enough not to risk having others know how he treats you. That kind of person knows he has to hide what he does from the general public."

Stephanie still worried. It just didn't seem possible that anything could *really* work out for her. Who was she kidding, anyway? Everything had fallen apart. Those were her feelings that she fought not to put into thoughts. "What if it doesn't rain?"

Arlupo grabbed Stephanie's shoulders with a confidence Stephanie didn't understand, proclaiming, "Stephanie, look at me! It will rain! In fact, it will pour!"

Looking at Arlupo, goose bumps climbed up Stephanie's arms and her head tingled. A feeling telling her something she couldn't understand inclined her to believe. But then she doubted again, "Then what?"

"Then you watch and see!" Arlupo's look was like steel.

Stephanie's tears pushed forth, as she searched her first *real* girlfriend's eyes. For some reason, the image of her little circular shelter she built back east in the woods flashed in Stephanie's mind. *I'm feeling so much I've never known before, just like when I used to meditate in my shelter.*

Holding each other in their gazes, they stood up and hugged each other and Stephanie, leaving the books on the table for an attendant to put away, left for home. As she walked, she drew up her memories of how she felt when she rebuilt her shelter and cried herself to sleep. Now, as tears kept flowing which she didn't understand, she compared this to her memories. *They're practically the same! But why?*

CHAPTER TWO
Past, Present, And Future

"*By a flood, rage dissolved. With a flood rage resurged. By a great quake the Earth divided more than the people but the Word.*" Mafferan frowned at his Queen's prophecy. "Yes, yes, we know this. It's past."

Yinauqua smiled, "Past, present, and future, my husband. Shall I finish?"

He sighed, and his wife knew she had given him another headache which was about to get worse. "*The sacred duty shall self-destruct. The Tree of Life shall turn to dust. No treaty made by man can protect that which he made not. Truer is the stranger at thy gate, than one from your own bowels whom ye know not. Beware the stranger, the bringer of death.*"

King Mafferan rubbed his temples.

The house was spacious with large rooms. Her father was a wealthy man, an important man. Many glass windows surrounded the new living room which had been added on for just such a show. The plush, cream color carpet had gold and dark brown patterns weaving through it. Three bedrooms meant Stephanie had her own on the second floor. They ate on a rectangular mahogany dining room table with cushioned wooden chairs to match. Stephanie didn't care for any of it. It made absolutely no difference to the quality of her life.

Jean, a pleasant, attractive woman, now around thirty, with long dark blond hair and blue eyes, hastily spoke, "Stephanie, have you set the table, yet? Your father will be home any minute."

"Yes, Jean…"

Her step-mother quickly corrected her, "Don't call me that. You know what your father said." "I'm sorry, Mom."

They heard the front door open.

"Daaaaady's hooome…Daaaaaadyyyy…"

"*No, Lana!*" They both screamed, but Stephanie got there first and scooped her up.

"I've got her Mom. Lana, Daddy doesn't like to be bothered when he comes home. Would you like to help me with his silverware?"

"Yeaaaaah…" she eagerly agreed to please.

Walking in, he ceremoniously held out his brief case, waiting. "I'm hungry. I *hope* you have dinner ready. I'm *tired*. I worked hard today."

Jean rushed over and took the case and set it in the corner behind the door. "I'm sorry Fred. Let me take your shoes off." He balanced on her as she kneeled over and lifted one foot at a time.

Lana desperately sought his attention. "Daddy...Daddy...*Daddy*, I...I...I put your 'siverare' on the table....Daddy...*Daddy*, I put..."

He spoke to his wife, "I swear, things just don't run like they used to. How am I supposed to get supplies to everyone if the recorders don't *clearly* mark the records of what they've received? I told them they need to have *men* in the warehouse. It's not women's work."

"Daddy...DAAAAAADYYYY..."

"But Fred, how do you know it was the wom..."

"You *would* ask a question like that. Everyone knows women aren't cut out to understand or be quick on industrial supplies."

"DAAAA..."

"Shhhhhhhhhhh...Didn't they get trained, Fred?"

"It doesn't matter. It's against their nature. They can't think like that."

"I guess you're right."

He pointed his big finger in his wife's face. "That's exactly the problem with women. They *guess* at things, instead of *knowing* things. But in this case, it's not natural for them to know *anything*.

Just like Stephanie here, she thinks she knows *everything*, but she knows *nothing*." Stephanie hated him pointing his big finger at her but she held her breath as she sat down next to Lana at the table. He sat down at the table's head.

Stephanie's heart tightened and her head ached. She spoke timidly, "Father? I'm sorry. Why do you think I act arrogantly?"

He pressed his attack. "*You see*? That's what I'm talking about. Just listen to how you speak to me! You think big words make you smart? Then you act like you don't know what you do."

She kept her head bowed. Yet, for all she had suffered from this man, she still spoke with the pain of longing for his affection, "Father, I haven't had much conversation with you." She fought the tear creeping into her eyes, lest her father be angry. She wished her father could know her, know that she still had love for him.

He attempted to correct her speech. "You mean you don't *talk* much to me. See how simple it is to talk plainly? And why is that, that you don't *converse* much with me? Because you think you know so much. I don't know what that woman I left you with put into your head young lady, and I use the term 'lady' *very* generously, but I expect a big attitude change from you."

Her mother redirected, "I'll talk to her, Fred."

"You had better. Stephanie, take Lana for a walk and don't be back until dark."

"Yes, Father." The children got up before dinner and began to go outside. It was usually pleasant weather where they lived on the West coast.

"Even the way you say *Father*. You should be thankful to me for giving you a place to live…working so hard for you. Listen how Lana calls me Daddy."

Lana figured this was finally her opportunity. "Daddy, I set…"

Her father snapped at her interruption, "Don't *interrupt*. It's not ladylike to interrupt a man. What's happening here? Ever since *you* showed up, my wife questions me, my daughter interrupts me. *Things* had better change around here. Now get going."

"Yes Fath…Daddy. C'mon Lana, let's go to the park and play. Don't cry."

As hungry as she was, she was relieved to be out that house. She never liked eating with him, anyway. *I wonder if he's always had that gray arm thing reaching inside his head.* Stephanie had toyed with the idea that moving across country would bring an end to the odd 'things' she was seeing. She recalled just four months ago, for the first time, seeing that transparent gray arm, a cross between a human arm and an octopus tentacle, reaching inside that little girl's head… *Right before that brat hurt that other girl.*

Stephanie shook her head, sighing, this time not able to keep the words from her mind. *I'm going to be sent away…if my father doesn't kill me first.* Of all the background feelings she now had, the feeling of impending death couldn't be ignored any longer. *Vaughn's right. Evil is an active entity. Vaughn…oh Vaughn, we're supposed to fight this together, whatever those arm things are, anyway, and what about those people still blowing up from the inside out? And that blackness I saw coming out of that monster?*

"Who's Vaughn?" Lana asked. "What monster?"

Stephanie hadn't realized she was thinking aloud while she walked Lana to a nearby park. She found an empty bench near the entrance so they sat down. The sun was low in the sky, but her father meant dark, not sunset. Since they lived atop a hill, it would be sometime before returning. Lana sat up on her knees on the bench so she could be at eye level with her sister. She tugged on Stephanie's dress sleeve, her own pink, frilly dress flapping in the refreshing breeze and her long, straight, light brown hair was blowing everywhere.

"Why does Daddy hate me?" The child's deep gray eyes bore the question deep into Stephanie's soul, like a fish hook stuck deep in the gullet that can't be retrieved without splitting the fish open. This was the trap that Stephanie dreaded, desperately wanted to avoid, but knew she couldn't.

If I tell her the truth, she won't understand, she's too little. If I tell her a little bit, that she can *understand…she'll repeat it and I'll get in trouble… If I don't explain, then there's nothing to keep her from being harmed. Oh God, what do I do?*

"*Stephie*, why does Daddy hate me?" She tugged insistently at her sister's arm to pull her attention. Finally, Stephanie couldn't resist turning around to within inches of Lana's face because the child held herself so close. Lana put her little hands on her sister's shoulders to hold her attention and to keep balance. Little children always love to be up close when they talk. They often love to touch the face they talk to. Perhaps it helps them to understand.

Stephanie spoke from her heart, since her mind was at a standoff, not knowing what to do. "Lana, he was my Daddy a long time before he was your Daddy. Do you see how much bigger I am than you?"

She nodded vibrantly, "Yeah, you're like Mommy and Daddy, 'cept you're their child like me."

Stephanie smiled. Then again, there was hardly an occasion when she didn't smile at Lana. Lana tickled her heart and made it giggle. "Well, that's pretty right. Well, Lana, I know things about Daddy that you don't, because he's been my Daddy a long time."

Lana's face turned serious. "Yeah, Daddy said you would say that and I wasn't to listen."

That didn't surprise Stephanie. She sighed, "Is it true what I said?"

"Yeaaaah." Again nodding, making her hair flop even more around.

Lana reached out, carefully pushing Stephanie's hair away from her big sister's face so she could see her better. But it kept flopping back, too. Stephanie quickly took it in both hands, rolled it up into a ball and twisted it somehow. It stayed all bunched up in one big lump at the back of her head so the breeze wouldn't just blow it everywhere. Lana paid close attention how she did it. Then Stephanie melted her gaze into Lana's eyes. Reaching out with her little hand to Stephanie's cheek, her little deep gray eyes stared intently at Stephanie's every detail.

"Daddy meant for you not to listen if I lied. Am I lying?"

Lana emphatically shook her head, "Noooooo, lying is very *bad*."

Stephanie nodded her head. "That's right. So you can listen to me if I tell you the truth."

"Oh yes, because Daddy always tells the truth. He's the best Daddy in the world, because he works so hard for us." She paused, looking down. "So, why does Daddy hate me?" Then, Lana looked up and locked Stephanie within her little gaze and was holding on.

Stephanie couldn't bear to break it. "Maybe, it's not that he hates you. Maybe he doesn't know how to love you?"

"Huh?" she shook her head in bewilderment.

"Some people don't know how to love, Lana."

Her little eyes opened wide. "Really? I know how to love. It's easy." Her little arms wrapped Stephanie around the neck, squeezing hard and Lana kissed her on her cheek. Stephanie's heart sang.

Oh, I so love it when she gives me these cute little hugs and kisses.

Then Lana pulled back to within inches of her face and informed her, "And, you know how to love, too, Stephie. Mommy knows how. How come Daddy don't?" The intensity flared again in her little eyes.

"A better question is, how can we teach him to love?"

Lana pushed back from her sister, her eyes as wide as could be. "*Teach* Daddy? Daddy knows everything."

Fear suddenly smothered Stephanie from all around.

Oh God, what have I done? He'll send me to the State Work Farm for sure. If she tells him what I said, that'll make him think even more that I think I know so much. But…but…I do know more than him…but…but…how can I hide what I am from him when my very knowledge makes me what I am? I can't unknow something…and darn it, I wouldn't want to. Then I wouldn't be me…I'm me. Even when I try to act ignorant, he sees right through it. Oh God…

Stephanie didn't realize what she was doing. Her thoughts seemed to transport her to another dimension. Lana brought her back by holding her cheek again. Love from her little hand entered Stephanie's private world, calling her to return.

"Stephie, don't *cry*. I'm sorry. I won't tell Daddy *anything*. I don't like it when he yells at us. I don't think Mommy loves me very much either!"

The shock of her childlike, frank admission brought Stephanie's head up. This little girl was as lost and alone as she had ever been. "Why would you say that, Lana?"

She scrunched her little shoulders. "I dun know. She won't play with me anymore. She won't sing to me anymore. She don't tuck me in bed anymore. She's always 'apolizing' to Daddy for me when I didn't do it."

Stephanie's heart broke as instant memories flooded her. She reached out and took both her little cheeks in her hands and kissed her on top of her little head, "I love you, Lana. But if you tell Daddy how we talk, he'll send me away to a very bad place."

"*Nooooo…*" Lana started to cry and Stephanie felt guilty. "Don't cry, Lana."

"I won't tell Daddy, *I promise*."

Stephanie's memories jolted her again. *A child's promise. Oh God, she reminds me of me! I remember making the same promises to…Oh God…my Mother! Oh GOD…I didn't keep them!*

❧ SACRIFICIAL WOOD ❧

Lana kept trying to push her light brown hair out of her face, but the wind kept blowing it back. Then she sort of harrumphed and sat back on her heels and thought for a second. She reached back and gathered all her hair up and spun it around and around as she remembered Stephanie did. She looked up into her eyes, waiting. Stephanie understood the request and took her hands and guided them. When she let go, her hair was done up like her big sister's. A huge smile spread across her face. She promptly undid it and made Stephanie help her again. They practiced together for some time, doing different girl hair tricks until Lana was able to do them for herself.

☙

The next day Stephanie went shopping, and Arlupo met her on the way into the massive store. Everyone from the whole neighborhood shopped there. Stephanie divided the list, and they went their separate ways, getting all the items in half the normal time. Many of them were from the most expensive sections. Then they headed for her house.

"Wow, I can't believe how *hard* it's raining Arlupo." It was unusual weather.

Arlupo just smiled from under her rain hood, but her black hair was still soaking wet. "Here, let me hold the door for you, Stephanie."

With one foot in the door, Stephanie heard her mother's harsh tone.

"Stephanie, who is *that*?"

"I'm sorry Jea…Mom, this is…"

But Arlupo never let her friend finish her words as she pushed by her and fell to the kitchen floor on her hands and knees bowing.

Arlupo's conciliatory tone accentuated the action, "Forgive me. Oh, I'm so terribly sorry for entering your house without showing respect. My people have custom to *always*, when first entering another's house, to show respect." *I know she knows nothing of my people, so she won't know we don't actually bow like this.*

Dumbstruck, Jean stared at the dripping wet girl, her sopping black hair sticking to the kitchen floor.

Arlupo pleaded earnestly, still bowing low, "Please forgive me. Show me where to put your groceries that I helped carry and I will leave *immediately*."

Stephanie's mouth dropped wide open, still with only one foot in her house. Her mother saw Stephanie's shock. When Arlupo briefly glanced up from the floor, Jean could see that Arlupo was a native girl. In fact… *This is the girl from the TV who told those strange stories of her people!*

"Ahhhh, please, get up off the floor. You're soaking wet and shivering. You helped Stephanie carry home the groceries?"

Still bowing, she picked her head up to answer, "Yes Ma'am. When I saw how terribly much she had to carry, and that she would have to make several trips in this terrible rain, I could not help myself but to offer to help her. With my people, it is a great honor to offer help to strangers."

Jean was overcome by it all. Strangers were more and more looked down upon, worse than just ignored. When she looked into Arlupo's face and saw genuine kindness, she could hardly speak. "An honor?"

"Oh yes. Forgive me for disgracing your home. I will leave…" Arlupo quickly got up to leave, but Jean rushed forward and grabbed her.

"*No*…please, forgive *me*. I was rude to you. I shouldn't have jumped on you like that. Please…"

But Arlupo kept the same vein, "Oh, you were not wrong. It is *your* house to do with as you like."

Jean grew more insistent, pulling her further into the kitchen. Stephanie was finally able to enter, also, shutting the door, and putting her packages down on the floor. She was stunned by what she was witnessing, her mind zipping faster than she could keep track. But something of Arlupo's approach made her think of Vaughn's lectures about fighting. Except this somehow seemed even more advanced.

Her mother kept pleading, "Please, I *was* wrong. What's your name?"

Arlupo bowed her wet head once. "Arlupo. My people are the Appendaho, who live in the Western Hills east of this city."

Jean took her by the shoulders and looked her straight in the eye. "I am very glad to meet you. Come…let me help you dry off and get warm, and then I would appreciate your help in putting away the supplies. Stephanie, you know where the towels are. You have a very nice friend. I'm glad for you."

Stephanie still stood speechless. Lana, who had been peeking around the corner, couldn't take her eyes from this beautiful stranger. She kept looking back and forth between her sister and Arlupo.

☙

The kitchen had an electric stove with an oven. Every burner worked. It shined white all around them. Jean and Stephanie kept a spotless home. Her husband spent lots of money to make sure everything was in top condition. Every electric light worked and every outlet. The beige tiles on the kitchen floor were new just this year. The light brown wood of the cabinets that encircled the kitchen showed off its grain through a high polish.

This was officially dubbed, 'the good life' by Fred, her husband.

Stephanie's mother's voice, truly pleased with Arlupo, had a pep Stephanie hadn't heard before. "Well, that was a lot to put away. We just got done in time to set the table for dinner. Arlupo, would you stay for dinner? Please, you've been so much help. If it wasn't for you, we wouldn't have it ready on time. I'm sure my husband will understand that."

She bowed her head once. "I would be honored."

Lana said nothing through all of it, but she couldn't take her eyes from Arlupo's face, specifically, her strange brown eyes… that seemed to have a glow in them. Stephanie had never seen Lana study anything so intently and so quietly. Even when Stephanie gave her the silverware to place, Lana kept one eye on Arlupo.

Finally, the front door burst open followed by the usual bellow. 'I'm home. Damn it. I'm all wet. Come get this. Who's *that?*"

But Jean was ready. She wasn't hearing any of this tonight. She overmatched his power and tone. He was instantly shocked. "*That* is the reason your dinner is ready for you, a hot bath waiting for you, and why I'm glad to see you!"

A rare occasion. He was almost speechless. "Huh? Woman…"

Jean didn't allow him to continue. "In this terrible rain, she found Stephanie struggling to bring home our food. Her people believe it is a great honor to help strangers, so she helped her bring home *our* food and then to put it away, and then to prepare the house for you to come home. Stephanie and I wouldn't have had it ready for you without her."

Totally disarmed, he felt strange. "Oh…"

But she wasn't done with him. "So husband, one thing a woman does know about is house manners. What are you supposed to say?"

He hung his head. "Oh…ahhh, thank you very much for your help."

Jean helped him off with his coat. Bewildered, Stephanie took his brief case. He began pulling off his own shoes!

Arlupo stepped forward, bowing low at her waist. "Arlupo is my name, Sir. I am *terribly sorry* if my presence has offended you. It is a terrible shame to my people for us to offend a stranger, *especially our women*."

He picked his head up from pulling off his last shoe. "*Oh?* You mean, your women, to your people…"

"Appendaho. Yes, Sir. There are many strict rules to make sure our women live properly so our men will be pleased."

Fred rocked back on his heels as if receiving revelation. "*Wonderful*, so God does answer prayers! You are welcome in my home any time! Maybe you can teach Stephanie, here, how to be a *real* woman." He pointed his big finger in her direction, as if pointing to any number of his other possessions.

Stephanie sat down at the dining room table and began blowing on her steaming beef soup. Sipping its rich flavor from the fancy metal spoon was soothing but demanded all her attention. She did notice her hunched over reflection in one of the many tall mahogany bookcases lining the walls of the spacious dining room. She thought about how she dusted them, yet, never saw anyone even glance their way. *But these are important possessions, Father always says. Possessing books is a sign of character. Hmm, well, it doesn't seem to have helped him much. Hmm, I wonder if actually* reading *them would!*

"Oh Sir, you do me a great honor. There is *nothing* more important to us than to be able to help people. And since you have been so kind as to offer me the food and shelter you have worked *so* hard for, I would consider it a *small* repayment of respect to you, if you would allow me to teach your daughter our ways."

The man positively beamed. Stephanie couldn't remember him ever being happier. In a way, she enjoyed it and smiled. He shouted with joy. "Wonderful, oh, this is *wonderful*."

But Arlupo turned, staring at Stephanie, shaking her head. "No offense, Stephanie," Arlupo frowned, "but since you are older, it will take *some time* to remove your ignorance."

Her father instantly burst in. "Take as much time as you need! This is wonderful. What about Lana, here?" He pointed his big forefinger at his little step-daughter.

Arlupo looked up ignorantly. "Sir?"

"You said since Stephanie's older, it would be much harder to teach her. Would you mind teaching Lana, too? It should be much easier to teach her since she's young."

"Oh Sir..." Arlupo slid off her chair to her knees. *Bowing now should just about make him fall off his chair.* "It would be such a great honor for my people to do so. If teaching Stephanie is small repayment, then teaching both would *almost* make me feel that I have repaid your kindness. Besides, a man such as you doesn't need *children* around all the time. You need time to be with your wife to teach her important matters."

The man couldn't control himself any longer. He pounded his fist down upon the table, making everyone jump, along with the soup. "I *like* this girl, Jean. No offense to you, but more and more, being a real woman has become a lost art. You just can't seem to teach it properly." He paused in his oration at some sort of feeling he couldn't quite make out. "I mean, you do O.K. It's not your fault, but, well, ahhh… I've been working with a special government agency to try to bring these ways back. That's why I'm always home so late. You didn't know that, but I'm telling you now. *I am becoming a very important man.* I'm going to make big changes here. When would you like to start, Arlupo?"

She hesitated. Once hooked, it was better to play a fish and let them tire, than to try and reel him in all the way, right away. "To do this properly, they would need to learn many things, and see how lots of other women act, because by seeing many different women act by the same virtue, they better understand it for themselves."

His eyes widened with understanding. "I see…so what you're saying is, they need to live with you for a while."

She hung her head in a continual bow as she spoke, "Well, Sir. I suggest that at first, they just come for the weekend. That will give my people a chance to show them our basic rules and ways, and then they can decide for themselves if they would *like* to learn."

Fred zeroed in on the word '*like*.' He didn't like it. It wasn't *their* choice. It was his! "The decision has been made for them. I have decided. Stephanie, Lana, you are both to go with Arlupo, to learn. Case closed." One could almost hear the gavel crack down on the judge's desk.

Now that the fish was hung on the stringer through the mouth and gills, Arlupo turned her attention. "Lana, did you know we have lots of little girls you could play with?"

Her little eyes beamed. She had no playmates except for her sister. "Reeeeallly?"

"Oh, yes, and puppies."

Lana's mouth dropped open, throwing her little hands to her cheeks and… "Ooooohhh, I looove puuuuuppiies."

Her father smiled! Turning to Arlupo, he directed her, "Alright. This weekend you take these two to see your people, and the following week they can stay the whole time. Then they can come here for a day or two and then return with you. I'll provide you money for their care while they're with you."

"Oh no, Sir. *We* have plenty, we don't…"

"I insist. I am not the kind of man that pushes *his* women off on someone else to care for. That's why I took Stephanie in."

During all this development, Jean kept shifting in her chair appearing to be more and more uncomfortable. She felt somehow betrayed, but couldn't figure out how the situation turned so. Fighting back tears, his wife meekly tried to gain his attention.

"Fred?"

An unusually soft tone replied to her call. "Yes, dear, what is it?"

"But…"

But the softness was quickly purged by the call of authority. "There are no *buts*. I have *decided*." The gavel seemed to slam again.

"Yes Fred." She excused herself from the table to tend to kitchen duties.

After dinner, Arlupo begged to clean up from the meal and Fred surprised Stephanie by telling her to entertain her guest in her bedroom until she was ready to leave. They even put Lana to bed together, since Jean wasn't feeling well.

Once alone in the bedroom, Stephanie sat on the plush cream carpet together with Arlupo and told her more about her father and some of her thoughts about being a woman person. "…but it's so hard, Arlupo. Because my father brings back all those terrible feelings that say I'm *not* a person and

I have to constantly fight them. But I know now that there's something so special about being a woman person. We refine life in ways a man cannot." Then, with a tear, Stephanie looked deeply into her new friend's eyes as she considered, *Should I show her? It's so special. So very special...but...Arlupo is special. Look what she has done for Lana and me. Oh goodie, we're going on a long sleep over! To see Appendaho.*

Stephanie jumped up, surprising Arlupo, and went to her underwear drawer and fished around at the back. When she returned, she hid it behind her, waiting a bit to increase the suspense. Arlupo's eyes widened in excitement and Stephanie answered them in all seriousness. "I want to show you the most precious, most special thing I have ever had." She solemnly handed Arlupo the poem, *The Helpless Finds Help.* "Vaughn gave this to me on our last day together and told me it was the secret to all his strength and love for me but that I couldn't open it until I was all settled here. When I finally opened it, I was so desperate. I felt like I couldn't go on. Then I read it, and I cried *so hard.* And then I prayed, and thanked God for all His goodness. Then I felt like I could go on again."

As soon as Arlupo touched it, tears came to her eyes. Her heart knew what was in it before she read it. But when she did, she sobbed.

> *What twisted forsaking*
> *has caused such a disease*
> *that I should be reared*
> *in ignorance and misery...*

❖ SACRIFICIAL WOOD ❖

Oh Light, this is their life*! Oh Light, how could they bear it? I couldn't bear it! Oh Light...*Arlupo sat quietly, holding the letter in both hands. She could feel the wonderful soul who wrote it, the strength, the striving, and yet, it was also Stephanie. As she handed the open letter and envelop back, Arlupo's earnest expression told Stephanie how she valued it. "Thank you so much for deeming me worthy to share this precious treasure."

Stephanie smiled, reverently putting the poem back into the envelope, and returned it to its hiding place. When she came back, she sat back down in front of Arlupo. Looking her straight in the eye, Stephanie's tone could not be any more serious. "I want to thank you for being my friend. I can't believe how clever you were tonight. I sat back in awe of you. I wondered how you came up with it. And if you'd told me what you were going to do, I would have thought you were *crazy*." Stephanie's seriousness broke out into hysterical laughter and joy. She fell over on her side in tears. Arlupo did the same, laughing at the irony of her Father and inspired at the hope for her friend. "Vaughn would have really appreciated what you did tonight. He's always talking about the art of fighting." Stephanie tried imitating Arlupo, shaking her head. "No offense, Stephanie...but since you are older, it will take some time to remove your ignorance." Stephanie rolled out in another fit of laughter. After all, who was the ignorant one, here?

Arlupo didn't want Stephanie's father to know she had a car with her. She wasn't sure if he would approve of women drivers. She had left it at the grocery store so that she could help carry the groceries in the rain. Her apartment wasn't far, but she hopped in her car and headed straight for her Appendaho home, some 60 miles outside the city. *I've got to talk with father tonight.*

As she drove home, she tearfully prayed, "Oh Light, You have given me so many wonderful gifts but I think by far the most wonderful is Stephanie! She is so much better than I am! I could not have lived through what she has lived through and I only know but a tiny bit of her life. Help her dear Light. Guide us all in what we must do. I know I cannot tell my father everything yet, but help him understand what I will tell him. He'll think I'm a child. But I'm not anymore. Not after tonight. I know what I must do. Help Stephanie to have the strength to face all that she will surely face. Help me to be the best friend to her that's possible."

Images from her new friend's past flooded her along with images of her future. They swirled together in torment until Arlupo wasn't sure what was past, present or future. Twice she had to pull her car over because she couldn't see through her tears. *How much of this is my imagination? I'll need to find time to sort it out.* "Oh Light, You've given me the perfect life… but she's had so much misery. Help me to help her so that she may become all that You have made her to be. She doesn't know yet. She doesn't know the power at her fingertips. Oh Light, when she comes to understand, don't, *please don't* let her be corrupted by it. Let her understand that all true power, for us, is simply in being a true person, that *that* is where the human gets their being." She felt the answer gently appear within. "I will. I'll teach her what she needs to know. We all will. Oh Light, so little time, but so much to do. Thank You for my wonderful life. Now help me to help her have hers. Watch over her loved one Vaughn. I'm sure he is living in hell without her. Give him strength and wisdom as You gave to our ancient forefather. He's a fighter like he was. But then, so is Stephanie."

☙

MASTER GRRRAGAGAG couldn't believe his Eye. He felt betrayed. Even he didn't see it coming. Plus, Arlupo's new tree posed unanticipated difficulties so he had to rely on what he saw through others to judge her.

"I can't believe that slut is just walking right out from under everything. That *idiot*. I've never seen a more *stupid*, *insipid* man in my life. What kind of man is he? He just turned *his* women over to strangers!"

"Master? What can we do?"

"Nothing, you *idiot*, not yet anyway. All we can do is watch. But perhaps this will work in our favor, because the longer they spend with those Appendaho, the more we can learn about them so we can destroy them."

Something just doesn't feel right about the way Master's acting. He knows more than meets the Eye. So then why is he acting ignorant? I think he already knew about the Appendaho. Why now does he want them destroyed?

What does that have to do with his secret file? They are glow *people...of course. They're the only ones with the potential to destroy the Black Essence. But how did the Blackness get to Earth? Why would Master want to hide its presence from the High Council ...unless...he's responsible for it! Oh my Great Eye! He broke the rules! Or did he? Master is very sly, indeed. But if he did put the Black Essence on Earth somehow, then that would mean he would have to have considered the Appendaho from the start as a threat...Master's been planning a long time...a very long time, I think. But what does Stephanie have to do with all this? How could he have known she would meet Arlupo? And that through Stephanie we could destroy the Appendaho. The only way I'll ever find out is to eat my Master. He's becoming tastier by the moment.* Scraback jerked back a bit, "Destroy them, Master GrrraGagag?"

"Yes, look at Arlupo's tree."

And now Scraback's Eye bulged in shock, "Master! She has a tree?"

His Master merely squinted at him the way one would squint at a speck of dirt on a clean dish. "You *idiot*, of course she does. Do you think I've just been watching her for nothing?"

Scraback's Eye twisted, not knowing what to say that wouldn't draw more invective comments. "Master?"

GrrraGagag was pleased to see how he had completely boxed his underling in. He couldn't do anything about the High Council, yet, but at least he could make fools out of their offspring. He smiled. "A very subtle trick. While we cannot touch the treeless directly in the present, we can touch them indirectly."

SACRIFICIAL WOOD

"Huh?" Scraback's grayness grew dull with spasmodic ripples. He remembered being confused about it the last time his Master alluded to the process.

Master GrrraGagag sighed, "It's *so obvious*. When looking at them through another's tree, I can touch the treeless in the present by connecting to them through the other's mind or heart. So as soon as they make contact with one of our tree-ed humans that I'm focusing upon, they also make contact with our reality and automatically gain a tree! Simple."

"Master, you are a genius." Scraback sincerely bowed his Great Eye to his Master.

Knowing the sincerity of the gesture, GrrraGagag felt quite pleased. "Yes, well, you would think it would be a very weak effect, one that would hardly work at all since we're dealing with humans. But this Arlupo Appendaho has a high degree of spiritual perception as demonstrated in her trunk, as well as extensive roots and branches, meaning her mind and heart are highly perceptive. That means she makes strong contact with others. Which means, before she realized it, she connected through the slut to our reality, strongly enough to foment not only her tree, but she will also produce a similar effect in all the rest. Her strength will lead them all to their speedy destruction, and to a marvelous feast for us."

"But master, why destroy them right away, since they're to become a part of our Forest?"

"Look at her tree." GrrraGagag pointed to a large ball of fiery glow where the tips of green, fully leafed branches could just be made out. It had stretched its branches over Stephanie's tree and their roots were connecting, even as Scraback watched. He had never seen such rapid change. He had never seen such a hideous sight.

He couldn't help but let out a repulsive shriek, "Arrgrr, Master, I have *never* seen such brightness, such pain….is that what *glow* becomes?"

"I believe the High Council has hidden this. I cannot believe the Father knows this ghastliness. But *we* will take care of it." His Master wrapped his long tail around him and drew him close. Scraback felt like he couldn't ripple as his Master whispered to him. "Scraback, for many, many years there have been those of us trying to find a way to replace the High Council. I think we just found it. How would you like to be a direct servant to the *new* High Council instead of being the tail of all their jokes and insults?"

Master is being very, very clever. He knows if I went out with such a wild story I would be laughed out of the ethereal, or, if it was true, that the Council does know, then they'd consume me before anyone else could find out. Scraback was desperately trying to ripple and to avoid his Master's Eye odor. "Oh Master, it is such a great honor to be in your grayness."

While being praised by his underling, Master GrrraGagag pointed his arm at Arlupo's tree, explaining, "You see, we have to destroy them. The *glow* will not destroy them because, if I am right about this, all their people have the same kind of trees."

His terrifying words made Scraback forget how uncomfortable he was. "Master, no…"

SACRIFICIAL WOOD

"We shall see. But I believe it to be so. The *glow* only destroys those who are surrounded by darkness, because it tries to force them into too much conflict. But these people all support each other. I am sure of it. That's why the *glow* is so sickeningly bright."

Scraback managed to twist his bulbous head to face Eye to Eye with his beloved Master. "Then Master GrrraGagag, how shall we destroy them?"

"You have a lot to learn, underling. *We* won't destroy them, not directly. The other people around them will!"

Scraback's Eye had done more contortions that ethereal day than any Alpha ever thought possible. He just added one more. "Master?"

"Watch Scraback, after we've learned from studying them a while and figured out the best timing to destroy the High Council and replace it, we shall destroy the abomination of the Appendaho, the girl, and anyone who sides with them."

"And the boy?"

Master GrrraGagag suddenly dawned one of his very rare, completely satisfied Eye smiles, "He knows reality now. Do you have any idea where he is?"

"He's on the Work Farm."

His Master gave him that speck of dirt squint again. "Scraback, how many times do I have to tell you? The outside facts aren't important. It's the mind and heart we're concerned about." He repeated the question in an instructional tone, "Do you know where he is?" Master GrrraGagag had forgotten to let go of Scraback. His tail still held him tightly.

55

Scraback supposed that old Alphas must be subject to forgetfulness or something, but now that the previous shock was wearing off, the Eye odor was becoming overpowering. Yet, for now, he was helpless to escape from his torments.

"Forgive me, Master, I do not. I only focused on the outside after I saw him put on the Farm."

That satiated smile returned to Master GrrraGagag's Eye. "He's surrounded by endless hopelessness. I could take him any time I wanted and he can *feel* that truth, but I'm feasting off of his pain. He wants to die, but I won't let him…not *yet*. There are still lower lows. I'm just maximizing the torment of his meaningless labor before I bring him down the rest of the way. And then…" Master GrrraGagag's Eye beamed blackness.

Complete thrill overtook Scraback with the thought of consumption. *Maybe Master will let me nibble.* "Perfect, Master, May your grayness cover me." Scraback extended his tail low and straight toward his clutching Master, begging for a blessing. Instead, his Master let him go and drifted off. *Thank the Blackness,* Scraback cried out inside.

CHAPTER THREE
Awaking The Mystery

"*Glowing times call for darker patience. We shall not always be so oppressed.*" Thus finished Claynomore's riveting oratory.

Underling Grrrag raised his tail in question and upon receiving the nod, "*Is there a way to approach the human problem other than directly destroying them, which seems to stimulate a strong glow response? What if we could...well...for instance, hybridize them?*"

Raucous laughter assaulted the underling from every direction. Underling Grrrag looked upon Claynomore's assistant, Gagag, who kept pointing his tail at Grrrag, taunting, mocking....

Never before had she experienced such things. So much meaning applied to the rest of the world. No longer sheltered, she was experiencing the consequences of her life connecting to the outside. So much responsibility to fulfill, and so little time to fulfill it, and she was only sixteen years old, just a year older than her new friend.

She hurried down the carefully laid ancient stone path in the center of her village. The last round stone cottage on the left was where she and her father, their leader, lived. She opened the beautifully carved old wooden door that was cut in a half circle on the top, with gold inlays on its front, depicting a tree. Quickly, she kicked off her shoes and crossed the round living room. She used to slide in her stocking feet across its polished oak floor when she was a child. Inlaid into the floor, a gold cross of perfect equilateral dimensions led to four doors around the room. She knocked softly on the left door and entered. Before even seeing exactly where her father was in his study, she began speaking. He wasn't at his desk where he usually sat.

"Father, I've met some very special people." Arlupo came to stand before her father, who was sitting in his favorite winged-back chair, relaxing. His graying hair imparted a sense of honor to his still young, ageless appearance. His face opened upon seeing and hearing his beloved daughter.

"My daughter, every day I see you is a day of greater joy than the day before."

Arlupo forced a frown to her lips. "Oh Father, stop. If it were so, then you would soon leave this Earth, because no one can stay here who would be *that* happy."

But he smiled broadly, knowing. "Ha! Reality is what it is, my dear, lovely, wise daughter. Tell me of your new friends and what you want me to do for you." Thoughts and feelings of others were clear to him, since reality is what it is, and all he needed to do was look. She leveled her eyes into his open face. She loved to trace its lines and study its continual flow of expression, but now she had the weight of responsibility on her shoulders and she felt it pressing.

"Father, Stephanie's come from the other side of the country. She's a year younger than I, and she has sight."

Her father's black eyebrows rose in question. "Are you sure, Arlupo? Many have a taste of sight, or happen upon it from time to time."

"I'm sure as I'm seeing you now, my beloved father. Stephanie's meaning is clear. And Father?"

"Yes Arlupo?"

"She has red hair."

He studied his daughter and realized there was much more going on here than typical childhood complications. "Red hair and straight sight…Hmm…a child's vision I see you have. Ha! You're playing with legend," he said while his eyes twinkled at her as if beholding a small child at play.

Arlupo persisted with a respectful, tender, but yet serious tone as she squared her shoulders and straightened. When she did, her father straightened. "Father, our people number less than one hundred now. You have broken covenant by sending us to school with the outsiders. Prophecy speaks of this time."

He rubbed his naturally smooth chin with his fingers. "Ha! I see. You're mixing legend *and* prophecy." He squinted, trying to appear more serious to his obviously very serious daughter.

"Father, perhaps there's a reason why legend and prophecy seem so similar, but truth has the power to discern from the inside what part is true."

He indulged her tenderly, trying to treat her more as an adult. "What's your reason for putting these things together?"

She was hoping he would ask. The key was in putting them together.

"Prophecy says we will die out. Where once we were great in number, the seed of an ancient, noble royalty, though offering ourselves to separation to be spared from destruction, we would, nonetheless, die a slow death. And when we find ourselves in the last hand…"

"And I take it that a hand means a hundred to you?"

"Yes father. The ancient king had ordered his army in groups of hundreds, and called each group a hand."

He nodded, "Continue my daughter."

"And when we find ourselves in the last hand, our leader, *you Father*, would break the covenant and join with the outside world…"

Her father found himself finishing for her. "…and we would once again find ourselves in The Forest. Arlupo, no one has had contact with such a thing except those from our legends."

Arlupo had ready an answer, "But Father, we know evil is…"

"But that doesn't mean the legendary Forest…"

Arlupo frowned in earnest this time. "Father, I felt the presence of the evil one touch me. I don't feel the same since that happened. I feel…sadness. You sit up now? I see you're beginning to wonder if there's more to this than just childhood fantasy?"

It *is* sad to say, but we are often the most blind to those we are closest to. But he knew this wisdom, and just to confirm he was right, decided to open his eye to look for what his daughter described, even as he began to speak. "We haven't had that kind of emotion since ancient times describe it to us. But now that I look at you...I..." His whole face changed from its very depths. Arlupo saw what she had never seen before in it... sadness. She knew now she would be taken more seriously. His tone, too, reflected his visage. "This *is* serious. Continue please, and teach this old man."

"Father, you're not old."

He just waited intently, trying to remember an old song he had heard when he traveled to a nearby outsider's farm. Something about having a daughter whose parents never wanted her to have tears, and the chorus, "You can't have all things to please us, no matter how hard we try."

Arlupo re-straightened herself, created a calm composure, as any mature woman would do, and continued, "Father, you broke covenant to join with the outside world because you thought that would help preserve us, but prophecy says that when we shall break our faith we shall bring upon ourselves the past tribulations. I'm worried. Prophecy says we will..." She thought she could just get through the whole sentence without crying like a child, but when beginning the last line, it was as if she could actually see and feel it happening. It stifled her. Tears slowly ran down her cheeks as her brow knit together. Her father shifted uncomfortably. He now felt a deeper sadness, but he focused on his precious daughter.

"Arlupo, your tears tell me this is more than prophecy to you. You believe this is the girl of legend and the legend is *true?*"

"Father, she gave me this paper from the young man she loves." She offered him Vaughn's list of research on King Metran, but instead of taking it, he focused on…

"She has a lover?" Her father's face changed back again, to something in between where he had just been, and where he had skeptically started.

Arlupo yet persisted, but couldn't help thinking, *Why is being a kid so hard?* "I don't know the nature of their relationship, except that she loves him with a woman's love. *Prophecy* says that when we shall break the covenant and disaster befalls us, that we must pass on the Tree of Life to one not of our people. *Legend* says the person will be a girl with a head of fire, with a woman's love, and the power over mystery, and that she shall be one with a boy with a man's love and a man's bravery, a great hero… And father…" She couldn't continue, being clearly overcome, and buried her face in her hands. He had never felt his daughter so.

"Please don't weep my daughter. I know the rest. And when we pass on the knowledge, the light will shine as it did of old and the world will see it and destroy the remnant of the people. Both from our legend and from prophecy."

She wiped her face with a tissue he handed her and continued, "Yes Father. She told me that he'd saved her from something terrible. I don't yet know the nature of these things. I don't know whether she's pure in her love as prophecy demands. But the feeling I get from her is that she *is*. She gave me this. I didn't tell her anything about it but said I would ask you. I don't think she knows me from the TV, either."

⁂ SACRIFICIAL WOOD ⁂

As he put his glasses on, he inspected the piece of paper while commenting, "The name is wrong."

"I know Father, but it's close, and many of the references are correct according to legend. Father, the prophecies are as ancient as the legend. They could be the same. We won't know until we open the sacred box!"

Her father looked up in surprise. It was not something he had ever expected to hear from his daughter, or anyone else of their people. He reminded her of their duty. "That box has not been opened since the time of the legend. It is said that at the time of the *end* we would *know* when to open it…so that the truth could be fulfilled."

Arlupo hung her head in shame with too much, now, going through her heart, her mind, to the point of bursting. "Yes Father. I'm sorry, terribly *sorry*." A sob broke through, and she didn't know what kept her still standing as unfamiliar weakness drained her from the inside out.

He raised a serious eyebrow. "And you believe…"

"That we will find the ancient king's name inscribed on something and the secret to waking the Tree. Father, the young man, Vaughn, searches for a book of wisdom. He can't possibly understand."

A presence seemed to flow into the room that made them tingle, bringing their eyes to meet in acknowledgement—the past and present merging with both good and evil extending their arms. Her father leaned forward, taking her hands.

"Tell me all you know of the girl and those around her and what you think we should do."

Arlupo pulled a wooden desk chair up to her father. She couldn't bear to stand any longer. *Well, at least I've gotten this far.*

All she described, every detail, was not as impressive as the unspoken commentary that her heart interwove into it. *The love that this girl has evoked in my daughter is obvious, and from only two meetings with her. Aside from Arlupo's feelings about legend and prophecy, there's a connection between them…I can see a fire in my daughter's eyes…the likes of which I've never seen before.* He gazed upon how very mature Arlupo had become. He wondered when it happened, and how he missed it.

"I do feel old," he said, after hearing in detail all his daughter's perceptions. Then his tone turned very serious, as she had never known it before, "But I want you to understand something. I did not break faith in the way you think I did. I did what had to be done. That word 'faith' in that context is more like the faith of tradition, an established set of ways and beliefs that have identity as such. But a person's 'faith', that has different meaning than the word faith when we talk of living by true faith. My daughter, as you can see by the light in me, I still live by true faith. Our true faith is based on our continuing connection to and understanding of the Light. Our beliefs flow from *that* faith. Anyone may pick up our beliefs but they will *not* understand them nor be able to follow them correctly if they don't have true faith to follow them from the inside-out. Your new friends may be taught beliefs, but we *cannot* teach them faith. They must find that for themselves, by themselves, within themselves by also finding and connecting to the Light."

"I know Father. I believe Stephanie already has! The young child, her sister, is special, too, but I don't understand how she fits into all this."

He raised an eyebrow at her. "Prophecy isn't meant to tell you everything, but just enough for those with true faith to act truthfully."

She nodded obediently to the truth of his words, "Yes Father." She bowed her head as her father sat up straight to give his pronouncement.

"We'll teach them how to handle the man so he's no trouble. Assemble the people, my daughter. Don't hold back any of your thoughts from them. Remember, truth and love with our people gives the right for any to speak their mind and to be heard as a leader." He paused, looking deeply into her, "Arlupo, what I did had to be done. Wherever this may lead, reality is what reality is. We've had a long and wonderful, peaceful history, but perhaps in our seclusion we have, in a way, suffered a kind of death other than decreasing numbers."

Her father's words pained her. She hadn't imagined anything like it. "Father, I don't understand. I see no *death* with our people."

He hung his head briefly then looked his daughter straight in the eye, "We had light to share with the world, but we hid it. A tree doesn't hide itself, but reaches ever outward. Perhaps we've lost the right to the Tree we so love, because we've dishonored one of its ways. Behold, we separated ourselves in ancient times and it's been asleep ever since."

His words fell like a mountain upon her, feeling a shame she'd not known before, though the wrong was theretofore unforeseen. Tears streamed down her face as the understanding sunk unabated ever deeper into her soul.

"Oh Father, I can't fight your wisdom. Why couldn't we see this sooner?"

Responding tenderly, he rose up to walk behind her. Putting his strong hands on her shoulders, he kissed the top of her head as she sat weeping. "Sometimes, my lovely daughter, tradition blinds even true souls with true traditions. We must accept the consequences."

She picked her head up and turned to look into his soft brown eyes. "Father, prophecy stops at the end of this. What does that mean?"

"It means, my daughter, that *they* will be the makers of prophecy, not the followers!"

Her eyes widened at the realization. "They will *become* the legend!"

"Perhaps."

Then Arlupo began to backtrack. "But Father, then you're actually fulfilling our faith by sending us to school, because you're giving us the chance to grow outward?"

His smile broadened. "You surprise me every day, and every day is more beautiful than the day before."

But Arlupo wasn't to be charmed away from her thoughts as she scrunched her eyebrows in confusion, "But then you may not be breaking covenant…oh…this is getting confusing."

SACRIFICIAL WOOD

He kissed the top of her head again and went to sit at his desk. When he was seated, he instructed her, "It's not for us to predict the future, but to act truly by accepting the ways of the Tree of Life in the present. The girls need help or they'll die. I'm so proud of how you conducted yourself. You went into the house of evil and spoiled its treasure and came out unharmed and you are yet a child! And a *girl* child at that!" His smile seemed to carry with it wisdom, understanding, and appreciation of the ages concerning what a mere *girl* could do.

༺༻

Arlupo's plan seemed to work perfectly. Stephanie felt she'd gone to heaven. From the first day, everyone knew her name without her even being introduced. What's more, the villagers didn't greet her like a stranger, but her name rolled out of their mouths being dearly cherished. Every time Stephanie met someone new, and they gave her that honor, she found herself asking herself, *Do I know this person? Have we met before?* And it wasn't just a custom, as saying thank you, or excuse me, which people often do automatically with no thought or feeling. From the first, Stephanie felt real feelings behind their greetings and words and more than once she had to scold herself from staring.

Stephanie and Lana came for the first weekend and then stayed for a week. They visited a single day at home and then returned for another week, repeating this for a whole month. *My God, this is what it truly feels like to belong…brothers and sisters for real.* Those thoughts kept playing like a sweet bird's song in her heart and mind. *It's so different than when I was in Gary's gang.* But every time that thought followed, she suddenly felt very out of place amongst the Appendaho.

Even Stephanie's father seemed to change towards her. In place of implied worthlessness, she thought she detected a hidden smile upon his lips every now and then when she passed by him. Just the thought of his daughter being transformed into the woman of his dreams, made him see everything about her in a different light. With joy, Stephanie accepted his happiness with her, but the joy had a companion lurking at its edges and in its depths…dread. But she need not pay attention to that, as she had found heaven.

Stephanie had met all the people in the village and had come to know some of them fairly well. Arlupo chose to live back in her village and Stephanie rode to school every morning with her. Every day Stephanie rose with joy, and after school she eagerly sought out whoever might need her help with some chore of the village's daily living. Whether it was tending the fruit trees, the goats, sheep, the gardens, spinning wool, or making cheese, it didn't matter. "Do you need my help? Do you need my help? Do you…" They all came to know and love the words that were going to come as soon as they saw her.

Her first working experience was in weaving. Stephanie watched intently as the elderly lady with straight, long gray hair, and a smooth face repeatedly took the heavy cross beam and pulled it down hard onto the threads she wove into a colorful native rug. "Weaving is like life, dear Stephanie. Each thread is like an experience, but it is up to the weaver what they want to do with them. If you order them properly, you come out with a beautiful rug to lie upon. Of course, you have to understand the meaning of the colors on each thread and how to adjust them to create the pattern of beauty you desire. Also, the texture of the rug depends upon how hard you pack the threads. The harder you pack, the tougher the rug and the longer it lasts."

I KNEW IT! I knew I was more than just a bunch of experiences all piled together. That teacher lied…I'm…a weaver, as well. "Can I try?" Stephanie's expression looked like she was five years old.

"Of course, dear," she replied and slid over on the bench to make room for her.

They began a whole new rug. Stephanie worked intently and forgot about everything around her. She found herself packing the threads as hard as she could. When her teacher finally told her it was past time to eat, Stephanie eased back and realized her shoulders ached terribly from repeatedly pulling the cross beam down to tamp the threads. She kissed the lady, thanked her, and bounded off to find Arlupo.

The next day it was making butter. Another lady of very similar features, except she preferred to have her sleeves rolled up and her hair done in a big ball, smiled when she saw her approach. Stephanie watched as she kept ramming a wooden handle down into a long, narrow barrel. She'd never seen such a thing and didn't know what it was.

"Excuse me Ma'am, what ya doin'?"

She smiled warmly. "I'm making butter, dear Stephanie."

Shocked, Stephanie's words rolled forward, "So that's where it comes from!" But then she realized she didn't understand anything more than somehow the butter came out of the barrel.

The lady read her look of puzzlement and laughed, "Oh my…you city folk take so much for granted. Making butter is like life, dear one. To get really good things, sometimes it takes a long, hard process with patience."

"Can I try?"

She handed her the handle with a smile and as Stephanie began the work, she explained to her how butter is made. "…so in the end, we get buttermilk too! Good for baking. Some people even like to drink it straight, but I don't. But in life, sometimes, nothing goes to waste. Every consequence of your labor is good for something."

Once again Stephanie realized she ached, but this time it was her chest and forearm muscles. Her hands were stiff, too. The lady opened the barrel, took a wooden spoon and scooped a bit of fresh butter for her helper. Stephanie's eyes rolled as it melted in her mouth. *Oh God, making butter is like life, too. You do all this work over and over again but you can't see what's happening in the barrel until you open it at the end and taste the product. But wait, how is that like life? What am I talking about? What product?* Stephanie shook her head at herself, feeling that this applied to her, but losing the picture of it.

The lady must have read her mind. "Making butter is like having true faith, dear. When you know what you put into the barrel, the work you will do, and the determination

※ SACRIFICIAL WOOD ※

and patience with which you will do it, then you can be sure of your outcome. But it all starts with understanding the basic nature of the milk you put into the barrel. That milk is like the spirit of life in us! The work is our attention to our thoughts and feelings and ways. The right determination is to seek the truth of all things, to live in it, and then be patient as truth, spirit, and work give you their finished product. Because we know the nature of all these, we, therefore, know what the result will be. This knowledge is true faith. Even toddlers learn it when they learn how to walk. There's a good reason even in their tiny minds for wanting to do so, and they don't question the wisdom of it. It just is."

Then there was making cheese as the old lady and Stephanie sat on a wooden bench at a wooden table with large bowls to catch the fluid from the bundles hanging above. "The harder you wring out the whey, the harder the cheese will be."

Stephanie loved hard cheese, it was her favorite, but the goat cheese the Appendaho made particularly delighted her. She noticed how much her hands hurt from twisting the wooden rod that squeezed the cheesecloth that wrung out the whey. "Whey isn't good for much. The outsiders feed it to their animals, but we don't think it natural to feed animal products to animals whose nature is to eat plants. So we dump it on our fallow fields, returning it back to the Earth from where it came. Sometimes, the consequences of our labor are only good for nothing more than that!"

I wonder what in life that would apply to. She didn't say. I don't think I'm supposed to ask. Oh God, I'm being taught so much…*Oh thank You Life, Thank You so much…* Tears of being overwhelmed gushed unexpectedly from Stephanie. She was a bit embarrassed.

Sitting next to Stephanie, the cheese-lady placed her hand upon her cheek, letting her tears run over her fingers. "You are the right one to have the world at your fingertips!" Stephanie just looked at her, being afraid, for some reason, to ask what she meant. "Cheese is a peculiar product, dear. It can only come about after the milk has been spoiled! The work applied to the spoiled milk gives us a product that is far more nutritious, lasts a lot longer, and is easily transported. Frankly, I think its taste is far superior, too." She looked Stephanie directly in the eye, the message being that she was applying this parable to her. *But I don't understand why that applies to me.* More tears came, but they were no release for her confusion.

Stephanie shook out her hands to try to ease the pain in them. *All that I've been doing is such hard work, but I don't mind it at all. It makes me feel so much more like a person. But I worked just as hard at Dad's. Why didn't it make me feel that way, too?*

"Thank you for your help today, Stephanie. You have brightened my day even more than it has been!"

Stephanie began to bawl from colliding feelings she couldn't identify, so the lady took her in her arms and held her. Stephanie felt motherliness wrap her up like a soft baby blanket. It made her weep that much more as she laid her head on the woman's shoulder. "There, there, dear child. Let it out.

SACRIFICIAL WOOD

There, there…" She stroked Stephanie's flaming red hair. "It's no crime to feel worth."

Stephanie indeed learned much from the Appendaho's words, but even more from their feelings, and yet more still by their actions. Everyone taught her something new, but she learned even more by just seeing and feeling the people themselves. It was as if they were all her family and she their common child. Such a tremendous family feeling overwhelmed Stephanie with joy, thanksgiving, prayers and more tears. Her heart burned inside with an energy all its own, as the word 'love' took on a continually deeper and deeper meaning. Every time she and Arlupo drove into the Appendaho valley, Stephanie's heart leapt with joy and excitement. *It's so different from my past and from my home with Father.*

She and Lana often completely forgot about their parents. Lana didn't have to go to school. She spent her days exploring, playing with other little girls and boys, and caring for her best friend, Puppy. She had painstakingly worked on Puppy's first responsibility as her pet. "Sit." "Puppy, *sit.*" Day after day she worked on it. She was about to give up, when one evening as she and her sister were sitting together at the dinner table, Lana was complaining, "Puppy won't SIT," and Puppy, who was climbing all over Stephanie, stopped, and sat! The expression on Lana's face doubled over Stephanie, Arlupo and Arlupo's father in laughter. "Good Puppy," Lana said laughing and squeezing her doggy. The rest of that night all anyone could hear from her was, "Sit Puppy." And Puppy sat. This was during the evenings, the time they cherished most, because they spent it all together.

The early part of every evening was spent with Arlupo, and her father and mother, and the latter part Stephanie and Arlupo spent alone, sitting on the soft bed. They spent hours talking and laughing together. Stephanie told Arlupo of all the lessons she was learning from her people and of how she interpreted them. She also told her of her past and they wept together. But she couldn't bring herself to tell Arlupo of her lewd behavior. She only gave hints, being too ashamed to speak about it. The Appendaho were obviously holy people. Yet, every time she felt like she didn't belong there, someone came up to her with a loving word, gesture, or passing feeling that drew her deeper into their community. It made it easier for Stephanie to forget what she had been.

When Arlupo finally heard how Vaughn had rescued Stephanie, her eyes were never wider, as she twisted on her nightshirt, listening to how they climbed out the window and almost fell. Then there was that terrible fight where the gang tried to kill them. "And you picked him up all by yourself?" Arlupo asked. Stephanie nodded. Spellbound, Arlupo asked, "How'd you do that?"

Stephanie shrugged, "I don't know. I had to. So I just did!"

Arlupo shook her head at her friend, hugging her.

They were more than friends, they were sisters. They were more than sisters. There was no word to describe the bond they had, except pure love, empathy, and appreciation for each other, and a boundless common hope together. Stephanie often found herself waking in the middle of the night in tears for just how much love she felt. She desperately wished Vaughn could join her. Everything she did, heard, learned, experienced, had the companion thought, *Oh, I wish I could share this with Vaughn. Maybe he could run away and come here. I'm sure he would be safe. He could work here.* She imagined what it would be like. *Oh, how he would love it here. How he would fit in with everyone. I can just imagine him listening to all the different stories and then discussing them, and maybe even asking questions and perhaps making* them *think too…* But there was a worry, too, just below the surface. *Is he guilty of my gang's deaths? What will that do to him? What will happen to him? Can I truly love him if it's true? To murder someone is terrible. Do I have a choice to love him?* It didn't seem so. Memories of Gary and her former gang ran shivers up her spine. Memories of her wantonness made her feel more than out of place with the Appendaho…and then the day arrived.

After three months, Stephanie and Lana were summoned early to Arlupo's father's study for assessment. He smiled broadly and joyfully at them. "Stephanie, Lana, you've been with us for a total of three months now. How do you feel? What do you think?" His hands were folded as he sat behind his desk, and his curious expression poured over them.

"Sir, I could *not* even have *imagined* a best friend being better than your daughter. She reminds me of my other friend I left, but he's a boy. But she's helped me to feel wondrous."

He nodded in pleasure and taught her. "Stephanie, with our people these feelings cannot go one way. If you feel that way, they are equally felt by all those touched by you. When love connects, all connected experience it and respond in kind."

Stephanie bowed her head to the Appendaho leader. "I also want to say that I *cannot* express deeply enough how thankful I am to be able to share in your community. All of your people have become so dear to me." She turned toward Lana, "How 'bout you, Sprout?"

Lana sang back her answer in giggles and bubbles of joy. Lana's nickname tickled her every time she heard it. When she asked her sister why she called her that, she would only say that she was *sprouting*. Lana tried to say she wasn't, but no, Stephanie said, "Oh yep, *sprouting.*" And then she would look behind Lana's ear, behind her back, or under her arm, "Sprouting, sprouting, sprouting…"

Lana peered into the leader's eyes and through her laughter answered straightly, "I love it here. I don't ever want to go back." She shook her head emphatically, "*No, never.*"

Stephanie reminded her of how she was supposed to act. "Lana, remember what we learned? How we must share love with Mom and Dad so that our friends will be honored, too? And how to bow to Daddy, to make him feel good?"

"I remember. It'll be fun."

"Good. We don't have to tell him anything but the little bit that will make him feel good."

"Right. I don't want to tell him *anything*. I don't think Daddy likes it when I'm happy, because when I am, he usually yells at me. So, I'll listen Stephie. Do we have to stay long there? I want to get back to Puppy. He's trying to learn *shake*. I have to make sure he learns his *responsibilities*."

"Just a couple days. O.K. it's time for you to go to sleep. There are some older person things I'm supposed to be shown now... Oh thank you for the big hug and kiss." Thus Lana did every night.

"I love you Stephie, Arlupo, Sir, and all your people...and Puppy too. Good night. Can Arlupo's Mommy tuck me in?"

"Yes dear, go find her." She broke from Stephanie's embrace and off her little feet patted away in a quick sprint, hop, and skip, and vanished through the doorway with a golden brown fur ball tripping, sliding and scampering to keep up behind her.

Arlupo's father promptly spoke, "Stephanie."

"Yes Sir?"

She'd never seen his face so intense. He replied with equal, serious tone, "We've shown you how we live, think, and feel." *Oh my God. That formal tone. This is it. They didn't tell me, but I expected it.* Stephanie straightened, holding her head level, looking solemnly into his eyes, swallowing. "Is this where you make me one of your people, Sir?" she replied with equal intensity, respect, and concern. But all of a sudden...

He burst out laughing! "Oh my...no, no, that's just story stuff!" He waved his big hand, laughing again, dismissing the idea as he tried to regain his composure. "Oh my!"

Stephanie sat befuddled while Arlupo hid her grin. He finally continued. "Life isn't about becoming another person or part of this or that culture. But I suppose you could say that if you wanted to *officially* be a part of our people, well, you have to live by the truth inside *you*." At that last word, he leaned forward, his eyes cradling her.

Me. I am me. I feel the meaning of that more every day. Inspired, Stephanie let her thoughts pour out, unafraid of recrimination. "It's easy to forget the truth of that here, Sir. There are so many of you who live that way, that I begin to think of truth as the way of your people, instead of the way *all* people must follow if they want to live. It's really not the way *of* any people, but the people being *of* the truth. A very important distinction, I think, because real truth is from the true faith *anyone* can find inside themselves, regardless of the culture or people. As soon as someone starts to assign truth as being of some people, then people start messing up by copying others' ways and things, from the outside in, instead of the inside out. At least, that's what I've been thinking about. I can feel the difference when I catch myself just doing something I've seen your people doing, as opposed to doing it because it's my feeling to do. The first feels hollow. You have to… No. *I* have to look at life inside me, and through that little life to the Life that is God. Meaning of everything for me must proceed from there. Ha, but then I end up doing a lot like everyone else anyway." She looked aside, but only momentarily. "I think I was kinda falling into that trap when I asked about being made one of your people, wasn't I?" Though she intended nothing more than to share her thoughts, she got carried away with them.

He sat back, rubbing his chin, relishing the power with which she spoke her words. "I so enjoy you! By the Light, I enjoy you every bit as much as my own daughter. Every day I see you two is twice as bright as the day before." She could see his appreciation and wondered at it.

Arlupo smiled but cautioned Stephanie. "That's Daddy's way of messing with your mind."

"I've noticed." Stephanie and Arlupo confirmed glances as they grinned together.

"Stephanie." He folded his hands atop the table again but extended his muscular arms to their fullest, sitting up straight as if planning on getting up.

"Yes, Sir?"

In a very measured tone, he said, "There is a great secret that has been handed down to us, and I would like to share it with you."

Stephanie became dumbfounded. She had just dropped her guard and felt comfortable. Now this! She had never seen nor felt him be more serious. Dwarfed by the implications, she stammered, "Oh Sir…I…I don't think…I mean, you've only known me…"

He waved it off with his hand and a twist of his mouth. "Time's not relevant when a heart's open to see. It's for you to know our secret, so that you can help protect it."

Stephanie's eyes flashed with the importance of it, "Oh Sir, I would love to help in any way possible." *These people have given me so much. Oh, whatever I could do for such an important thing. But what* could I *do?*

"Come, and I will show you."

The Appendaho leader went to the back of his study and opened a door with a gold tree engraved into it. Stephanie looked at Arlupo, but could get no hint of what was to come. But instead of Stephanie directly following the Appendaho leader, she stepped around the open door to look at the gold tree more closely, touching it, running her finger over its branches and trunk. Then it flashed in her memory. *Oh my God, the glowing tree at the church back east. FIND ME! it said. I wonder...* Prickles moved in waves up and down her whole body. She remembered how annoyed she had been, not understanding what had been happening. Even wondering if she was crazy hearing the image of a tree talking to her.

Stephanie and Arlupo followed him through a low, narrow hallway that traveled a good hundred feet. The very closeness of the hallway shouted *secret*. Stephanie's secret shelter, its specialness, flashed in her mind. *But this secret is much, much greater, I know.* The slow walk seemed slower as the word, *secret,* no, *great secret,* rang louder and louder in Stephanie's head. Her steps became strangely reverent and every breath taken with care.

Finally, emerging from the very dim hall, the setting sun blasted into Stephanie's eyes through open windows from across a thirty foot round room. Encircling it, beginning three feet up from the stone floor, were three foot square, wooden shuttered windows, each butted against the other. Pairs of shutters, hinged to each window frame, opened inward all around. Their effect gave the impression of being inside a great wheel with spokes. The beautiful colors of an evening sky shone through a shallowly domed ceiling of clear glass tiles. His expression made it clear she was supposed to tell him what she saw and thought of the object in the center of the room.

"Sir? It's…it's…a dead tree with lots of gnarled branches in a huge brass crock."

The tree stood a mere seven feet tall from the base of the crock. Its trunk was wide at ground level, perhaps twenty-four inches wide, but quickly tapered to a point seven feet up. The first three feet had no branches, but the thickly barked trunk seemed to be covered in many knots and subtle twists. From its complexity, it seemed like a very long lifetime had been compressed into the trunk. The first branches seemed to go straight across in all directions, and the ones above that, and the ones above them, all seemed packed closely together, but all seemed to possess the same subtle twisting and turning. The only difference was, that the closer to the top, the shorter the branches became. All the branches seemed to have many smaller branches radiating in all directions crowded together. There were old, dormant buds all over the secondary and finer branches, making the tree appear as if it was studded with black beads. The leader directed her attention.

"Look closely at it. Details are very important. Don't just look with your eyes, Stephanie, but with your *life*."

Arlupo studied her intently, holding her breath. Stephanie understood her father's meaning and opened her feelings to touch the tree so she could see.

"It's very twisted….*very old*.......may I touch it?"

He and Arlupo were stone silent for some time, as if frozen by the question.

"Sir? Arlupo? Why do you look so strange?"

"My sister, no one has ever asked this before, or even thought to ask."

Stephanie became embarrassed, ashamed, and afraid she had offended. It completely overshadowed her friend's calling her 'sister' for the first time.

"*Oh no*, I'm so *sorry*. I didn't mean to…"

But Arlupo's father comforted her, "No, no, child, you did no wrong. Don't worry about it. Of course you may touch it if you desire."

Relieved, Stephanie's full attention immediately returned to the tree.

Arlupo raised her eyebrows at him, speaking softly, "Father?"

"Reality is what it is, my daughter."

Stephanie was too enthralled to pay them any mind now. Pulling her long, dark blue Appendaho dress up a bit, she sat on the crock's broad brass rim. It encircled the tree like a round bench. Its soft luster seemed to encourage Stephanie to sit, to be comfortable, to rub her hand across its smoothness. As she did, she monitored all the new feelings pouring into her. *It's like I'm being introduced, and at the same time, introducing myself. It's as if the tree* wants *me to touch it.* She bent under the branches to feel its trunk. She placed her right hand flat upon it to gather sensation and feel with her

SACRIFICIAL WOOD

heart. At first there was a gentle softness, and then stronger impressions began to inundate her.

"Oh….*oh my*…this is…*very old*….I…" She wasn't dizzy, nor was she moving, or spinning, but… "I….*see*…*visions*… of…long ago…this tree is *alive*…but…asleep… so sad… it is asleep…but…now it is…" Suddenly, Stephanie broke off from feeling the trunk, turning to her friend, feeling that she shouldn't be touching this, this… "Arlupo, what is this?" she stared, asking almost accusingly.

Her friend's faraway look was of ages gone by as the history of the tree flashed in her knowledge. "Legend… Prophecy…this was passed down to our people to protect. It is called the Tree of Life. It is as old as our people and we don't know how old that is. I believe it is older…and, it is sacred."

Stephanie *knew it* and sprang up in mournful plea, her heart pounding. "*Oh my God, you let me touch a SACRED OBJECT?*" She threw her hands to her mouth, her eyes wide and filling with tears, her stomach turning over and over.

"Yes Stephie. Why are you crying?" Her friend's strong reaction startled Arlupo. Her father nodded, sighing deeply.

Stephanie wailed, "*Because I have no right to touch a sacred object!*"

But Arlupo's father, the leader, replied as if it was an everyday occurrence. "Reality is what it is. It was as much the Tree's choice as yours!"

"But…I…*Oh God…*" She continued to wail, clutching her stomach with one hand, covering her face with the other, and easing down to the floor, her strength failing her.

"What is it, dear child?" he asked her, already knowing.

She answered from her knees, shaking her head as she bent over. "You don't know what kind of person I've been, what I've *done*."

He spoke tenderly. "The Tree knows, child. You wanted to touch it because *it* called to you to do so. It has called no other, not even me!"

Stephanie looked up from being on her knees not comprehending, "But…why would it call to *me*? I'm…"

He felt tears at the corners of his eyes and heartache. "The Tree knows all about you. Look at it deeply. It has reached its size and age, not by sticking to the past or being chained by it, but by building upon it. It has *many* gnarls from the wounds of mankind, but the gnarls add beauty to life's overcoming, as life found a way to overgrow anything that got in its way."

Stephanie bent lower to the floor, weeping. More than anything she wanted to overcome all the evil in her, but to have her scars turned into beauty seemed too much to ask… but she felt the desire for just that, anyway. His words sank unrestrained into her breaking heart, breaking it further. Feelings of deep life were flooding her, as the connection she established to the Tree had not been broken when she took her hand away. Now, depths of goodness flooded her and she became acutely aware of the evil she had done in her life. He waited a bit before resuming instruction.

"I think it called to you because your tree is very much like this one."

◆ SACRIFICIAL WOOD ◆

The ridiculousness of his statement brought her to respond. She picked her head up again. "Oh no, that can't be so. I'm hardly as old as the tiniest twig, here." She had absorbed knowledge from her encounter with the Tree without even realizing it.

But he countered her thought with wisdom. "Even this Tree was young at one time."

She looked up again, straightening her back while still on her knees. "What did you mean 'my tree'?"

"Dear child, that is a very good question, but one that our people never answer to another because the answer is within!"

"But, why..."

"And that answer is also within. When you come back, though, we can teach you how to rid yourself of your shame so that your wounds may heal and become a part of your beauty, even as this Tree has beauty." Strength poured into her through his hands as he helped her to her feet and held her eyes in his.

She found the courage to tell him her thoughts. "It's not a dead tree at all. That's just for eyes to see. But it's the most beautiful tree I've ever seen, like all trees are represented by this *one*. How will you teach me? Is it hard?"

"Yes and no. Something in you produced death from within. This Tree, here, has no death from within. Though even now it suffers greatly, it is the outside it battles to overcome. This Tree lives inside of you, also. You must find it inside yourself. Think about this and it will prepare you for your lesson when you return."

She held his arm. "Sir, I love you so, and you Arlupo, and all of you, and your Tree. I love the way you live, the way you relate. The way you support yourselves..." Stephanie began to ramble, overcome and unable to process all she had just soaked in. "...and I think tending mountain goats and orchards is the most beautiful way to live. You don't need anybody but yourselves."

But he shook his head sadly. "No Daughter, if that was really true, our people would not be dying out. It certainly seemed true for a very long time. But perhaps some truths take a very long time to be understood."

Stephanie's arms were each being held, Arlupo on one side and her father on the other. She spoke as if in a daze about many things she felt when she touched the Tree, not realizing that a certain connection had been permanently established between them. "You know, all life is a whole. It's all connected like that Tree is one tree. You know, there are so many variations of life, but all based on the same qualities, just like each tiny little branch comes from the *same tree*. You know, I think I'm on that tree! No. *Really!* One of the tiniest little twigs near the top...somewhere..."

They led her down the main stone path to her little private cottage. The stars twinkled now. The night air was comfortable, laden with many different sweet scents from fruiting trees and wild flowers. At the door, they let go and she promised them. "When I return, I look forward to your lessons. Good night."

Arlupo stared at her sister, her best friend, and more. She was in awe of her! "I'll turn in also, my sister." Arlupo's tone was solemn, reverent. The full moon shined on their presence and its very light seemed like a blessing.

☙

The time had come. *I knew it was really just a matter of time. I was doomed the moment I set foot here.*

Every boy was required to be a woman for a weekend. They had passed him up thrice since he was there. But all the boys who serviced wouldn't hear it any longer. Ralph was particularly insistent. Besides that, the suspense made Vaughn more desirable to everyone.

I love you, Stephanie. I will *always* love you. *But I just* cannot *go through with this just to preserve my* existence. *I probably should, because with time there's also hope, small as it may be that we could be together. But I just can't go through with this. I just can't.*

"HEY, we're talking to you." Another boy boisterously barked and a crowd of a dozen older boys and young men began to gather in front of the beds,

Vaughn thought about going back out through the door. *But what would that do?* The last rule, the twenty-first, to *The Art of Fighting* was that it was better to die fighting honorably than to die a coward and in disgrace. It was fitting that it was so similar to the first rule. It had made a nice conclusion to the series. But the last rule was advanced because it pertained to what honor and disgrace really were. The first rule warned against losing the battle from within and could be applied from the very beginning. The last rule could only be honored after understanding the many principles that make one honorable. The first rule dealt with the crippling effects of fear conquering a person before they even enter battle. The last dealt with a *choice* that wasn't obviously crucial as the first rule: Choosing a battle because honor required it even though it could be avoided. A true coward is one who will not defend honor. He had the self-responsibility to choose honor but refused. Someone who runs away from battle simply out of fear is weak. Some say that is cowardly. But the disgrace is much greater when they choose not to defend honor, because to defend honor is to defend the standards of life.

Vaughn shook his head, smiling at them. He put his hands on his hips and counted. *Thirteen and more coming.* He raised his right hand, beckoning for them to come to him. He knew they didn't know his fighting skills. He purposely hid them. That was why, when he first arrived, he only punched the man out instead of kicking him. But he knew he couldn't beat them all, even with all his skill.

"Hey, the runt's crazy," the largest young man laughed, coming to the head of the pack.

When just fifteen feet away, Vaughn took two running steps at him and jumped into the air. Faking his left foot to kick him in the gut the big man dropped his arms and Vaughn's right foot snapped up, flattening his nose into his face. The man's arms splayed outward as he fell back, each arm knocking a man down to either side. But Vaughn now found himself surrounded. Upon landing on his feet, he spun and swung his backhand across one face. He spun the other way and swung his other arm up and over a hand that grabbed his shirt at the shoulder, wrapped his arm around that arm, flexing, spinning, and snapping the man's bone in two. Crouching, he drove a backhanded elbow up into that man's gut. Then he spun and threw a backhand up under his chin, knocking him up. He followed it with a severe punch to the gut, doubling him over again. It was all in an instant.

He sensed everyone closing in on him from all other sides, so he rolled up onto the bent over man's back, and as he rolled off, he cocked his foot and kicked his only opposition in the gut, sending him flying backwards. The pack became enraged as they smelled blood.

Vaughn made it to a bed and leapt onto it, turning his back against the wall. He desperately needed a weapon. He ran to his right, jumping from bed to bed as quickly as he could until he had some distance. The pack seemed in no hurry. They had made up their minds as others blocked every door. Vaughn tipped a bed over to look underneath to see if there was anything he could do to rip a board or something out. But the beds were metal frames. He grabbed a sheet.

"Ha, what's he gonna do with that sheet?" one grossly pock-marked face spat out.

"Make the place where we all get to do him," another laughed. Vaughn waited atop one of the beds across from a door. He decided escape would be better than staying and fighting. He violated the Fourteenth Rule: Never make a battle plan against overwhelming odds that you will change while fighting. They came for him.

He jumped up as high as he could, throwing the sheet outward. It unfurled perfectly, blocking their view of him. In that instant he landed back on the bed and sprang off it, up and forward, with all his might. Tucking himself into a summersault, he spun over the mob. It was a move he had only done in his imagination. He cleared the mob as they cleared the sheet, and were dumbfounded that he'd vanished. But Vaughn landed wrong. His feet weren't under him when he hit the floor. He tumbled across the smooth concrete out of control to the feet of a boy guarding the door. Worse, he was disoriented from the spin.

Vaughn picked his head up and saw Ralph. Hope flashed before his eyes. Ralph kicked him straight in the face. As the pain hit him...*I knew I should have killed Ralph earlier.* Ralph had tried to con Vaughn, so that Ralph wouldn't have to service. Vaughn should have killed this drug dealer even earlier for what he tried to do to Stephanie. But after the fiasco with Gary and gang, Vaughn had lost his stomach for killing.

"He's over here." The pack descended, less interested now in sex than in blood. Vaughn curled into a ball, knowing it was over. Blows and kicks rained down from all sides. He was alone in his thoughts.

Pain...darkness...can't give up...what am I fighting for?...I have nothing... Stephanie...I'm sorry...at least I die before they...pain....Pain...PAIN...

Master GrrraGagag finally leaned back away from the orb satisfied. His Eye relaxed and he sighed. "Now Scraback, send her word." Scraback got busy with the orb. He was being

SACRIFICIAL WOOD

trusted more and more with unmonitored assignments. He knew his Master was leaving. He would do his job well.

☙

"Well, well. What do we have here?" Gary wheeled himself over to Vaughn's bedside. He mused as he examined the unconscious, barely recognizable form. "You know, I could kill you right now…but why would I want to end your suffering so quickly. You know, I waited here for you. That's why I didn't come back to school. I knew you'd show up eventually." Gary stood up! "Look at me." He jumped up and down. "They think I can't walk yet. But it looks like you're in worse shape than I ever was. When is the best time to kill you? They say you're dying anyway. Glen's father had you sent back here. Wasn't that nice of him? He's made sure you won't get any care that might help you. Word's out that anyone who messes with us will end up *just like you*."

Gary hockered up a thick wad of green phlegm and spit it into Vaughn's face. It slowly oozed down his swollen, discolored cheek. Gary reached over and grabbed Vaughn's crotch. "You know, these things work whether you're awake or not." He laughed. "No thanks, I really was never interested like you." He sat back in his chair and wheeled himself out. Just before he left, he said, "You'd never believe who was responsible for setting you up. You *idiot*. You never could watch your mouth. You didn't know who you were talking to." Gary left.

☙

Waverly sat by Vaughn's bedside at his hometown's only hospital. Vaughn's parents wouldn't spend the money for the advanced care he needed. The doctors told them it would only prolong the inevitable. The ambulance brought him in two days ago. Waverly heard that Gary bragged about all the horrible things he heard were done to Vaughn.

As soon as Waverly found out, he tore out of school and rushed to the hospital. Vaughn lay swollen, black and blue and brown all over. Waverly had to check his name tag just to make sure it really was Vaughn. The doctors said that, remarkably, there were no broken bones, but the internal injuries were numerous. He was bleeding inside, and all they could do was give him occasional transfusions and hope the bleeding stopped. But Waverly didn't see anything hooked up to his arm, and he never saw them bring any extra care at all. Waverly wept at his bedside.

"Oh God, I can't believe this Vaughn, you've always been my friend. You have to wake up. The doctors say you're dying. I don't believe it. I'm going to… write Stephanie! She loves you, remember? You have to pull through… for her… *Vaughn!*" He shouted. "I don't care how much money it costs to send the message. You've been a true friend. I'll send her the letter."

☙

Scraback didn't realize his Master had come back and was watching over his shoulder. He had been engrossed in his work. His Master put his tail on Scraback's shoulder, patting it.

"Job well done. O.K. We've got time now. We might as well review what she's been up to. Oh what fun. You know my trusty underling, sometimes I love my job. I just received the latest Report of Ages. If things go according to the Father's plan, this generation of humans will be the last to be troubled with the *glow*. The old ones have all died except for those Appendaho. Besides them, there are only these random occurrences that we're now stamping out. Every chief Alpha such as I are contending all over the world to make it so. Our work here is far more important than you could imagine. Just wait till the slut gets that letter. I want to be watching at that *very* moment. See it *live*."

CHAPTER FOUR

Becoming the Mystery

Chapter 29 — The Forest

Part 1 — Harvesting

The key question asks whether sooner is better than later. This directly relates to the skill level of The Forest tender. Proper husbandry will produce superb food quality that may be tasted ever after consumption, enhancing strengths, rounding out weaknesses. Yet, such a long term investment risks losing to competitive forces all time, effort, and desire.

Case study: Ancient Alpha Allintime was the most patient of all. Having consumed enough to establish his power, he set to raising the best crop of any Alpha. Naturally, it made him a target according to our natural order. But he expected this, and instead of hunting to feed, he waited cleverly to be hunted. In short, his food came to him, and he consumed his rivals. Thus, his crop had two purposes: To provide long term quality food and to draw to himself short term food. Thus he solved the problem of forgoing early harvest by substituting in his enemies!

SACRIFICIAL WOOD

Footnote: So desirable did his crop become, that the Father himself consumed him. Thus, the Father has All in time (Allintime) within Him.

Falling, falling, falling…how long…what does it matter… falling…hold… no hold… die, no death… hope…. hope…where…falling…hold… no hold…falling… how long…forever…hope…no hope…Stephanie…forgive me… die…no death…why…

☙

"I'm home. *I'm tired…*"

"Let me take your boots, Sir." Arlupo bowed, clothed in a full length, black velvety dress, with golden Appendaho embroidery at its hem, neck, and sleeves. Her long, thick black hair hung down freely, gracefully. The young lady more than epitomized the spirit of true royalty.

"Daddy, I…I…I take your hat." Lana bowed and smiled. Her long, colorfully printed white dress had different animal patterns frolicking about.

"I'll take your coat, Father." Stephanie bowed, smiling. Her dress's velvety dark blue material flashed with finely sewn flaming red patterns running the length of its long sleeves, up the middle in the front, and around the neck. Her wavy, red hair hung in two thick braids. She didn't mind the short visits with her father. Treating him in such a fashion allowed her to imagine giving and receiving affection. *Perhaps, in time, he'll learn to lighten up.*

"Here's your supper, Fred." Jean dropped a plate of food at his table spot with a clang. Sitting down upon his dining room chair as a king sets himself upon his throne, everything seemed delightfully in order. He began to chew on a piece of roast beef. He chewed hard. Lately, Jean's cooking, which had for so long been positively scrumptious, seemed to have taken a turn for the worst. For the children, however, she prepared her special glazed chicken in which they delighted.

Everything finally began to live up to his expectations, and now the time was at hand to move them along. Jean sat opposite her husband at the long end of the table with Stephanie and Lana beside each other, Lana closer to her father's right. Arlupo sat alone on the other side, opposite Stephanie.

He waved at Arlupo a strip of beef speared on his fork as he spoke. The beef emphasized his gestures as he inflected his words. "Arlupo, someday I'll have to visit your people. This is marvelous. Finally…some sanity. I don't blame your people for secluding themselves and protecting their ways from outsiders. I want you to know, I'm very grateful."

Arlupo bowed her head once. "We are honored to be helpful to such an important man."

He felt important, looked important. His hair was freshly-cut-important with perfect shape cut out around the ears. His bald spot on top shined like a beacon. He had just come from a very expensive barber. He picked up another piece of dry, overcooked beef to help him communicate to his subjects.

"I've told the people I work with about you. Your people could be model people for what we are trying to do. We would like to visit you." A knot jumped into all three children's stomachs. All eyes turned toward Arlupo.

"That is wonderful, Sir. But you must give us a week's notice. It is sacred to us to receive guests and we cannot receive you without the proper preparations."

The beef waggled in circles as if some tortured, impaled life form. "Of course…of course. When you come back in two weeks, I'll let you know. The progress you've made is phenomenal."

"That would be very good, Sir." Again the head bow.

Lana looked to Stephanie, and Stephanie looked to Arlupo to see if she had the same feeling that they did. They had become almost completely in tune with each other's thoughts and feelings, and usually knew them without much being said. But the only thing Stephanie sensed now was that she couldn't tell. It disturbed her. More and more, Stephanie became aware of a powerful sense she had to…*feel* things. But this time, in fact, Arlupo even avoided her gaze. When Stephanie redoubled her efforts to see past her friend's cover, she still came up empty. Her father's cruelly tinged words jolted her concentration.

"Jean, where's my wine? You know I always like to start with some white wine."

She had expected him to notice it earlier and had begun to worry he would forget altogether. Her response sounded hollow, dry, and overlaid with servility. "I'm sorry, Fred, I forgot."

He blew up, his shining beacon turning red. "Forgot! How would it be if I forgot to do my duty to you? If it wasn't for your little daughter, I swear..."

With the children gone, she had become the sole focus of all his homely intentions for perfection. Stephanie could feel every fiber of Jean's pain. Besides, Stephanie knew her father wasn't so noble as to stay for the sake of any mere child, especially a *girl* child. A ball of fire ignited inside her. Arlupo's eyes quickly flashed to her friend as she sensed it. She could see Stephanie's thoughts.

I've had enough *of this... Arlupo, don't* kick *me, I'm... ouch...*ouch!

Jean began to bawl uncontrollably. The worst thing she could have done. Like setting fire to dynamite, he exploded, "WHY ARE YOU CRYING, WOMAN?" His big black eyebrows bore down onto her.

She looked up into his eyes, pleading, "I miss my daughter."

Hearing her mother's loving confession, Lana's eyes grew wide. She began to move in her chair but Stephanie grabbed her hand under the table, silently praying for her to keep quiet. She understood.

The king decreed his best judgment, pointing the way with that big finger, "GET OUT! Go to your room until you can stop embarrassing yourself."

"Fred..." She wailed as she left.

He turned red-faced in shame to Arlupo, "I'm sorry, Arlupo, this must be very difficult for you, an *enlightened* woman, to see this."

Arlupo held her head down, biting her lower lip before she could speak. Her head felt like it would burst, trying to keep track of everything. Never mind her heart. "I suppose some people can't help themselves. Would you excuse me, Sir?"

"Oh, of course, dear." He hoped she would go talk some sense into his wife.

Arlupo slowly climbed the stairs, pulling herself up by the shiny, dark brown banister to where the bedrooms were. *There's no time for anger, now.* In the back of her mind, she supposed she saw this coming, but with so much to attend to, she hadn't given it thought. She thought now. All reality was connected. It was dangerous to ignore that. *I shouldn't have ignored it. Being young is no excuse. I don't think I wanted to look. I hope Stephanie and Lana can control themselves. I hope I can control myself!* She knocked softly and poked her head in.

"Excuse me, Ma'am, is it all right to come in?"

Jean sprawled on the bed as their eyes met. "*You!* You've *stolen* my daughter!" Arlupo gasped inside as the hatred she saw in Jean's eyes entered into Arlupo, stabbing her in the heart. The pain of it had her holding tightly to the crystal doorknob for support as her vision temporarily blurred. Never before had she felt such evil directed at her. She caught the full intensity of it without defense, having never been in such a battle or faced such weapons. But Arlupo regained focus, pressing on with a look that could heal, while thinking, *Oh God, is this what Stephanie has had to face in her life? This is the way it feels? Oh God, how did she bear it?*

"May I come in?"

But Jean responded with mocking. "You are the *important* one, here. Come and go as you please. If you're not careful, Fred will throw me away and marry *you!*"

Arlupo answered softly, "Whose choice was it to marry him?"

But that only brought out her rage to lash Arlupo. "CHOICE! CHOICE! *WHAT CHOICE?* I couldn't take care of myself. The government would have taken my daughter… you *bitch*, you know *nothing*!"

Arlupo was learning war. She placed her hands upon her hips, narrowing her eyes at Jean, but she still spoke with kindness. That was her nature. "How many men were courting you? You're very pretty."

Jean hung her head. "My husband died. He was a *good* man. I didn't care who was courting me. I just needed…"

Arlupo's lips flattened. Her tone became dry. She couldn't help it. "*That* was your choice. I was going to tell you all about Lana, but I see you don't want to hear anything from this… *bitch!*" Arlupo backed out and began to close the door behind her but Jean screamed after her.

"WAIT…*please*…*I'm sorry*…" Entering the bedroom, she shut the door behind her. As soon as she turned to Jean, Jean confronted her. "I just don't understand how you women can act the way you do!"

Arlupo, shocked at the absurdity, looked dryly at her again, "*Really*. And why is that?"

"Because, you're nothing but slaves, bowing down to men!"

"I bowed to you, too, out of respect. I helped you with your housework, with your daughter…"

The hatred came back into Jean's eyes, overpowering her. "Oh, *you help* alright…"

Arlupo decided to challenge her, grabbing Jean's eyes with hers. She held the woman's gaze with the power of her will boring into Jean, reflecting what Arlupo saw, that Jean, in part, had created her own problems. After several long moments, Arlupo redirected. "Lana has a puppy."

Jean hesitated but something in her allowed her to pick up Arlupo's lead. "She does?"

"Yes, she's named it."

"Oh? What does she call her?"

Arlupo reproduced the way Lana said her pet's name. "Puppy."

Jean's hatred collapsed as she heard her daughter's delighted voice reflected in Arlupo's answer. Surprisingly, Jean laughed. "Oh dear, that's Lana." Arlupo repeated it several more times in same fashion. Jean broke into fits of laughter. She wanted her daughter to be happy more than anything.

Arlupo softly chuckled, sitting on the bed next to Jean. She placed her hand on Jean's shoulder. "She misses you terribly, but she's scared."

Jean's head snapped up. "Scared! What are you doing to her?"

Arlupo's calm stare weathered the onslaught. Moments passed as the incongruence of Arlupo's caring defied Jean's evil characterization. Arlupo squeezed Jean's shoulder. "She thinks you don't love her."

Staggered, Jean fell silent.

Arlupo waited for it to sink in. "Because you stopped singing to her, tucking her in, and you let Fred yell at her, and you 'appolized' for her when she *wasn't wrong and didn't do it.*"

It was clear to Jean that those were her daughter's words. Arlupo glared at her to make her next point. "That was *before* I met you!" Then she softened, "How does Lana seem to you now?"

Jean's shoulder's drooped. Shame crept into her. Also, her inadequacy began to be visible. "She does seem…happy."

"Is she any less loving to you?"

Jean reflected for a bit, trying to push away the crushing weight in her heart, "Oh, she's still my lovely daughter."

"Is she getting yelled at by your loving husband?"

"*My what?*"

Arlupo just stared at her, allowing reality to make its own point. *I think that should do it.* She didn't want Jean's spirit crushed. The simple truth was, though, that Fred was a lot better now with Lana and that oddity finally struck home in Jean's awareness.

"You are right, though. She's not getting yelled at. Actually, she's getting his love…somehow….but everything I do… it's never good enough."

Arlupo squared herself in front of Jean. Arlupo's anger at Fred's behavior came through in her tone. "You are a good woman! It's better if you add wisdom to your goodness."

The compliment further disarmed Jean. She felt helpless, not being able to solace herself in anger or rage or grief for any harm done to her daughter. Her own selfishness felt sick inside her. *If Lana is happier, then I shouldn't...* "I don't understand. Wisdom?"

When Arlupo heard it, she raised her eyebrow at Jean's ignorance. "It's interesting to me how people lie to themselves when they convince themselves that they have no choice to do something and then choose to do it…and then blame everyone else for the consequences because, of course they had to be innocent because they had no choice!"

Jean's silence betrayed her conscience.

Arlupo spoke softly into that silence, "You sit and stare at me. Look into my eyes, if you dare, and see yourself." Arlupo opened her eyes wide but Jean collapsed on the bed in tears.

"No…I can't…"

Arlupo bent over her, not willing to let her escape. "You weep, and you can't look, because you already know what's there. You already see yourself, and you don't like it. Now you're faced again with choices, and you must find the strength and wisdom to live with dignity." Arlupo put her hand upon Jean's back. The comfort, the meaning of it, racked Jean with sobs, bringing a spark to a word to which Jean used to fiercely cling. *Dignity! Oh God, how could I have forgotten for so, so long!*

Jean turned around, sitting up, looking into Arlupo's eyes with amazement. "How can you speak so? You're but a child, yourself."

Arlupo shrugged. "Ehh, children are idealistic by nature. And, reality is what it is. It doesn't cloak itself. It's there to see. I wasn't taught to run from it. In fact, I was taught *how* to keep from running from it! How to not blind myself, how to be truthful to myself, so I could be true to others. Don't think you won't have your daughter back. She'll be back much sooner than you believe! And only you will be able to save her!"

Now Jean felt the grip of something greater than her. She felt small, helpless, and very ignorant and something much more… "What? What are you saying? Why? I don't…"

"I'll tell you a secret that not even my father knows!"

Jean was overwhelmed. People just didn't relate like this, but… "Why would you do that to a stranger?"

Arlupo repeated, hoping it would sink in and mean something this time, "Reality is what it is. A tree needs sunlight to grow. You need my secret to believe."

Jean shook her head, her heart perceiving something her mind had no way to comprehend. "I don't understand."

"That is your choice! Are you ready?" Arlupo's look was like steel, but Jean's wide eyes were caught between terror, awe, and confusion.

"I guess so."

"I understand you have many conflicting emotions that make this, your choice, seem like a guess. But you're not guessing. You've made the right choice." She paused to let Jean catch her breath. "I am the daughter of the great leader of my people. But with my people, it is law that only truth and love may be leader, so that anyone who speaks it, has right to speak as leader! Men, women, even children!"

Jean swooned. Nothing was as it had seemed. "But, but…I had no idea…"

"Wisdom has guided me in what I do for you. When I told my father and my people of your trouble, they agreed with my desire to help you!"

Jean's eyes couldn't draw wide enough. Her heart pounded. "Oh my God…you mean…all this…is *your* idea, a *child's* idea?"

Arlupo shrugged. "Reality and truth and love are what they are, and my people will not argue against it. But in order to help you, we had to approach your husband as we did. We have never lied to you or acted falsely, but your eyes saw what they wanted to see, not what was truly there. Now, at risk to me and my people, I take your blindness away if you choose."

Tears kept running down Jean's face. "But why would you *do* that?"

"Because I *cannot* say that you are any less valuable than your daughter or me or my people. Your life, also, is on the line. Choose for your life and your daughter's." Arlupo placed both of her hands upon Jean's folded hands.

Jean shook her head seeking escape and finding none. People just didn't act like this. "Oh God, I don't understand."

The pain of Jean's chosen ignorance shot through Arlupo. She could see what would come if Jean decided not to change. Arlupo hung her head. "Your ignorance is your choice and you will die with your daughter in your arms and she shall be raised by your husband until the day she kills herself! She does not have the strength of Stephanie."

Jean pulled away angrily, "How can you say such a *terrible* thing? What craziness…"

Arlupo's tears were falling onto the bed. "Sometimes I wish I couldn't see or *feel*. But my secret is real, nonetheless. I am a prophetess! Some things are shown to me; past, present, and future. You are now the only one who knows this. I haven't even told Stephanie, or my own father."

"Shown how? You're just deluded. What have you got my daughter…"

With tears increasing, almost to the point of sobbing, "In visions with understanding. Your former husband didn't die a natural death!"

Jean reeled, "Wha…"

"You loved him very much. He was a good man. You used to have secret discussions with him about the government and God. When you were pregnant with Lana, you wanted to flee the country, but your husband said it was too dangerous! You used to be a thinking woman! Your husband was crushed to death in a supposed factory accident but they never let you see his body."

Jean shook. "How can you know such things?" *There are no such things as future telling…but how could she possibly know about our discussions? They were secret. We wouldn't dare have told anyone.*

Arlupo just stared at her. "You think your husband was murdered…but you don't know who did it."

"Was he?"

"There is no such thing as future telling and how could I possibly know the past? Why ask me?"

"Oh God, those were the exact words…"

"Your current husband has terrible dreams. He smashed your bathroom mirror. You hear him crying out at night for his *mother* to save him!"

Oh God, no one knew about the mirror. No one. "Stop, stop..." Jean wept, "Do you know if he was murdered?"

"I know he wouldn't want you to be next! Can you look into my eyes?"

From somewhere, Jean didn't know how, but somehow it seemed as if many scattered pieces of a huge puzzle were beginning to slowly fit themselves together. She hesitated and then drew upon her new feelings. "I think so."

Without smiling, heart breaking, Arlupo responded, "You have made the right choice, again."

Jean let herself flow into Arlupo's eyes. It worked both ways. She felt comings and goings. "...Oh dear God...*dear God*...she speaks the *truth*...what am I to do?" Jean wept. Arlupo wept. She could no longer help herself. She felt undone. *How do they go through this day after day? Oh God...* They held each other's hands and Arlupo finally spoke because time was growing ever shorter.

"It's begun."

"What?"

"Yours and your daughter's path to salvation. If you continue on it, you'll raise your daughter to have the strength she will need to save thousands, maybe more. Now, go and bow to your husband and beg his forgiveness, not because he deserves it, but because it does no harm to you and because it's wise. In this way, you're at least offering some goodness to him that he can receive. He's a very weak man and can't bear strength in a woman. Yet, the more he acts as he does, the weaker he gets, so the more he must debase you. Let him see what he desires to see and that will keep him from seeing the real you!

"When wisdom bears fruit, that fruit will justify its actions because it comes from a good tree. That fruit is your and your daughter's free lives with dignity. Whatever you do in life, first do it unto yourself in truth, and then there will be no shame when you do it to others. If I humble myself before the Light even within me, I can humble myself before others for the cause of the Light. It doesn't matter if others think I am bowing to them. They choose their blindness, and it will kill them in the end. But when you're true to yourself, *reality is what reality is.*" Her words seemed full of thousands and thousands of years, and they swallowed Jean up in time. Her whole body, her whole being, seemed to be vibrating.

Jean whispered, squeezing Arlupo's hands, "I have much to think about."

Arlupo leveled her gaze into her. "You keep making all the right choices. I knew I didn't risk my life for nothing! If you chose to tell your husband about me, I'm sure he would have me put to death!"

The two women went to the small bathroom off the corner of the bedroom and refreshed themselves. Then they came down stairs together. Stephanie was having Lana recite school lessons to her father. It was an innocuous procedure.

Jean drew near to her husband. "Forgive me, Fred, I am

a foolish woman." Jean bowed and his mouth dropped open.

He looked up at Arlupo with a mixture of love and reverence, "Arlupo, I swear, if you weren't a child, I would...Oh, Stephanie, there was a letter for you from your hometown. I'm afraid it bears bad news."

"Excuse me, Father, how do you know?"

"I read it. I'm your protector. You don't know how evil and tricky this world is. I wouldn't be the *man* I am if I let harm come to you. Here."

Stephanie took the opened envelope and pulled out the piece of school notebook paper. For some reason, she started shaking, even before she unfolded it. She sat at the dining room table, unfolded the triple-folded, ragged-edged paper and read.

Dear Stephanie,

You may not remember me, but I am Vaughn's best friend, next to you. I am sorry to tell you that many terrible things have happened to our friend since you left. I cannot afford the space to tell you of them, only that Vaughn lies near death.

Her hands weakly fell to the table with a bang, as tears fell from her eyes and memories flooded her. Suddenly, she could feel Vaughn gently holding her the last night they spent together, smoothing her hair. His words, *I like your eyes...What don't you understand about being a person?* Her chest heaved. Arlupo, who was standing next to her, touched her arm, "Stephie, what is it?" But she didn't answer. She found just enough strength to shakily pick up her arms and finish reading.

The doctors say he may die at any time. I told Vaughn I was going to write you, but he's unconscious, but maybe he can hear because he did say something. But it didn't make sense. "Through our prayers." But I wasn't praying. I am now. Perhaps if you could somehow reach him, you will give him the desire to live.

Your friend too, Waverly

Stephanie wailed, "*Oh God, no…*" In that instant of time, a single feeling picture engulfed her of every aspect of the realness of her life that Vaughn had inspired. It proclaimed itself loudly of her feelings about herself, her understanding of *everything*, her added ability to help others, her ability to be with the Appendaho without running away from herself. Painfully now aware that she had continually within her a connection to Vaughn that was both his and hers at the same time, and in that connection how much she loved, cherished, and adored that goodness that is Vaughn, all of that convulsed together in helplessness. All strength was now gone and Stephanie collapsed, falling out of her chair and onto the floor next to Arlupo.

For the first time in her life, Arlupo was scared, actually terrified. It felt as if her dear friend had just been torn apart and lay there dead, and with it, a continual connection within Arlupo screamed in agony. A thick blackness suddenly, stiflingly, descended upon Arlupo making her gasp inside. All hope was gone…there was no meaning any more. Severe pains in her chest took away her breath. *Oh Light, save me from this evil!* Arlupo did her best, grabbing the chair for support, but she couldn't hide her shaking.

Stephanie's father scolded, "Stephanie, get off the floor. That's no way for a lady to act. Crying, always crying like your mother. Pathetic!"

Oddly, Fred's outburst was exactly what Arlupo needed! She desperately needed something else to focus on. Though shaking, she mustered every bit of strength she had to hold her composure. Arlupo turned bright red. Fred thought it was from embarrassment because of Stephanie. Jean's mouth was hanging open. Lana was about to cry. Arlupo knew if any one of them acted foolishly now, this could blow up terribly. She quickly turned to the tyrant. "Sir, let me take her to her room and try to correct her!"

He waved his hand off in a kingly fashion. "Please do, Arlupo. The problem with her is that she's been with too many *boys!* I don't know if she told you, but when I was back East, some of her concerned friends told me a *great deal* about her. She's not the kind of girl you are. I really don't know what man would seriously want her if he knew her past."

Arlupo turned seething red, gritted her teeth and with all her will spoke softly. "Well Sir, *for your sake*, perhaps we can hide it from the world and she could live a dignified life, so *you* don't have to be ashamed."

Jean was about to tear into Fred, but hearing that word, *dignity*, kept her from speaking as she remembered Arlupo's wisdom. "How wise you are, Arlupo. Incredible! Please take her away and don't blush because of her. It's not your fault!"

Never before had Arlupo experienced serious anger, no… rage, and never before had she known anything so ferocious and consuming. She hurried away with her arm around Stephanie's waist, lest her feelings cause her to say something she would regret.

It was an arduous climb up the stairs but she finally set Stephanie down on her bed and sat next to her. She was still clutching the letter in a daze. Arlupo grabbed her shoulders, but Stephanie paid her no mind. She shook her, "Stephie, what is it?"

Stephanie's eyes were distant, as if she had gone somewhere.

Arlupo was still shaking from both her rage and fright over her best friend's condition. In the back of her mind she knew that Jean and Lana were still in danger downstairs, but there was nothing she could do. Her heart was in her throat. Another new experience along with… "Pleeease, Stephie, you're scaring the hell out of me! May I see the letter? Thank you." Stephanie really hadn't offered it, but her friend took it anyway.

Arlupo fought back her tears as she read it. But there was no time for tears now. *This doesn't make any sense. This isn't supposed to happen.* "This isn't right." She voiced her thoughts in anger or as a plea, both. "NO!" She shook her head violently, her raven hair spraying in all directions.

Then, a moment of stillness as she realized she had let herself be overpowered. Another new experience. She shook herself again, but this time to clear away that awful feeling. She directed her entire will to help her sinking friend. She needed to find a way to make her face reality.

"STEPHANIE, I'm afraid we don't have time for you to cry now. Do you want to help your lover?"

SACRIFICIAL WOOD

For some reason that question, that *word*, dug at Stephanie. She heard it as if in a distance, then came rushing back to herself as if through a long tunnel, back into the open. Her eyes snapped up. She answered dryly, twisting away in anger from her best friend, "He is not my *lover*." Then she realized where she was and connected the meaning of Arlupo's words to what she now vaguely remembered her father saying.

What Stephanie had hidden was now out in the light. She hung her head. "What Father said about me is true, but not about Vaughn. We never..." Arlupo grabbed her arms hard and spun her around to face her. "That *bastard* knows no truth at all, least of all about his daughter. I don't care about him. I care about *you* and *Vaughn*. Do you know why Vaughn said, Through our prayers?" Stephanie shook her head to clear it further, not knowing why Arlupo was so interested in it. "Yes, but no, I mean...I'm not supposed to tell anyone. It's a secret between me and Vaughn."

"I was sent to you by the Light, Stephanie. Do you believe me?"

"Yes, I do."

"Then trust me. I swear I won't reveal your secret to another." Arlupo's heart pounded so hard it felt strange inside her body. Having not experienced anything like this, she wondered if she might die herself at any moment. There was so little time.

If Vaughn dies, then what good is our secret? But what good is it to Arlupo? But there's no one I trust more than them. "Vaughn said that we needed a way to trust our communications and that those words, through our prayers, should be used naturally in every communication we exchange so that we would know it's true."

Arlupo's eyes went distant. "Oh my…a wise young man…he foresees…" But then she sharply focused on Stephanie, "But why that particular saying?"

"Because I had said that would be the way we would communicate with each other, even if we couldn't write much or talk. We would feel our prayers for each other in our hearts. Oh Arlupo, I prayed for him after we agreed on it and I could feel our life together, not just then, but in the future, while I prayed. I believe he could, too. That feeling was so wonderful, and we knew then that we had chosen just the right, meaningful words…through our prayers. That was like an answer to my prayer that through our faith we would come back together. Oh Arlupo, it didn't feel…like *this*." She took the letter from Arlupo and shook it.

Arlupo squeezed her friend even tighter, her own thoughts and emotions beginning to overcome even her best efforts at control. Insistently, Arlupo pressed, "You prayed? And you could feel it, truly? Like you were actually there?"

"Yes." She looked at her friend not understanding why her strong emphasis.

Arlupo leaned back, letting Stephanie go, leveling her eyes into Stephanie's, searching. Arlupo seemed to have made up her mind about something. *She* touched *the Tree of Life. No one has ever done so except…* "You are a very special woman, Stephanie. We need to get back home right away."

Stephanie scrunched and raised her eyebrows, "But...I don't understand."

"Have you been thinking about what my father told you?"

"Yes, quite a bit."

"Good. That's what's required. If you have found the true tree within yourself, and are able to free yourself of the dead one, you may be able to save Vaughn's life!"

Stephanie sat back, dazed, daring herself to accept what she heard, not understanding, but Arlupo had proven herself to be true. "But...but how?"

Arlupo was hoping. She wasn't sure...it was a feeling. *Is this a feeling because I just want it to be real, or is it a true perception? Oh Light, I don't have time to discern it. But that doesn't matter now. I have to hope it's real. I have to hope in Legend.*

"I can't tell you how, because I don't know! Only you can know this, because you have the gift. I felt it in you all along, but now I *know* you have it! I don't have that gift. So I don't understand it, and I can't tell you how it works...except..." Arlupo cut herself off, holding back. She knew this was way over Stephanie's head.

Oh God, I never told Arlupo about any of my strange abilities. Stephanie's wide eyes told her that she wanted to hear more. "What? Except what?" Stephanie grabbed her arms. "Except *what* Arlupo?"

Arlupo sighed, "When a person steps into the complete unknown, and the only thing they carry with them is true faith..." Arlupo stopped again, but not by choice this time.

Stephanie was hanging on the edge of her friend's words, "What…*then what?*"

Arlupo pleaded with her with her eyes, "I don't know! *God help me*, but I really don't know. It's only a distant vision, a feeling. I can't know this because I don't have that gift. Only one with the gift of special faith and the gift of special prayer combined can see clearly what they must do at each exact moment. And Stephie, if you want to save Vaughn, you will have to do the right thing at *every single moment*, or you will be lost, too."

They were squeezing each other's arms so tightly each felt pain, and Arlupo realized she was putting her best friend's life in horrific danger. She hadn't even thought it through…but there was no time to think. Stephanie began to recoil from the impact. "I don't understand…I'll never…"

Arlupo redirected. "Did you and Vaughn ever discuss faith?"

"Yes, quite a lot."

"That's because it called to each of you, just like the Tree of Life and you called to each other."

"But aren't the gift of prayer and faith the same?

"The gift of prayer uses only a *part* of the gift of faith, that part that pertains to the prayer. But the gift of *faith* goes much, *much* farther."

Arlupo's eyes widened at the awesome knowledge, remembering the stories of legend her father used to tell her. She remembered how rapt she was when she heard them, and how, when her father had finished a story, she had begged him to go back and retell it all over again.

◈ SACRIFICIAL WOOD ◈

"For what? To what? How does the gift of faith go much farther?" Stephanie tried to pull her friend out from her thoughts.

Arlupo refocused, gazing deeply into her. *I'm becoming more and more sure my feelings are correct, not just because I want them to be. I can see it burning in her eyes.* "It wouldn't be good for me to tell you, because it's not any specific thing, but of endless possibilities. If you fixate on any particular thing, you'll limit your gift, and I don't know if by telling you something, that'll cause you to limit the very thing you'll need most. I'll tell you this. Your being able to touch the Tree and see the visions are part of your gift of faith. What is real faith based on, Stephanie?"

"Vaughn and I discussed this. He says real faith is not blind, but is based on *understanding* of what is true, what is real. That you know, by virtue of coming in contact with Life's ways, its principles, you just know by their nature what Life will do and what it won't. I agree with this, but it's more than just an intellectual thing…it can be…kinda in everything, knowing by feeling how things are, or may proceed. It's more than just an intellectual understanding. It's more than just a feeling. It's a real understanding on a much deeper level.

"Vaughn and I believe everything has meaning…I think true faith thinks in terms of this deeper meaning, with intellect *and* emotion supporting and understanding each other perfectly…and…and…puts together chunks of these deeper meanings like we put together words to form a thought. That's why it's so hard to describe. It's like looking at a lake and not just seeing the surface, but being able to see the whole lake, like we see it from ground level, like the fish sees it in the lake, and like a bird sees it from above…all at the same time, in one big understanding that makes sense!"

That awesome picture that her best friend so eloquently and accurately painted swallowed Arlupo. It brought her to tears. Good tears. The power of that picture, which Arlupo absorbed in full, direct from Stephanie's heart and mind, staggered her, and Stephanie became aware that her friend was overwhelmed. It was an odd moment for them both.

Arlupo finally responded, "My God, I have never, *never* heard such words in my entire life, not even from Father. But I know they're as true as I am looking at you right now. What you are saying is simply that you are able to see reality for what it is, as a *whole*, and that seeing only the surface is not seeing truly, as the surface is connected to the depth. The only true sight is to see it all as one. Stephanie, the gift of faith allows you to not only *see* this way, but to *move* through reality in this way!"

Stephanie's mind reeled. Her face scrunched up in helplessness. She didn't understand Arlupo's words about the gift, but she realized her heart definitely did, because it told her that exactly made sense. But what did? "Huh? Arlupo, all this is way beyond me. I just now thought about what I told you. I never thought that before. Vaughn is the one…"

Arlupo squeezed her very tightly now, being even more sure, and raised her voice. "Dying, if you don't help him. But to help him, you have to first forget all about him!"

Too much now, way over the top. "WHAT? I could never..."

"We must go, now. My father will explain this to you. It is his gift to do so." At least Arlupo had figured out how she would get Stephanie back right away. Poor Lana would have to fend for her little self for now.

They came downstairs, and Stephanie did as Arlupo had told her. Stephanie was huffy. Lana was teaching her father her counting lessons that Arlupo's mother had taught her. He was listening as if he were her student, making sure she was correct on everything.

Arlupo came before Stephanie's father with tears. "Sir, forgive me...but..."

He was shocked to see her, of all women, crying. "Arlupo, tears from you? I would not have expected..."

"Tears Sir, because I have failed you."

"What? Oh child, poor child, how have you failed me?"

She wagged her finger at Stephanie. "This...this...*girl*, is so stubborn. I couldn't make her see what she needed to see. I'm afraid only my father has the ability to straighten her out."

It didn't require thinking on his part. It was obvious what needed to be done. "Well then, take her to your father. If he can, he will be a better man than I am."

Stephanie fought back! "Don't send me to her father!"

He gave the predictable reaction. "You will do as you are *told*," he yelled at her, not willing to put up with a moment's more rebellion.

"I won't!" she answered snottily.

"*YOU WILL*," he roared menacingly.

She yelled back, "FINE, I'll GO *NEXT WEEK*."

Without a moment to spare he slammed the gavel down, "YOU'LL GO NOW. RIGHT NOW OR I WILL GIVE YOU TO THE GOVERNMENT."

"WHAT KIND OF FATHER ARE YOU?"

"ONE WHO LOVES YOU! GOOOOOOO!" he bellowed.

As the two girls left the dining room, Jean and Arlupo exchanged quick glances. Jean gave her the slightest nod and Arlupo knew that Jean was now seeing reality for what it is. Arlupo let out a soft sigh of relief.

As they packed up their things, Jean and Lana came into Stephanie's bedroom to say goodbye. Lana gave them explicit instructions on how to care for Puppy, reminding them to practice *sit* and *shake*. Arlupo drove Stephanie immediately back to her village.

☙

Master GrrraGagag growled softly, "What legend? It must all be locked away in the secret files. Scraback, you worked in the records department..."

"Master, but history wasn't my field. Shouldn't we get back to…?"

"I can't believe this. We were so close to having her. I could have just grazed her with my touch and she would have fallen off the edge. But I was so sure she would do it all by herself and didn't need my help. I almost had her friend, too. I'm going to take extreme pleasure in watching both her *love* and her *best* friend die. Then I *will* push her over the edge, if she hasn't fallen off by then."

Scraback still couldn't figure out why his Master seemed to be putting on an act. *Why act ignorant of all these things? What Legend? Did someone mention Legend? What secret files? Hmm…*

CHAPTER FIVE
Minds That Are One Endless Heart

Grrrag could hear Gagag calling him but knew his Master would never suspect him hiding here. He picked up another ethereal stone and hurled it across the Black River, watching it skip, watching the black vapors bubble up at each touch point. But it would do no good to inhale them now. He called out to the now grey wisps, "First I have to consume many before I can give you full life." The wisps turned toward Grrrag and began floating toward him but before they arrived they were reabsorbed by the river.

Arlupo arrived in her village around two in the morning. Unexpected, the watchers noted her. They looked over as she got out of the car in the parking area. But since she made no sign of desiring attention, they went about their business. Their post had been created since the beginning of their being a people. Twenty-four hours a day, there was always someone who did nothing but watch over the village.

☙ SACRIFICIAL WOOD ☙

Arlupo sighed with relief at being home. Part of her felt like a little child who wanted to run into her mother's arms, be comforted, and forget about the world. She shook it off quickly. She felt drained, but knew she was a long way from being able to rest. Nevertheless, it was comforting to be back in a community of human beings. She remembered how it had been her idea to have the apartment in town before she had moved back with Stephanie. "I want to feel what it's like to live with them. It will help me to better understand," she had told her father. She shook her head at all that she now understood.

As she nodded to the watchers, she realized how much she took for granted…those who continually prayed for the village's purity. By herself, in her apartment, she had often felt the walls closing in. She realized now, just how much true people praying together made a difference to the general atmosphere. In contrast, it made what Stephanie had become to her all the more impressive. *How could she make it, all by herself, facing all that anger, hatred and, and, and…?* She had no word for the continual assault by evil in spirit, in people, and, and…now that she had felt the full force of what it was to be thrashed by such evil, only for just a brief time, she was confounded even more at how anyone could maintain their integrity. *By the Light, I love you Stephanie.*

Hundreds of round stone cottages were once occupied, but now only around thirty. The rest were, over time, carefully sealed up and set aside, in case one day there would be others. Now, only the ones near the village square were lived in, except for a few who preferred the privacy of a hillside cottage.

Arlupo sighed, *If father is right, that we've died out because we secluded ourselves…But it seems impossible to live a true life on the outside.* She shook her head, for the first time not being able to reconcile her thoughts. Tears crept into her eyes and then she looked over at her dear friend. Arlupo tingled all over. Somehow she knew the answer to her conundrum was Stephanie. *If she can make it, she'll be able to bring the strength of goodness to this world even we could not.*

Stephanie made note of the shining, golden tree inlayed into the front door. It had so much more meaning to her now. *I remember seeing that so many times, but now that I know, it doesn't look the same.* She reverently ran her fingers across it before entering. She remembered the tapestry in the government church, how she poked at it. Her thoughts vocalized. "What a difference!" Arlupo looked at her in question, but she shrugged it off.

Just inside the door, they kicked off their shoes, and Arlupo made her way to her father's study. How she knew he would be up at this hour, Stephanie couldn't figure out. As they walked across the living room, Stephanie took note of the golden cross pattern on the floor leading to different doors. *I wonder what other meanings have been right under my nose unawares to me. I'll have to remember to ask about this.*

Arlupo knocked softly at the study door and went in without being invited. Her father was sitting behind his desk.

"My dear Father, we are sorry to bother you so late."

He seemed to be expecting them. "It's alright, I couldn't sleep. What's wrong? Why are you back before…?"

Arlupo handed him Stephanie's letter. "Read this, my father."

He took the letter, looking hard at his daughter. She looked torn up inside, wounded. So much was different about her. Even the way she carried herself was different. He knew, she, at sixteen, had surpassed him in knowledge of many things. A pain shot through his heart as he gazed into her eyes. He sighed and then read.

He sat silently for several moments, a stillness that seemed eternal.

Setting the letter down, he folded his hands with gravity and another sigh. The two girls grabbed folding chairs from the corner and set them up in front of the desk.

"What is it you want, my children?" Somehow, that word, children, suddenly seemed out of place to him.

Arlupo looked straight at her father. "Will you hold her hands Father? Will you see for yourself? Then maybe you'll believe me?"

Stephanie studied her and her request. She didn't understand. He looked over to her sitting next to his daughter. He loved seeing them together. They were as sisters. They were more. His face opened to Stephanie as never before. There was softness in his eyes of which she had not seen the likes.

"Stephanie, my daughter wishes me to use a gift that the Light has bestowed upon me. But I cannot do so without your complete permission. To give it, you must understand what the gift is. If I hold your hands and let your mind and heart flow into me, I will know everything about you, *everything*.

It's not just the knowing of ideas. I will know you like you know yourself, maybe better. I will feel all that you have felt, and think all that you have thought."

Stunned, Stephanie didn't know why such a thing should be done. "How...why..."

"I really don't understand that myself. I've only used this gift twice in my life. I'm sorry. In a way, it's a terrible gift."

Stephanie turned to her beloved friend. "Arlupo, why do you want your father to do this?" It wasn't only a question for knowledge. It had a growing flavor of protest.

Arlupo didn't hesitate. She knew what had to be done. There was precious little time to do it. *If it really can be done.* Her face was pleading with them. There was so much she knew that she wasn't telling them. Even her father didn't know the extent of her foresight. He only had an inkling of it, and then he wasn't sure she really had that gift. She took Stephanie's hands in hers. "Because time is short. Vaughn doesn't have the time it will take for me to convince Father, nor the time it will take you by yourself to understand all that you need."

Caught between her tremendous love and her great shame, those two terrible forces rending Stephanie in two, she lodged a deeper protest. "But...oh Arlupo, you don't know me..." She broke down crying, shaking her head, castigating herself for her past indiscretions because they now interfered in what was truly important. Memories of feelings and vial actions now assaulted her and she felt out of place even just remembering them. *But to have it all exposed, so vividly...*

Arlupo put her hand on her shoulder. Her father leaned his elbow on his desk and propped his head upon his hand, watching and waiting. He wasn't sure he would be able to succeed even if she agreed. He didn't know if he could hold on. And he wasn't sure what he needed convincing about.

"Please don't cry, Stephie," Arlupo begged, but Stephanie aired her doubts.

"Knowing me would only convince your father not to bother...*at best*."

All three sat silent for a time, because her statement was so final in tone and her shade of red deeper than any ever seen.

He studied her. *The Tree called to her to touch it. If she's good enough for that...* He reached out his spirit to touch her and felt her heart and mind. He knew how to free her.

"Arlupo, I hear much in your sister's words. Stephanie, if I use my gift, I will experience your pain as you feel it, but worse."

The words shocked her. She couldn't conceive of... "Worse? But..."

"Because I'll still be me, and I'll hurt for you as deeply as my understanding can feel for you."

Her eyes instantly widened. She couldn't fathom that type of pain. She shook her head forcefully, "But...you understand so much...no, no, I cannot allow you to..."

He asked softly with words and face, "You would let your loved one lose his chance to live?" He didn't understand what chance that would be, but he knew that his daughter did, and it involved her request.

But Stephanie already knew her answer even before he finished the question. "Both Vaughn and I could never accept help if it meant loss to someone else. He would not accept this, so I cannot either, even if it means his life or mine. When we were in great danger, our lives threatened by others, and it would have been right to kill them, Vaughn said it was better that they had a choice to save themselves, and if they chose evil, to die by their own choice, rather than us bring harm directly upon them. If he wouldn't bring harm to his enemies, how much less would he bring harm to those who would surely be his friends?"

He sat back in his chair. Tears flooded his old eyes to see reality unfold before his heretofore unknowing eye. *She is powerful. Perhaps Arlupo is right. This is a* dear *child.* When she turned down his help, he saw the bright light shining in her. He still wasn't totally convinced of her connection to prophecy or legend, but he didn't have to be, since reality would follow its natural course.

"Arlupo, I don't need to hold her hands. I believe in you. What is it you want to do?"

But Arlupo wasn't satisfied. "It's not just that I want you to do something for me, Father. I need you to *understand* Stephanie. I need you to understand her as only you are able to do, so that you can help her be pure, to find her Tree of Life, and destroy the tree of death, and…help her understand her gifts so that your love will give her the courage to use them as only I and my mother know you are able to do." Arlupo became aware of just how much she had strung together in a single request.

Stephanie put her hand upon Arlupo's knee, leaning forward to look at her. "It was you and your mother that your father held hands with?"

She nodded and he explained it. "Dear child, the gift works both ways. My love for them desired that I be able to give myself completely to them. Not only are the others' lives fully known to me, but my life is given fully to them in help. To the extent that they are able to benefit and understand, they gain from me. It is a great honor for me to be allowed to do such a thing. The honor outweighs the pain! It is said that in the secret book, it is written that when two are joined in such a way, they become as if they were real sisters or brothers or fathers or children to the one with the gift and to the one being helped. Would Vaughn approve of this?"

Stephanie smiled with tearful understanding as she remembered how Vaughn had told her it was an honor to be wetted by her tears. "It sounds just like Vaughn, in a way. What book?"

Her father didn't mean to make mention of it. There were too many other things needful. "That's not important right now. You already have too much to focus on. Let me help you, child. I am willing. I *trust* my daughter."

Arlupo took Stephanie's hand. "Stephie, do you know what this means? If you do this, you will become my true sister."

Stephanie leveled her eyes and spoke of a surety. "I am already your true sister, and more so you, than I. I cannot believe I'm receiving such love, such goodness." Stephanie zoned out and they waited for her to return. *What does this* *mean to me? If I am ever to get rid of my terrible shame, this tree of death, I have to face it sometime...But...no one need know it but God...but...Arlupo says time is short. Vaughn could die any moment. Oh God, what if I'm too late? What if it doesn't work? What if I can't...? Stop it. Just STOP IT! Sacrifice...*true *sacrifice. Oh Vaughn, you were right. The word does have true meaning.* Her presence returned to the room.

She looked at Arlupo, then at her father, holding his eyes. "My life has been...you will know it." She bowed her head to him.

"Good," he said.

"Good, Stephie," Arlupo said.

"Arlupo, wake the town. For such things..."

"I know Father, all must be awake."

He instructed Stephanie. "You must bathe. We will give you special garments to wear. Arlupo will fix your hair into three braids, and then you must be alone for as long as you need in the back room and sit before the Tree of Life and do whatever comes into your heart and mind in that time. Then we will hold hands until the joining is complete. There is no timeline for this. Then, I must sit before the Tree of Life, also. Then we shall proceed as the Light leads us."

She picked her head up, feeling as if she were heading into the unknown. "Father, may I call you Father?"

He smiled his broad smile. "Yes, child, you *certainly* may."

"May I go *now* before the Tree of Life...I....I...want to pray there now."

"I see your eyebrows raise, my father," Arlupo questioned.

"Yes. I see why you have requested such things. Stephanie, you may certainly do so. No one has the right to deny a request of the Tree of Life. Remember, it calls to you even as you call to it. No one has the right to step between the Light and another heart or mind. No one can even make such requests unless it was given by the Light. They just wouldn't feel comfortable."

She bowed her head. "Thank you, Father."

Stephanie knew the way and left them in the study. She slowly, reverently walked down the hall, asking God to let her be able to even enter the same room as the sacred tree. Then she realized, *In a way, I guess this is exactly the kind of shelter I was trying to build…a sacred shelter only for goodness. It was even round like these…* When she came to the end of the hall, she paused before entering the room. She could see the Tree and felt it accept her. *This is the presence that was missing in the government church.* She understood how God was working through the Tree of Life. Approaching with her head down, she fell on her knees before it. She folded her hands upon the brass rim and leaned forward over the soil so that she was under its branches above. Stephanie wept and prayed.

"Oh Tree, let not my prayers trouble you, they are to the God that created you. But when I touched you, I knew you knew my life. But you are not a person. But now another shall know my terrible life, my *terrible* shame. Oh God, I don't know how to bear it. For the sake of all your goodness that is possible to bring forth through me, help me, because I am not worthy to live! I have caused murder! I have caused a good man to become a murderer! I can feel their lost lives! I have been perverse and lewd beyond description! I have disrespected You on so many levels! But if I do not go through with what has been goodly offered to me, then who would help Vaughn, if I can even help him. He deserves to live, in spite of what he has done, he loves You dearly, I know. For Goodness sake, Oh God, help me, so that I may be able to help him and anyone else possible. Help me to bear my shame and do what You require, for Your Goodness sake. Is it not better to cause me to truly do Your will than to leave me as I am? I cannot be good without Your forgiveness to take away my sin, my shame, and to make a true nature in me."

An invisible shower, as if sparks, began entering into her. She could feel the little bursts of heat all through her. But it wasn't physical heat. She felt a glow all around her and the feeling of it was as the sight of the glow around the glowing tree that had called, *Find me,* in the church back home. She looked up at the Tree. "Oh, *my*... ARLUPO, FATHER, COME SEE THE TREE!"

Stephanie fell backwards and crab crawled several feet away. Her heart was pounding. The Tree was no longer asleep! She could feel its power radiating outward and directing its full attention... to her! Stephanie wanted to hide, but there was no place in the room to do so. She felt unworthy of such attention.

Arlupo and her father came running in and Arlupo grabbed her father's arm as they entered and beheld the sight. "Father!"

SACRIFICIAL WOOD

They stood staring in captive sight of prophecy and legend. He answered Arlupo's exclamation, understanding now just who Stephanie was and is meant to be. His daughter was right all along.

"My daughter, Stephanie has wept on sacred ground and watered the Tree with true tears. It has brought life to a twig."

There, before their eyes, were green, tender, young leaves sprouted from a small twig, high up on a tree branch that had hung over Stephanie.

Arlupo began speaking without thinking, "Prophecy says, Father, that…" He cut her off.

"I know."

Stephanie was still in her crab position sitting on her backside and propping herself up from behind with her arms. She twisted herself to look at them. "Prophecy?"

But he redirected her in a serious tone. "Too much now, daughter. You must concentrate on what you need to do."

They came up behind Stephanie and grabbed her under the arms and picked her up. Arlupo was staring at her, again in awe. It made Stephanie feel very uncomfortable.

They're making too much out of me. It's the Tree they should be inspecting. Besides, they still know so little about my real life. I don't deserve all this attention. How can they be so kind to me and invest so much in me? It's not right.

Stephanie pulled away, turning to face them, spreading her arms out from her sides, palms outward, "You barely know me, and you've never even met Vaughn, how can you do all this for us?"

He stepped in front of her, taking both her arms in his hands. The tree of death was trying to force her to run away from her calling by making her identify herself with the fruit the corrupt tree brought forth through her. She had just been blessed through the Tree of Life, and now the tree of death was fighting back, fighting hard for its survival in her. He could see that the two trees were tightly intertwined, and Stephanie lived in the space between them.

He answered her question, and hoped to God she would be able to overcome the consuming evil that threw itself against her to destroy her. "I have faith in Arlupo. She has befriended you to the depths of her very soul. I know the meaning this has to her, and it's not honorable or right for me to question that. I can also see you for myself, and I know by the things you communicate, you are worthy of our attentions. With the Appendaho, it's not so much about time, or even the past or other external qualities of the world, *it's about meaning*. We see, think, and feel meaning continually. We would not be *what* we are if we did not help you as much as possible.

"We see the meaning Vaughn has to you. Because Arlupo is meaningfully connected to you, and in turn you to Vaughn, we *must* help him, too. Not helping him would be to injure you. In a way, we already know Vaughn through you, because meaning crosses the boundaries of the physical world." He leaned forward to gather her attention even more. "Remember this: You always have a choice after having done wrongly. You can focus upon the wrong or upon that part of you that desires good. Which is greater? Which is the *real* you? *Which* will you choose to become in the future?"

Stephanie felt the beautiful picture of his words absorb into her and become a part of her understanding. She felt his utter respect for truth and dignity, and something else she had never known the likes of from anyone except Vaughn. They had *faith* in her because they saw something real in her.

She realized…*I'm being an* idiot. *Why should I run from being blessed?*

Stephanie motioned for them to wait as she ran back to kneel before the Tree of Life.

"Forgive me for being such an ungrateful *idiot*. Thankyou Life for blessing me through Your presence through this wonderful Tree of Life and thank you Tree for sprouting for me. Thank you for my dear friends. Make me worthy of such honors by guiding me to keep all Your ways." Then she got up and they all went to make preparations for the joining. The sun peeked over wooded hills as another day began.

ಊ

Scraback beheld the many new hideously glowing trees in their forest, especially *that* man's and daughter's trees, and he began to question whether his Master really knew what he was doing. He felt it might even be dangerous to himself to be associated with all that *glow*. All this talk about the girl being a legend made him nervous. *But we know the humans have many foolish legends.* Scraback remembered when his Master had shoved him into the orb and *glow* leapt from Stephanie, stinging his precious Great Eye. *No, Master is not aware of that particular power she has, otherwise he would have destroyed her and not played games about it...he mustn't be aware...but all that* glow...

"Master, I don't know, shouldn't we tell the High Council ...?"

Master GrrraGagag growled deeply. He realized he had been far too calm for too long. But it was hard to maintain his act when things were going so well. He drew his Great Eye close to his underling. "And let them have the glory of destroying all this? They have one defective tree on Earth. Look at our Forest. It's a *forest*. You speak as a fool. If you speak again of such things, *you will speak no more!* The girl has only a glimmer of understanding. WE have moved through reality at will since the beginning of time. If she attempts it, we'll trap her there. Do you know how delicious it is to trap a living soul in the depths of our reality?"

"No Master. Has it been done before?"

"My dear Scraback, there is nothing you have seen or will see of this decimated world that has not been done before, and most has oft been repeated."

Master does know. It'll never work. All that planning for nothing...or does he know specifically?

CHAPTER SIX
Seeing in the Lake

The Ancient Prophecy of the End

"When true tears shall water the tree, life shall begin again, and our people shall be no more. The Earth shall be in the hands of the Faithwalker. When she dies, hope dies with her, for there is no one left for whom the seed will grow," prophesied Queen Yinauqua.

"Are you sure?" King Mafferan asked her.

Her helpless stare answered his question.

He shook his head. "There must be more to it than that."

"Reality is..."

For the first time, he interrupted his wife. "I'm not saying that reality isn't, just that there is more to it"

"Prophecy ends there, my husband."

As Stephanie bathed, her prayers were that she should be cleansed within. Rinsing and then patting dry were like an 'Amen', which means to let it be so. Running the brush through her hair seemed to cause her life to play back for her. As she slowly drew it down her long, thick red hair, her past came clearly into focus. Feelings, thoughts, actions…ways of thinking…growth… *My hair, it's so long, it's been with me through all I've done. In a way, I'm carrying my life on my head. God, now my hair feels different to me…because of its meaning…* She called to Arlupo who waited outside.

Arlupo fixed her hair into three long braids. The middle braid was the thickest, and the other two hung from each side. *My life has been put in order,* she thought as she felt the meaning of the braids. Arlupo handed her a box.

Stephanie pulled a long, royal-blue, velvety dress out. She couldn't imagine anything more beautiful. She hugged it to herself looking at her dear friend. Her eyes did all the talking, *A new dress for a new life.* Arlupo confessed that she had it secretly made some time ago!

Stephanie tingled all over from feeling so special. She knew great power was surrounding her, leading her, calling her, as they walked out the door heading for the sacred lodge. When she entered the sacred room, her eyes played over a special rug that had the same colors and designs as her dress.

A thick, round rug of royal blue embroidered with deep red and gold in complicated, but balanced geometric patterns laid below the Eastern windows of the sacred room. All the windows had been opened wide. The town, all ninety six souls, minus one, gathered around the sacred lodge. Arlupo sat on the brass bench beneath the Tree of Life facing them. Stephanie stepped onto the rug, opposite her new father. Her toes sunk lavishly into its thick yarn. Looking at the rug, she ran her fingers over the patterns on her dress, wondering at their meaning. He had similar patterns of gold upon a white tunic and pants.

He spoke with a loud, sharp, and clear voice so that all could hear. "Hear me, Appendaho. This child we all decided to take into our hearts to help. This Love we serve now requires of us great sacrifice. We are not the whole tree, but simply a small branch upon which we, as leaves, eternally hang, if we forsake not its calling. Let any voice of dissent speak now against the joining, the responsibility and the consequences that shall follow."

Permeating the silence, a sweet, gentle breeze seemed to blow into every window of the round, sacred lodge. Stephanie felt like she was floating, as the prayers of the whole village lifted her up. Yet, there was also a part that seemed sunk in the bottom of some deep, dark lake. Experiencing both at the same time brought on helplessness and some disorientation.

Her father spoke as before. "Stephanie has been through great troubles. This will not be a joining as we have experienced before, but one as we were told of in the beginning of our history as a people. How can we shun our roots? A tree cannot live if it shuns its roots. No matter what you hear, no matter how great the suffering, the bond must not be broken. Stephanie, no matter what, you must not remove your hands from mine if you want to be bonded. I am not allowed to restrain you at all. Both of us must hold on by our own free will, but we must not restrain the other from withdrawing, otherwise the bond is broken. Therefore, I will sit with my palms open and up and your hands shall be placed on top of mine. If any has objection, let it be voiced now."

The same silence, the same gentle breeze, the same still presence that was greater than all, but somehow seemed so small it was hard to find. That presence pervaded the breeze, the white tile floor, and themselves, everything. It was the feeling of reality being what reality is.

Her father spoke again. "Arlupo, bring the sacred water to the tree. No other is allowed within the sacred lodge until the bond is completed."

Arlupo stepped close. "Yes father. I love you Stephanie. No matter what, I will always love you *dearly*. I cannot begin to tell you how much I have already learned from you!"

"But…from me? I don't…" *How can that be so?* She had never felt smaller and a large part of her wanted to run. She had made all her prayers. Poured every ounce of strength into this, but she still wanted to run and didn't know if in the next moment she would!

Arlupo explained with the same voice as her father but her tone wrapped in a purely feminine blanket. "You have faced the tortures of evil, drank of its destruction, and fought against it with whatever you had. And now you are at the door to become free. None of us has faced what you have faced. I have only tasted a tiny, bitter bit, and that was incredibly difficult. We cannot imagine it. We are in awe. We have been holy our whole lives. It is told that the father and mother of our people were as you are, and fought against terrible evils and overcame them all. Prophecy has said that in the time of the end we would return to our roots." Arlupo then left to retrieve a special leather pouch with the sacred water.

They did? Time of the end? What end? What roots? What are they hiding? Something she should know. And yet, the love she felt was real through and through and it brought automatic, unquestioned trust.

The Appendaho leader sat down upon the sacred rug and turned his palms upward, leaning the backs of his arms against his knees, his hands extending halfway beyond them. His loving eyes beheld her. "I offer my hands to you in love. You may place your hands upon mine if you wish. You may withdraw at any time, but if you do, it may not be offered again."

Stephanie sat down on the soft rug, her knees a mere hair's breadth away from his. She rested the palms of her hands upon her knees. With tears streaming down her face and her chest heaving…she wanted to run…she wanted to stay…she felt like she was dying…she felt like she could live…she had no choice…no, this was all her choice…she let go…she prayed for all to hear her…

"Oh, God, forgive me for what I do. Forgive me, father, for doing this to you. Honor or not for you, I feel ashamed. But I know I must do this. I want to die…and yet…I want to live. So…I place my whole life…in your hands…"

At first, nothing, and for a few brief moments…stillness. The first sensations, pictures of basic feelings crossed through each…back and forth…and then meaning was added to the pictures, and then the pictures became like simple words, and these meaningful words were put into sentences which were immediately changed into more complex pictures, which were again strung together into sentences, which became pictures...and so the process repeated and repeated until the Appendaho leader wailed mournfully. His hands shook. Reflex had him pull away a thousand times just in the first second, alone, when the searing pain first clamped down upon him. But a thousand and one times, before he could really pull away, he held them in place. And so it continued second by second by second...

Oh shame...my whole life is...opened...want to die...I want to live...help me...oh, I feel your life...I see through your understanding...your love...so much in the way...

And they continued like this for hours, the process comparable to waves flooding and receding upon a beach...adding and then taking, reforming the beach to look much as it does every day, but no single grain of sand remaining in the same place as before.

Arlupo had heard over and over the historical, legendary descriptions of the bonding between their first king and queen. But it was clearly an extremely abridged version compared to seeing and feeling the real thing. She began to worry at how very long it was taking. She knew her father would hold on even to death in his attempt to help Stephanie. *Oh God, have I done the right thing?*

Just then her father's hoarse voice startled her. She saw they were holding each other's arms tightly. "It's done. The bond has been completed. You'll be forever my daughter, Stephanie."

◈ SACRIFICIAL WOOD ◈

His tired, red eyes told the story of his ordeal. His hair looked much grayer. His face's wrinkles, which hardly seemed noticeable before, were those of an old man. Arlupo took the sacred water and poured it at the base of the Tree of Life.

"And you, *my father*." Stephanie's voice rang with a clear, mellow tone. She stood up slowly, carefully stretched and walked behind her father. Then she hugged him tightly, pressing her cheek against his head as he still sat where he was. She kissed the top of his head and held him in her arms from behind, not wanting to let go. She had felt the heart, the mind, the soul of this *true* man, who was father to her best friend and husband to her mother. Stephanie understood the truth of these things now, what a real father was, how a real husband was, and what it was to be their daughter. She felt life pouring continually into her from all sides. He rasped out a response to his new daughter.

"Go with your sister and she will prepare you for what is next and so that I may be alone with our Tree of Life." Stephanie kissed his head again and smoothed his gray hair, then left. All the people followed them, jockeying for position to get a closer look, to hear any words Stephanie might speak.

As soon as they were gone and he knew he was alone, he helplessly collapsed onto his side. Time disappeared. Weeping, weeping, weeping…seemingly without end. Beyond painful. *This is our roots! We were born from such pain.* Every point in his heart was shattered into unnumbered pieces, as he felt evil's violation of her life on a grand scale. The attacks from her biological father and mother, the manipulations by her so-called friends, the unseen evil stabbing, probing continually at her. But, even worse, was her collapse into degradation and her wanton destruction of herself. Yet, in spite of all this, came a tremendous appreciation for Love. This, too, he received from Stephanie! His knowledge of Love was taught by hers! For in spite of all that evil had done to her, and all the evil she had embraced, and all the evil still fighting to hold her down, she now valued Love and Goodness above all else. She felt life had meaning. He felt smaller than the smallest child, having experienced what Stephanie had lived through and what she currently is. Barely managing to crawl over to the Tree of Life, he was unaware of how he had any strength left at all, as the words of his prayer drifted from him of their own accord.

"Oh Tree, you contain the lives all the living. You called to Stephanie and brought her to us, to You, so that she should live. Never have I...never could I...imagine such horrors, such pain, such mighty love and faith as she possesses. Oh Tree, your root is strong indeed. You have chosen your new heir, if she will accept you. Nature teaches us that the forests shift and change locations over long periods of time. This is wisdom beyond my understanding, except that I know it's true. Help me to fulfill my part in You, that you may fulfill your part in me, even as the Light is bestowed upon you."

Arlupo came by way of the hallway and called in unto her father. After a moment, she entered the room, and froze in astonishment. Yet, seeing her bedraggled father drew her into helping him to his feet, all the while pointing to the Tree. "Father, the Tree has sprouted buds at the other side."

SACRIFICIAL WOOD

He smiled with understanding, "It's a sign, Arlupo, of balance. What we're doing is right."

She looked at him like a needy little child. The meaning of the prophecies that were coming true was undoing her. He could feel it as they wrapped their arms around each other.

She whimpered as she revealed her thoughts. "Father, all I have ever known is our people until you sent me to school and I began..." She was trying to tell him much, much more, but couldn't bring herself to say the words. She knew she had been the catalyst for all that was happening, and would happen going forward. *Maybe, if I hadn't...*

But he comforted her with new found meaning that he knew she would recognize. "The surface is not seeing the true reality, daughter. We have to see the lake from all perspectives in one. The truth hasn't changed. The people will always be the same, whether they be of the Light or not." He had learned much from bonding with Stephanie. Particularly that he had made the right decision to send the children out to school.

"Yes, Father. May we help her begin her journey, now?"

"Yes. I'm able to help her, as you have so deeply desired."

☙

The villagers never went back to bed. Instead, they congregated in the village square commons. The beautiful old stones seemed to radiate ancient commentary upon their current events as the people discussed legend and prophecy while the midday sun beat down upon them. There were many ancient stone benches with very old, well pruned trees that hung over them. Each tree was blocked in with beautifully carved stones. Many of the Appendaho were planning how they would put their houses in order, while others confirmed that prophecies were always hard to predict in the present. The men, women, and children were all in awe at prophecy and legend being fulfilled together. On almost one accord, all offered up their full mind and heart to the natural course that Goodness should take in their lives. However, one soul was missing.

They had called him to come in from the city, but he refused, citing other more important matters. They explained the urgency of it, but he still declined, saying only that what he would be bringing them would be explanation enough. Their leader told them to let him be. No one had the right to interfere with another's will. He sent word that he wished the young man well. Being the first student to be sent out into the world, he knew more about it than anyone else. He must surely have encountered something vitally important to the village's welfare, otherwise everyone knew he would not be missing such momentous events at home. There were reports from some of the students that he had been on TV, just like Arlupo, and that he was fighting against some evil. This made them proud, a good show to the world of the Appendaho.

Arlupo gathered the people back to the sacred lodge as before, and then went to retrieve Stephanie from her own private lodge where she had gone to freshen up. Stephanie loved the sacred dress and decided to continue to wear it.

SACRIFICIAL WOOD

Arm in arm, they sauntered down the narrow, long, hall that led to the sacred lodge. Arlupo held her tightly, almost as if she were afraid of losing her. Stephanie contemplated her life in the past three months since she had moved west, and the three months before with Vaughn. She would be fifteen soon. All that growth, all that wonderful new knowledge vibrated in her heart and mind. She squeezed Arlupo's hand, thinking of how Arlupo maneuvered her out from underneath her biological father, again. *So clever.* And then she thought about Vaughn, how at any moment he could die. *The key to the chance to save his life is to save mine first. Vaughn taught me to 'Say I first, then You.'* She remembered her promise to him, that she would not let herself down, and *then* she would not let him down. If it was to be a last battle, she determined there would be nothing left to spare of her strength, of her whole self, in fighting it to win. *The tree of death in me has to go.*

They entered the room, and their father motioned Stephanie to sit on the brass bench under the tree. Arlupo left through the direct exit from the lodge in the western section of the wall. Alone with his new daughter, with his new understanding of her, he could see only one way for her to accomplish what needed to be done within the time it needed to be done. But he didn't know if she would be able to face the challenge. The strength she needed to win was not in her. *She has to go get it. Reality is what it is.*

Her father, still wearing what he wore when they bonded, began to pace around the room, as if gathering strength and determination with every step. Stephanie saw him begin to glow brightly. It would not be easy for him to do what he had to do but he had somehow recovered his voice and spoke loudly, clearly, and sharply for all to hear.

"It's time. All the windows are open to the sacred room and the whole town sits around in prayer for you, Stephanie. You sit before the Tree of Life as it has desired of you. Much of your life has seemed an endless torture. But you dangled lost in the midst of that tempestuous sea with a hidden love. Preserved in you was the root from which your faith now springs, a certain goodness. Great evil has been done to you, and you have done evil to yourself and others, but more to yourself than to others. Whether to you or to others, it is wrong, and part of the tree of death. I know your heart, that you wish to overcome all evil and live pure and bring goodness to people, and that you love others even more so than yourself. Yet, there is no goodness in devaluing yourself. You devalue yourself because you feel the tree of death in you and are ashamed. It is the reality, the nature of death, to be of such little value. The tree of death has its roots sunk into you so that you feel it and cannot argue that it does not force you to act on its behalf in some ways. Are these words true to you?"

Sitting under the Tree of Life listening intently, inside and out, she answered clearly. "Yes Father."

"Since you cannot argue against the tree of death, *you are beaten by it!*" he spoke sharply.

She had no idea he would say such a thing, with such *meaning*, and in such a definite, final way. It cut her heart. It didn't feel right. She gritted her teeth, listening inside. *Is this something he learned from the bond? That I'm doomed? Then why this charade? No, no, I'm not here for anyone but God, Himself. Not for some stupid ritual. I must seek only Truth, no matter what. That much I am sure of.* After comparing her father's statements to her own self-knowledge, she held up her head, resolutely responding, "No, Father!"

Good child, good. "This *child* disagrees with her leader."

A burning in her chest ignited at the implied meaning. She tried to restrain the force of her answer. *What is going on?* "Your daughter taught me when we first met that truth and love are the Appendaho's leader."

An official tone carried his next words to everyone, "The child speaks *truth*. She is *not* on the surface. She walks with *meaning*. She is ready to begin her journey."

"AMEN, AMEN…" Everyone intoned which echoed through the windows with the late afternoon breeze.

Stephanie hadn't slept last night, yet the energy of her love and the task now at hand fueled her alertness.

"The people have added their blessing to your journey," he pronounced.

Stephanie raised her voice with the fullness of life.

"With all my heart, I could never express the unbounded meaning your people's love has to me. Every one of you has contributed to my being."

Warmth mixed in with his official answer. "The child walks with meaning and has seen the truth of our people. She comes to us not to belong to a people she sees with her eyes, but to belong to the Tree of Life to which all the living belong. But you cannot argue against the tree of death, dear one. Even now you feel it."

She returned the warmth of his tone in her own. "Yes Father." His lure of warmth worked and her heart was vulnerable. He pressed the attack again, with extra sharpness! "Then how say you that you be not *beaten* by it?"

Before she could moderate her answer, anger shot it out of her mouth. "I'm beaten by it only until it's *gone!*"

"The child speaks two voices in one. She speaks with courage and faith. How will you rid yourself of the tree of death?" He stared at her intensely, pressing his point, but her meditations had prepared her for this part.

"I cannot," she spoke clearly for all to hear.

He responded with dispassionate, calm finality. "Then you *are* beaten by it, and it *will* eventually consume you."

Fire burst into her eyes as she felt her soul and that fire become one. "The Tree of Life is also in me. The Tree of Life is my beginning. The tree of death is a weed that makes many people believe in it…simply because it exists in their field. When all that people can see and feel is that tree of death, they believe that it is the tree from where they came and it defines them. *The tree of death is a liar.*" She snapped with even more power. Her eyes were taking on sharpness.

He scrutinized her. He saw her reaching. *Yes child, that's it. Go get it.* "Think hard, Stephanie, what gives the two trees power in you?"

She was quick and even sharper to answer, "*I DO!*"

SACRIFICIAL WOOD

He was silent, stepping back, waiting for her to explain.

"The tree of death lives, no, exists in me because somehow I have let it. I don't know when or how this happened, but somewhere, at a very young age, it began to grow its death in me. I know I had to have given it power over me because death does not grow on the Tree of Life and the Tree of Life is my beginning. So, the Tree of Life did *not* bring death to me. The Tree of Life made me to live, not to die. Therefore, I, only *I*, had to give death power over me when it originally had *none*."

"How can you say that you give power to both trees, life and death, when life is the only power?"

"Because the nature of the Tree of Life is as the bond we have…no, that's backwards. The bond we have is as the Tree of Life. I placed my hands upon your palms and chose to hold them there and you also chose to support me. True love is only true when it's free, no matter how painful. That's the nature of it. That's one of the wonderful gifts and truths about the Tree of Life. It's made us to know it by making us free, so that we would be able to love truly, so that we would be able to live of the Tree of Life. Because the Tree of Life has made us free, in order for it to fully live in us, we must *allow* it to. We must, with deep understanding, freely choose it to be so. Our ability to choose gives power to both trees to be inside of us. *But it is the Tree of Life that made it so, not the tree of death.*" Her eyes gathered ever more intensity.

"The young woman speaks with righteous anger. So, what! Big deal! What does it matter?" he chided, throwing up his hands, pacing.

All the villagers were looking at one another holding their breath as they watched and listened through the open windows. None of them had ever conceived of such proceedings. This wasn't the way it was supposed to go. Appendaho don't treat people this way. Their hearts were pounding, but none were led by the Light to interfere.

Stephanie's determination only strengthened and she stood up, which was not protocol. Words were pushing in her of their own accord. But this *was* the right time to let them have their way. She followed her father around as she returned her answer. Putting her hands to her chest, and raising her voice, she replied, "It *means* that everything that's truly me came by the *first* tree, the Tree of life. The other things in me are *not* truly me. The evil things that I thought for so long were me, are *not*. They are a *lie*." She followed him like a lion hunting its prey, waiting for his next move.

He whirled on her. "But they are you, NOW."

She stopped in her tracks. His few words carried the clear picture of where, how, and why death held her captive. She had utterly turned away from natural born goodness, coldly forsaken it…as if goodness never existed at all. Her willing, joyful, whole-hearted participation in lewdness claimed her. She still had those same desires and remembered when she boasted of her sexuality, taunting weak boys, and sadistically enflaming other girls' jealousies. She still knew she was '*hot*.' Her complete choice, through drugs, to disregard any natural born goodness proved to her she had no right, now, or ever, to return to that natural goodness she so insulted. And the evil began to snowball with one after another and another and another insult. One after the other irrevocable claim of ownership of her soul.

Overcome with sudden guilt and grief, not being able to avoid what she saw, knowing of a surety that evil had a legitimate claim upon her, everything changed. It felt like the floor opened up, and she fell deeper and deeper into the darkness. She remembered her dream of being sucked into the maw of eternal damning blackness. Her throat tightened… and she couldn't…breath. Her heart was breaking with one last primal cry for help. She threw her hands out from her sides bawling, pleading, begging, "OH FATHER, that's why I've come here. I don't want evil to be me."

He didn't want to have to say it, but it was necessary. This crossroad would determine which tree had victory in her, and whether she and her loved one had a chance to live. She had to choose now. *Oh God, be with her.*

"The evil *is* you. It is the way it *must* be. You can FEEL that. Death can be no other way." It was as if a gavel slammed and pronounced the official judgment. His speech reminded her of her real father when she was a child, reminded her of her helplessness. Her mouth dropped open, but no sound came out. She felt death squeezing her, backing up his words by showing her the force it had over her. She wanted to wail, but no cry came forth.

Yet, beneath this maelstrom an underlying feeling began to bring a single word to her mind, its voice becoming her internal voice. *Purpose.* But that single word conflicted with all the rest she was now feeling. *No purpose.* Then, *PURPOSE.*

Something caught in her throat. Everyone held their breath. They could see time stand still. Her father desperately tried not to show any emotion, but he could see light and darkness swirling around her, in and out of her. He knew light had power over dark, but Stephanie was correct in her explanation, *she* was the one who gave them *both* power over her. *She* had to choose. That was the battle swirling inside her, a battle for her choice. Light and dark making their cases, vying for which she would believe and choose.

She kept hearing his words echoing maliciously in her head, *The evil is you, the evil is...* Images of her biological father danced around her, his big finger pointing, stabbing her in her face, *The evil is you, The evil is...* the more she heard it, the angrier she got. And the angrier she got... she grabbed her head, shaking it violently. *No...NO...NOOO...* and then, throwing her arms down, with all her might, "*I DO NOT BELIEVE THAT,*" she screamed, her heart pounding, fire bursting from her eyes. "Evil does not have to be me. Life has *Purpose*!" she shouted sobbing, melting to the floor. "Evil has none!"

Her father stepped back. He could feel the tremendous power she was automatically summoning to fight the evil. He could see the fire dancing all around her. *Come on child, it's not in* that *power, it's in your choice. It's up to you now. Your father drove that worthless feeling into your heart. You couldn't help it then, but now you can. You have to choose to get rid of it. It's been with you as long as you've been here in this world! A color painted as background on your canvas. But it's not the real you. Don't define yourself by your pain which feels empty, but by the love that's hurting. The answer's in your heart, not your mind, dear child.*

He threw open his arms, spinning around, addressing everyone in his official tone. "The young woman has made the challenge. We must leave her now. Lock all the windows. Shut the door, but do not lock it. She is free to stay in the sacred room or leave."

"AMEN, AMEN…" Everyone repeated over and over with tears streaming down their faces, young and old. Never had they ever imagined such a thing. Their hearts broke as one for the battle Stephanie was fighting.

Left alone in silence.

After a while, she picked herself up off the floor to pace back and forth around the Tree of Life, looking down at the floor, desperately thinking out loud, searching, then gazing at the Tree that had sprouted for her, and then peering into her inner turmoil again. Back and forth she struggled.

"Why do I not believe that? I spoke with such certainty. But why? It felt true because Life has purpose. But what does that *mean*? Because it's not in Life to leave us hopelessly chained to death. It's in Life to make us pure. Then there must be a way to be rid of this death tree. If I pass away from this world with the death tree controlling my will…oh God, I can't live forever on the tree of death because that was my choice to die. How does one die eternally? I mean, forever dying?"

She paused, shivering all over at the thought…the picture of dying more and more and more for eternity until that picture got so black she couldn't stand it.

"I need to refocus. The Light will not tamper with my choice because it won't tamper with my freedom because it's Love. After I die…I get no more choice for life! Because the Tree of Life will no longer be in reach, because I'll have given myself over to death. That was my choice. Only if I'm free of the tree of death will loosing this earthly body not matter because I live in *meaning*, able to cross the boundaries of this world. Death is meaningless, a waste. YES, that's why I spoke with such certainty. Life has to have a way for us to escape meaningless death because Life *is meaning*. But why is Life meaning? I feel it, but what are the words so I can *understand* it?"

It was easier for her to put into words why death is meaningless, than to say why Life has meaning. At first, just focusing on the human feelings such as love, started out feeling right, but when it was pointed out that her love for Vaughn failed so many times, and besides, they couldn't be together, she lost the feeling that love had purpose. But this conclusion didn't feel right. She began again.

"Why do I feel my love has purpose? Obviously, if I act out of mere lust or other evils, there can be no true happiness. Those things are dead, vanities, false senses of the power of life. But why does goodness feel otherwise, and why did I just lose this feeling? *Hmm…just because I fail goodness, that doesn't mean goodness has failed me.* YES! So, I have to look at what pure goodness is, just what it is, to be able to understand. Then, once I understand it better, maybe I won't fail it! YES! The problem is, when I started out with my love for Vaughn, I failed that love by not appreciating the justice by which he

SACRIFICIAL WOOD

treated me…Justice. Love…Vaughn said there could be no love without justice and no justice without love. I see this. They're distinct, yet they're one. This must hold true for other qualities of Life. Virtues. Yes, that's what those qualities are called, they're called virtues. Peace, understanding, truth…Yes."

Suddenly goose bumps prickled all over her. Pieces of a puzzle came together into a picture consisting of feelings and thoughts.

"Oh my God. Just like every part of a tree is meaningful to the whole tree because it supports its life, so is every aspect of goodness that makes up the spirit of life. Life is meaningful because every part of it supports a meaningful whole, and yet, every part has its meaning because of the whole, and the whole supports every part. And…and that whole is an everlasting, living, growing tree continually bringing more new life. What could be better, more meaningful than that? Death is like a canker, a blight…it's something that offends the whole in any of its parts, then it's robbed of the meaning of that part. That's the death tree I must get rid of.

"But how? Can I just not choose death? Not if it's already a part of me. Once the tree of death has root, how can it be pulled up? Can I untangle its roots from around my will? Is that even the right analogy? What if it's not tangled, but one substance? What if, instead of light and dark twisting in a root mess, my will is just gray? Either way, gray doesn't live on the Tree of Life, either. Gray doesn't feel right.

"It's not the evil in me that despises the evil in me. It's not the evil in me that is *ashamed*. God respects this goodness in me because it *is* goodness. Evil knows no shame. Shame comes from understanding that Goodness has been violated. It's goodness feeling pain. So, the purpose of shame is to turn and reach for the good, not to keep beating me up over the bad. I mean, if I burn myself, I jerk my hand away. Yes. None of that is gray but clear cut. Goodness is the real me and the other is trying to destroy me. This…this terrible *feeling* in me…of…dejection…it has to go.

"My ability to choose failed me because I was too weak, too ignorant. I don't understand how to be free of this. How could I? A fish only sees the inside of the lake. A bird sees how it fits into the land. We take notice of how the water and earth mix together. Only God can continually behold all reality. *Only He can fix my soul.* Then what do I need to do to let Him?

"I must *let* God do so. But it's my very will that needs fixing! OH GOD, *how do I let You,* when as long as I try to choose You, I'm still using the very will I want You to fix! As long as I control my will, You can't fix it, because I'm using it, and Your Love won't tamper with me choosing, but it's my very ability to choose that needs fixing. Then, somehow, I must give up my ability to choose? How do I, as my last choice, give up the ability to choose? My last choice with this will must be to return my whole being back to the Light, to Life, to Love, for God to do whatever God desires. But even something as simple as breathing can be choice…Oh God…

"But if I give everything away, I'll cease to be me. I'll be nothing…*no, wait,* that's a *lie*. God is Goodness. Goodness never fights itself. God wouldn't destroy the original me that He made out of whatever goodness pleased Him. Anyway, that goodness is all I really want to be. Then what would He do? He would add to it what I was lacking before, so I wouldn't fail Him. Why didn't God just do this in the first place? I don't know.

"Hmm, the life of the Tree of Life is different than God's life, because God's life hasn't battled evil, at least not in direct contact as the Tree of Life obviously has. What if there wasn't evil like there is now? Then God couldn't have strengthened us against that which didn't exist…yet. We would've had no way to relate to evil, and it would've taken time for the Tree of Life to build extra goodness against all the evil in the world. Does this make sense? I think so. But is it the *truth*? I don't know. Well, one thing is for sure, somewhere along the line someone didn't appreciate goodness enough and then…well, I don't know. Everything got all screwed up. And how could God make us appreciate Him better anyway? Isn't that up to us? Yes, it is. Hmm, but after we lose…YES! Then we learn how to appreciate better what we lost. Hmm…"

Stephanie felt progress in her thoughts, though the course was not of her mapping. She felt her faith growing stronger as the feelings of Life, Meaning, and Understanding grew clearer. She looked up at the Tree with its green sprouts now growing on each side. There were comings and goings between them.

"I can almost feel this Tree as if I were a part of it, sensing everything else about it. Wait a minute, I *am* a part of it. This Tree, look at it, so gnarled and scarred and yet so beautiful.

This Tree has gone through evil and has overcome it. It lives with all its scars…"

Stephanie sat again on the brass bench surrounding the Tree. She knelt under its branches, placing her right hand flat upon its trunk like she did before.

"Oh my, I touch your life. This Tree does have a *different* life than the life of the very beginning, because it's overcome death. Is that your *meaning*? That your life is different than God's Life? In that God made you to confront death and overcome it? Is that why the Appendaho say all the living must live on you? God made you to do what He could not? To have a life in *this* world, where you could face all death and overcome it so that you could give us mortals your strength when we are weak, knowledge when we are ignorant, wisdom when we are foolish, comfort when we are miserable… not just passing down a command or a thought from above about what is right, but passing to us the very experience of the confrontation itself?

"Oh my, God of Love, it makes sense, it has *meaning*. It has *faith*, but what does this *mean* to me? How do I gain this new life, this new will? As long as I breathe this life, I make a choice.

"Three braids. Why three? I have a heart. I have a mind. They live in my soul that connects the two. There has to be a soul, otherwise my heart and mind couldn't…Ha, talk to each other. So, my will is not just my mind, not just my heart. I must give both up together, and to do this, they have be one, they must both understand each other. The heart must love and trust what the mind believes, but the mind must believe what the heart trusts, just like before when I was so sure I had said the right thing but my mind had to figure out and see why. Only true meaning and understanding that proves itself to heart and mind can accomplish this unity. Oh my God, I have *this*. But what do I do with it?

"How do I give back my whole heart and mind when it's by them that I choose? How can I be will-less? But goodness has a will of its own. Vaughn mentioned that, too. If I let true reality be in me, *it* will change me *without me choosing to do so*. *YES,* all I have to do is *let it*. YES, my *little* goodness will gladly give itself over, agree to be taken over by the Greater Goodness. That would feel *right*. That would be my last choice with my old will, to let Goodness fully enter me, *after that, it is God's choices doing the changing in me!* True faith unites heart and mind into one. It really does.

"But as long as I have the breath of life in me, my will is still holding on to this life, choosing to breathe. Choosing…a life I must let go of…breath…our life on Earth from my very beginning here….breathes…Hmm, I can see the lake from the outside, but maybe to receive the new life, I have to be…on the inside? Use only my spirit life? Yes, because the tree of death entered during my breathing life…but my spirit life was given to me…Oh my God, while I was in my mother's water…"

She had forgotten she had her hand on the Tree for some time now. In fact, while deep in thought, she had leaned over without thinking and was holding the trunk tightly with both hands, lying on top of the sacred earth. That's when it suddenly became vividly clear to her. All the different parts of meaning seemed to assemble together into a complete picture. *So clear...so beautiful.* She pushed herself up from under the Tree and while brushing clinging soil back into the urn she called out repeatedly. "Father! Father! I need you to do something for me! *Father!*" She ran to an eastern window, unlocked it, and pulled it open, shouting her request. Her father came to the window in surprise with Arlupo beside him.

He still spoke in that ridiculous official tone. "The young woman has called out from the sacred room with a request. What is it that I could possibly do for you that you cannot find in the sacred room with the Tree of Life?"

She was tired of this, the formality, or the *whatever*. Stephanie stood up straight, leveling her eyes at him through the window, speaking surely, pausing only an instant with the realization of how strange it would sound to him, but then pressing on with knowing determination. "I want you to... take me to the lake and hold me under the water!"

He was truly shocked. So were Arlupo and everyone else. There was complete silence from all. None knew what to do. This wasn't protocol, nor was it anywhere in their history. Everyone looked at one another but came up blank. He remembered a distant reference to such an outside ritual being done before the Great Religious War, but their people at that time had stayed isolated and would have nothing to do with *any* outside ways. Direct knowledge through the Tree of Life was far superior to any of the outside religions and traditions, because their religions became a hazard to true knowledge of

God. Besides, they killed too many people over them. The Tree of Life had protected them from all the corruptions the outside world had suffered.

They all stared in silence as all minds rushed in thousands of different directions trying to find the true meaning in what she had requested. But there was fire in Stephanie's eyes now. She knew what she'd been shown and wasn't backing down. It was so clear.

What is going on in this child?

"I know it sounds crazy, but I need you to do this for me. There's a prayer I cannot pray except from under the water… where I cannot breathe. Father, you must hold me under the water…for as long as it takes!"

Her father looked worried, even scared would not be an exaggeration. *Has she lost her mind? I shouldn't have pushed so hard.* "Daughter…I…how am I to know how long?" *Yes, that's a good argument.*

She pressed him in spite of his obvious doubts. "I don't know. I don't know how long it'll take. Don't worry, I won't fight you or struggle no matter how long. There's something I *must* do under the water. I have faith in you Father, that you'll know when the time has come to pull me up!"

Oh God, I can't drown *this child! But if I pull her up out of fear, it would surely not be the right time. This is impossible!*

He looked very doubtful. Arlupo watched them both and then placed her hand on her father's arm. "Father, do this for my sister, *please!*" Arlupo had him by the arm, imploring him with her eyes. She had faith in her friend. Even if Arlupo didn't understand with her mind, her heart was sure of her. But her father's battle between heart and mind went the other way and he countered his daughter's request with a plea.

"It's written that peace must be found in the sacred room. If they leave it before then, the process is discontinued. They can't come that way again." During his protest he didn't quite look her in the eyes, but a bit down and away.

Her hand tenderly guided her father's sight into hers. "Are you looking at the surface, my dear father? Even if she walks out of that very old building, she won't have left the sacred room!"

The power of her words sent vibrations all through him. *The Spirit of Life backs her. She speaks truly.* He paused as he gazed at his beloved daughter who made each day brighter than the day before. His eyes widened with understanding. He assumed his official stance again. "My daughter speaks truth! Is there any here who disagrees with it?"

For such a strange thing, it had to be put to the whole village, giving opportunity for any further insight. There was only silence, amazement, tears, and secret prayers.

Her father turned to Stephanie. "Come, Stephanie, I shall do as you have requested." She opened the eastern door and left that old building. He held out his arm for her and she took it reverently.

They walked down the southern path through the apple orchard with everyone silently behind them. Many special varieties of fruit were almost ready for the late harvest. Apples in shades of red, gold, and green weighted the trees down with limbs bowing as they passed by. The smell was glorious. Even a person with a full stomach would yearn to taste them. But not this time, because all were focused on matters beyond this world.

They finally came to the edge of the orchard to the eastern shore of a peaceful, clear lake that had a strong stream feeding its northern shore and another draining its southern end. The large setting sun was almost even with the water's surface, shining a bright, golden swath across it. Stephanie and her father kicked off their shoes, the silt immediately squishing between their toes as they waded out into the pleasant golden path down the gradual slope to waist deep. Little fish darted away. The people stood still, captivated by the sight of them silhouetted in the brightness. *Or is that fire surrounding them?* Arlupo went into the water up to her ankles to watch more closely. *Oh God, this is so sacred. Look at* that!

Stephanie looked her father in the eye. "Remember Father, you must not pull me up until you *know* it's time. My life here is at an end."

He stared at her. *She's in charge*, he thought, then corrected himself. *Life is taking its natural course. All I can do is watch it unfold and take its leading.* "Yes, my daughter. We are bonded. I'll know when." Then he turned to the villagers who had all gathered on shore. "Behold, everyone, this child has come to this lake to give back all that the Creator has given her. I do not know the prayers she will say under the water. It is not for us to know. No one has the right to come between the Tree of Life and a soul…*I must do this.*" He turned to Stephanie, a greater presence now seeming to have descended upon him. "Stephanie, for the sake of all goodness that the Tree of Life has endured this world for, I place you under the water to make your prayers..."

And under she went. She immediately disengaged herself from all physical feeling. She wasn't in the least bit interested in it. What she was seeking was not of the physical world. What she most needed to pay attention to was on the inside, an inside narration.

"Stop thinking, stop feeling, everything I do with my will, stop it, I only want to feel Light. Vaughn, I love you, but if I truly love you, I must forget about you, so that I can truly love. The only true act I can do, because of the goodness that is surely inside of me, is to give my whole life back to You, God of Life and Truth, to do with me as You choose. I am *not* the evil that is in me, a part of me. I must get rid of it, but in order to do this, I must give my whole life back to You. In You there is no harm. You will not destroy the goodness in me, but I know I cannot even wonder a single thought as to what You might do, because then I am still holding onto my life, using my mind, my life. From the time I was born, the very beginning of my will, all that I ever chose, right or wrong, was done using this breathing life. I can't breathe under the water, so I can give my whole life back to You under here. I do not know when I shall be pulled out. It is no longer my concern, because I give my word to You that my life is no longer mine, but Yours. Forgive me Holy God, from the very beginning of my will through my whole life, forgive me and do with me as You choose..."

SACRIFICIAL WOOD

To be truthful she has to mean it. She does. To be truthful she has to be it. She is. No designs on the future. No attempts in the present. Completely handing over, waiting…

Suddenly, she felt a different presence try to squeeze her, telling her she can't breathe. Her heart burst with fire as she addressed it directly with her mind and heart speaking as one.

"NO *FEAR*! I told *you*, *I gave my word*, I'm not going back on it. I stop thinking, I stop feeling. I am Yours, God of Life. Where are You? Oh, I must also *let* Reality enter into me and change me. The Tree of Life. I felt it. It just *IS*. I feel it now. My heart…Oh no, what is this tightness I now see? Oh my, I've had this feeling for…as long as I remember. Fear is the opposite of what just IS… it's the fear that's holding me away. Ignore it. Let go of the tightness. Disbelieve it. Focus on the Tree of Life. I feel the Tree of Life as if it's *right beside me!* If it's the last thing I ever do, *I want to appreciate you*."

She felt a stillness beside her. The more she felt, the more she looked deeper. The deeper she looked, the more she was drawn into that stillness of spirit… and her heart began to let go of her past life that still kept clawing at her, that kept trying to hold onto her even though she determined to let it go. But the comfort of that Stillness made so much sense that she discovered ability to feel she had not known before. Suddenly, it became crystal clear to her heart how to let go of that last shred of destruction… an impaling presence that had been with her as long as she had known herself. Even though that darkness desperately fought for its claim on her, its reality in her began to disintegrate, unable to survive the total lack of attention to it. In feeling the Stillness of the Tree of Life, it made perfect sense to just BE, so Stephanie let her heart surrender completely to that new sense of stillness in places inside her she had never known before. Her mind agreed, and became completely quiet. It was as if she began to slow down, and then time itself just stopped. Yet it was eternal. It made sense to her mind. *Because there is no fear in this stillness. It totally just IS...* She realized, at this point, it was better to just totally feel rather than think. Then, so simply, her heart agreeing to fully feel that stillness, that Stillness was in her. They became one. And the Meaning of Being became so very clear.

"*TRUE REALITY IS THAT IT JUST...IS...ohhhh, soooo beautiful......in my heart...it's in my heart...oh my, and it's that easy? Oh, I feel my mind...at peace in the knowledge of my heart...Oh so beautiful...Where am I? Like I'm not under water...*"

Her father saw her smile and could feel through his hands that she had changed. Never had he been awed like this. He wanted to cry. He wanted to shout. If it wasn't for him still holding her under the water, he felt as though he could have jumped a thousand feet in the air. Finally though, he came to himself. *Oh!* He picked up his head, loudly proclaiming, "THE CHILD SMILES...IT'S TIME!"

And up she came, the water quickly running off and down her three braids. The sun still shined a sliver of gold disk peaking across the lake. Stephanie stood transfixed, not wanting to move, not wanting to have left where she had been.

SACRIFICIAL WOOD

"Ohhhh….sooo beautiful…I didn't want to come up…I…could have stayed under there forever."

Her father looked hurt as fear stabbed his heart. "I waited…you were under a long time."

When she realized how he had interpreted what she said, she came to her senses, taking hold of his arms and squeezing. "Oh, you did right. You waited just the right amount of time. It's just that anyone who goes there…would *never* want to leave."

Relief flooded through him, turning to joy. He turned back to the waiting people on shore. "The child shines. BEHOLD HOW THE CHILD SHINES," he proclaimed, his voice cracking.

Stephanie smiled. *He's so cute! HA!* "You didn't drown me, Father!" She looked at him with an impish grin and he burst out laughing. Such hard laughing he felt he might fall into the lake. Stephanie held him tightly to keep him up.

Arlupo was on her knees in the water. Her head bowed. She was in her own private world, crying. The visions were too much for her to endure. Powerful relief and overpowering grief found no way to mix within her, so she just had to wait for it all to subside. *But it's better to always honor the joy. My thankfulness is real, nonetheless.* She picked herself up just as Stephanie and her father reached her.

Everyone broke out in ecstatic cheering and shouting. When Stephanie reached shore the crowd mobbed her with hug after hug after hug. But she received all that attention willingly and gladly and didn't feel at all like it was misplaced or that anyone was making too much out of her. However, after a short time, she requested that she be allowed to go home to sleep, and all nodded in serious, single understanding. It had been a whole day and a half since she last slept.

◊

Never before had master GrrraGagag been so brutally forced out of someone's soul. He felt a part of his essence 'limp home.' Yes, occasionally he met resistance…True. But that was just in relation to a particular thought or feeling. *This* was different. He was *gone. Completely. No inroads.* Shaken to his ethereal core, he guarded his expression so his underling wouldn't know. Now he needed to present this as a lesson to his student, but carefully so as not to be embarrassed. Master GrrraGagag finally moved out of the way of the blue orb so he could begin teaching.

"Quick, check her tree, Scraback." But he knew.

Scraback was never angrier. He had wanted to see but his Master had been blocking him. He now knew what an earth child felt when someone rudely grabs something away from them. He flipped the orb back a bit in time to see how everything happened. He saw them put the girl under the water. And then…his Master blocked the orb again! He tried squirming around him, but Master's tail kept deflecting him. Scraback was even sicker with defeat when he finally saw it. "Master, SHE'S LOST TO US, HER TREE GLOWS AS THE OTHERS…*EVEN MORE SO!*"

Master GrrraGagag comforted him, but he couldn't look him in the Eye or pat him with his tail. He was still in pain

SACRIFICIAL WOOD

from being so unfairly treated, having been cast out of the girl. "She's not lost to us as long as she still has a tree in our Forest. We may not be able to use her now to create more trees for the treeless, though. Patience Scraback. We've still gained far more than we've temporarily lost. When I send the great affliction and the *glow* in their trees falters, I'll bring our reality to them and then destroy the High Council by bringing my victory before the Father. They'll pay for hiding the existence of these *glow* people." *Now Scraback can't go and report this to them. If he tells about the girl, he would have to tell about the Appendaho. He knows they'd immediately consume him to protect their secret.*

Scraback wasn't sure if he should be comforted, but the vision of the plan sounded glorious. Still… he scrutinized his Master without him knowing it. He could see he was hiding pain. *The girl must be even more powerful now.* Scraback hid his deep thoughts, his deep pleasure! "Brilliant, Master, may your grayness be turned into blackness, so that you may truly be a High Councilor."

"And you shall be my aid, Scraback, because *you* have been with me from the beginning of it."

"Anything I can do to help your grayness become blackness, Master." Scraback wrapped his tail over his Master's shoulder. GrrraGagag was too deep in thought to consider it. After all, Scraback was *just an underling*.

CHAPTER SEVEN
Faithwalker

"Where is your Master, Grrrag?" The High Councilor demanded.

"I ate him. And my name is not Grrrag. It's GrrraGagag."

The three High Councilors eyed him, whispered something to each other, and then unceremoniously left, leaving GrrraGagag alone. GrrraGagag whispered to himself. "Phase one complete." He transported himself to his favorite place, the Black River.

He would never be an underling, again.

Oh god, so beautiful, but I haven't slept in... how long? But I just have to wash this dress out first. She began to sniff the air. *Ug... it smells like...* She sniffed a couple more times.... *Fish!* Through her exhaustion Stephanie labored to pull off her lavishly embroidered blue dress. Next, she stripped out of her underclothes and set them in a corner. *I just want to wash you, my dear, favorite dress.*

Placing it in her little kitchen sink, she poured in some soap and ran warm water. As she gently kneaded the soft fabric, her thoughts revisited her underwater experience. *Oh God, so beautiful! I could live there forever… it's such a different world now, and everything looks different somehow… everything… just IS.* Then she looked at all the bubbles in the sink, realizing she didn't know how long she'd been washing. Smiling, she emptied it, ran the rinse water and gently squeezed and re-squeezed, and hung it up to dry on a hook above the sink. She could still feel the Holy Spirit's presence in the garment from when she had been under the water.

Then she began to sniff the air again, and then she sniffed her arm. "*Ugh, FISH…*" She looked over to her bedroom, then over to her little bathroom. Sighing happily through her mortal exhaustion, laughing at it, she went to shower. *No bath. Ha! I might fall asleep and drown!* She burst out laughing, remembering the hilarious look on her father's face worrying he would drown her. *I am sooo bad. The poor man! Oh my. Just a quick shower. Oh God, I'm so tired.*

As she rubbed herself with soap, she became aware of her body. *Oh God, it's my body. But… it feels different somehow, like I'm washing it for the first time. Strange… everything feels new.* She wanted to explore all this, to understand better, but her mind rebelled against any more additional effort of any kind other than falling into bed.

When she finally crawled into the soft comfort under her sheet, and pulled up the quilt she'd made herself, her body instantly surrendered to its most basic need. Now that the crushing burden of the immediate battle had been lifted, her residual strength quickly drained away. Her last thought was a promise to Vaughn. As soon as her strength returned, she would plunge into the unknown for him. Her night prayer was short, and only two words, *Thank You*.

She slept till mid-afternoon. In her dreams, all she saw was beauty. The beauty of Vaughn, of Arlupo, and of the Appendaho leader whose bonding had made her his daughter, too.

☙

To tell the truth, being the Appendaho leader consists mostly of boring accounting duties and making sure the outsiders don't find some devious way to start stripping away ancestral land. Keeping them believing Appendaho were primitive and subsistent on valueless ground went a long way towards this. But also the prayers and the presence of the Holy Spirit made most quite skittish about ever drawing near.

Spiritually, everyone is their own individual, with only minimal need for a leader. The Spirit of Truth does fine for all, from the inside-out in each person, in the department of *leading*. True, there is the leader's own private access to the Tree of Life, but it isn't the only access. However, the biggest responsibilities for many generations had fallen upon this leader, especially as their population declined to less than one hundred souls.

For many generations, only a single child was born to each of the Appendaho families. The Leader knew their decreasing number was making it difficult to sustain their village. That prompted him to send many of the remaining young people outside to school, which was a momentous decision. But even that paled in comparison to what they *all* had experienced because of Stephanie. To commemorate the extraordinary

SACRIFICIAL WOOD

event, the village agreed to throw a party, better than any in the memory of their people. But as they all discussed the nature and timing of the celebration, their leader stood with a look of apprehension.

At first, everyone just ignored their leader's attitude, and thought to themselves, *He's probably just thinking about another land problem,* but then he surprised everyone by saying the party ought to be right after Stephanie awoke! "But what about Vaughn?" they all asked. All he would say is, "I know." And indeed, they knew he knew. So after Stephanie had gone to her lodge, they organized how they would do it, and then went straight to bed so they could rise early and surprise her.

When Stephanie finally came out fresh from her lodge in mid-afternoon and went down to the common square, she couldn't believe what she saw… Everywhere, tables, chairs, and colorful canopies had been erected. There was probably food enough to feed a thousand. Pies of all sorts, meats cooked six different ways for each kind of meat, and more vegetables than Stephanie even knew existed. *But what about Vaughn?* she thought, not yet knowing how to bring it up, and not understanding how he could be ignored.

People kept lovingly giving her things, not allowing her to find the opening she desired. She felt their realness, their love, and in ways she had not known before. *So clear a connection, so deep,* she kept repeating to herself. And her instant response, too, was so deeply perceptive, with a clarity that made her feel she was experiencing herself for the first time. She felt larger, not in her body, but in the amount of feeling, thought, and information that effortlessly materialized. *This is how life is truly meant to be… to feel. I love it! Oh I how I love it!* In spite of her immediate goal to save Vaughn, she couldn't avoid truly enjoying herself, truly appreciating.

This newness sent her mind scurrying to understand what great change had come about her. She remembered how new her body felt while washing it. *These feelings I'm having now are also just like that, only different somehow.* Everything happening within her and to her became a learning experience… as if it was her first day on Earth. Yet, with the familiarity of all her past experiences intact, it was that strange difference between her past and present that made her feel, in a way, ignorant. During all of this self-examination, her Appendaho wardrobe now went from a few pretty, long dresses to everything from absolutely exquisite regal apparel to harvesting overalls, whatever the people thought she might need, use, or enjoy.

Oh, I wish Lana could be here to see this wonderful celebration. She would love it so. I'm sure Puppy misses her. But I need to help Vaughn. But… how? Stephanie began sneaking up on her father to give him a kiss, but long before she met him, others saw her and started fussing over her. Soon she found herself surrounded by a large escort of people, all making a huge commotion over her, each vying for who got to feed her, or show her this or that first.

"Just come over here one second and try…" one would say, before being interrupted by another grabbing her other arm and saying, "No, this is closer. Better to do this first…" Then another would interrupt…

◆ SACRIFICIAL WOOD ◆

The irony of such deep love literally pulling her in so many different directions, pulling her potentially apart, in a loving way of course… well, judge for yourself! "I taught her how to make butter." "Yes, but I taught her how to quilt." "Yes, but I taught her how to prune trees." "Yes, but I taught her how to make cheese." "That rug on her floor, she made it because I taught her." Well, as Stephanie's arm was gently pulled in one direction, and the other in that direction, there was yet another person in front of her trying to hold her shoulders, she couldn't help feeling how loved she was and how much she dearly loved them all, in spite of her growing concern for Vaughn. Finally though, she collapsed onto an ancient stone bench in laughter at the chaos she was causing. There was no restraining it.

Yet, even more so, her laughter was an open celebration, the deepest of Thank You's, the reveling in her new life, peace, and internal freedom. She rejoices at being *what* she now *is!*

A thought drifted to her: *First say 'I' Stephie, and then 'We'.* And that thought made her reach out with all her heart to embrace the party thrown in her honor, as if somehow, by accepting this to its fullest, she was also making herself more capable to say 'We', more able to help Vaughn. *I first have to be 'Me', before I can be 'We'.* Funnier still, was them surrounding her, not knowing why she was laughing.

When she finally got control over herself and picked her head up with tears of gratitude, they seriously asked her what was so funny?

She smiled. "Maybe you should just divide me in pieces and…" she burst back into uncontrolled laughter, unable to complete the thought about putting her back together again after the party. They all just stared at each other still not comprehending, confounded at her laughing spectacle. Finally, her father and sister noticed the commotion and managed to wiggle through everyone.

Stephanie, glad to see them, wiped her tears of laughter from her face. The crowd quickly explained what they'd been doing and how she broke into these laughing fits. "We were just trying to show her around when she started laughing uncontrollably. We're not sure she's alright."

As one explained they wanted her here, and another interrupted that they wanted her there, little innocent squabbles broke out again concerning where Stephanie should go next and Arlupo and her father looked at each other knowingly. When one pulled Arlupo aside and earnestly asked if she thought Stephanie was O.K. concerning her laughing fits, Arlupo immediately sat next to Stephanie and broke out laughing. One in the crowd made supposition that perhaps it was something like a cold virus. A laughing virus! The seriousness of the remark brought roaring laughter from their father, who collapsed at the feet of his two daughters. Someone in the crowd was heard saying, "Yes, I think it's contagious!" Finally, Stephanie was able to do the thing she wanted, and she wrapped her arms around Father from behind and kissed the top of his graying head. She felt like he had always been her father.

Holding him, she gave him her daughterly advice. "I love you father, but as your new daughter, I feel it is my duty to

SACRIFICIAL WOOD

inform you that if you do not administrate quickly, I may be the cause of a great war among the Appendaho."

He nodded, then motioned everyone to step back and said that Stephanie would simply go in order, from left to right, and visit everyone. They should all just go and wait at their respective tables. He and Arlupo would escort her to make sure no one *cheated!* With that implication, many huffed humorously and ambled to their stations. Stephanie put one arm around her father and the other around her sister as they walked to their first stop.

"I love them all so much. I probably shouldn't have laughed so hard." They both just looked at her, scrunching their eyebrows as if to say, we couldn't keep from laughing, too, so don't feel bad.

Awed by what they all had done, Stephanie squeezed them both. "Such a celebration, Father… I've never had such a thing done for me, nor would I ever have dreamed it."

Stephanie was glowing. Happiness and such a still peacefulness like nothing she had never, ever known or imagined washed through her like the gentle rolling of waves onto a beach. Each wave seemed to bring a little deeper insight, a deeper feeling of '*Reality Is*'. Everything seemed new inside her and she perceived through this newness everything on the outside.

"Nor us, daughter. We've never celebrated our own blood the way we've celebrated you, and with good reason."

"Father?" She looked over to watch his answer.

He smiled that broad smile, but his eyes carried a deep knowing that hinted at his pain. "The meaning is different.

You were all but lost to life, dear child. But you found your way back to the Light even though many, many of your fore parents' generations were lost. But for the Appendaho, we have been of the Light for as long as we remember, and raise our children to be so. The celebration takes place for them when they come of age to think for themselves. But they haven't gone through the pain, the torture, the evil that you've gone through. Mostly, they've faced the ignorance of youth and the questions associated to that. Hardly to be compared to your tribulation."

Stephanie meekly smiled. But what he said got her thinking. "Father, what will happen to the Appendaho as they come more and more in contact with the world?"

"That's why I've sent Arlupo and the others to school. They come back and teach us of the world again, so that we'll be able to endure it. Eventually, I expect, we'll end up marrying back into it, or hopefully they'll marry into our tribe."

Stephanie's heart twinged, *I know the world*. She looked at how beautiful all the people were now. She couldn't imagine them retaining this beauty if they married outsiders. But she didn't say anything. Those troubles were still in the future. Vaughn needed her *now*. Fire began to burn down deep. As much as she loved this joyous celebration, eagerness to fulfill last night's promise to Vaughn grew steadily more urgent.

He saw trouble cross her brow. He knew she wouldn't be able to hold back much longer, so he asked before she did. "Stephanie, what is it? Why should you be troubled after such joy?"

She sighed. "It's not the same kind of trouble as beset me before, Father."

"Then tell me, what is it?"

She looked up with pleading eyes. "You know, Father. God has preserved my love in me and made it more understanding, so it seems to me that I feel even greater pain. It's time to see what can be done for Vaughn. I need your help."

"Yes, the greater the love, the greater the pain. It *is* the nature of reality. But always remember, so the pain doesn't destroy you, that the love must *always* be first. Without the love, this kind of pain couldn't exist. To keep the pain from destroying you, be thankful that you are able to truly love. For without love, you are dead inside, but with it, even when in pain, you live."

Nodding deeply, she remembered Vaughn speaking similar words. She brought her heart to him. "Yes, Father. Remember you also said that after I found the Tree of Life inside me, there was a possibility I could help Vaughn? Now, more than ever, I desire to do so."

"Yes. Let us pay a short visit to all the people so we don't have a *war* on our hands." He smiled. "Then we'll see to your request. Please understand, I'm not simply delaying for a mere party. You need the time to let your wonderful blessings settle into you. Normally, with one such as yourself, I would imagine, you should take at least a week…"

"*Oh Father…!*"

"I know, I know, Vaughn needs you now. Arlupo, after we finish here will you reconvene everyone at the sacred room? Open all the windows?"

"Yes, of course, Father. But first I need to do something, then I'll do as you ask. Stephanie, let me get another hug from you first. I feel so good in your arms." Each buried their face in the other's neck and shoulder, Stephanie being only slightly shorter.

Stephanie cooed. "Ooooh, it feels like we've always grown up together." Stephanie leaned further in, squeezing her even tighter. *This woman pulled me from utter death. How can I ever repay her?* As they embraced, memories of how Arlupo stood by her, brought her back to herself after reading the terrible news about Vaughn, how she convinced her father to bond and to put her under the water, all this Stephanie's heart remembered and combined it with Arlupo's utter beauty and integrity, and that generated an overwhelming love for her. Stephanie's new heart and mind brought it all so clearly and sharply into focus that she took even more note of this tremendous difference within herself. *I loved her before I changed, but now even much more so. Oh God, what have You done to me? Thank You!*

Arlupo felt Stephanie's love flow into her and cherish her, as Stephanie held her preciously. Stephanie felt the same from Arlupo but also felt Arlupo hold her in a way Stephanie didn't understand. *It almost feels like she's clinging to me for dear life… but whose? Mine or hers?* They didn't want to part. Then Arlupo broke off the embrace without looking at her friend and headed home.

Stephanie went to each table receiving various foods, garments, and blessings. At her direction, her father carried the growing stack of clothes. After two long hours, she was

SACRIFICIAL WOOD

stuffed full of meats, vegetables, pies and delicacies. She realized it had also been a long time since she'd eaten. But more so, the wonderful settling of her inner workings that her father had spoken about was strengthening her resolve as she began to be familiar with her new intensities, perceptions and abilities. Her newness was like gazing at a beautiful landscape for the first time, eyes roaming over its beautiful hills and streams, smelling its wonderful scents, knowing it belonged to her and being more and more comforted by it. Yet, she also knew she was supposed to walk through it all before she did anything else. She had only walked the first few yards in a territory that extended miles. *I think he's right. I probably need at least a week…or more…but Oh God…*

☙

Arlupo knelt before the Tree of Life weeping. "Oh Tree, there is no one dearer to me than Stephanie. What have I done to her? She's about to do something because of me. There are warnings concerning what she's going to do. Our ancestors' stories tell of others who have been *lost. I didn't really think about this before!* Oh God, what am I to do? She won't fail to attempt it. But she's not ready. Oh, God, I can't see her outcome. Why can't I see? *Why can't I see?*"

☙

When Arlupo reappeared, Stephanie smiled, always comforted by her presence. A nod from her father had her announce to the people to come to the sacred lodge. They all looked at each other in surprise, wondering what other fantastic things were to come.

Once assembled, the Appendaho leader, his daughter, wife, and two elders with their wives sat in a semi-circle surrounding Stephanie sitting under the Tree of Life. Stephanie rubbed her hands across the brass bench's smoothness, remembering the last time she did so. Back then she had been fighting to understand how to be free of the tree of death. Now free, she searched for how to help Vaughn, while outside, all the people encircled the lodge wondering. Only those seven knew the purpose. The people outside whispered their guesses. Their leader answered their fervent curiosity in his clear, sharp voice.

"Now, this is a sacred ceremony that has been written about in *legend*." Gasps and Ooohs and Aaahs instantly went up from the people and their leader paused till they calmed. "None of us has ever accomplished it before. But as Arlupo has pointed out to me, there may be very little difference between legend and prophecy. We are all sitting in this circle around the Tree of Life because of love, because of the young man Vaughn, whom Stephanie loves with all her being. The young man is near death." Only Arlupo and her father knew the exact nature of Vaughn's dire need. The rest had just been told merely that he was in trouble.

All the people moaned as one, some putting their hands to their mouths, others had instant tears. Some of them, while holding their husbands or wives in their arms, remembered marrying when not much older than Stephanie. They clutched each other more tightly. She had become dear to them, her presence a continual presence in their hearts. Now it was transformed into pain, which they had not known before. They looked at her now, not only as a daughter, but as a young woman in love, facing the most terrible, the brutal destruction of her most precious love.

"Stephanie, you must go before the Tree of Life and ask it to bring us the vision of your loved one, as he is in the present. When the vision appears in place of the Tree, we may pray for Vaughn and….." He stopped mid-sentence as if at a loss for words.

"Why are you hesitating, Sir?" Her concern was obvious.

His gravity even exceeded her concern. "Because that is all I can tell you. The legend says that the *faithwalker* must continue alone from there. None of us has that gift or is able to give you counsel."

Alone. Ignorance. *Very* alone.

Her eyes widened, looking up at her father. "Faithwalker?"

His thoughts more than nagged him. *Am I doing the right thing? Arlupa, if you weren't so sure of yourself…* Comfort radiated from his eyes but they maintained their intensity. "Yes, remember we are bonded, so I know all about you. You are a legend, my dear, lovely daughter… a real live legend… you are a *faithwalker*." The sobriety in his words could not have been clearer. It was reality, as if being officially proclaimed by the Light itself, her father merely reporting what was so obvious.

Still looking up at him, Stephanie's gaze transformed into a helpless plea. "But… but what does that mean?" Her heart was pounding. *I'm not able to do this. Whatever it is I'm supposed to do… But this was my idea… I think.*

"As Arlupo explained, I'm not allowed to tell you what little I know of it. It's the very nature of the gift that you must walk alone when you use it. Anything I would tell you could hinder you."

Stephanie's eyes grew wider by the moment. Fear as she had not known fear before inundated her. Vaughn's life depended on her new found abilities that she knew nothing about. She *needed* to understand as much as possible. At least as much as they did.

Her father saw her trepidation and decided to reveal some of what he had learned through the bonding. "You have already used your abilities at least four times before!"

She leaned forward and… "*What?*"

"Four times before, your heart, mind, and soul were joined in a singular purpose. When you healed the little blond girl at the playground." He waited for her to remember.

Oh God, blood without injury…

"When you climbed out the window and fell, you used your abilities to keep from falling further!"

The ladder!

"When Vaughn was lying in your bed badly hurt and bleeding inside, you used your ability to heal him, too!"

That's how he recovered so fast!

She sat back in utter amazement, recalling those instances. But now, since she was born anew, she was able to see them even more clearly than when they actually happened. She remembered her feelings and actions that had been hidden or taken for granted at the time she had them. She leaned back further, her hands reaching behind her for support, again her eyes widening. Her father could tell that she could see it for herself.

"Oh my God," she said in response to her reflections. "The fourth time was when I touched the Tree of Life and saw the visions." Her father nodded. But this wasn't enough to satisfy Stephanie. *How is any of that to help me now?*

"What about the fire that protected Vaughn from the evil creature's black essence?" she asked, knowing her father knew. But all the people were shocked to hear it. Arlupo's mouth dropped open. *She never told me…*

"That's a different gift! You can use it in combination with your others, just like Vaughn told you!" *My special sight and the fire…*

"Others? How many others? No. Wait. Let's just focus on the main one for now. You do know of the legend. Surely everyone knows. So, it couldn't be harmful for me to know it… could it?" Her raised eyebrows were pleading.

He deferred to his daughter, since all this was still under her authority. "Arlupo?"

"Yes, Father. I think she has a point." Arlupo turned to her sister and smiled. Love. Knowledge. Giving. Stephanie imprinted her face into her memory for all eternity. "Oh Stephanie, the legend has a beautiful story to it. Long ago, there was an evil lord with great powers. He was *very* cruel, and took many women and did *terrible* things to them. There was a boy whom he'd made his personal servant for *many* years. The boy fell in love with a young woman, and she with him. When the evil lord discovered the romance, he took the girl for himself, and in the young man's presence, this evil king did horrible things to her. Then the evil lord hid her from the young man so he couldn't find her, nor was he allowed to search. The evil king rejoiced at the terrible pain he caused the boy and girl. He taunted him every day. But the boy was as you are, a *faithwalker!* The evil king's abilities were similar, but far more advanced. He never expected anyone else might have such abilities. The legend says that sometime in the boy's life, the boy discovered this Tree of Life…"

Stephanie broke in, "Oh my, it must have been quite a young tree back then."

"We don't really know. We don't know how old the Tree of Life is. The boy discovered the Tree all alone at the top of a desolate, dead mountain. Nothing grew there, and any creature that drank the waters of the mountain died. The Tree is said to have looked very much as it did when you first saw it. When the young man discovered this lone tree, he wept bitterly, because the tree reminded him so much of how he felt about his own life and of what had been done to the young woman he loved. When he was done weeping, he looked up at the tree and it looked much like it does now… with living sprouts upon it!"

Stephanie's mouth dropped open. Everyone kept still at hearing the great legend recounted. Stephanie broke the silence. "You're kidding?" Their devout quiet answered her question.

Suddenly realizing what she said and being ashamed, she quickly amended. "You're not."

"Then the boy's vision was opened, and he discovered that this Tree was not as it had appeared to his eyes. He was afraid if he visited the Tree too often, others might find out, so he went just once a week. Legend says that the Tree taught him the ways of Life because he had faith in Life.

"One day, he missed his loved one so much that all he could see in his imagination was her. He wept before the Tree, and the Tree disappeared and became a vision. Legend says he reached through the vision and touched her and healed her and gave her knowledge. She was also a wondrous woman of great virtue, in spite of all the evil that had been done to her. She was able to perceive what he'd done to her and she somehow escaped her prison and became his Queen. Legend says that we, the Appendaho, are their descendants!"

Stephanie's tears streamed down her cheeks unabated, as she held her head high. "Oh my God… that's the most beautiful story," she sobbed.

"My daughter, I see that you appreciate it greatly."

"Wait… Queen? What happened to the evil king?"

"The young man killed him!" Arlupo chirped out the answer.

Stephanie's eyebrows jumped up, her head jerked back. "What? But how?"

"Legend says he killed him by his faith, that he brought down a mountain upon the evil king's head."

Stephanie's face relayed her shock. "He moved a mountain?"

"That's what the legend says. The limitations of a *faithwalker* are not known."

"But why did the young man wait so long to do such things?"

Arlupo gave her a wry look. "Why have you?"

Stephanie saw how foolish her question was and silenced herself. It only made her feel her ignorance that much stronger.

But Arlupo knew her friend's feelings and sought to assuage them. "The evil king ruled not just by his great power, but through fear as well. Our forefather had to first conquer his fear before he could conquer the evil king. And he had to learn the truth about his life and the Light. There was no one to teach him."

Stephanie maintained her silence.

Arlupo turned her hands outward toward her sister. "Do you see, my sister, why we love you so? You have the same qualities as our forefather had. We could have no higher respect for you."

But Stephanie felt like only two years old, a toddler having just realized she could stand up straight and walk, with all the precariousness that implies. *That's why they're called toddlers.* Her shoulders were shaking up and down from her sobs, but she still held her head up to meet her fate. These were not tears she was ashamed of. However, she just didn't feel she deserved to be mentioned in the same breath as their great legends. "Ohhhh, *please*, that's going too far, I'm not…."

But Arlupo cut her off. "Reality is what reality is. Even if we never had the legend, we would respect you the same way because of the meaning of what you are and what you have already done. It's not about the 'who' Stephanie. It's about the 'what.'"

Overwhelmed by such appreciation, but not knowing how to live up to it, she looked around wishing for some place

SACRIFICIAL WOOD

to hide, knowing there was none. All eyes were upon her. Expectant of something. They didn't know what.

But there were more important things to consider than old or new *legends*. *Vaughn*, she heard her heart call out. Determination flooded into her. It didn't matter if she wasn't even a fraction of what some legend was. She had to try to help Vaughn. *No matter what*, she heard his words echo in her mind. Fire suddenly flared brightly in her eyes and the people saw it. Their own eyes widened, then they silently nodded to each other. "Thank you Father, Sister, all of you… now, what must I do?"

Her father now answered her. "That is up to you child. When Arlupo first came to us on your behalf, we gave ourselves to her for direction. We now give ourselves to you!"

Stephanie never expected such a statement, such an absurdity. She held out her hands in reflex and…"But… but…" But they all waited upon her instruction.

Struck dumb, frozen between ignorance, terror, and legend, she sat as the situation sunk deeply in to her. Then her hands, as if thinking for themselves, because the rest of her was still frozen, slowly wiped away her tears. She felt a fire descend over her from the Tree of Life. It reminded her of the coolness of the oak tree that bathed her and Vaughn that summer day… that now seemed so long ago. *That* reminder snapped her out of her deadlock and she suddenly could see Vaughn's face before her. *But I'm the only one with a true feel for this situation. Feelings! It has to do with feelings. That's a start.* She bowed her head and asked the Light for guidance because she felt so unable to follow through with any of what had been placed before her. All the people watched through the windows and prayed. They all loved her as one.

Stephanie, determined to speak from her new heart, mind, and soul, and from her new found joy, love, and understanding, thought to herself, *I am me… more me than I have ever been.* So she held her head up, and spoke clearly. "Oh people of the Appendaho, I have been so honored by you. Because of your love for Life, you have helped save me from bitter hell. I *live,* now. Every one of you has talked to me at some time, and shared a piece of your true lives. What I have become now, is because of *you. You* all live in me. Everything you taught me, from milking goats, to making cheese, picking apples, and so much more, gave me *deeper* meaning… of *everything.* But there is another, who is far more worthy than I, who needs your help. I love this young man, and no other *forever.* Will you beseech the Tree with me so that it may listen?"

They were enthralled by her words, and couldn't respond fast enough. "AMEN, AMEN, AMEN." All had tears in their eyes, taking hold of one another's arms or hands.

Then Stephanie turned around, and knelt under the Tree as before. With her knees on the soft rug from her bonding, she leaned on the brass bench surrounding the basin and leaned further over under the branches, and began her journey as she wept. "Thank you, Oh Tree of Life, for doing the Light's will and holding us all to you. I *know* that somewhere upon you is a tiny twig where Vaughn lives, but I don't know where. I also know that you value the tiniest part of yourself as you do the largest, for you are True. He is near death, but you are Life, and he cannot die except you let go of him. Please, since you love him, let my tears be for his tears before you, for his soul, for his life. For I know if he were here, he would surely weep for you. So *Please,* open a way to save him. Look deep into my heart, my mind, and my soul. You will see that the love I have for him is not selfish, but that I love him for the goodness he has of you, and that *that goodness* should prosper. I would give my own life for his, if it were possible, not because I value mine less, but because he is worth the price of my life now, as I value my life so *very* much…" At hearing her words the people all collapsed to their knees. *A woman. A true woman,* they wept in their hearts.

Sparks falling from the Tree again began to enter her, but this time she did not run from them. Instead, she stretched her arms out and raised her head to receive their fullness, and that's when she saw what began to happen. "Oh my God…"

Arlupo saw the Tree change. "Father, the Tree! Just like the legend."

When everyone heard *that*, they all stood up, pressing at the windows. All were amazed by the vision they saw… the condition Vaughn was in. "*Oh my God!*" Arlupo cried, as if a knife had been twisted in her gut. And, in fact, she grabbed her chest and abdomen and fell over. Vaughn's pains, Stephanie's pains, had become *her* pains. It was not just the physical pain she was experiencing, but the spiritual condition as well.

As Arlupo cried, Stephanie was thrown back onto her backside as before, and her whole body was shaking. Not just from the energy of the tree, but this time because of the terrible sight and pain of Vaughn. Gasping in horror, hardly able to breathe, everything began spinning. She could feel *everything* about Vaughn.

"Oooohhh Vaughn, *my love*...oh no...what has happened? I see you... I FEEEL YOU..." Stephanie's awareness and concentration was drawn deeper and deeper into the vision, and she became less and less cognizant of her surroundings. She forced herself back to the brass bench as before. "No Vaughn, I'm *here* to help you. It's *not* hopeless... you must remember Vaughn, YOU *MUST* REMEMBER YOUR FAITH!" *He can't hear me. I've got to get closer... reach into the vision...* She leaned forward. The people gasped. Her father saw her reach into the vision, and the part that reached, disappeared!

"Be careful my child, the vision's a mystery. Don't reach in too far."

But it was too late. The outside world was no longer real to her. Her entire focus lay right before her. Her words began to echo. Everyone looked at the other to confirm their hearing. "Vaughn, remember how you taught me faith. My life would be *nothing* without you. Remember how you saved me from that terrible... *Vaughn, Vaughn."* He can't hear me... OH GOD, *HE'S GOING TO GIVE UP! I CAN FEEL IT. NOOOOOOOOOOO...*

They all saw what she was going to do. They felt it in their gut. Their mouths dropped open. She sprung herself up onto the sacred soil. They cried out as one... "STEPHANIE, NOOOOOO, DON'T..."

SACRIFICIAL WOOD

Arlupo fell over on her side again, wailing, "OH FATHER, *SHE'S GONE! THE VISION'S GONE!* WHAT SHOULD WE DO?" But she already knew. She had no feeling of what would happen because hope was gone. Arlupo felt as if she were dying. "It's my fault. *Oh God…*"

Her father and everyone else were shaken, and they all trembled. His words weakly tumbled out. "I don't think there's anything we can do. She's beyond us now."

One of the elders asked, "Can't we call another vision?"

"I…don't think so. The *faithwalker* has made her choice, and we cannot interfere."

"Now Scraback, we have her. She's in *our* reality now. Let's go get the *poooor* child," Master GrrraGagag hissed with venom and delight. His eye drooled. "Harvest time is here again, is here again…" he began to sing. "It's a little ditty I picked up from the humans. Finally, my plans have come to fruition! Get that Scraback? Fruition? Fruit? Harvest time? Never mind, it's an Earth sense of humor called a pun. Alpha's ought to have more of a sense of humor!"

"Yes Master, I agree!" *So, Master intended this? So did I!* Scraback's eye drooled, also.

CHAPTER EIGHT

Good Dreams and Nightmares

"What is time to us? The humans count days, weeks, and years. We know no temporal changes except our evolution into our perfect form. Do not be dissuaded by the human's marking of time for we are timeless. What is it if we shall wait one hundred-thousand years, if need be, until the glow be purged and the Earth be ours. We shall have billions of their years ahead with no limit. Patience is one of our chief virtues."

GrrraGagag listened to Claynomore's oratory unmoved, eyeing all of the other Alpha's slapping their tails and waving their arms in praise of his speech. GrrraGagag kept tossing a black rock up and down as if bored until it irritated Master Claynomore. "Just what kind of comment are you trying to make, Grrrag?" He used his former underling name on purpose.

"None. I just prefer actions to words. Have a piece of the Black River." GrrraGagag tossed the rock at Claynomore but *he didn't know how to catch. It bounced off his bulbous head, and GrrraGagag vanished before they could see his laughter.*

Misty dim light enveloped her. *Where am I? Oh GOD, Where am I?* Her fright seemed to shake the very essence of wherever it was she was. She immediately clamped her fear because of it. That cut off the expression, but not the feeling.

She was in the Ethereal Corridor that connected the physical Earth to both the Ethereal and Paradise. The corridor of common travel for all those who were able. But she knew none of this now, for she was sure she was lost forever. That was the feeling of it. There were no longer any recognizable perceptions of the world she came from. *But I gave that whole life up anyway.*

She thought out loud. *"What am I going to do? Oh, I've made a mess of this."* Then she got angry at herself. *"You idiot! The Tree of Life didn't send you here to cower!"* She felt ashamed and refocused. *I'm supposed to be here. THINK! Oh Vaughn, where are you? I am… a faithwalker. Why am I called a faithwalker? Because I can travel by faith. I not only see reality as a whole, but I can move through it. I understand now, Arlupo. That's how I can find him. Feelings. My mind and my heart meshed into one. Feelings. Concentrate on my love, My Vaughn…* There, *in the distance through the mist.* There. *Walk by faith to him because Love would have it be so, would approve it to be so…* "Vaughn, my love, can you hear me?"

In a mere few moments she had zipped through what would have been nearly two thousand miles in the physical world. But she wasn't *in* the physical world. Now she floated in that part of the Corridor that paralleled where Vaughn was lying. She could see and feel his thoughts, as real and as easily as people in the physical world see bodies.

…Hope…what? Want to di…live…What?…Stephanie… I miss you sooo…

She spoke tenderly to him. "Vaughn, I'm here. You *must* have faith, or you can't be saved."

…Hopeless… falling… forever…

She screamed at him, angry to hear such words in his mind, in his *heart*, "No! No!"

She realized *faithwalkers* can cross boundaries. *I've left the physical world and entered a different one. That's a boundary.* She tried to reach through from where she was now, back into the physical world to touch him.

At first, all she did was simply reach within the Corridor. Then she realized that wherever she went was the Corridor! It could even occupy the same space as the physical world. *But how do I make contact with the physical world?* She focused on the physical world, on that part of it which was Vaughn. She reached out, but it was as if something pushed back. She gritted her teeth. Anger at being prevented mixed with the urgency of love.

Waverly felt a tingling sensation, and picked his head out of the crook of his arm that was leaning on Vaughn's hospital bed. His wavy blond hair a muss, his blue eyes widened at what he could not yet see. His knees began to tremble at the resounding thunder…coming from everywhere, nowhere…

◆ SACRIFICIAL WOOD ◆

"Huuuuh? OH MY GOD, DID YOU HEAR THAT? Vaughn, didn't that wake you? It sounded like the thunder was in the *room*... oh my Go..." Waverly's thoughts began to jumble.

A bright light began to shine in the air above Vaughn. Waverly fell off his chair, onto his back beside the bed, his eyes widening yet further, as he looked up. Shaken even more, he squinted, rubbed his eyes, and tried to refocus. It was as if the air were splitting above Vaughn. Hands! Then arms! He scooted backwards until he could see Vaughn again. He couldn't stand. Hands were reaching inside Vaughn's chest and head.

Waverly had hardly heard his friend's voice since before Vaughn had been sent away. But he heard him now, but couldn't hear Stephanie.

"Stephanie? Where... are you?" Vaughn said.

"Faith Vaughn, I am in *faith* where *you* need to be also."

"I'm dreaming..."

"Have you dreamt this before since you were hurt?"

"No. This can't be real. No hope..."

"Through our prayers, oh dear Vaughn, through our prayers I have come to you. I don't know how to return back, but I'm here for *you... no matter what!.*" She waited, but it had no effect at all. *I thought for sure our special phrase would touch him.* "I have gladly given my life for you, so *please*, take hold and remember your faith." Her power swirled all through him, trying to join with him, but without his choice to take hold, it slipped off... as if he wasn't even there. Never had Stephanie had an emptier, more sickening feeling.

199

He could *feel* her. There was no mistaking it. If any dream were ever as real as this, he would have to *live the dream*. It really *was* her… But…

"No. No hope… Dream too good… It just increases the pain! I can't take any more… *death,* come *for me!*"

Waverly hadn't a clue as to what was happening, but he heard himself cry out. "NO Vaughn. Whatever it is, if it's a good dream, *then live it! Don't die!*"

Stephanie turned from glowing gold to deep black. Waverly saw the light turn to deep blackness. *Oh God, death is coming for him.*

No words could have angered her more than *death come for me*. No words were more the antithesis of both their lives than those. Without thinking, she reached into his mind for the most powerful memory they shared…

He saw her smile at him, walk up and *slap* him as hard as she could, knocking him down. He felt it again! She leaned over him and . . . but the words were different this time, "*Faith. Men talk about it ALL THE TIME but they haven't a single* clue *as to what it really IS. Especially when they have to live it* beyond *what they think they* know. *MEN ARE JUST PLAIN STUPID!*"

Stephanie and Waverly heard him mumble. "Wow, what a woman!"

She began to withdraw from him. "Well, *this woman is leaving, since you don't believe me!*"

He felt her comfort begin to fade, and the terrible darkness of his torments creeping back in. Waverly saw the blackness turn back into golden light, and then it began to fade. His heart jumped for his friend. "Whatever's going on, Vaughn, it's better than what you've been having. *Don't let that light leave!*"

"NO… OH GOD… DON'T GO… *PLEASE…*"

Her voice trailed off, "Only your faith can keep me." She continued to withdraw.

"Oh GOD… PLEASE…" *Faith. All of it feels right. But can I have faith in just a dream? Maybe… if it's a* good *dream. Goodness has a will of its own. It's a doorway into another world. My escape? I can have faith in the goodness… because goodness is always real, whether in the imagination or in reality.*

Suddenly, she felt her power begin to touch him, and her heart leapt. "YES…" She poured love into the connection.

He felt a surge of life! "Oh God, I feel her… like before… getting stronger…" He focused his heart and mind to travel more deeply into the goodness he felt. *There's no doubt that this goodness is real. That's all that matters.* Then he could *see* her, as when he saw visions in his meditations… but different. None of this was symbolic. *This is really happening?* "Stephanie, *it is you!* OH GOD, I've been in the hell of hells. I wanted to die but I couldn't. Forgive me, *I've failed you.*"

Fire burst all through her, even though she was in the Corridor. Thunder sounded again in Waverly's ears, and he fled to a corner of the room.

"You'll fail me if you don't *WAKE UP* and be healed. Feel me, my love, in your heart, *feel* the truth I bring you, let your mind *see*." Though she'd somehow mysteriously been able to reach through to him, it was more like she'd extended another part of the Corridor into him! Or perhaps become a bridge between them. These things only the *faithwalker* has the power to clearly explain. But one thing was clear, unless Vaughn connected to her by faith, it would be as if she had done *nothing*! She had opened the door on her side, but he needed to open the door wider on his.

"Stephanie. Your love. My love. I remember… *the meaning…*"

As soon as he said the word 'meaning' she felt his heart and mind burst open. *Of course! Vaughn's faith is in meaning.*

As conscience once again flooded his being so did deep shame. "Oh my God, where've I been? FORGIVE MY LACK OF FAITH! *No matter what*, that's what I'd promised. How could I have allowed myself to fail you Stephanie?"

Stephanie thought of all the times she failed. Vaughn pulled her back. "You couldn't help it, my love. But there are people, the Appendaho, far to the West, deep in the mountains, just east of the Great City. You must go there. They'll help you so you *never* fail again." She placed the picture of the Appendaho and the place in his mind.

"Oh God, I feel alive again. My strength. I *feel* your prayers. I feel you *inside* me. But how?"

She chose to answer his question with a prayer. "Thank you Tree of Life, thank you for providing me passage. You'll be all right now Vaughn. You must find a way to go where I showed you."

Now he focused on the future. *Future.* What a wonderful word compared to hopeless.

"I feel you inside of me, Stephanie. You… you are so beautiful… so much more than when you left… so much more… What are you Stephanie? Are you still alive? How have you come to me?"

Realizing how strange this must be, even for him, it made her laugh to imagine it from his end. She felt him healed, so she gently withdrew herself from inside him. Relief flooded her, as she simply wrapped her arms around his chest, in the position that in the physical world would have held him.

"Very much alive, my love, they say I'm a legend." She laughed. "Something called a *faithwalker*. But I really know almost nothing about it." *Oh my God, I came by faith, so I should be able to leave by it. Could I even come to Vaughn in person? But if I do that, I won't be near the Tree of Life. Would I be able to travel back West by faith without the Tree? I don't think so. I would be caught in the wrong place.*

Stephanie screamed! It was the kind of sound one makes at severe, unexpected pain, but then she was stifled in mid-cry. Her connection to Vaughn was abruptly severed. Her scream chilled him to the bone as he sat bolt upright. When Waverly saw it, he almost fainted.

"Stephanie? *Stephanie?* STEPHANIE!" he cried out.

☙

Back in the sacred lodge, Arlupo still kept vigil, still kept praying. She alone kept the watch, as she insisted no one else be around. This was all *her* fault. Guilt and grief vied for which tormented her more. The ancient stories echoed in her mind of how others were lost. *But these are only stories,* she kept repeating. *Only stories.*

She begged the Tree of Life to let her see her friend. She extended the powers of her gift beyond their maximum, almost feeling as if she were trying to force the Tree to comply with her will. She received only glimpses of terrible visions that tore her heart out, only to have the Tree of Life put it back together, only to be torn out again. *This is my punishment,* she thought. She could see Stephanie's sweet face and her flaming red hair, as well as hear her full laughter. But she saw this as one would think of those who've passed away.

She remembered the horrible dream Stephanie had described to her. The hideous snake sucking her into a torturing blackness forever. She shivered when she heard it, rubbing her arms briskly. But now, in her visions, glimpses of those snakes kept flashing before her. "Oh Light, why do these visions keep coming before my eyes?" she cried out. "Are they just my worst fears, my guilt haunting me?" She wanted to believe so. "OH GOD! Forgive me! If they're just my fears, then why do they seem so *real*? Oh God! If she's swallowed by that evil, she'll have nothing but eternal torment!"

Arlupo hadn't had much experience with fear, so she wasn't too sure what it could or couldn't do to her. Heretofore, her visions were always real and she never doubted them. *Can fear make things seem real that are not? But then how would I tell the difference?* But it was that realness that drove her deeper and deeper into torment. For the first time in her life, she knew what it was to wish to die!

※ SACRIFICIAL WOOD ※

All day Arlupo knelt under the Tree. Actually, she was lying in the sacred dirt, grasping the Tree's trunk, begging. As the daylight in the room dimmed, she looked past the Tree of Life and saw through the low windows that the sun had but a sliver of gold quickly disappearing from above the horizon. There was no one who had a greater presence of mind and heart than Arlupo. All of that presence came forth in a shattering wail that could be heard throughout the village. A cry like no other ever heard, reserved only for a single, devastating meaning. Every muscle convulsed as she curled into a painful ball and began to completely die inside. The stories said no one ever returned after sunset.

༺༻

In bed, Vaughn rolled onto his face in tears, praying, while his friend watched in utter amazement from the corner, where he had fled after the second booming thunder.

"Oh God of sweet mercy, oh God of sweet Truth, Oh God of sweet Love and origin of faith, thank You for restoring my life. Forgive me for failing You and Stephanie. I was too weak. Please make me so that evil will *never again* be able to overcome me, no matter what the situation or circumstances. *Pleeeease.* I must figure out a way to go to Stephanie. How am I to do that? As soon as I leave this hospital, they'll put me back on the State Farm. I'm *not* going back there. I don't belong there."

The feeling suddenly came to Vaughn that he should take account of his life.

"I can't believe my parents. All my mother ever cared about was money. Even when she supposedly did something good for me, she told me over and over how much it cost, how much she sacrificed for me. Oh God, I want to say I hate her, but isn't it wrong to hate your mother? I hate what she is and has done. I would love her to have better ways, but I just can't help loathing her. She's a disgrace to the human race. If she's not making slurring remarks about different groups of people, she's telling everyone how much she *sacrifices*, how undeserving her love is. HA, what LOVE?

"My father never, in his pitiful life, stood up to her. Even when he knew she was wrong, even when he knew she was hurting me. He didn't want me to be sent away, but he let that *witch* send me away anyhow. It would *cost too much*. They are completely worthless!

"Oh God, am I wrong to express myself this way? Surely their actions deserve to be called exactly what they are, and they to be called exactly as they have acted? Their actions were wretched. They're wretched, even if they are my parents. Reality is what reality is. It is a disgrace to lie about it.

"All my life I had to listen to my mother's fears, her put-downs, her constant screaming, demanding for more and more money. Oh God, she's *pregnant*. She's going to put another child through that hell! What can I do? But my life is with Stephanie. I have to build my *own* life with *no* looking back.

"Stephanie and I will build a beautiful life together. Not the life our *wretched parents* gave us… Stephanie, what happened to her? That was a *serious* scream. I can't believe anything really bad happened to her. She felt so beautiful. I think she knows much more than I do. I felt it. She's wiser, stronger. Oh God, *please* protect her, let no evil be able to overcome her. I have to get to her. How could she come to me like that? Through our prayers? Oh God, I love You so. Faithwalker? She was almost making a joke out of it? What's a *faithwalker*? She's so beautiful."

Vaughn pushed her scream from his memory. That was something that was simply impossible to deal with in light of all that just happened. *She's alright. She has to be. She just healed me. I owe my life to her. I feel alive again. My heart, my mind, ALIVE. Now, I ought to be thankful and rejoice. I have to. Stephie would want me to.*

Vaughn rolled back over, looked at his friend still shaking in the corner, and spoke as if he had just woke from a little nap, nothing more. "Hi Waverly!"

"Vaughn... Oh God...I... do you know what I saw?"

Vaughn smiled calmly as if nothing out of the ordinary happened. "Stephanie."

Waverly sat up from his slumping position. "WHAT? That was Stephanie?"

Vaughn smiled again. "Why? Who'd it look like to you?"

With eyes wide, Waverly crawled across the floor. His strength still hadn't returned. Reaching Vaughn's bedside, he propped himself up. "Vaughn, I heard this terrible thunder in the room, and you didn't even wake up. And then... the air split open and light poured out, and then these glowing hands and arms reached inside you." His face seemed as though it would burst, and he still hadn't completely stopped shaking.

Vaughn continued to act as if it were a normal day. "Yeah, yeah, like I said, Stephanie."

Waverly leaned even closer to his friend. "You're kidding, right?"

Vaughn just stared at him with that same, continuous, calm smile. "I told you we really love each other!"

"Oh my God, I... I..."

Vaughn decided he needed to redirect his friend, for his own good. "My friend, how long have you been here?"

"How long have you been in the hospital? For weeks, I think. I lost track. You went in only six weeks into the school year. It's late fall now." Vaughn shook his head. *I was in that hell for...* he shuddered. He didn't want to calculate it.

"Waverly, I have to leave. Will you help me?"

"LEAVE! You *can't* leave. Where would you go? You know as long as we're kids, the State demands..."

Vaughn leveled his eyes at him. "Waverly, after what I've been through, I don't feel like a kid anymore."

But he cut him off in earnest. "That doesn't matter. It's what the State..."

But Vaughn's solemn demeanor even exceeded his friend's, as he grabbed Waverly's arm. "Then help me get around them."

Waverly's face turned apprehensive. "What? You'll get me in trouble."

Vaughn poured his compassionate gaze upon his faithful friend. "Waverly, you didn't sit here all this time just to see me sent back to where this all happened." That reality shook

※ SACRIFICIAL WOOD ※

Waverly, forcing him to see the conflict in his emotions. "I didn't even think about…"

Vaughn squeezed his arm, focusing even more deeply into where his friend's compassion lived. "I need your help, my friend."

The conflict increased. "What could I possibly do?" he pleaded.

Vaughn told him as fast as the thoughts were forming in his own mind. "It's got to be getting cold out. I need warm clothes… boots for the winter. I have an idea. All those things are at my home. Go to my house and tell my *loving* mother you would like to try to sell my things. You can sell all the stuff I don't need now, but bring me the things I'll need to travel. Oh, and the last book, book seven in my fighting series, *The Art of Fighting: Advanced Future*. If you can stick that in, I'd be grateful. I've only read the rules, but not studied it yet."

Waverly looked at his friend like he was insane. "TRAVEL! WHERE?"

"Take a week. I'll need time to further regain my strength, but don't tell anyone I've recovered."

"I don't know. Don't tell anyone? Vaughn, everyone probably knows you're awake already."

He waved it off, "Nah. You said it thundered. Sooo?" Vaughn's gesture and smile conveyed the simple truth. Waverly realized that as much as the experience had impacted *him*, it really must have been just self-contained in the room otherwise folks would have been rushing in. But he looked back at Vaughn with serious question, and Vaughn read it.

"It's best you don't know where I go, my friend. There's an old oak tree standing alone on top of the hill west of the town. It's got a big hollowed out area in back. Place my stuff in there."

Waverly's worry made his look change from serious to somber, as he was actually thinking about helping Vaughn.

But... how will you survive?"

Vaughn rolled onto his side to face his friend better. "Love!" When he saw Waverly didn't look pleased, he asked, "Waverly, do I really have a choice?"

In short-sightedness his friend jumped with an answer, "YES. There are always choices." But he paused when he realized that, "...just sometimes none of them are very good."

Vaughn's wry smile blended well with his friend's words, but determination came to the fore. "All right then. I *choose* to leave because the only place there's any chance of real life for me is far, far away. It's far more meaningful for me to at least try, *even if I die trying*, than to submit myself for one single second longer to this abominable, meaningless death of an existence here!"

All Waverly could do was stare at his friend in awe. "Vaughn, I wish I had your bravery. All right, I'll do as you ask. I'll wait for you at the tree."

"No. I don't want to risk you getting into trouble on my account."

Waverly couldn't believe the realization setting in. All this time, all he had thought about was his best friend's life. He began to choke up, "Then... after this week, I'll never see you again?"

Vaughn looked away. "I don't know, Waverly, maybe, somehow in the future. If they sent me back you wouldn't see me anyway."

Waverly grasped Vaughn's right arm with both his hands and pulled him out of bed to stand up. He threw his long arms around him, squeezing him tightly. Vaughn was swallowed up between his friend's broad shoulders, and slapped him on the back as he was being squeezed. Waverly didn't want Vaughn to see the tears in the corners of his gray eyes, so he held him a bit longer, hoping they would clear.

Waverly was only able to speak a few, soft words. "My friend, then to the future."

"To the future," Vaughn slapped him on the back again. Then Waverly left quickly, without turning around. Vaughn froze his friend's chiseled face with those questioning gray eyes into his memory. He never wanted to forget him. But even more important at the moment, Vaughn's concentration focused ahead, and on what he needed to do.

The week passed excitedly for Vaughn. Waverly continued to visit, so as not to arouse any suspicion of change. He brought Vaughn real food. They talked softly, and Waverly thought he might finally understand some of Vaughn's ideas. The last day's visit was the hardest. All they could do was hug, as they first did when Vaughn revived. To the future, they both pledged.

Vaughn contemplated many things during that week. He wondered why he had his own private room, since it cost so much. Then he realized guilt must have finally gotten the better of his parents, so they decided to make up in his death, what they loathed to give him in life. *Oh how angry they'll be when they realize they've wasted their money!* He didn't know yet, they hadn't paid for any of it.

Vaughn was careful to always be in bed whenever anyone came. Since he was at the end of the hall, he always heard visitors in the rooms next to his first. At night, when no one came in, he exercised to further strengthen himself. But what he relished most was that he could think and meditate again… although he kept having to push away the sound of Stephanie's scream.

It was clear that everyone expected him to die any day. Since they thought he was still unconscious, they often said so right in front of him. He had to restrain himself from laughing. They never bothered to examine him anymore, and he wondered if they ever did!

The hardest part was still doing a bit of his private functions in bed as they expected. Or maybe, it was even harder keeping still when Gary came to spit on him every night. That first night, after being healed, as he was exercising, he heard the door begin to clang open. He barely made it back to bed in time. It took all his will not to jump up and kill Gary on the spot, and to let his hocker slowly ooze down his face without showing any sign he knew. He hated being dirty, and had always kept himself clean with teeth brushed twice a day, face washed at least twice a day, but none of that was wise right now. When the week was finally up, he had butterflies in his stomach.

It's been a week. I'm sure Waverly did as I asked him. Well, time to say goodbye to this wretched town and leave my old life behind. He paused a moment. *But I met Stephanie here. I found much truth here.* He paused again. *The truth, the love, I carry away with me. The wretched town I leave behind. But I'll miss Waverly. And what about my unborn brother or sister? Oh God, I'm powerless to help. I have to first help myself. Stephanie said something about a special people. Perhaps they're the reason Stephanie's so much stronger, so mysterious. No, I'm sure they helped, but Stephanie had that in her all the time. It just needed to take firmer root and grow. What about me? What must I do to grow into what I really should be? I feel so cut off, so separated from life... and yet, I don't.*

Vaughn shook his head. *How can I know so much truth, I know it's truth that I know, but I still feel so separated from it? Hmm, I suppose Life would first have to teach us that it's Real, before we could somehow really be alive. Hmm, but what must I do to make that change? I've been studying hard the things Life shows me, trying to keep every feeling, every thought of it within me. But the moments of revelation, inspiration, direct connection are yet only for short periods. Too short. But I think that's how I should be continuously. Stephie said those people had helped her. Mmmm, I feel pulled,* a strong pull, *like the time I had to go rescue her. I have to go to where she told me. I have to. O.K., then like I planned out. But first, Oh God, let me take a quick shower and wash up. Tonight is the* last *night that bastard will ever spit on me again. If I ever see him again,* I'll kill on the spot!

Vaughn felt he just had to risk cleaning up. He wouldn't start such a momentous journey being filthy. *This will be a new life for me. Let me wash away the old.*

There was nothing left to do once out of the shower, but put on the flimsy hospital gown and leave. As Vaughn proceeded in his escape from the hospital, he continued to think deeply: *Out the window, across the ledge, and down the fire escape. No one is around a hospital at night. Brrrrrrr, it's cold tonight. I should have taken a hospital blanket...no, I don't want anything that doesn't belong to me. Do the things Waverly got for me really belong to me? My parents bought them, except for my fighting books. But all children need to be taken care of. There's no theft, no wrong in that on the child's part. Even my parents had to have things given to them that became theirs. Still, if I could, I would like to pay every cent back to my parents that they ever spent on me. I don't want to have any connection, nothing* to do with those wretched people.

...Brrrrrr... it's freezing...

ఌ

"Glen, you were right. He's leaving!"

"How do you know? Are you *sure?*"

"After you suspected he was out of the coma, I stole a stethoscope and I've been listening through the wall. I heard him open the window. Hell, he even got up and took a shower."

"I told you Waverly didn't sell all his things for nothing. It didn't make sense for him to sell them, and keep visiting the way he did. Normally, you wait 'til they're dead. I just *knew* he was going to make it!"

SACRIFICIAL WOOD

"Well cousin, don't worry. I'm goin' after him."

"NO! I mean... that won't be necessary. I've got it all worked out. We can use him."

"Look, he's getting away. I've got to go now or I'll lose him."

"NO! Don't worry about it."

"What are you talking about cousin? How can anything work out if we lose him? He's not going to stick around, or they'll just ship him back to the Farm."

"I know where he's going! I followed Waverly around."

"Look, either you tell me right now, or I'm hanging up."

"To the big, lone Oak tree up on the hill due west of here. Now will you just listen a minute?"

"O.K., for a minute. You know, I've got a score to settle with him."

"Look, he's got some kind of special power."

"I heard about that. Your father told me you'd gone nuts. Look, if your old man wants him dead, and someone bigger than him wants him dead... what the *hell* is wrong with you? Did you forget he knocked you out, too?"

"You weren't there in class, I was. He stood between me and that, *whatever* it was."

"Sorry cous', your father told me not to listen to you if you got wacky."

"But Gary, I've got it figured. He'll have to listen. No choice. I'm on my way right now to put the plan in action."

"Hey, you do what you gotta do, and I'll do what I gotta do. Bye."

"DAMN. He'll ruin everything for me!"

◆ DARRYL MARKOWITZ ◆

☙

Vaughn made it down to the ground with the thin hospital gown flapping in the wind. If it wasn't for his modesty, he would have gone naked, although, truth be told, there wasn't a whole lot of difference. The gown was really useless for warmth.

He stuck to the shadows across the large parking lot, although there was no one in sight. The hospital was on the southern edge of town, and even though the main road would have been a straight shot west to the hill, he decided his best escape route was to leave town at its southern end, then travel clockwise around the town, from South to West.

Cold as he was, the crisp smells, even the chilling breeze, spoke of life. A general path worn through the country grass and foliage circled around the town, and he followed it. His hospital slippers fell apart halfway through the journey. In the crystal clear night, the stars and the diminishing full moon shined brightly. A welcome sight after so long.

With teeth chattering uncontrollably, *Oh, God, I'm freezing. I never thought it would take this long to get to the tree. Ahhhhhh, THERE'S MY STUFF!*

He desperately pulled the pack from the mouth of the opening and laid it aside. A long knapsack was actually shoved upward inside the tree's hollow, and he had to struggle to loosen it. He fought his eagerness to get it out quickly, lest he rip the sack, which he couldn't afford to have happen. He was sure the things he now wanted most would be in the knapsack.

◆ SACRIFICIAL WOOD ◆

Oh, coat on top, YES. Brrrrrr…ehhhh, might as well wait just a minute more. Come on, where are you? Ahhh… underclothes, shirt, pants.

He threw off his hospital gown and donned his undershirt and shorts, red flannel shirt, and heavy brown pants… then finally, his thick, wool winter coat. Instantly warmer, the shivering began to calm. Lacing up his boots, he felt like a man again. He turned to inspect the backpack.

Oh, my camping gear. Awesome. Oh, food! Bread, a chunk of roast… mmmm, smells fresh. Mmm… so good. Ahhh, my canteen, and filled with water. Oh thank you my friend. I probably shouldn't build a fire, not here. I'll go off into the woods and finish eating. Set up my tent. Then, tomorrow I'll head west.

He repacked the knapsack and backpack and threw them over his shoulders and began heading down the western side of the hill to the woods. But he paused to look back at the tree and smiled. He wondered if the squirrel was still around. He took a piece of the bread he was eating, and threw it back to the base of the trunk. He remembered holding Stephanie under that very tree.

His heart pounded with eagerness. Tears stung his face in the cold breeze, as he could still feel Stephanie in his arms. Now, hope had been transformed into action. He spoke to himself in an oathful tone, *I'm going to be with her.* Laughing a loud laugh of confirmation, he remembered, *She was right about the squirrel, though. We were separated just like she…* A sudden hit to his side drove him to the ground! His knapsack flew off.

DARRYL MARKOWITZ

When he came to his senses, a fist hit him in the face, as someone sat on top of his stomach. Jammed awkwardly, leaning left, as his backpack was still on under him, his arms struggled, as the shoulder straps partly restrained their movement. Dazed, his eyes filled with different tears. He couldn't make out what was happening, but the *Art of Fighting* kicked in automatically. His legs were free, and his attacker sat on him above his waist. Instinctively, sensing their freedom of movement, his right leg swung up and hooked a foot underneath his attacker's chin and pulled him backward.

"You *pig*," he cursed.

It was Gary. Vaughn took the same foot and kicked him under that ugly chin. Gary rolled away, and Vaughn rolled up to his feet. As he did, he slipped out of his backpack and tossed it aside. Gary tackled him again. But this time, Vaughn was unencumbered, and he used Gary's momentum to roll over several times and he spun away from him. Gary was slower getting up this time. He shook his head to clear it.

"I don't know how you got well. We did everything to make sure you'd die, short of killing you outright."

"Maybe you're not in charge of death like you think." Vaughn needed time to regain his senses. His head pounded from Gary's unrestrained punch.

"Yeah, well I'll *prove* it to you." There was no question that Vaughn was going to die. Just a pip squeak compared to Gary. Gary rushed at him again.

SACRIFICIAL WOOD

Vaughn grabbed Gary's extended arm, pulled it in the direction Gary was moving, twisted, ducked, and threw him over his shoulder. Gary went rolling down the hill, cursing.

Vaughn taunted him, "You're still the same dumb old, fat slob you ever were. Falling two stories hasn't improved you at all!" Vaughn knew he was easily bated.

Gary came up fuming. "Did I ever tell you how I used to make Phanie squeal when I banged her? That's what your *love* loved to be called, you know, because of her tight ass. She used to ride me all night… among other things."

Part of Vaughn fired, but his training squashed it. He'd practiced these kinds of things over and over again in his mind. In fact, he often fought Gary in his imagination. Gary said very close to what he imagined he would say. So Vaughn had a better answer back. "Yeah, and when she came to her senses, she told me how embarrassed she was. She said she'd rather lie next to me for the rest of her life, than to even *think* about you. You just don't have what it takes to be a real man!"

Gary ran up the hill at him. It was easy for Vaughn to kick him in his face. Gary went rolling back down the hill. He came back up even more enraged. This time he knew to be ready for the kick, but Vaughn knew it as well, so he faked the right cross kick, and hit him with a left rising roundhouse up under his chin. Gary went rolling back down the hill again. "Hey, ya know, this is kinda fun. *Can we do it again?*" Vaughn burst out laughing. He really thought it was funny, and wasn't just trying to bait him.

Vaughn had to fight to regain his composure, he was laughing so hard. That made Gary go crazy. When Vaughn faked his kick again, both of Gary's arms went up to block. Expecting Gary's reaction, Vaughn kicked him in the gut. But Gary was so angry, he plowed through it, and tackled Vaughn again.

This wasn't good. Vaughn went down hard. Rule four of the *Art of Fighting:* Never let an angry enemy tackle you. You have two enemies, the opponent and his anger. Vaughn's hands immediately clapped over both of Gary's ears, which disoriented him. Both of Vaughn's legs swung up and rapped under his chin, then pulled him back. Vaughn was angry at himself for having been tackled. Rule five: Determine your outcome, then determine your enemy's. *I'm being sloppy. What do I want to accomplish? If I just escape, he'll either come after me himself or alert the authorities. Either way, I won't get away. I have to have time to get away. He's got to die.* Vaughn had Gary pinned. His feet had his head locked, and his arms held his legs fast but now that he knew Gary was going to die, he had to determine how.

Gary's anger broke Vaughn's hold, as was to be expected. That was OK because Vaughn was stalling while he thought what to do. He somersaulted backwards and came to his feet. *I need to try and make this look like an accident. If I rip out his guts, choke him, or break his ribs, they'll know for sure he was murdered. But… if his neck breaks…*

As each vied for position, Vaughn spun low, and swept Gary's feet from under him. As soon as he went down,

Vaughn went to the ground with him, wrapping his powerful legs around his neck. "I'm sorry Gary, but you've left me no choice. But really, you deserve to die for what you did to my future wife."

As Vaughn spoke, Gary suddenly realized he might actually die. The thought had never really occurred to him… that Vaughn had it in him. During that thought, Vaughn abruptly jerked his legs. It took only a second. But in that second, shock hit Gary that it would be his last. His neck snapped.

For an instant, Vaughn lay still, but as soon as Gary's neck snapped, Vaughn's stomach turned over and dizziness swept through him. He began to shake, but this time… not from the cold. The decision to kill him was calculated, it was necessity. But this reaction was none of those. *Stop it.* He scolded himself. *You're affording him a luxury he never would to you. Do you want to see Stephanie again?* That question helped him refocus.

He got up. There was no time to waste. Gary's body was still shaking from its death throws as Vaughn shouldered him up, grunting. As he did, he could still feel Gary's quivering mass, as if it were trying to fight off death. Vaughn shuddered as he carried him back to the tree, fighting the sudden weakness in his legs. He finally laid him down, then stepped back to examine the position of Gary's body. His flesh still crawled from carrying the dying soul. He nodded to himself, *Looks right.* Then he turned to examine the tree, finding the branch he needed. He climbed up the tree and began bouncing on the branch. "Break DAMN IT," he yelled at the tree. Finally, the branch snapped, but it still hung on by the bark. *Good enough. It looks like the idiot climbed the tree and 'cause he was so big... yeah.* Vaughn went back down the hill for his stuff, but paused, and turned back, "I'm sorry beautiful tree for breaking your branch, and leaving *that* underneath you!" When he turned away, he hoped for finality, only to feel a growing uneasiness, as if something alien had become an inextricable part of him.

After heading deeper into the woods, he found his old camping site. The fire pit, piles of firewood, the kindling and tinder, still remained exactly as he'd left them months ago, so he pulled out the dry grass from his pocket, which he'd tore up from the hillside, and laid it down in the blackened pit. Putting the tinder and kindling on top, he wiggled his metal sparker into the pile, rasping it back and forth. He could see the sparks fly out through the dark spaces in the wood. And then, almost like a mystical experience, a tiny glow caught his eye.

Kneeling down, gently blowing, the little glow produced a hint of flame that for an instant seemed to tentatively wonder at its birth. Like life, though, it reached out and enjoined more grass in its quest then burst into a full fire. Quickly, the tinder was consumed, the kindling turned to little red coals, and the heavier wood was aflame. Vaughn greedily gathered in warmth. Finally, he sat down to finish his first meal in freedom since... he couldn't remember.

Some amount of time had been stolen from his life. Never had he appreciated tasting food so much. After he got warm, he relieved himself in the pit he had also previously prepared. Then he came back and set up his tent, rolled out his sleeping bag and crawled in. Warm, sated, and in the place he loved most, the countryside, he returned to his thoughts.

I'll go to one of the farmer's I worked for this summer, and work there a couple days to get enough money to, yes, make it to another farmer. Yes, farmers are good folk and they know each other round about. At each stop, I can ask who they know, who would be good to work for, maybe they would even give me a note. Yes! That actually sounds like a good idea! They don't much care for the government. Farm help is tough to come by. I don't think they would ask many questions. Farmers aren't like that anyway. They don't try to pull people's lives down like city folk.

Hmmm, at least the farmers I've met. And, they're used to people traveling around asking for work. Ahhh, but there won't be many like that now, since the cold weather is already here. But I know there's still a lot of work to do on a farm; barns to be cleaned, hay to be stacked and un-stacked, pre-winter tilling, and oh yes, gathering and chopping firewood. Oh how I love to chop and split wood. Tree pruning can be done now, too. A bit early, but it can be done. Oh, I so enjoy this kind of work… it makes me feel so alive! It's hard, but I actually like it to be hard. How come so many people don't like hard work? Ha, no one much likes the countryside. That's good for me.

Night sounds from the trees rustling in the breeze mixed with his expanding thoughts, and somewhere in that continuum, sleep claimed him. *What? No! …No! What am I seeing?* "Oh Gary, do it again to me, mmmm…" Her hands clutched him. Her moans of passion increased until it seemed the whole world filled with them. Her heart, completely given over to them, savoring them, called for more, more… Every burst of sound, fired his own passion with equal intensity. As he saw her muscles tense with pleasure, his tensed. He abruptly woke feeling sick.

"STEPHANIE! Oh GOD, what a *horrible* dream. Arrrrrrrrrrrrrrrrrr… terrible, TERRIBLE feelings in me, like I was *him*." A thought pushed itself forward, *You are me, now. You have to be. You killed me. Now you must live my life!* Vaughn shouted back, "NEVER!" *Oh God, feeling, wanting Stephanie so badly, but… she wasn't connected to me at all, she wasn't even, Oh God, it's a dream. But it seemed so real. But, how? Why?* He heard Gary's voice in his mind, again, "I used to make her squeal." *Oh God, there's no win in this.* But the most painful part was the element of truth it had. Tears ran down his face. He didn't want to put his feelings into words. But his oath came to mind, *I'm going to be with her.* His oath didn't feel the same as when he spoke it before. He hadn't really been confronted with her past until he killed Gary. *No, no, I can't let anything convince me our love isn't real.* But within that short time of his escape, something had forever changed in him, and therefore, Stephanie no longer felt the same to him. Something was different.

CHAPTER NINE

Consumption

"Father, you actually met a demon?" his twelve year old's' eyes couldn't be wider.

Mafferan considered the question. "I wouldn't actually describe it as a meeting."

"What then?"

"Well, more like when... a mouse 'meets' a cat."

His son turned to his other younger siblings. They all whispered together, then they began nudging him to speak. "Ask him." they urged.

"Father, which were you... the mouse or the cat?"

"That's an excellent question still open for debate! But there have been others no longer able to engage in it. I wouldn't recommend the 'meeting'."

The children looked at each other in silence, afraid to inquire further.

Master GrrraGagag wrapped Stephanie up in his long, ethereal tail with her head sticking out at the top, just like a constricting snake. The shock of overpowering malevolence, along with a fine mesh of scales, dug into her all over, choking her in mid scream. *Hmm, delicious.* His Great Eye never smiled more broadly. Somehow, his pleasure registered in her scattered mind, which quickly added to her terror and helplessness. His coils could taste her, and Stephanie sensed *that*, too, the most hideous feeling of violation, actually experiencing being tasted for *consumption*. Unable to move, unable to think, and too scared to feel, Stephanie felt her heart would stop at any moment.

"Adding her will multiply my strength considerably, Scraback. There are precious too few humans able to do so. I'll be the talk of the Ether. Perhaps this alone will give me a seat on the High Council." He'd hidden from his underling just how great an effect consuming one such as she would have. He held his Great, black, glistening, drooling Eye over her. Scraback watched in excited delight and amazement. *This could be it. Yes… Yes.*

His Master spoke in a pleasant voice to the human! "Well, well, what do we have here?"

Stephanie felt she needed to breathe, although she hadn't had the need since she entered the Corridor. Probably, unlikely then, her heart would stop. *Please stop!* GrrraGagag squeezed tighter and tighter. It wasn't just his physical force constricting her, but the demon's presence as a whole had a totally anti-human malevolence. And his *stench* was unimaginably nauseating. Excruciating pain tore at her mind, making it run away into a thousand different directions at once. Her heart felt as if she was disintegrating. Equaling her torments, dear Stephanie finally found her voice ridden with horrendous screams. Screams generated from a place that few humans know, or discover too late, or sometimes wake with from nightmares. *Oh God… my nightmare… it's REAL!*

Master GrrraGagag figured there was no time like the present to bring the past back to light. Playing with food had become a fine art to him. It improved taste to work the meal up into the perfect state of mind and heart. "Having trouble little *slut?*"

His voice sounded like her biological father's voice confronting her. In spite of her growing pain, his words ignited an explosion of anger in her. It gave her focus. She wasn't *that* anymore and she *knew* it. The pride and evident knowledge with which the demon posed that question into her very depths, gave Stephanie the distinct feeling that Master GrrraGagag was taking personal responsibility for her degradation. This angered her even further.

"What? *What did you call me?*"

Through her awful demise, she answered him back! Scraback was delighted. There was always hope. *Yes, yes, that's it.* Stephanie felt a wave of fire begin in her center and burn through her. It seemed to burn away the fear that was aiding in suffocating her.

Master GrrraGagag ignored her inconsequential gibber, and decided to teach his underling a lesson in actual progress, "Oh Scraback, she is a *feisty* one." Master GrrraGagag rippled and shimmered with ecstasy. It had been a very long time since he had feasted so, feasting on a special soul and body together. In fact, Stephanie bore resemblance to the last one! But that seemed so long ago.

Scraback could never have imagined so many different kinds of ripples and shades of dark gray. Scraback's Eye longed to taste her, but that would come later. *Come on, come on, you can do it.* He urged her in his thoughts. "Yes Master GrrraGagag, feisty indeed, and there is *so much* of her… her *spirit.*" Scraback's eye was drooling. He could almost taste his Master.

Stephanie's pain increased tenfold. Her head pounded. She couldn't keep from shrieking. Her eyes stung, as tiny blood vessels began to pop in their whites. Master GrrraGagag relished it. *This is* just *like the last one.* His eye was putridly dripping now.

Physical pain. Mental pain. Emotional pain. Pain from parts of her yet to be identified, it all blurred together. But she needed to maintain her ability to *think*, because here in the Corridor, thinking was like life itself! The other demon's words played in her mind, *Spirit… so much of my spirit.* Stephanie involuntarily heaved as wails pushed from her very depths. But the fear was gone, and the screams came from just pure torment. *He's squeezing me… to death.* Fear came back.

Master GrrraGagag slowly increased his taunting, easing back on causing pain so she could think about his next provocation. He sounded like Vaughn this time, "You know, dear Stephie, I know all about you. If I had a phallus, I'd pleasure myself with you." Only moments before she had been touching Vaughn's spirit. *Ripping her away just when I did was just right.* "The art of torment brings to the big picture all of the victim's hopelessly, unfulfilled desires. A wonderful sense of final failure increases the prey's helplessness, making them ready for smooth *consumption*." He winked his Great Eye at his student.

He winked back. "Yes, yes, Master. Keep playing."

Scraback eased back a bit, intently studying them both. He didn't want to be too close. This was like the glorious stories told to him when he was just a baby Alpha. But Stephanie was far less appreciative.

It took a while for Stephanie to be able to see anything in the Corridor. Gross shapes were finally coming into focus now. But the demon's words gave her all the focus she needed. It reminded her of the party that Vaughn rescued her from. But this violation felt a thousand times worse.

"Phallus!" *No, no, no…*

"Forgive me, I've forgotten my manners. Allow me to introduce myself. I am the Master of Reality, Master GrrraGagag. You have an eye. Use it to see me. LOOK into my Great Eye." His Eye drooled even more as he anxiously awaited her to heed his command. Master GrrraGagag always consumed his food as they watched. *Yes, any second now and I'll slowly begin to consume her.*

His command was forceful. This too reminded her of something *No… no… something wrong with his command. Gary commanded me to look at him, too, and I became helpless. NO… NOT THIS TIME…* Anger, pain, she twisted her head away.

Scraback became doubtful. Suddenly, he felt his plan would fail. *Master is going to consume her any second. No, no...*

Master GrrraGagag sensed she was becoming used to his pressure, so he tightened his coils even more. Dear Stephanie's insides vibrated with her screams. Blood dripped from her ears. *This is the dream I had!* Her dream of the giant snake sucking her into eternal blackness, feeling her very essence being swallowed up into pure hell. *Oh God, it is real!* Panic increased as she realized what closed in on her. Worse yet, she could now see clearly in the Corridor! They were more hideous than giant snakes. The sight of the demon's sickeningly rippling grayness wrapped all around her, holding her helpless, stifled her will, and that *odor* they omitted was like inhaling vomit. She gagged and wrenched uncontrollably, helplessly. The food from her party came up.

"Perfect. This is better than I hoped for, Scraback. She can see us clearly. This is even *better* than last time. I told you they can seeee ussss."

Master GrrraGagag slowly snaked his smirking Great Eye around into her view. Her nightmare had become reality. The dripping, putrid, shining, huge black Eye in the center of his huge bulbous head felt like the gaping maw of a great lion closing in. Its deep, endless blackness was like the mysterious black hole in the center of galaxies that swallowed everything into eternal darkness. She felt its pull upon every essence of her being. *There's no escape from a black hole,* she remembered learning in school. The fine tip of his arm gently flipped her red hair from her face, much like one would flick the seeds from a watermelon.

Something about how he did it galled her. It centered her focus, again. *I'm not a damn piece of food!* Violently jerking her head from side to side, she avoided looking directly into his Eye. "NO...*hideous*..." She tried to work an arm free. *If I could just poke at his eye...*

But Master GrrraGagag proclaimed proudly, triumphantly, "No, I'm not going to let you poke my Great Eye. I've eaten far more dangerous meals than you." Then he squeezed a bit tighter and tried to twist her so she had to look into his Eye.

Panic. Suffocation. Pain. She ignored them now. His words angered her further. *I'm* not *your damn food! Me being food for pure evil?*

Determined, Stephanie strained with all her might, screaming as much from battle as from pain. But except for her head, she was paralyzed by the hold he had on her. As she twisted her head back and forth, trying to avoid the huge suffocating Eye, a new plan of attack came to her. She lowered her head and tried to viciously bite a coil. But as soon as her mouth made contact, she gagged. The stench was bad enough, the taste was worse!

Master GrrraGagag's Eye drew slowly closer, overpowering her. His coils slowly crept over her shoulders, and her head movement became more and more restricted, and the huge black Eye became too big to avoid. The tip of his tail flopped over her head and became forked into two fine hooks. Each hook grabbed one of her eyelids, and he held them open. "You see, Dear, how well we are made to eat you? It's the natural order of things. Accept it. *Meow!*" he laughed.

Even through all her helplessness, the depth of the constant insult infuriated her. *Think. THINK. You've got to do something.* She remembered the fire that she used to drive away the gray arm thing. *But how did I do that? Oh God, it just happened at the time.*

"Yes, yes Master. Now I understand what the forks in our tails are for."

Master GrrraGagag barely paid his underling any mind.

Think, Stephanie, for God's sake, THINK. These... are... demons! Oh GOD, HELP ME! Oh LIGHT!

Master GrrraGagag felt the time was almost at hand. His Eye ached to begin sucking in her spirit, her every essence, and to possess this *particular* soul for eternity inside his inner torment. He was like a cat playing with a mouse... and loving it. Her eyes were held open. Her head could barely move. *But let's not be hasty. This final moment of her life is the best.* He held her there with her knowing she couldn't avoid being eaten.

She tried to blur her vision. To throw it out of focus but it didn't work. She realized her eyes were connected to a greater kind of sight that she couldn't distort.

"It's time. When the prey fully realizes it's doomed to be eaten, it can't withhold anything of itself from consumption. Look me in the Eye while I *slowly* consume you."

She had no choice. With her eyelids held open, and she couldn't distort her sight, she had to peer into the black hole of eternal torment.

◆ SACRIFICIAL WOOD ◆

Scraback rushed up and tugged on his Master's arm. It distracted him. "Master, and then we'll destroy the Appendaho?"

"Yes, yes, Scraback." Master GrrraGagag hurriedly spoke, trying to pick up where he left off. This was a rare moment, and one that needed to be savored properly. It was the equivalent of smelling the finest of wines. His Great Eye spasmed with the effort of holding itself back for just the perfect time, and now it was evident that perfect time had come.

Scraback, excitedly bouncing up and down, tugged harder on his Master's arm. "Can I eat her *best friend Arlupo*, Master?"

Irritation began to gnaw at GrrraGagag. *Totally frustrating. This must be what it feels like to the humans when their sex thing is interrupted.* "Yes, yes, Scraback. You can eat her. *Now leave me alone.*" Master GrrraGagag's whole bulbous head pounded with desire.

Stephanie's eyes opened wider.

Scraback, completely overcome and out of control, grabbed him even harder by the tail. It caused him to lose hold of an eyelid. "*Oh, thank you Great Master.* I shall delight in eating her *slooowly*. That was very clever of you to kill her *mother*. Perfect. It brought this girl to the Appendaho, so we can *consume them all.*"

"*SCRABACK!*" Master GrrraGagag bellowed. He shook his underling off him. His fork worked its way back under her eyelid and pried it open again.

Come on, come on. What's it going to take? I studied you... Ahhh, I know. Dare I risk it, again? Scraback's Eye drooled to consume his Master. He couldn't help himself. He tugged on his Master's lower eyelid. "Master, are you going to keep *Vaughn* all to yourself?"

Master GrrraGagag turned his head toward his underling. Never had Scraback seen such an angry Eye. GrrraGagag focused his ethereal power, grabbing his underling and squeezing him. In a menacing tone he yelled, "If I hear one more sound, feel one more tug, even a touch, *I'll consume you NEXT.*" Master GrrraGagag's Eye was tearing and out of focus as he looked back at his food. *I can't believe he tugged my Great Eye!*

Stephanie's heart cried out because of the threat against her loved ones. She wept. She couldn't be responsible for the Appendaho's destruction because they helped her. Fire burned hotter inside her. She couldn't bear Arlupo to go through this torment. The fire glowed even brighter. *He had my mother killed!* The blackest blackness mingled with the intensifying fire. *But what do I do? How do I fight this evil?* A single question spoke softly in her mind, *How do you prove your love?* She answered, *Vaughn, to prove my love for you I had to…yes.* As she did when she gave her will up to the Light to destroy the tree of death within her, and to receive her new will, once again she looked away from the outside, away from the terrible pain and attacking fear, and into her very depths of desire to live. There, in her passion for goodness, she gave her whole will to feeling, to thinking, to weeping only Love, only Life. There… her mind, her heart, and her soul became fully conscious of their power swirling, burning, raging inside her. It erupted from depths she knew not. Instantly, it burned its way through her mind and heart in natural reaction against the threatening evil. *LOVE, MEANING, LIFE, JUSTICE. From the inside out. That is God's will, not this damned demon.*

It was the threat against Vaughn that finally allowed her to find the connection, to understand how to do it, to apply the inside to the outside, just as she did when she came to heal him. "*Vaughn?*" She spoke through gritted teeth, more as a threat, or even a challenge than a question!

Master GrrraGagag's eye finally came back into focus. But GrrraGagag didn't realize this mouse could fight back.

Dear Stephanie's voice sounded like a thousand ages were speaking in judgment. "No, you bastard of creation, *you look ME in the eye!*" She wasn't using her physical eyes now at all. Things look different through the eye. Focusing deeply into Master GrrraGagag's Eye, facing the ultimate of anyone's fears, withholding nothing of herself, she locked him in her stare. Once common sight establishes, it's a two-way door. Loud thunder, and a bright flash...

For some reason, he never had time to understand why he couldn't resist her command. Perhaps it was just curiosity to do so and he wasn't really *compelled to obey.* After all, he had her wrapped tightly in the coils of his tail, in the coils of his dark ethereal presence, with his ethereal fangs sunk into her being. Then why was he suddenly screaming in *pain?* All he could see, all he could feel was abomination, *Glow...*

In a way, she had looked him in the Eye as he requested, but not to see what he had to offer, but to release from within her the goodness and love that expanded exponentially in the very fiber of her soul that was reacting naturally to the evil imprisoning her, and threatening her loved ones. The explosion knocked Scraback backwards, as he felt waves of pain emanating from the struggling pair. Worse, from the corner of his Eye, he glimpsed a bright *glow* burst from the girl.

Yes, YES "MASTER!" Scraback cried out as he hid his Great, black Eye. The so called Master GrrraGagag dropped the girl like a hot potato.

Stephanie instantly felt relief. Even more, tremendous power still hummed all through her. It searched to be released… somehow, but how? Feeling *cheated*, she yelled for the demons, "THE TWO OF YOU! COME *BACK HERE! I'm not done with you yet!*" *Where did they go? Hmm, faithwalker. I could maybe find them. What? Are you* nuts? *Don't let your gift go to your head, Stephanie. Focus. On what? Yes, the Tree of Life.*

The demons had quickly fled from the Corridor. So called Master GrrraGagag could no longer hide his predicament. Now he needed his underling's help. GrrraGagag wailed as excruciating pain and humiliation forced it out of him. A small helpless part of him knew he shouldn't be doing so.

"OHHHH SCRABACK, my Eeeeyyyyyye, *my pooooor Eyyyye…* help me!" GrrraGagag's arm was gingerly touching around the outer edges. His tail curled around his aching, bulbous head. He only had slight peripheral vision.

Shock inundated Scraback. *My plan actually worked! I think.* His Eye was never wider. It drooled profusely. His ripples froze. But his color began to vibrate. Could it be? *Could it be?* He timidly tested the ephemera from a distance. "Master?"

GrrraGagag wailed again, "Help me." Then he changed his tone. "You *idiot*. Bring me some of the sacred black oil next to the sacred blue orb."

Scraback kept testing. He had sensed the girl's potential. What she had done to him in the blue orb, only he had known. He even dared imagine she could... Still, he kept his distance and his meekness. "Master... is your eye hurt?"

But Master GrrraGagag matched every bit of Scraback's timidity with ill temper. "*Just do as you are told.*" Master GrrraGagag's growl never sounded more threatening.

Scraback lifted up his bulbous head as he had never lifted it before. *Idiot, huh? Master's eye is* hurt. *I'm tired of being told . . . watch him a bit, make sure...* Scraback slowly floated toward his Master. GrrraGagag kept turning his head from side to side, using what little vision he had around the edges. But his eye teared so badly, even that little sight seemed distorted. Scraback made sure he stayed directly in front of him, no matter where his Master turned. *In patience we possess them,* he reminded himself of his Master's words. Finally, close enough, he hovered above his Master. Scraback's coil slowly straightened. Looming over GrrraGagag... watching... watching... slowly lowering his massive Eye . . .

GrrraGagag sensed something was wrong. *Scraback's being awfully quiet. He's* never *quiet!* The Master's rippling went sickly, as well as his color... but... *but... but, this can't* be happening, not to me. *I've been so patient, planned so long. waited to bear offspring. I started the Earth's transformation ahead of schedule. No other demon dared even consider it.* The pain of all that is dear being ripped away felt like a thousand deaths. "SCRABACK, *WHERE ARE YOU?* I TOLD YOU TO..." And then, he felt something drip onto the top of his head.

That was it. It was now or never for greatness. "YOU WILL TELL ME NO MORE! YOU HAVE *FAILED*. LET A LITTLE EARTH GIRL PUT A *GLOW* IN YOUR EYE." Now Scraback was playing with *his* food. But he wasn't going to be foolish and prolong it. "BUT MY EYE IS JUST FINE... LOOK INTO MY EYE AS I LOWER IT UPON YOU." Former Master GrrraGagag had no choice because without his Great Eye, he was defenseless. Unwillingly, helplessly, he was compelled to look up, because he had no way to resist. A thousand, no... a million deaths... and the *humiliation*.

GrrraGagag shrieked a prolonged, hideous cry. His essence began being sucked into eternal prison, eternal torment. He became acutely aware of who and what he was. Of his greatness! Part of him was already lost. But the part that wasn't lost, watched as it too became less and less. He tried to hold back something, anything of himself. *How could this be? Where is the* Justice *in this?* His cry died out as his last essence was sucked into his underling's Great, black, glistening, delighted Eye. It was such a large meal, that after he totally consumed his Master, Scraback wobbled as he floated, almost as if he were drunk.

✥ SACRIFICIAL WOOD ✥

Images, thoughts, feelings, knowledge from his former Master inundated Scraback's ethereal consciousness. It was like a thousand Earth movies all playing in his bulbous head simultaneously, but he could follow each one. His body began to lengthen, to thicken, to *darken*. His arm grew powerful. Even his bulbous head grew larger, and his Great Eye became even darker. He began to roll over and over in the ethereal chamber that now belonged to him.

Ecstasy. Sweet ecstasy. Sweet Justice. All of Master GrrraGagag's former meals now belonged to Scraback, including GrrraGagag himself. When Scraback's transformation was complete, his rolling ceased and he floated up high, as if on a cloud, and he stretched out his very long coil to float horizontally. *So much knowledge. Mmmm... he was so tasty. Buuuuurp. Except for that glow I just belched up. No more leftovers for me. Hmm, I guess I'm Master now. Those are the rules. I should know, as I rewrote them. My new name... yes, reality is what reality is. BEHOLD, SCRABAGRRRAGAGAG ...It's a bit too long. BEHOLD, SCRABAGAG.*

Oh my, that little rat. He hid so much from me! What? What's this? He knew about the Appendaho way before he told me! But why the... Oooohhhh my. You had more in mind than just replacing the High Council. Oh, you weren't allowed to do that. *The rules. Ahhh, were meant to be broken! Hmmm.*

☙

As Arlupo saw the sun disappearing, and her death wail consumed her, she became faintly aware of sparks floating upon her and entering into her. More out of thoughtless reflex than hope, she looked up at the Tree. As she did, an energy impact knocked her off the brass basin and flat onto her back. The Tree of Life seemed to be on fire, but it didn't burn. A brilliant fireball burst from the Tree's crown, hovered in midair and then floated down, hovering beside her. Arlupo's heart pounded. Her mouth naturally dropped open. A tremendous thunder resounded that brought the whole village running to the lodge from every direction. As the blinding light began to fade, she could begin to make out the form of a person. For some time, though, the glow was still too bright to look at.

People began arriving at the windows. Arlupo's father burst into the room. And then Arlupo, gasping, propped herself up, recognizing her. "Oh my God, Father, a fireball came out of the Tree of Life. Oh *God*, it's Stephanie!" Arlupo collapsed back onto her back unable to hold herself up any longer. Then Stephanie materialized as she extended her right foot through the glow and onto the lodge floor from the very spot she'd left. By now, everyone either encircled or stood within the lodge. When they saw her appearance, they fell wherever they were, saying prayers of thanksgiving and wonder. However, Stephanie was quite ordinary in her pleasant greeting, as if she had just strolled in from a walk! *I'm not going to let them treat me like some special person.* She looked around at everyone and… "Hi everyone!" She waved and smiled a regular smile as if it was an ordinary day's greeting.

Arlupo was still agape, as she was sure she had died. In fact, she had just moments ago miserably resigned herself to it. When Stephanie saw how terrible her sister looked, her tear stained face quite drawn, her long brown dress covered in dirt, and that she remained flat on her back, she reached down and picked her up from the floor. She lifted her like a feather.

Arlupo looked into her soft, rich brown eyes and gingerly put her hand to Stephanie's cheek. She wanted to grab her, hug her and never let go, but instead, she just stared at her with great concern. "Stephanie, you're… bleeding! You *smell like vomit*. And your beautiful dress is all *torn!*"

Stephanie didn't even realize how she looked, or *smelled*. There was blood coming from her mouth, nose, and ears. She realized it must have come from the terrible force of her screams. She looked down at her favorite dress and saw how shredded it was, with vomit clinging in places.

With a great, great frown, and serious shake of her head, "Darn! Oh well, I'm O.K. Just had a little run in with a couple demons! Vaughn is going to be fine. I told him to come here." She took her sister by the arm and began to walk her out of the lodge, not realizing what a tremendous impact her words had on everyone.

Arlupo spoke for them all. "Demons! Father!"

"Daughter…"

Stephanie sort of shook her free hand around to calm them. "O.K. Just let me change my clothes, get a bite to eat, and I'll tell you all about it. Geeee, *I'm hungry*."

But Arlupo's mind grabbed onto what she'd said and was running with it. "Demons! Are there really such things, Father?" she asked wide-eyed.

"Apparently so, apparently so." His eyebrows rose exceedingly high, in response to Stephanie's statement.

Stephanie went to her lodge, washed her pathetic dress and cleaned up. Though none of her sensory perceptions from the Corridor transferred themselves here, she scrubbed extra hard at the memory of the demon's stench. Her ribs were bruised, but she scrubbed hard anyway. Then, she sat at her little, wooden dining table devouring a whole apple pie, washing it down with fresh goat's milk. *Food,* she thought. *He was treating me like food!* She shook her head and shuddered, staring at the last bite of pie. Then she popped it into in her mouth.

She recognized the delicious pie as one from her celebration, and was delighted they brought it to her. She looked in her refrigerator and found it packed full of the various delicacies from her party. Her heart burst with thankfulness for everything. Never had so much gone right in her life. Vaughn was healed, she beat the demon, she now knew she was a *faithwalker,* whatever that really was, and she had a real family. She felt strengthened physically, mentally and emotionally.

But more than anything else, she enjoyed the new will the Light had supplied to her from the Tree of Life. She knew without it, she never would have made it back alive. And still, everything seemed so new to her. She began to wonder how long it would be before that newness wore off. *Hmm, maybe it won't!*

She walked over to her tattered, shredded dress that she had spread out on the floor and wondered how it happened.

She thought to herself, *Oh darn, this dress is my favorite dress. It's not right that it be torn apart by some* demon. She knelt down and held its hem. She could still feel the presence of the Holy Spirit in the dress from when she received her new will under the water. She closed her eyes, thinking with all her heart and mind, that such a garment with the Good Spirit in it should not be destroyed. The image of it in her mind and heart felt real. And then, the image felt like it entered reality.

Her hands holding the hem knew. When she opened her eyes, the dress was whole. *It worked! It really worked! Oh my gosh, it really, really...* She paused, talking to herself, "No, it's not vanity. This is special. Besides, now that I know I can do something like this, Hmmmm…"

And, then, it occurred to her what she had done way beyond bringing her dress back to life, *Oh my God! I was about to be eaten by a real, live…dead…existing demon. And I BEAT IT!*

Astonished, bowing to the floor, flooded with tears at the memories, her whole life also flashed before her eyes, and she whispered, "Thank You Light, for blessing me and making me what I am. Able to fight demons and win! Look at what you have taken and made to do such things! Me! Of all people… Me!"

After a while, just before she picked herself up off the floor, it occurred to her, *Hmm, I wonder if everyone at school will notice the difference. I mean, would I look as different to them on the outside as I feel on the inside?*

CHAPTER TEN
Stories Of Life

Their eldest son had requested an audience. Both the King and Queen sat before the Tree of Life. As he presented himself before them with a war axe strapped to his side, Queen Yinauqua covered her mouth with her hand. His father sat up straighter. "I wish to go into the outside world and find our lost sister. I shall take her back from whoever stole her."

His mother spoke first, "How shall you find her? When they have already stolen you?" she looked away.

King Mafferan informed him, "You know we gave pledge to be separate from the outside. But more important than a pledge, we cannot subrogate another's will. You may go!"

"But if I leave, I'll break your sacred oath for all the people."

"It was only as good as all the people."

Their son hung his head, his heart pining for his sister.

Queen Yinauqua placed her hand upon her beloved husband's arm. "Key to oaths is their purpose, which each side interprets to their benefit."

The King nodded. "You are certainly breaking it if you leave." He looked upon his son's axe.

◆ SACRIFICIAL WOOD ◆

His son dropped his weapon in the sacred room and left to find his sister.

Sighing, she squeezed his hand, "We have found our son again. The oath remains."

The High Council summoned Scraback post-haste. Everyone felt very strange vibrations coming from GrrraGagag's sector. Since Master GrrraGagag didn't respond to their invitation and couldn't be located, they summoned his underling.

Ready for them, having not only his own deviousness, but possessing all of his former Master's, ScrabaGag solaced himself, *They're in my backyard now. Well, not really, but that sounds nice! Hmm, maybe I should pop down to the Black River and pick up a rock.* He chuckled to himself positively delighting in all his new knowledge.

Even though he was High Councilor Premion's offspring, he had no love for him, and neither did they at all respect him. He was, well, a nerd among demons. *They'll see how much nerd... shortly!*

They didn't believe him. They had already asked him the same question three times with the same answers. They were on their fourth attempt now, when ScrabaGag answered.

"Yes Sir, I ate him."

"*You* ate him?"

"Yes Sir, I ate him."

A High Councilor leaned forward with a dubious Eye. "YOU, ate him?"

ScrabaGag held his head up proudly, "Yes Sir, I ate him. *But only once!*"

Another Councilor scrunched his thick black coils up, hovering Eye to Eye with ScrabaGag. It was Premion, his sire. "*How* did you eat him?"

ScrabaGag smiled. He knew they weren't going to like his answers, but he also knew they couldn't do anything about it. "Ahhh, Sir, section three-thousand-six-hundred and forty-four, paragraph eighteen, lines two through eight, specifically states that an underling is not required to inform how he ate his Master, only that he did, and that he assumes all the rights thereof of his Master and position. Would you like me to quote them specifically… Sir?" The other two High Councilors floated backwards at his answer.

Premion, who had always been embarrassed by him, began to huff, "*Rules.* I've known GrrraGagag for, well, for a *very* long time, I can't even imagine… what did you say your name was?"

ScrabaGag, throughout the inquiry, kept straightening his arm out, and showing off his now very dark gray coils. He did so again with even more flair. "Behold, SRABAGAG!"

Alphas are not readily given to amusement or untoward displays, unless they're enjoying the employ of their occupation. But for some reason, the High Councilor members burst into howling laughter.

Finally, his sire spoke again. "Rules are just words that ebb and flow. Alright, so you think you can fill his grayness? Just remember, we of the High Councilor will be watching. If your work doesn't measure up, we'll have you serving in some far away corner under most unpleasant circumstances."

ScrabaGag assumed his normal coil. "YES SIR. I think you will find that having some new darkness around will be most beneficial. New insight…"

Another High Councilor growled and snapped at him, "There is no *new* insight…YOU ate him?"

ScrabaGag's Eye smiled widely, "Yes sir, *I* ate him." ScrabaGag really began to enjoy saying it. When he left, he kept repeating it to himself, until he, too, broke out laughing. A happy Alpha. He thought to himself, *Hmm, I see why GrrraGagag wasn't anxious to tell the High Council anything. I don't like the blackness of the one who sired me. Hmm…yesssss… I'll make reports every day, in detail of everything I do and plan to do. Well… almost everything. I'll send them to* that *High Councilor, although I know he won't even as much as look at them. Then, if anything goes wrong, I'll say he approved of everything. Section four, paragraph one, line one is very explicit, "No disapproval from a High Councilor concerning the plan of an underling shall be deemed as approval. The High Councilor shall come before the Father for judgment if…" Ha, this way, if the plan fails, I still win and get rid of him, but, if I succeed with GrrraGagag's…no, ScrabaGag's plan, then I get rid of him. HAAAAA, old demons, they think they know everything. I think I know a way to get rid of a lot of them. That girl could be most useful. How can I get her back to our reality? Hmm… but in the meantime, let me have some fun with those two. That old demon didn't have the subtle touch.*

☙

Their father led Stephanie and Arlupo to the western edge of the harvested plumb orchard where some very rocky, colorful, ancient hills rose up. These hills of sparkling pinks, purples, black, white and grays projected all the ways back to the village on its northern side, finishing into sheer cliffs. Impatient, their father beckoned them. But Arlupo and Stephanie lagged behind, holding hands, giggling.

Stephanie was on her third retell of how she smacked Vaughn, and then used that memory to smack him again into realizing she was real. Arlupo couldn't get enough of it. Something about using a smack to do good… and about how hardheaded men are… but also, Stephanie's stories were as the legendary stories of her youth, which she had made her Father tell over and over. She had already listened to Stephanie's demon battle six times, until Stephanie had mentioned the story she now told again. Stephanie didn't mind. To see how Arlupo enjoyed it so, she would tell them over yet again.

Behind a huge, whitish boulder, there was a crack just wide enough to squeeze through. Their father disappeared into it. It opened up into a narrow rocky path that wound its way up the hills around various outcroppings, and all the way back toward the village. The girls were glad their father made them put their blue overalls on. More than once they slipped on the loose rock and gravel. When they came to a ledge with a huge, dark overhang, he disappeared, again. From that ledge, Stephanie looked out to her right, surprised to see the village below.

"In here, daughters." Following the sound of his voice into the deep blackness, for it was quite a bright noon day sun outside and their eyes hadn't yet adjusted, their father immediately started explaining. "These caves are ancient. This, my lovely daughters, seems to have once been a sacred room! I brought you two here to show you something. Light all these torches." Arlupo strained her eyes to see what he was speaking about. Attached to the four corners of the square stone table in the middle of the room were, indeed, tall torch holders." He pointed to a lighter resting in a carved recess in the wall beside the entrance. Turning back toward the light blinded Arlupo again, so she groped her way about. Stephanie, for some reason, didn't have any trouble shifting between light and dark, and probably wouldn't have thought anything about it except for her friend's obvious blindness highlighting the difference. *Hmm, that's odd. I can see and she can't.*

"I'll get it, Arlupo." She took the metal cap off the old fashioned lighter that had a small wheel inside. She flicked the wheel several times, seeing sparks fly out and catch the wick on fire, which she used to light the torches. Having never been here, Arlupo was surprised her father never even mentioned the place. But what really startled her was the beauty.

"Father, the walls... so beautiful."

All around the somewhat square cave, were murals depicting people and...

"Yes, Arlupo, I thought it just decorative art, but now, since Stephanie returned, I'm not so sure!"

Stephanie looked at him raising her eyebrows. "Why?"

"Because Stephanie, you said you encountered demons. While we have, from time to time crossed paths with evil presences, we've been secluded from such things a very long time. But demons are legends. Look here on the walls, over in each of the corners."

Stephanie went to her right and then to her left, inspecting two of the corners. "Oh God." Stephanie put her hand to her mouth in recognition of the dark coiled figure with the bulbous head and huge, black eye. She thought she could smell it, and her stomach became queasy.

Arlupo too, found her stomach churning. "Hideoussss." Arlupo hissed and thought she might be sick. Their ugliness projected through the demonic portraits, giving them an unwanted, realistic presence when gazed upon. "Father, why are they painted at the far corners?"

He threw up his hands, while saying, "I don't know. But legend would have it, their part of reality is a spirit world that's at the edges of our part of reality." They both looked over to Stephanie, to the *faithwalker*.

Stephanie walked around to each corner, nodding her head, and then came back to the drawing where they were standing. She pointed at it. "Father, this one here, I think I recognize… *his eyeeee!* What's this writing down below it?"

"I don't know."

"You don't know how to read it?"

He raised an eyebrow, sensing this was important to her. "No, why?"

"Oh, I heard them call each other by their names…"

※ SACRIFICIAL WOOD ※

His and Arlupo's mouths dropped open simultaneously. They spoke as one. "They called each other by name?" The image of demons actually having a persona, with names, talking to each other as people talked to one another unsettled them, to say the least. Stephanie didn't realize she'd left that part out of the story. Come to think of it, she'd left a lot of that conversation out.

Stephanie looked at them oddly, as if to say, of course. "Well, yes, the one wrapped around me talked directly to me. In fact, he introduced himself, and, each called the other by their name. He introduced himself as…"

Raising his hands, her father blurted out, "NOOOO! Don't call the name of a demon."

Stephanie backed up, startled by the rebuke, "Why, Father?" She wasn't worried about any demon. She still felt cheated and wanted to finish the job she'd started!

"Because Stephanie, legend has it that when we call the name of a demon, we give him passage to our world."

She wrinkled her nose at him in skepticism. "Father, is this legend or superstition?"

Upon reflection, he got an 'I don't know' look on his face, but then found a wise answer. "Well, are you legend or superstition?"

Noting it with a, "Hmmm," Stephanie went to explore the ancient pictures on the wall between the first two corners. Her childlike tone of discovery drew Arlupo's attention away from examining another wall. But upon beholding, awe captured her, also.

"She's so beautiful," Stephanie whispered, gazing at a life size picture of a woman with long, rich, wavy brown hair that went down to her waist, and with rich brown eyes, the color of Stephanie's eyes. Her royal dress looked almost exactly as Stephanie's most favored dress, except it had more gold in it. Arlupo had heard descriptions and seen art work depicting her ancestors, but none captured their feeling as these pictures did. Although the physical aspects of the pictures were truly beautiful, it was the feeling they somehow emanated that was exquisite.

Arlupo broke the spell, straightening up proudly, pointing to the woman. "That would be Queen Yinauqua, the mother of our people."

Then Stephanie pointed to the man, his flawless exquisiteness took her breath away. "And who's he?"

Arlupo smiled, noting his striking handsomeness, strength, and nobility that simply radiated. "That would be our other legend, King Mafferan, the father of our people."

Then it dawned on Stephanie, pointing again to them, barely able to get the words out because she remembered their story. "Are these the two you told me about?"

Arlupo folded her arms across her breast, straightening again and holding her head up. "They are *indeed!*"

Looking very much like a three-year-old child now, and Stephanie's questions reflecting it, she asked, "Do you think they *really* looked like that?"

Their father couldn't pass up the opportunity. He came up behind his daughters, and put his arms around each of their shoulders, and hugged them together.

SACRIFICIAL WOOD

"I don't know. Do you think in two thousand years someone might ask the same question about your pictures?"

"Father, don't be ridiculous," was their common reply.

But his silence said so much more. Stephanie wandered over to the table in the middle of the room. There, on the ancient stone table, appeared to be an equally ancient stone box, with intricate carvings of trees and creatures. The elaborate patterns increasingly enticed her.

"What's this *beautiful* box?" she pointed, immediately thinking about touching it, even opening it.

Coming up beside her, her father smiled. "Legend, my daughter, legend. But it's passed down that none may look inside until the time of the end."

Stephanie's heart skipped a beat. She'd almost gone straight up and opened it! If it wasn't for a second thought, telling her to ask first . . . Then she realized there was no visible lock to such a special box, and she grasped by the way her father explained the legend, he seemed to be implying none would be necessary! Standing next to Stephanie now, Arlupo was also riveted by the box. *So this is where it's been kept!*

Stephanie couldn't help her words, nor her tone, so she just pressed forward. "You mean, the box isn't *locked*? So there's something mystical or something about it? Right? I mean . . . to keep people from opening it."

He laughed. "You must've read too many fairy tales. No, there's no 'magic' with the box. And no, it's not locked. But to the Appendaho, a word given is a word kept, no matter how long ago it was given. Thousands of years ago our ancestors gave their word they would not open the box until the right time. That was enough."

Goose bumps spread all over Stephanie, yet she found it hard to believe. "You're kidding?"

Again, his silent, warm smile said more than mere words. Arlupo kept staring at the box, almost as if to stare right through it!

"You're not kidding. And no one even wanted to peek?"

He laughed again. "Well, I wouldn't go that far. Probably all of us have *wanted* to look, but we honor our word more than our curiosity. We've kept this room secret, though. Only the elders know of it . . . and now you two." He looked at Arlupo, and then at Stephanie again.

Stephanie felt a deeply warm presence calling to her from all around. She now recognized this extra sense as part of her *faithwalking* abilities, and wondered what it meant. She instinctively turned to her father for knowledge. "Father, why have you brought me here?"

He took her by the shoulders so they could face each other. She stood up straight, looking into his dark brown eyes. "Because there are some things so old we don't know if they're mere legend or true prophecy. But your recent experience is confirmation that much of what we thought to be just beautiful legend is indeed prophecy and *history*." And he said the word, *history*, with sacredness.

Stephanie started shaking her head as her eyes went distant. *History!* A sense that history wasn't random, but reigned over her life flooded into her. One thing lead to

◆ SACRIFICIAL WOOD ◆

another giving her a sense of something preordained, and somehow she was part of this long process. Her goose bumps became like mountains as a sense of purpose overran her. A new found knowledge of the bigger picture of her life suddenly became apparent, *her history*. Her head tingled. She backed away from her father, doing a slow turn around. Stephanie felt as if she were almost transported somewhere far above. "I can't believe my life!" *Everything I've lived through had some purpose. All the bad, all the good, has brought me to be exactly where I am now, to be standing right here, now . . . but confirming prophecy? Ridiculous!*

"Stephie?" Arlupo came over and put her hand on her shoulder because she could hear the emotion in Stephanie's shaking voice.

"Arry, I just can't believe my life!"

Their father's brow went up, and he squinted a bit at Arlupo. "Arry?"

His daughter noted his amusement. The Appendaho didn't create nick-names, but she'd grown to love the name her sister had given her.

Now Arlupo began to look and sound like a little child. "Oh yes Father, Stephie nick-named me, Arry. Seeeee? Stephie and Arry." She stood up straight, shoulder to shoulder with Stephanie, and threw her arm around her giving a big smile. "Stephie, Arry. Arry, Stephie."

His big belly laugh echoed in the cave. "I see. Every day I see you two, is surely a day filled with more laughter than the day before."

Then Arlupo remembered Stephanie's emotions and squeezed her shoulder. "Stephie, what do you mean, *you can't believe your life?*"

Tears of understanding rolled down her cheeks, as she collected her breath. "Well, it wasn't that long ago that I was just a lost . . . well . . . I was just a . . . I was a mess. A nothing! And now you're joking with me about my picture in two thousand years, and about me confirming legends . . . about me *being* a legend. It's ridiculous! I mean, I understand how one thing must lead to another, but *even so...*"

Their father walked around in front of them, folding his arms across his broad chest. "My daughter, people are only used to seeing the glorified in a story, because a story is only a tiny, tiny piece of a person's life. Legends, sacred writings, they're all like that. But I assure you, dear child, every one of those people up there on that wall felt like, thought like, and suffered like *you!*" And when he said the word, *you*, he nodded his head at her for emphasis.

His glowing tenderness, commingling with profound meaning, entered into her and absorbed her until she felt so small she'd wondered where she went. It wasn't a bad feeling of small. But it was the kind of humbling that was difficult to process, to find footing in the real world. Stephanie couldn't help beginning to cry, with deep sobs bubbling up.

"Stephie, why are you crying?" Arlupo asked, getting watery-eyed, and not even knowing why.

There are some messages that are only meant for hearts to feel, the mind still learning how to think of such things.

SACRIFICIAL WOOD

For Stephanie, in spite of all she's seen both inside and out, her image of herself just would not accept the position in the world Life seemed to be offering her. Perhaps, because in her deepest of hopes and dreams, she could not have desired anything more wonderful than what she had actually been made and appointed to by Life.

Stephanie turned back around and pointed at the pictures of the king and queen holding hands, lovingly gazing at each other and at whoever looked at them. "Because they're so beautiful. Not just their features, but their *expression*. So much *love* in their eyes, bravery, strength, yet . . . tenderness. When I think of even the little bit you told me they went through, the terrible pain, I can't help it. And these are your ancestors, from where all of you came. But I'm not . . ." Tears poured down her cheeks, but she held her head up straight. Something was trying to tell her something, but it was far too large for her to do anything about but let it flood into her.

Arlupo saw the cave begin to glow. "Father . . . do you see?"

"Yes Arlupo."

"What's happening to the room?" Stephanie asked through her tears, no longer surprised at such things.

"Prophecy, Stephanie, legend becoming prophecy," was his answer. "It means that the spirits of this sacred room have accepted and welcomed your presence."

Arlupo began to speak gravely. "Father, it means that Stephanie is the…"

But he cut her off. "I know, dear. She is the *faithwalker.*" But that wasn't what Arlupo was going to say.

DARRYL MARKOWITZ

When Glen saw the body at a distance, he half expected it to be Vaughn, and knew his hopes were dead. It was a strange mixture of feelings when it proved otherwise. "You *fool*," Glen cried over his body. Since Gary interfered with his plan, he decided to take his time with Tracy. He always loved squeezing out every last drop of excitement. Glen looked up at the tree, shaking his head. "No Vaughn, I don't believe this. I know you killed him. You're *mine* now!"

Kneeling over his cousin, grabbing him up by the coat, "You stupid son of a bitch. You didn't have to die. Why didn't you let him GO?" He threw him back.

Glen knew nothing would come of Gary's death. He wasn't even supposed to be able to walk and his being way out here was too suspicious. It was best just to leave it as Vaughn set it up.

Glen couldn't wait to catch Vaughn to tell him what he'd done. Plans to make him and Stephanie suffer were already taking shape. His thoughts spoke over his beloved cousin's corpse as an epitaph, or was it an oath? "*I intended on letting Vaughn go, you know, to use him. If he's not able to get rid of this Jargon guy, I'll have to find another way. He has* no *choice now. I needed an excuse to become a gov agent. There's a murderer on the loose, and only I know him. I'm going to catch him. I'm going to enjoy it.*"

Stephanie rushed into her sister's bedroom with tears, falling on her knees, leaning on her bed. Arlupo opened her eyes to Stephanie's face… mere inches away.

"Oh Arry, it was terrible."

Arlupo reflexively stretched. "It must have been to wake me in the middle of the night. Tell me Stephie."

Stephanie looked away. Arlupo noted her reaction as something she hadn't seen from her sister since she was freed from the tree of death. Still looking away, Stephie said, "First, I was remembering, oh, *reliving* being with a hideous young man. Arry, I used to be a *very* bad girl. We were . . ." Stephanie wanted to crawl under the bed, she felt so ashamed.

Her friend finished for her. "You were being intimate."

"I don't even think that it deserves the word 'intimate' but, I hate to say this, but I was enjoying it, *really* enjoying it. But there was another part of me watching, that was hating it, too, *really hating it!* But, in the dream, I was only enjoying it. Oh, Arry, I feel so ashamed." She buried her head into the bed weeping. Arlupo put her hand upon her best friend's head, smoothing her hair.

"It was a dream, Stephanie, trying to call you back to what you no longer are."

She picked her head up. Arlupo pulled her red hair out of her face. "Oh, but there's more… then the dream switched, and it was Vaughn, not with me, but with my friend Tracy, whom *I* made him promise to try to help. OHHHH ARRY, I MADE HIM PROMISE," she wailed, and reburied her weeping head upon the bed.

It now became clear to Arlupo the full extent of how deviously Stephanie's mind had been twisted. She kept smoothing and re-smoothing her friend's hair. Arlupo leaned into Stephanie's ear, and softly spoke. "Stephanie, you talk as if this really happened. The first part of your dream made you feel worthless, so it made you more vulnerable to believing the second part. From what you say of Vaughn, not even willing to be intimate with *you*, when you know he loves you, well… he *certainly* would *not* go with someone else."

Stephanie shuddered when the light of her words illuminated reality. In that moment, her heart seemed to stop beating. She shook her head forcefully, scolding herself. She looked into her friend's eyes. "Oh God, what's wrong with me? Of course you're right. How could I even think…?"

Arry put her hand to her dear friend's cheek, hushing her. "Shhhh, I think, Stephie, that when we're asleep and then just wake up, we're only really half awake, and we perceive things in our minds and hearts that aren't correct, things in combinations that we would never allow to be a part of us in reality. Sometimes, too, things just hit us faster and harder than we can catch up to, and then BAM, they're just there." Arry raised her eyebrows and tilted her head forward to touch Stephie's forehead to give the understanding a little push.

But the evil now clawing at her mind fought back with doubt, "I don't know. It seemed so real to me at the time, and I feel so *ashamed*."

Arry took her forefinger and lifted her chin back up. She held her chin between that finger and her thumb and softly nodded or wagged Stephie's head at key points to emphasize what she was saying when she said it. "Stephanie, look at what you've been through to be free of that death. The answer to your question, *How do you know what you really are now?* doesn't lie in consulting the memories of filth nor dreams. They'll only lie to you and testify of *their* nature. Your answers rest in the goodness you've chased after, and have come to know." She gave her chin an extra tug and let go, waiting for her words to sink in.

Then Arlupo pulled her friend up into bed and they both sat up straight, face to face. They pulled their long hair back behind them. Arlupo had a grave look on her face, and she grabbed her friend's arms and squeezed. "Stephanie, look at me and listen carefully. I'll tell you a serious truth, a rule, if you will, of Reality. The Reality of both good and evil. Evil cannot understand at all the things of goodness, as it has no connection at all. It can't understand its feelings, or its ways of thinking, even though it can predict a bit of good behavior. But, Stephie, goodness can see both sides for what they are, especially you, since you've lived in both sides so deeply. And goodness sees evil for what it truly is, but all the while has the ability not to *be* evil."

Arlupo squeezed her tighter, intensifying her piercing stare into her friend's eyes. "That's how you know, Stephanie, what you *truly* are. Let *Goodness* show you the truth of your dreams this night, as Goodness sees it. Let *Goodness* show you about the goodness placed in you that *is* you. Then, you have to decide whether you believe what you see!"

Stephanie looked surprised by that, and Arlupo knew it, so she continued to explain, "Stephie, *listen carefully* to me. Believing doesn't create or determine reality. Whether you believe correctly or not about something, reality is what reality is. *But,* correctly believing allows you access to reality, whereas believing falsely blinds you to it. It's your choice! The goodness in you will explain itself to you because goodness is made out of true understanding. Goodness can prove itself worth living for. How do you think you've come to be what you are now, and to do what you've done?"

Finally, Stephie began to feel better. Never had she experienced such a great and rapid qualitative shift in her conscious knowing of everything than what that dream had done to her. It was as if she was only now waking up from that dream!

"Oh, Arry," Stephie grabbed her in a massive hug, kissing her cheek. Arry was glad to have her sister back.

"I couldn't have asked for a better sister or friend in you, Stephanie. I love you dearly." Arry kissed Stephie's cheek. "Come over here, here's a pillow, there's room enough on the bed."

A childlike glee burst from Stephie. Her voice squeaked in delight. "Ooohhh, a sleeeep over. I looooove sleep-overs."

Arry rolled her smiling eyes at her. "You're funny."

"No, *really*. I'm not talking about when I was older, and just wanted to be out of the house like I told you about. But when I was a little girl, my… Mom, real Mom, used to let me have a friend over, or go to a friend's house to sleep over. We talked all night long, had pillow fights…"

Arry scrunched her brow together, backing her head away a little, wondering. "Pillow what?"

Mischievousness subtly crept over Stephie. She squinted. "You don't know what a pillow fight is?"

Arry's eyes went wide as she shook her head in ignorance, "Huh?"

Stephie put on a congenial helping demeanor, "Here, let me show you... you see, watch very closely... are you watching?" Stephie held up her pillow, and when she was sure Arry was focused on the pillow, she hit her square in the face with it! Then burst out laughing, pointing at her friend.

Arry, being a fast learner, grabbed hers and retaliated. "HEY..." Her side blow across Stephie's head almost knocked her from her knees, but Stephie quickly recovered, and chose her close fighting strategy of the two-handed jab. With a hand on each long end of the pillow, she jabbed it back and forth into Arry's face. Stephie laughed with its success, confident in her battle hardened experience.

Arry was driven back against the wall while protesting her ignorance. "Hey! How do you win at this?"

Stephie paused, realizing, "Ahhh, I never thought about it too much. Maybe, ahhh... more quick jabs." Her friend would just have to figure it out!

She did! With two massive swings, first a roundhouse left and then a backhand to the right, she knocked Stephie off balance both times. Then, *stealing* Stephie's strategy of the fast two-handed short jab... Arry began to get the hang of it, as Stephie tumbled backwards onto her back shouting, "I give...I GIVE..."

Arry wrinkled her brow again, "Huh?"

"I give means *I give up!*" Stephie burbled through a mass of tangled red hair that had also gotten into her mouth. She was unsuccessfully trying to spit it back out. But she dare not let go of her pillow until her friend acknowledged her surrender. The way she began the fight made her less inclined to believe she'd accept it so soon! Arlupo might want to have more strikes because of the surprise attack. Stephanie stared into her eyes attempting to discern her intentions.

The sight of her poor friend lying on her back, miserably defeated, making various futile spitting sounds brought Arry to squeal in laughter. Then she raised her eyebrows, her eyes sparkling with pleasure. "Oh, so does that mean I win?" Arry anticipated her first pillow victory.

"I guess so, but I'm not… good at pillow fighting… or anything when I'm laughing so hard." Her laughter, unfortunately, drew more hair into her mouth until she had to toss the pillow aside to pull it out. She made yucky face as she did so. When Arlupo saw *that*, there was no control left.

Each one's laughing infected the other even more, until they were laughing at each other laughing. Arlupo cried that she couldn't stop, but that only made it worse. When Stephie's ribs began to hurt, she forced herself to calm. Arry was glad, because her sides also ached. Laying still for a bit, gasping to regain their breath, Arry managed to speak, "I've never laughed so hard in my entire life. Oh Light, I never have." But when Arlupo finally got enough courage to look over at her friend, she saw deep thought on her face. "What is it Stephie, you suddenly look so… pensive."

What can be said to adequately describe what true friendship means? To look into another's eyes and feel the finest, most delicate aspects of their life, to know their deepest thoughts… and experience them as if they were your own. To be able to gain instant strength from them because of what they are. But, most important, to be known and appreciated by them in the same way. As they both gazed deeply into each other, they knew it.

Stephie spoke intensely. "I just can't say how much I love you. How much I respect you. You're so strong. And you've given me your strength tonight. You're always thinking about everybody else. I would be so lost without you. I've never had a friend like you." Stephie's words impacted far more than she knew. Arlupo was thankful her friend continued to speak. "You know what's been happening to me at school?" Stephanie sat back up, and Arlupo did the same.

"No. I'm a grade above you."

"*You won't believe it.*" Her tone stoked Arlupo's interest.

"What?"

"A number of girls who've been bugging me, who're getting more and more to join in with them every day, have been calling me . . ." Stephie hesitated.

Arlupo's interest escalated. "Calling you what?"

"A prude."

"A WHAT? Is that some kind of fruit or something?"

Stephie looked at her, realizing she really didn't understand. *Hmm, why would she understand that word?* "No silly, it's someone who… doesn't like and doesn't have sex."

Arry's brow went up again, and she leaned a bit back thinking, "Oh! Well… I guess they got that half right, huh?"

Stephie leaned back, too. "Huh, I never thought about it like that. That's actually kinda funny."

But Arry's interest began escalating. The outside world fascinated her, particularly if it had to do with her little sister. After all, Arlupo was a grade above her. "So?"

"So what?" Stephie was stringing her along on purpose to intensify the suspense.

"STEPHIE! What did you say to them?'

"I really thought about how ironic all of that was, because they had no idea of the kind of past I had. Then I saw that in a lot of ways they were trapped by the same *stupidity* I was, except I don't think a lot of them had the screwed up home life I had. I think… I think they just think being a slut is a good way to be!"

Arry fidgeted with the hem of her nightshirt. "So?"

"Well, I told them."

Arry slapped her hands down on her crossed legs, "STEPHIE TOLD THEM WHAT?"

"Some about my past!"

Wide-eyed, Arry straightened. Her heart began to pound, but her words were subdued. "You're kidding. Really?"

Most serious, Stephanie leveled her eyes into Arlupo's. "Yes, really, and you know, when I told them, I really wasn't ashamed. And that's when it hit me. I thought it odd that I wasn't ashamed until I felt what was in me, that that part of my life *wasn't in me!* I actually had to pause a minute and consider how truly different I am, and I didn't even realize it until then. I felt clean inside, free. And since my past wasn't in me, I could freely talk about it without it having any claim over me. So I wasn't ashamed, because my past is no longer me, even though the memories still are. Does that make sense?"

Arlupo beamed at her sister. "Perfectly. I'm so proud of you. That's exactly what I was trying to tell you to do earlier. Look through the goodness in you to see what you are. But you see how evil tried to even take you away from what you already knew? Anyway, so what happened next? What was their reaction?" she urged.

"Well, they didn't believe me! They teased me even harder, saying, 'PRUDE, PRUDE, HATES BOYS,' bla…bla…bla… So, I even told them I used to have a nose ring that Gary gave me, and when I went to show them the hole where it used to be… you won't believe this!"

Her poor friend felt like strangling her. She'd balled up her fists in her nightshirt, squeezing them hard. "STEPHIE WHAT?"

"It's gone! I couldn't find the hole or any sign of it. So then they *really* didn't believe me. But then I got kinda mad at myself. Because I said to myself, You *idiot*, why are you trying to prove to them that you indeed were a *slut*? *Idiot*, what good would that do?"

Arry nodded. "You have a point there."

"So, I switched tactics on them and asked how they could possibly even think that being *sluts* was good for the person they were born into the world to be? Since all that sex stuff didn't at all involve being a person, being respected, loved, or really cared for."

Arry's eyes widened even more. The power of her story showered over her, and her whole body tingled. "Oh my, you didn't? You did?"

"Well, yeaaah." Stephie leveled her eyes into her sister's wide eyes and waited.

Arry shook the balls of nightshirt at her best friend. "SOOOOO?"

"Well, some just stared at me with their mouths open. A couple got really, *really* angry, saying, I thought I was better than them. A couple started crying…"

Arlupo began to grasp the magnitude of just how many people Stephie was dealing with. "Stephie, how many were there?"

She shrugged her shoulders. "I don't know. A lot! They just sorta gathered around when I started sticking up for myself and explaining things. One even said I was right! But they started teasing *her* then. But she wouldn't back down. I was so proud of her. But they made me angry. So I turned on them, saying, 'You poor excuses for human beings! Since you got no good answer to what I said, you act like little brats, calling names, 'cause you *know* you're wrong.' Ahhh, I kinda said that forcefully. It actually surprised them how I said it, I think, because everyone just shut up!"

Arry had major goose bumps. "Oh my God, you're kidd… OH, I'm not going to say that." She tugged more at her nightshirt.

Stephie leaned forward. "No, I'm *not kidding*." She chuckled. "I think I actually got them all to see the point, because one after another started turning red. But one girl laughed. Oh my God, you'd never believe what she said." Stephanie waited again, just long enough for Arlupo to heave a sigh. "She said, she wanted to have sex with her teacher!"

"NO!"

"YES! Even the other girls said, 'Yuck.' But she said, 'What's the dif? Our parents all agree we're gonna do it anyway. Hell, they give us condoms like candy." Stephanie waited again, but this time, not to stoke her friend, but to let the meaning sink in. "Then she said, 'Since we sex anyway… well…what's the dif if we wanna do it with someone other than just boys? Really, I think I'd prefer a *man* to bang me rather than some *boy*. And… I like my teacher. What's the dif, we're doin' it anyway!'" Arlupo's mouth dropped open. There were a few sixteen years old's in her village that married men six, seven, even eight years older, but for the Appendaho, the level of maturity, love, respect, and responsibility way surpassed the outside world.

But then Stephanie said, "I'm not done!"

"Not DONE?"

"She continued to explain herself, saying, 'The only reason they don't want us younger women to bang the older guys is 'cause the older women are afraid we'll steal their men away! After all, they're like twenty-five or somethin'. All dried up, probably, by then! You know the older guys always lookin' at us anyway!"

Arry's mouth fell completely open. She'd heard and seen some outlandish things, but this . . .

"Arry, I was just about to reply to this when some of the boys who had been listening at a distance must have gotten worried, so they pushed their way in and started groping the girls, telling them they know they love it." She paused to check more deeply into her friend's eyes. "And Arry . . ."

Arry grabbed her friend's hands and pulled impatiently, "Yes STEPHIE, YES… don't stop, just keep telling."

Stephie kinda wagged her head from side to side, "Weelll, I got angry. And I, well . . ." Stephanie looked down and away with a wrinkled up face and scrunched up her shoulders, and that put Arry over the top.

"S T E P H I E!" Arry had grabbed her wrists now and was pulling.

"All right, all right… I grabbed one boy and hauled him out of the crowd. I chased another. And well, one acted tough, like he wasn't going to move, and he was holding a girl and *she didn't even want to be held*, I could tell . . ." When Stephie paused again, Arry threw her friend's hands down and folded her own arms tightly up, pouting and sighing . . .

"I hit him!"

"You WHAT?" she jerked up so hard the bed bounced.

Stephie grabbed Arry's hands, blurting out… "KNOCKED HIM OUT!"

Arry's eyes were near to popping out of her head, "STEPHIE, YOU *ARE* KIDDING NOW."

Stephie leaned back and relaxed to regain her composure, still holding her friend's hands. "In a way, I wish I was. I balled up my fist, like I saw Vaughn do one time even before I met him, and I hit him as hard as I could under his big, fat, ugly chin. But when I was doing it, I did it so quick, I don't know, it felt like, well, like there was this force with me. That it wasn't just *me* hitting him, but me and some unseen force together."

"OH MY GOD." Arry had both hands to her cheeks.

"Actually Arry, I think you're right! I think God was with me."

All Arry could say was, "WOW!"

Stephanie continued in her modest tone. "Yeah, because all the girls were like hangin' with their mouths open, the boys too, before they fell over laughing that a skinny little girl had knocked out that fat, ugly slob. Then all the girls started cheering me! And we all walked off together. They wanted to know how I knew so much. So I told them about how Vaughn had saved me. This time, they believed me, and I began to explain a whole lot of things to them about sex and real love and stuff. Arry, they had respect in their eyes for me! I've never in my life had an experience like that. I mean, the Appendaho, of course, but it's different for them."

"I understand. That respect is coming from *your* people, regular people, so to speak."

"Yes, it somehow felt very meaningful. I still wouldn't go as far as to say any of them would be my friends, but, I don't know, to me… it was a completely spiritual experience."

"You have got to tell Father all about this. I think he would enjoy it very much."

"I don't know. Do you think he would be interested in girl talk?"

"Stephie, clean life can be anyone's talk. He'd appreciate this girl talk because it'd show him a deeper understanding of the goodness growing in you. I talk to my Dad about everything."

Stephanie raised her eyebrows. "You're right. But he already knows everything about me."

Arlupo corrected her. "No, not at all! He only knows up to the point of the bond, but you've grown way past that point."

"But it hasn't been that long."

"Reality is…"

"What reality is."

"Right."

Stephanie mused about her father listening to the story and chuckled to herself. "I suppose he'd be very happy to know how his help has affected me."

"He would *indeed*."

Stephie yawned so long and so wide that Arlupo caught it, and then Stephie recaught the yawn. "Oh my, I guess we'd better get some sleep. Wow, I feel so great now, and just think about when I first came to you tonight, how messed up I was."

Arlupo touched her arm tenderly. "Stephanie, you need to be able to do this for yourself, in case you've no one to talk to." But something in her touch and surety sent chills all over Stephanie. Arry laid down, curling up, but Stephanie still sat there, staring.

"Why? Why would you say that?"

Arlupo gave a sleepy answer. "Well, just think. If you can do that for yourself, alone, then you're much stronger than if you always need someone else."

It was a good answer, but it didn't sound right, "Yeah, true, but why?" Stephie leaned over to peer into her friend's face, "Arry? Arry, are you asleep?"

It seemed as if Arlupo had dozed off and then reawakened, "Huh? Oh, sorry, Stephie. Oh, I almost forgot to tell you. I've done something special for you." Stephanie laid down face to face with her best friend. "You've been doing something special for me from the time I met you."

"No, this is different. I've opened a bank account in both our names. Either one of us may put in or take out what we want."

Dumbfounded, Stephanie said, "What? But…but… why?"

"First of all, the money your father gave toward your care has been placed in it, but a lot of the money came from what I sold."

"Sold? What did you sell?"

"Besides the orchards and the goats, we find precious stones in the hills. But we haven't let the outside know of such things, because of their terrible greed. But when I went to school, I found out that I, and the others like me, would need a lot more money than we were able to get from just selling goats and fruit. So I began taking a few stones, here and there, to different places to sell. I make sure that these places are far apart so that they don't suspect we have much treasure. They only think we have a few. I know they pay much less than they're really worth, but even what they pay is a lot."

"How much did you put away?"

Arlupo rolled over and away from Stephanie and leaned over the edge of the bed to reach under it. She came up with a little booklet and a small leather pouch.

"Here is your bank pass with our current balance listed. Just check at any of this particular banking institution's branches and they can tell you how much money is in there."

Stephanie opened to the first page and her eyes almost rolled onto the floor. "OH MY GOD, THIS IS A FORTUNE!"

Arlupo looked doubtful. "Is it really a lot Stephie? I'm not sure what a lot is."

Stephanie grabbed her upper arm. "Arry, this *alone* makes your whole people rich. Money is tight, has been for as long as I have known about it. You all could live like kings and queens."

Arlupo looked puzzled, staring at her friend, "But Stephie, we already do!"

Stephanie realized the *stupidity* of what she just said. "I'm sorry, Arry. You're right. You're lives really couldn't be better, couldn't be happier. I just meant that there's enough here to live in the luxury of kings and queens. Luxury… that is *really meaningless*." Stephanie shook her head.

"Stephie, I'm not sure, but I think this bank even has branches in other countries."

"Really? I thought our country kept it all to itself?"

"But they still have the government to deal with the outside, and because they travel outside, I think they have these banks outside as well. I think so, because once I was in the bank and a government official was asking a teller if the branch bank in another country would know he had put money in that bank, and she told him it was automatically available at all branches."

Stephanie was overwhelmed. She couldn't believe it. Now, added to every other blessing she'd received, she was rich, too!

"Wow!"

"Also, Stephie, I wanted you to have this." She handed her an old leather pouch.

Stephanie scolded her. "ARRY, does this little pouch contain what I think it does?"

Arlupo frowned, looking away. "Just open it and see."

Her breath was taken away. "OH MY GOD! They're beautiful. Sooo beautiful! I've never seen so many different colored stones before."

But Arlupo explained further. "Stephie, they're not just stones, they're finished jewels. Some of our people are skilled at making them. That's another reason why when I sell them, it doesn't raise suspicion. The outsiders would never expect us to possess such skills. So they figure they're just part of some old collection, like when an old person dies and leaves behind a few things."

Stephanie shook her head over and over. It was tempting, but she didn't deserve any of this wealth.

"Arry, I can't accept this. There's a fortune here, also. I barely do enough work around here to earn what you've already given me just in regular life. Since we began school, I work even less…"

But Arry insisted. She pushed her friend's hands back toward her. "No, I want you to have this, *too*. You mustn't wear these when you go to the outside, and be very careful that the outside doesn't even know you have such a collection. *You understand?*" Arlupo stared sternly.

"Of course, but Arry…"

Arlupo was strangely firm with Stephanie. "*No buts* Stephie, no buts. You're my *sister*, as close to me as if we shared the same womb. I'd be insulted if you don't allow me to express my love for you."

Stephanie knew she was hemmed in, but… "Arry *please!* What have I done for you? I don't deserve all this." Tears welled up in Stephanie's eyes and she began to sniffle.

Arry squeezed her shoulder. "You've shared all your truth with me, your whole heart, soul, and mind, and that's *everything* you have. You've shared your wonderful insight into life, words I could not even have imagined for beauty. Nothing else can even come *close* to that value."

Stephanie put the jewels back in their pouch, pulled the drawstring tight, and buried her face in her hands as she lay beside her friend, the jewels resting between them.

"Oh Arry, will you ever stop making me cry?"

"Well, at least you don't have any makeup to get all runny like all the other outsiders. That's one of the first things I noticed about you. How really pretty you are."

Stephanie giggled. "Oh my, you and Vaughn should talk."

"Good night, my *dear* sister. I will always remember this night. You hit him? KNOCKED HIM OUT?"

SACRIFICIAL WOOD

Stephanie smiled, reaching over and caressing her sister's cheek. "Good night, dear Arry."

The night was far spent, but their sleep was never sweeter. They awoke mid-morning.

CHAPTER ELEVEN
Live By Love

Inviting him in was a kindness he desperately needed. The warrior pulled the wigwam's flap open, and he sat before the Shaman. "Thank you. I have come…"

But he held up his hand for silence. "From very far away and you are not supposed to be here at all. Go home, young man, before you destroy all our futures!"

"Shaman, I perceive you have sight, but what of this understanding? I am but one man."

"In my vision I saw your arrival and I made you this." He removed a cover from a framework. An elaborate structure of wooden pieces rose several feet. He pointed to one piece in the center, several layers up, but well below the top. "Pull this one." He pointed to a string attached to it.

When he pulled it, the whole structure collapsed. The Shaman laid his eyes upon the young man, again. "Go home."

The young man hung his head, sighing, nodding. "Thank you Wise One."

SACRIFICIAL WOOD

One of the farm dogs that remembered Vaughn met him in the field and accompanied him to his home. The large, black, shaggy dog had floppy ears hanging from a big face, with a white spot over his right eye, and a white belly, with a white paw at the right front and the left hind. He carried a stick in his mouth and Vaughn understood, instantly forgetting about his troubling thoughts.

First, tug of war, and then toss and retrieve. Vaughn noticed how smart the dog really was, because every time he faked a throw, the dog just stared at him as if to say, *You're being stupid*. Before Vaughn knew it, he was knocking on the old, heavy wooden door as the sun just peeked across the field.

A tall, elderly, gray haired gentleman, with a cleanly shaven square jaw, and bright blue eyes opened the door, a little at first and then swung it wide. He was already dressed in blue overalls, although the sun had just come up. Vaughn stood there with a very full pack on his back, and a long knapsack slung over his shoulder.

"How are you doing, Sir? I've decided to be a traveling worker. Do you have work for me?"

The old man smiled broadly, happy to see him. "Vaughn, of course I do. You could stay all winter if you liked, but, you know the rules. You need to be in school."

Vaughn had prepared for this. "Well, actually, they say 'in school', because we can't be causing trouble or mooching off the government which is really mooching off hard working people. But I'm not mooching or causing trouble. You see? I'm really not breaking the rules, because I'm not breaking their purpose. It doesn't make sense to make a rule and then forget about the meaning and purpose of the rule. Does it?" Vaughn looked up into the tall man's eyes. He always felt like a boy when around him, but this kind of feeling wasn't at all disagreeable. In fact, he relished it.

"My boy, *you* are amazing. If you ran for government, I'd be one who would vouch for you. Ehh, but they have no respect for farmers. So I just stay out of their way, as do most of us. Did you know that's the reason most people don't ask or give their names anymore?" The old man took Vaughn around the shoulders and guided him to a large, wooden dining table in a room off the kitchen. Vaughn set his things in the corner. He would take them to the guest room later.

"Ahh, I don't think I understand."

"It's a form of *rebellion* that goes way back to when this government took over by force. They needed to keep track of people, and so they needed the identities of everyone. Unconsciously, or purposely, people stopped using their names much!"

"Hmm, I don't think it's very effective. I think the government knows everyone anyway. You see, I even think they know I've run away, but they're so arrogant, thinking that I've no place to go. So they're assuming I'll turn up somewhere, and I'll have to get caught, because all kids must be someplace. But I think they never figured like I'm figuring. I can work the farms and keep traveling."

"My boy, I think you just may have something there."

"But Sir, I'm sorry. I would love to stay long, but I can't."

SACRIFICIAL WOOD

"I understand. You'll need to keep moving for a while until they forget about you. If you don't show up after a while, they'll probably figure something bad happened, and that you're dead."

"Yeah, that is right. Wow."

As Vaughn ate a breakfast of fresh eggs, milk, and muffins, he began speaking without even thinking. Before he knew it, he told the farmer about his school troubles, being sent away, and being in the hospital. But he left out all the mysterious parts.

The old man listened intently, but calmly. And when Vaughn finished his story, the old farmer had nothing to say! Perhaps because he knew Vaughn had already worked it out. Vaughn realized he hadn't even paid attention to what he'd eaten. In fact, he couldn't even remember what he ate! Then Vaughn went to work.

He helped put the cows out. Then he joyously cleaned out the barn, and carted the wagon load off to the compost pile and dumped it. He noticed how good the natural manure smelled. Before he knew it, he heard the old man call him in. Lunch time.

All through his meal preparations and dining, the venerable old man was quiet, but there was something being spoken clearly in his patient care, the purposeful way he forked his food, the frequent wipes of his mouth with a napkin, and the way every single action seemed meaningful. Vaughn couldn't seem to take his eyes off of him. He wished he could put into words what he was seeing. In fact, Vaughn felt like a little child simply given to watching and absorbing . . . *something*.

After the elderly man cleaned up the table, he brought out an old box that had been taped together more times than was recognizable. Checkers. A very, very old game. He handed the box to Vaughn, and he eagerly set them up. Last summer he didn't take a single game from the old man. *Hmm, maybe this time. Maybe my luck has changed.* Upon further consideration, *Nahh, nothin' to do with luck.* He noticed a sharp gleam in the old man's eyes as they began to play.

Vaughn couldn't figure out what the old man was studying on so hard. *Is he thinking about my move or his?* Vaughn lost all the games. The old man just smiled with that glint in his eye, but… *Is that a subtle challenge behind his smile? But for what? How'd he beat me like that anyway?* There was a look of knowing in his face but… *Knowing what?* That was it! All his moves, whether in the game or preparing food seemed to be carried out with *knowing. What?*

After, Vaughn hitched a different trailer to the tractor, then he went down a dirt road into the nearby woods. The half dead trees he had felled in the summer dried considerably. He sighed. Back then, he and Stephanie were still together. Bringing back the logs to the farmhouse to cut up into firewood was like bringing back his past with Stephanie. Looking at the dead wood, he shook his head. *We're going to be together, again. Just like this wood, our experiences together will be to kindle a fire.* He was pleased with his analogy. *Yes, an everlasting fire.*

He'd gone through only a third of the long logs. Even though the cool of evening had set in, Vaughn had his shirt

◈ SACRIFICIAL WOOD ◈

off with the setting sun glistening off his sweating muscles. The farmer strolled up with a serious face.

"Hey my boy, where'd you learn to chop wood like that?"

Vaughn smiled with gratitude, glad to hear the farmer's voice. "You ought to know, you taught me."

If there was any adult he could say that he loved, he came close to saying it of this particular farmer. The old man pulled a freshly cut stump over on its end and sat on it, as Vaughn kept chopping. He rubbed his chin between his thumb and forefinger. "Yeah, that *is* right, isn't it? I remember when you didn't know one end of a pitch fork or axe from the other."

Vaughn laughed at himself. "Well Sir, I'm so glad I learned all these things. I enjoy working with my hands so much. But how come you don't have the modern things a lot of other farmers have?"

A laugh popped out from him, "Don't need 'em. All that terrible noise those chain saws and other contraptions make. There's really not that much time saved by 'em. Anyway, that's only if you really know how to use a good hand tool. They think because these tools are old-fashioned and simple, that they're no good compared to their complex machinery. It's just not so. There's a real art to using an axe or saw correctly that just makes it flow. Before you know it, your work is done, and there's a certain beautiful feeling you can get while doing it. You don't get that from a noisy, stinking machine. C'mon, help put this log on the sawhorse so we can saw it up together. You know, I would race any chain saw with this two man saw, or even my other long one man saw… *and I'd win."* The old farmer's eyes shined with a knowing smile.

"I believe you, Sir."

Vaughn helped him lift the heavy oak log up onto the sawhorse, leaving the right length to fit in the fireplace hang over the edge. The farm dog sat off a ways, watching them calmly as they began to cut off the piece. Every now and then other dogs could be seen in various parts of the farm, like sentries.

As they were pushing and pulling the two-man saw together, the old farmer began his exploration. "Which do you like better: sawing, chopping off the branches, or splitting?"

This got Vaughn thinking. "Hmm, I don't know. I like it all, actually. But now that I think about it, I like each differently."

The farmer's whole face focused to put the next question to Vaughn. His seriousness seemed akin to considering the secret to life itself. "And why might that be? Why do you like each differently?" All this while sawing barely fazed the man. The effort was as if he were just out for a pleasant walk.

Why! He asked me why! "Huh, let me see. Chopping off the branches is the preparation work. The tree worked all its life to put them there, reaching out in every direction. I chop them off. Make a clean cut. Sometimes one swipe with a sharp axe takes off the whole branch, strips the tree down to just its trunk. Hmm, I guess it's kinda like getting down to the fundamental part of something. But there's a feeling I can't explain, too." They sawed the log through, and the piece plunked to the ground. Vaughn bent over, grabbed it, and tossed it a little away.

As they both were resetting the position of the log, the old man answered with a questioning look. "I see."

They set the saw's new position, and the farmer's nod began both the sawing and Vaughn's continuation. "But sawing up the big trunk, well, that's like opening up the tree's whole life. Its whole life is in the trunk. I actually feel a kinda deep respect for the tree, because, well, all those years, all those rings the tree has. I get to see 'em, and it's like I'm becoming a part of those years when I open the tree up. Sometimes, I stop and place my hand on the freshly sawn surface… across all those rings. It almost seems sacred." Vaughn was a bit winded, and had to take deeper breaths between his words, but not the old farmer.

"Hmm, I see. Hey boy, this isn't a race. Just relax and *walk* through it. The saw has a natural pace. Don't fight it. Let it do the work. You just guide it a bit. Why do you look so sad?"

Vaughn relaxed his arms and changed his stance a bit, trying to apply the sawing advice. He readjusted his mind and approach. "Because, well, in a way, I feel bad cutting it up, invading its life. But more respect than sad." Vaughn paused to consider his own answer.

"I feel more respect because, well, it's still leaving something substantial behind. All this wood. Also, it's a tough life, I think, being a tree. Standing out there naked against all the elements, and yet growing, strengthening, becoming such strong wood. Too bad they die." Another piece dropped off, and the main log got shorter still. Vaughn, again, tossed the loose piece aside. As they reset the log, then the saw's position, the nod came and the sawing began, again, along with the farmer's reply.

"Since almost the beginning of time, when evil entered into the world, living things have been giving up their lives for the sake of others to live. That kind of death is not the death of the dying, but a living sacrifice for the living. Watch, even when an animal catches its prey, it's almost a sacred act between them. Sure, the prey fights to live, it has to. But when you look deeper at each, you see something there, as well, that's almost reverent. How the prey gives a final act of submission, how the hunter peacefully sits for a bit over the prey it just caught and killed. And there's no evil glee on the part of the hunter." The old man looked deeply into Vaughn and could see there was nothing lost on him of the lesson. Another piece fell, and the routine proceeded almost unnoticed while they conversed. "How about the splitting?"

"Oh, I love to split the logs, too. I don't know. It just fascinates me how some wood will just split so cleanly with one good whack of the axe, with such finality. Others, you got to really work at… sometimes use a wedge. I guess I would say, when you split a log, it's kinda like putting the tree to its final rest. Until you split it, well, it still seems like a tree to me. I mean, you can see all its rings go around into a complete circle, the way it grew in life. Once I split the round shape into pieces, it's like putting a final end to its being a tree." Vaughn paused, listening to his own words, again. *Hmm, freeing it from this world, or completing its sacrifice, or both.*

SACRIFICIAL WOOD

"Kinda like letting its spirit free?"

"Maybe so. I'm not sure, but I guess so, because until I split it, I still think of its tree life. But after, it's just wood to be burned up. So, maybe the difference is that the spirit of the tree has left. It certainly has a different meaning after I split it."

The farmer nodded with understanding, but Vaughn wasn't exactly sure what that understanding was. The old man then asked him a pointed question. "So what you're saying is that sawing, chopping and splitting each has a different meaning to you, and you like the meanings?"

"Huh! I never thought about it like that, but I would say that must be correct. I mean, that's really what I just described, isn't it? Hmm, strange that I didn't realize all this when it was me that was doing it all along!"

The farmer leveled his eyes at Vaughn to impress the next point. "Just because we do things doesn't mean we have the perspective to see the true nature of what we do." The last piece fell and the widest piece was left atop the sawhorse.

Vaughn went over to a half stump that served as a chopping block, just past the pile of pieces, and pulled out the axe where he'd buried the blade. "Yeah, I guess because you're on the outside of me looking in, you can see the bigger picture."

But the farmer shook his head. "Young man, I couldn't know anything about you like that if I first didn't look at myself from the inside out! How many city folk looking from the outside into you would have been able to see it? To see the care, thought, and feeling behind your everyday actions such as this!" He waved his hand indicating what they were doing.

Vaughn was about to strike the axe into a freshly cut piece to split it, but out of the corner of his eye he saw the farmer holding his hand out, waiting for Vaughn to see and take in his point.

Meaning seemed to stop time. Vaughn paused as he looked at the farmer. *No, city people don't understand me at all. They haven't a clue who I am. But he does!* "I see your point. I guess at any given time or place, whatever a person does is really the sum total of all that is inside him. I guess we really should be able to see it, if we had eyes to see the whole picture."

The farmer slowly nodded. "They can't recognize all the feelings you have because they haven't recognized them first in themselves."

Vaughn leaned on his axe handle, fully turning to the farmer. "So what you're saying is that to gain the perspective of seeing the true nature of myself or others, I must look deeply into myself first, and then out to others."

Again, with a slow nod, almost like a royal dispensation, or giving permission to perform some noble right. "Yes. All you have to do is ask simple questions like, why am I feeling this way. If your whole heart is set on goodness, it will connect to the greater meaning of things, and through that greater meaning, you will gain the greater perspective to see truly."

Vaughn rubbed his fuzzy chin. "Hmm, from the *deep* inside of me, outward into my regular insides, and then to outside of me. Truly from the inside out."

The farmer smiled. He seemed greatly relieved, and raised his leg and slapped his knee with a sharp crack. "You've got it, my boy, you've got it!"

SACRIFICIAL WOOD

Pride surged through Vaughn at the farmer's show of satisfaction. He noticed he had never had such a feeling before. He truly loved this old man. "You know Sir, I think I already do this a lot."

The farmer surprised Vaughn even further. "*I know!* That's why I spoke to you so. You think I would've wasted a single breath on those others from town? I know 'em all. I find more comfort with my chickens, as *they* make more sense!"

Vaughn laughed heartily. A larger picture of this man's life suddenly flashed in his mind as he felt love for him burn in his heart. And then it occurred to him. "Sir, how come you never married?"

Pain shot through the old man's eyes, and Vaughn instantly regretted asking him. The farmer bowed his head while folding his hands, and spoke at the ground. "I did. Even had children, but that was a long time ago. We all used to live here. I was going to leave my farm to my son and daughter, but about forty years ago the government decided it needed young people elsewhere, so they told us our children had to go."

Vaughn became indignant. An angry darkness grew in his eyes. "*You're kidding*… well I know you're not kidding… but…I'm sorry, Sir, I didn't mean…." Vaughn hung his head, his fury oddly mixed with embarrassment.

The farmer waved it by with his hand. "The government has actually calmed down a lot from what it used to be. It's still not great, but better."

Vaughn just had to know, as if recording it in himself for some future purpose. "Sir, may I ask?"

The farmer knew. "My wife was heartbroken. She loved the children so. It ate away at her and she just died one night, some months later. Died young."

Vaughn hung his head more heavily, feeling as if his own heart had been ripped out. His love for Stephanie was as this man's for his wife. But Vaughn picked his head up. He had to ask. This man went for so long after her death. He had to ask. "But Sir, how did you find the strength to continue? I don't know if I…"

The farmer picked his head up, leveling his wet eyes into Vaughn's, but Vaughn couldn't continue, as he had never seen the old man in tears.

"It's that perspective we were talking about. I realized I couldn't foretell what life might bring my way, what good I may yet be able to do in the world. I knew my children would be out there, somewhere, too."

Vaughn hung his head. He knew the answer somehow, but asked anyway. "Have you heard from them?"

"No, but I thank God you've come my way, my boy. Even just to share with you the little I've shared, has given meaning to all these years I've endured!" His smile didn't last long, but seemed to fill an eternity in Vaughn's heart.

Humbled by such a grand statement, Vaughn shook his head. "Sir, please, you bestow me too much honor."

Standing up even straighter, the farmer walked over to Vaughn, and placed his strong right hand on Vaughn's shoulder. "No, I don't young man. I know what I'm lookin' at. Maybe one day…" then the old man cut himself off.

◈ SACRIFICIAL WOOD ◈

Vaughn still bowed his head. There were tears in his eyes for many reasons. "What Sir?"

"Well, it wouldn't be right for you, but I was going to say I would leave you my farm. But you'll be a long ways from here by then, and besides, I just don't think you're meant to live your life isolated on a farm."

Vaughn shook his head in wonder, thinking, *How amazing this is, to be disinherited from my real parents, only to be offered an inheritance from someone better.* "I really don't know what my life is going to be. I'm just living it day to day."

"That's what you think right now, young man, but just as every part of these trees we cut up is attached to the trunk through *something*, your life is attached to a Tree of Life. When the wind blows, the tree moves as a whole. You, as a little leaf on that tree, only feel yourself moving for now, as if you were alone, living day to day. But in reality, it's not so. Right now, you are moving with that Tree holding tightly to you. Believe this, my boy, have faith in it, so you don't fall off that Tree." The farmer squeezed his shoulder.

Vaughn could only stare at the old farmer he wished would have been his birth father. But then he realized that if he had, Vaughn would have been the one the government stole away from him. Vaughn shook his head at the utter confusion he was feeling, and decided to refocus on what was just told him. *A Tree of Life. Stephanie thanked the Tree of Life for . . . what were her words? Giving her passage to me. A Tree of Life. I use that analogy, too. Is it just coincidence? Is it just an analogy? Let me see what more he has to say.* "But all leaves fall off eventually, Sir."

The farmer pointed to the forest across the field. "But *these* trees are only partly like the Tree of Life. The Tree of Life connects to your eternal soul. It supports the young, the ignorant, even bears with the evil, as it holds onto diseased leaves for a while. It even holds *this* old man. But I have learned that I can hold onto it as well, because the Tree of Life is a Tree of Goodness. There's no death in goodness. And what connects me to this Goodness? My depth of understanding of the nature of Goodness, thereby enabling me to love it that much more. *This* is where *true* faith comes from, from understanding what is real, and the natural love this invokes."

The farmer squeezed Vaughn's shoulder again so that he picked his head back up. Then the old man continued with his gaze melding into Vaughn's heart and mind. "Love and understanding do a beautiful dance together. In this way, there is no fear of the death of this body. Nothing can convince my love that its understanding isn't real because Goodness is its focus. There is a reason goodness feels so alive. Because it *is*. I am *not* this body, but the *person* inside. It doesn't make sense to believe the dumb body has pre-eminence over the conscious person, especially when the person sees that only goodness is the life of that person.

"When the Tree of Life decides it's time to let go of this body, I have no say over that. But the person inside me sees no sense in letting go of that Tree of Life, even through my last breath, because the ways of goodness have been the real life of the person inside this body for some time. If I have already lived many years here on this Earth, countin' that as

SACRIFICIAL WOOD

my real life, why would I then make my life a lie by fearing when I face the death of this body? No. To my last breath, I will appreciate and be thankful to that Goodness, and I shall leave here in that peace as I entrust myself to the Greater Good. I will not make my life into a lie at my dying breath."

Vaughn didn't even want to speak, being spellbound by the feeling and power of this old man's words. *The Tree of Life is not* just *an analogy. I can feel it. I can see it. It's the very nature of the Spirit!* Vaughn had to tell him his feelings, the only thing he possessed that had any value. "Sir, you have put me in awe of you. I… I hope I can be as you are."

Satisfaction beamed in the farmer's face and he motioned to Vaughn to pull up a stump to sit across from him as he did the same. His hand tightly grabbed Vaughn's knee as he again fixed his eyes into Vaughn's. "No, Vaughn! While I may demonstrate certain qualities that are good for you because they're common throughout the Tree, you're not supposed to be like me or anyone else! You are a different leaf on a different part of the Tree. As each part of the Tree grows according to the nature of it, so must you take the natural course that the Tree offers you. Don't let yourself become diseased like so many others that trouble the Tree. I've watched you, my boy, for a long time. You're doing just fine!"

Surprise dropped Vaughn's mouth open. "You… watched me, Sir?"

He laughed. "Of course. Who do you think got you your private room at the hospital? Oh, I was given the run around. I had to bribe an administrator and a doctor. Seems, for some reason, they were intent on sticking you in a corner of the basement next to the morgue, *by God!* Fortunately, money under the table talks."

Vaughn's head swam when he heard it. *My parents didn't do it after all.* He held his head up, tears gushing. But he didn't care if his tears were seen. He had to look this wonderful man in the eyes.

The old man continued with a peppy voice, his eyes burning brightly. "I've watched everyone in the town. What else would a lonely, old man do with all his time? *Talk to chickens?*" The old farmer made some cackling chicken noises and the chickens in the distance responded in kind.

Vaughn burst out laughing. The continued sight of this virtuous, serious old man acting like a chicken, and the chickens thinking he *was* a chicken, caused Vaughn to roll off the stump in uncontrollable laughter. He was just a boy, and he loved it. The old man stood over him and cackled some more, with his arms bent and flapping like a chicken.

Vaughn pleaded. "Stop. *Stop!* I can't laugh anymore." Vaughn looked up from lying on the ground. "I'm going to miss you, Sir."

He reached down, they grabbed hands, and the dear old man pulled him up like he was no more than a feather. "And I'll miss you, Vaughn. You've hauled me in a good store of firewood. My barn's never been cleaner. *Spot* has taken a real liking to you. I want you to have him!"

Vaughn was shocked, yet again. He had never had a pet. "Oh no, Sir, I couldn't."

"You've got a long way to travel. After this week, you'll have earned enough money to care for yourself and Spot for a while. *I trust you.*" The old man leaned closer to Vaughn, sharply focusing on him as if to impart another important life lesson. "Spot has dog sense. That's a sense we *don't* have. He'll help protect you on your journey. Besides, you see how many dogs I have here? *Too many.*" He scowled and waved his hands around in mock annoyance.

Vaughn was shaken from all the wonderful blessings he'd received over the last few days. It was so very different than what his life had ever been. He felt very much like a small child. "Oh Sir, I've *always* wanted a pet doggy."

Vaughn looked over at Spot lying against the freshly cut wood. Spot pushed himself up and walked over to Vaughn. The large, beautiful dog, made flapping noises with his black, floppy ears when he shook his head. His square snout housed an endless tongue whenever the dog decided to lick someone in the face, which was now. His long, bushy, black and white tail created a comfortable breeze, if one positioned themselves just right. Thick, black fur with a white spot over his right eye, and a small triangular patch on his chest earned him his name. Vaughn scratched him behind his ears, and his tail almost seemed to tap out a tune, indicating the intensity of his pleasure.

The farmer finally interrupted them. "C'mon, let's eat. You'll spend just a few days here and then I'll drive you to your next farm. I know the man. He's an honest fellow, with no love for the government, either."

Vaughn looked up from his pet. "But, Sir, I'm headed West."

The farmer rose from his stump. "I know. You told me. He's due west about fifty miles from here."

Vaughn worried for him. "But Sir, the government check points."

The wise old man shrugged. "Are nothing to us farmers. We just cut through the fields and go around them. We've had our own little secret road system for some time now. We don't use it much, so it never draws attention. Besides, there just aren't enough of us anymore. Most of us are too old, anyway, so the government really doesn't care. I guess, eventually they'll control all the farmland as we die off. Spot, c'mere boy." Spot moved to his master, looking on attentively, arfing loudly, panting with excitement. His old master rubbed his head firmly, "Good boy. Spot, I want you to go with Vaughn. You belong to him now. Here…" He took Spot over to Vaughn in a very formal way and patted Vaughn on his shoulder, then patted Spot again.

Spot panted with even more excitement, arfed and jumped up on Vaughn, putting his front paws into his lap and his big doggy face into Vaughn's. And there it was, again. The tongue from which there was no escape. Spot seemed to understand, and was extremely happy. Vaughn tried to dodge it, but ended up having his face thoroughly washed.

"Ahhggg, O.K., O.K… you can come with me, Spot." Spot eased down, sitting at his feet. He arfed more softly this time. Vaughn rubbed his head as he spoke. "Yeah, there, there. He's a big dog for a mutt." He rubbed his ears right where Spot loved it.

SACRIFICIAL WOOD

"Part Great Dane, part Shepherd, part Lab, part… ahh, I don't know what. He's only two-years old. Still a lot like a puppy, but make no mistake, he'll protect you with his life. I've trained all the dogs the same way."

It was getting dark as they headed inside. The farmer cooked him the best meal he had ever had. Freshly butchered chicken, fresh parsley and thyme from a protected herb garden, with tomatoes, potatoes, onions, and carrots from the root cellar. Vaughn thought, *If anyone would know what to do, he might.*

Sitting at the table, Vaughn told the old farmer of his vision, of the man that blew up, and about Tracy. The old man sat with all his usual calm until he heard what Vaughn did with Tracy. He could picture the girl hideously transforming into a human demon and the brave lad jumping on top of her. But his head spun as he tried to imagine Vaughn's internal battle against himself being possessed and mutated. The old farmer's eyes widened with admiration.

Vaughn shook his head, mistaking the man's reaction. "You probably think I was pretty stupid, huh? Maybe I'm jumping to conclusions. Maybe I got lucky. Maybe…"

"You're going to 'maybe-ing' yourself to death if you let that continue! Trust the goodness that's leading you, Son. It's what allowed you to save both your friends. Yes, I know about how you saved Stephanie, too! What was her reaction to the man that blew up?"

Vaughn decided to tell him about Stephanie's abilities. Again he was calm until he heard how Vaughn was healed in

❧ DARRYL MARKOWITZ ❧

the hospital. He shook his head with tears in his eyes. Deep intensity filled his voice. "You listen to me, young man, and you listen *real* good. You two are meant to be together. I just know it. And you're meant to do things in this world that have never been done, *ever*. Because evil things are going on, and if they're not stopped, well, never mind. I believe that Tree of Life has put your lives together for a purpose. But I'm not telling you anything you don't already know. I believe you've already figured this out. Trust that Tree of Life and trust each other. You *have to* find each other again."

The old man paused, mulling over something, but then decided to speak. "You listen to me, and listen *real* good. Evil has been around almost from the beginning. Since then, it has acquired more and more wisdom to do its thing. You find your love, and you give yourselves time to grow. You have to let that Tree of Life *prepare* you first. It may take years. *Listen!* Before you take on the evils you've described, you need deeper roots. You need to be a much more developed tree." He paused again, and his look got harder. "You *listen* to me, I *know* you! You're going to want to fight before it's wise. That's a *trap*."

"But what do we do in the mean time?"

"If you have to, *run!* There's no shame in that now, because you're not running to avoid battle, but so you can fight and *win* later. But the hardest thing for you may be to turn your back on helping others *now*, so that you'll be around *later* to make a real difference."

Vaughn's head hurt and with elbows on the table, he leaned it into his hands. He felt older. He sighed. The old man rose up quietly, patted him on his back, and went to bed. Vaughn sat a long time with his head in his hands. *I just don't think I can do that. I don't think I could ignore someone needing help.*

Vaughn woke well rested but noticed his pillow was wet again. It had been the same for all three nights he spent at this farm. He remembered weeping in his dreams. He remembered that little girl from his vision surrounded by blackness. "*I have to save her,*" he heard himself say.

That morning, that dear old man drove him to the next farm and dropped him off. As Vaughn watched the old farmer drive away into the distance of the field, his heart ached from the separation. Spot howled a mournful howl. He nudged his head against his new master's leg for a pat of reassurance. *Oh God, Stephanie, I have to find you. Why did you scream? How are we meant to stop all this evil?*

☙

Early in the morning the old farmer's front door burst open. Harsh words followed its crash as he stayed seated at his table. A large young man with curly black hair entered boisterously.

"O.K. *old* man, where's the criminal?"

"And who might that be, *boy*?" he said with a steady, cautious gaze.

"Don't call me *boy*. You know who I'm talking about. I'm Officer Glen. That's all you need to know."

"And how is it someone still wet behind the ears has such an important job?"

DARRYL MARKOWITZ

Glen leaned over the other side of the table peering into his eyes. "My *father* is a chief administrator and he's personally appointed me to find Vaughn because I know him so well."

"Yeah, right, well, why don't you go back to school and learn a little…"

Glen slammed his hands down on the table glaring at the farmer. "I've been given a special certification to be employed. I'm to bring the murderer in."

The sound of it made the old man's gut lurch, and Glen could see he was shaken.

"Murderer?"

Glen hissed back. "Yesssss. Didn't you know?"

The old man paused to catch his breath. "Know what?"

"I thought you old timers knew all about the town. That's what they tell me. It was *your* barn where they found all those dead boys."

"Yeah, well… they shouldn't have been there. Vaughn didn't…"

"Oh, I think he did, but that sniveling boy that was left is just too scared to tell the truth. But I'm not here about them."

The old man eased back, not liking how this was developing. "Then who?"

"A girl named Tracy was found murdered not long after Vaughn escaped. We found some of his things with the girl. It's clear he killed her, and I'm to bring him back for trial, or kill him *with government sanction*."

The old wise man shook inside, but he kept it all within. "You know, *my boy*, I've been raising hogs a long time."

Glen shook his head in disbelief. "What the hell does that...?"

He cut him off. "That's a good question. I'll tell you. When the litter is born, you can almost always begin to tell right away what kind of *pigs* they're gonna be. The runt..."

Glen played along, being curious. "That's Vaughn, a runt."

"The runt you have to pull out of the litter and raise it special, or else the others will push it aside from the sow and the runt'll die."

"He *is* gonna die."

The farmer stared into him. "But if you raise it right, it comes to outgrow all the others... to be the strongest out of 'em all."

"He's done growing, and a short time to live."

Squinting, with his blue eyes blazing, the farmer hushed him with a killing glare. "*Boy*, I'm not done telling you about *pigs* yet. You see, others in the litter you can tell whether they might make good *pets*..."

"A pig as a pet?" Glen scoffed.

"Oh yeah, they're smart... just like dogs. Others, you can tell will make good stock to sell for meat, and the others ya breed. And then there's usually one *mean little bastard*, who you just know you might have to put down, because he'll disturb all the rest too much."

Glen laughed. "That would be me, *one mean little bastard*, but it's me who's gonna put the runt down."

"Anyway, as I was saying, there's this one mean little bastard, that when you even just look at him, you know that the name *pig* had to have come from him."

Glen's nostrils flared with anger. He reached across the table for the old man, grabbing him firmly by his neatly pressed shirt, then tugged him forward. "All right *old* man, I've had…"

Three, large, jet black dogs bearing pearly white teeth seemed to appear out of nowhere, just inches from behind Glen and on each side. They didn't sound friendly. The old farmer spoke softly. "I would advise you to take your hand off my shirt *very* slowly, or in just about two more seconds, there won't be much of you left to bury."

Glen eased back. "Where the hell did all these damn dogs come from?" Glen said incredulously.

The farmer patiently, carefully straightened his shirt. "Thank you. Hmm, didn't you see them? They've been watching you sneak up here for the last half-hour. I had to tell them to let you come up, or they would have torn you apart out there in the field! There's a certain *smell* they don't like, and it drives them wild."

Glen so badly wanted to pummel this old man's face in, and watch him suffer. "I'll be back *old* man… we'll see about this."

"Indeed. *If I let you!* I'll let you leave, but don't count on being able to visit again! DOGS, show the man OUT." After he was gone, the old man hung his head in his hands as he leaned his elbows on the table. He had only one thought…*Damn…*

SACRIFICIAL WOOD

❦

He knew what he had to do. He felt good that he finally passed down his sacred understanding of life. He figured it out when he was young. Life is a goodness tree. He knew Vaughn would treasure it and allow it to grow. So, having fulfilled his purpose for living here, there was nothing more he could do except this final act of rebellion. He wasn't surprised when the black vehicle that had followed him raced in front of his truck and cut him off. He only hoped waiting till evening was long enough.

"O.K. *old* man, get out," Glen ordered, waving his pistol at him.

"Well, if it isn't Mr. Glen. I didn't know you liked driving in the country so much."

"I don't. Especially driving through fields. These aren't even hardly roads. But you messed up. I was sure you took Vaughn somewhere. That farm over there must be it."

"I don't know what you're talking about."

"Well, it doesn't matter, because now that I know, I don't *need* you anymore. Hey, where are your dogs?"

"I gave them all away."

"Yeah right. You know that story about the pigs you told me? Well, I have one to tell you. It's about what they do to old horses after they've outlived their usefulness."

❦

Glen burst into the farmhouse the old man was heading for. He questioned the other farmer, but he didn't like what he heard.

"What do you mean you don't know what I'm talking about? All you old men are the same. What'd you do, send him further North? You're about to have an accident, *Pops*, just like your friend did."

☙

Three days, that's what Vaughn told himself, no more than three days before moving on, until he had at least several hundred miles between him and his former home. And he wouldn't use public transportation. He didn't want to take any chances of being returned to that Hell Farm. But there was so much to learn from this old man, he just had to stay the week.

But finally, Vaughn felt the pressure build up too much and he *had* to go. What he had learned here, though, was the perfect practical knowledge to go with the life lessons from the previous farmer.

This sturdy old man knew how to fight. Fight with weapons. After chores were done, he seemed to enjoy teaching Vaughn the staff, the knife, and sharp-shooting. He also taught him hand-to-hand moves… moves that Vaughn had never even thought about. When he told the farmer how he'd been in a fight and almost escaped, but fell flat on his face, the old man laughed, shook his head, and took him to a barn. There, he piled hay up and had Vaughn practice jumping off an old box spring until he landed properly. When he took the hay away, he smiled, saying, "O.K. Let's see you do it for real! Don't break your neck!" When Vaughn landed correctly, elation sent him doing backflips across the floor. The old man walked out laughing. "I'm going to bed now. You should too."

◆ SACRIFICIAL WOOD ◆

But Vaughn stayed up, practicing his midair tumble over and over until, *Wow, I feel kinda like a bird now!* Bending over, panting, finally realizing his exhaustion, he dragged himself to bed, too. Having learned the one move that would have saved him, he fell quickly asleep, brimming with confidence.

In the morning, well rested and ready to travel, his pack and knapsack once again upon his back, and Spot at his side, Vaughn stood just outside the front doorway as the sun was rising behind him. He thanked, yet, another graying elderly man for his help.

"Thank you, Sir, for the work, the wonderful wages, and all you taught me."

"Well, our friend recommended you quite highly. But I was listening to the TV last night and now I'm thinking I should turn you in!"

Startled, Vaughn tentatively looked deeper into the farmer's eyes. He didn't know what to make of his words or harsh tone. "Just because I left home without telling anyone?"

The tall, muscular, old man stood just a few feet away within the doorway and folded his arms across his chest. "You're not a man. Are you? You're really only fifteen?"

Vaughn's mind began to race. *He knows my age. But why does it matter to him?* Vaughn was polite. "Do I do a man's work, Sir?"

The farmer answered dryly. "Oh yes, and apparently you do a man's worth of evil, too!"

Fright began to move Vaughn's mouth, sensing something had gone terribly wrong. "What are you talking about? I've worked hard for you."

DARRYL MARKOWITZ

Cold green eyes bore into Vaughn that seemed to fillet him like a fish. "Tell me about Tracy. Nice little hometown girl?"

Off guard, and now completely unsettled by the man's brutal tone, all Vaughn could do was try to comply with his inquisition, "Huh? What about her? What, oh, she must be mad because I left and didn't tell… no, I don't think that would be it… how do you know her?"

The farmer pierced him with a deep stare that seemed to turn him inside-out. After a long pause, he spoke from deep thought. "You didn't do what they say you did."

Vaughn dropped his knapsack behind him, blurting out, "Do *what?*"

The inquisition continued. "Were you close to the girl?"

Helpless, Vaughn continued to answer respectfully. That's all he could feel for this man, which made the old farmer's mistrust even harder to bear. "In a way, we were close. I promised someone I would help her."

"She was horribly murdered, tortured, sadistically raped, and the government says you did it."

Vaughn staggered backwards then fell over his knapsack while the pack on his back made him land awkwardly. He couldn't stand. With his breath hard to draw, he blurted out, "Oh God… *Tracy!*"

The man silently watched him, waiting.

Vaughn slowly struggled out of his pack. Hollowness and crushing sorrow only allowed Vaughn the ability to whisper. "Why do they think I did it?"

"Apparently, it was the same night you *left*. You're an escapee from the Farm. They found your things with her."

Vaughn's head snapped up. "*My things? My things* were sold before I got out of the hospital."

The old man stepped up just a foot away from Vaughn, who was still on the ground with his legs draped over his knapsack. The old farmer's stare bore down upon him again.

"They've assigned a special government agent to track you down. You were on the local news last night. They say you tortured her all night long, judging from the number of cuts on the girl… and other things."

Nausea overpowered Vaughn. He barely managed to pull himself to his feet to stagger around the corner of the house to throw up. All he could see was him and Tracy locked in a death grip as he battled the demon that had taken her until he plunged his love deep into her soul to drive the demon out. A special bond had formed between them then, and he felt connected to her in some way. "*Tracy,*" he moaned. When Vaughn finally came back, weakly sitting down on his knapsack, the farmer hadn't moved an inch. In the back of Vaughn's mind he heard the word '*Think.*' He hung his head. *Can't think.*

"You'll make life for us very difficult if they suspect we've helped you. I'm not sure we should."

Vaughn felt like a little child again, like the bottom fell out of his beautiful world, and all he wanted to do was cry. But he shook it off. He didn't like feeling like *that* kind of child. Something nagged in the back of his mind and it grew louder. Spot sensed his pain and from behind nuzzled his head into his limp right hand. Vaughn looked up at the farmer while holding his breath inside his heart. "Do you *really* think I did it?"

The man's stare intensified even further, if that was possible. Vaughn decided not to run from it, but to meet it with eyes wide open, letting his soul be seen.

Then the old man's demeanor suddenly relaxed. "No. I don't. You don't have it in you. I can see that. C'mon, I'm going to drive you a good two hundred miles from here. As bad as this is, it's local. I don't think any news of it will make it even half that distance. You're just not important, and neither was the girl." The farmer took his keys from his pocket.

Vaughn couldn't help it. "She *was* important." And he began to weep. All he could feel was Tracy's soul fighting for life. He remembered her begging him. 'Please don't die.' Vaughn was ashamed that he was in front of this stranger like *this*, but he looked up at him and spoke through his tears. "She was a *person.*"

The tough, old farmer assessed him again. "There's more to you than meets the eye, boy."

Vaughn figured he might as well tell him. He wasn't sure why. There really was no good reason. But judging from the farmer's last statement, he felt the truth was his only ally. "You're right, and you're wrong." The farmer waited with raised eyebrows. "There's more to me than meets the eye, *and I do have it in me.*" Vaughn's expression turned cold as he stood up. "Sorry Spot, I don't mean to insult you, but *I killed the only son-of-a-bitch that I know that could have done that to Tracy. I killed him that night..."* Vaughn's voice trailed off, "... so it couldn't have been *him*."

The farmer crossed his arms over his chest nodding. "Like I meant before, there *is* more to you than meets the eye. But I wasn't talking about something like that. I was talking about an excellent character! Before we leave, I have a few more things to teach you! And, a little gift that will come in handy."

Vaughn's eyes watered. He couldn't believe it. *Is what he's acting like real?*

"Come on back in and wash out your mouth from throwing up. You need to eat again and be a *man*. You have a lot to face if you want to live. People like you are *supposed* to live!"

People like me! "Thank you, Sir."

After Vaughn washed up, he sat down at the table and the farmer made him breakfast again. Vaughn's mind began working. "But then why appoint a special agent?"

"Probably just talk to make people feel safe. We'll need to load up some cans with gasoline. I don't want to stop while going or coming back."

"Sir, ahh, I'm headed West. I can't go..."

"Hmm, you're real intent on that direction, aren't you? You shouldn't have told me. Tell no one. When you leave from your next place, first go in a direction other than west, and not opposite to where you want to go. Once they figure out you went another way than you really are going, they'll figure you went in the opposite direction to fool them."

"But if I never go west, won't they figure it out?"

"Good point. You'll have to use your best judgment on that."

"But if no one is chasing me…"

The farmer scrutinized him. "I saw the look in your eye. *You* believe there is."

Vaughn nodded. "Yes. It's just a feeling… a *sick* feeling. But I believe he won't stop."

"Why?"

"Because there's only one other person who would have killed Tracy, and only this guy who would set me up, and he's the only one able to have a special agent appointed. If he wasn't my age, I'm sure he'd come for me, himself."

The steely farmer raised an eyebrow. "That's some pretty tough stuff, young man. What's this boy's name?"

Vaughn's head shook. "The less you know, the better."

The farmer gave him a deep look of appreciation and appraisal. "You're thinking of me when your own neck is in the noose. Let's get everything together. I want to get you safely out of here and on your way."

༄

The next day the door burst open to the old man sitting at his eating table for breakfast. Glen figured this was the best time to visit.

"Well, well, well… *another* old man. Don't tell me. You don't know what I'm talking about, either. Tell me, do you have any *dogs*?"

SACRIFICIAL WOOD

The old man's tone was steady and calculating. "Who might you be, to be so rude as to start asking a passel full of questions before you even introduce yourself?"

"Special Agent Glen, see my certification here?" He shoved it in the old man's face and waved it around. "Now, *old man*, I already know what direction that murdering Vaughn is going. After I thought for a second, I realized he would head south to find the girl I heard about."

The man put a fork full of scrambled eggs in his mouth, methodically chewed and then swallowed. He washed it down with some coffee, took his time wiping his mouth with a napkin, then said, "West!" The farmer noted the surprised look on Glen's face. "Are you surprised I told you the truth?"

"Why would you tell me the truth?" Glen immediately realized he'd been outsmarted. *Damn, I didn't want him to know I knew.*

"So then, you already *knew* where he was heading." The farmer saw it in his eyes.

Damn. I'm not the one who should be questioned. "Listen, *old man*, I want to know how long it's been since you saw him. When and where…"

He slowly pushed his plate to his left, since Glen was at his right. His glaring green eyes had death written all through them, cutting Glen off in mid-sentence.

"You know, you're not only *not* impressive, but *stupid!* First of all, I'm also a member of the secret service! Not *your* junk, but back during the *Third* Border War. And once a member from *that* war, always a member. I wasn't much older than *you* when I joined. You know what they called us?"

Glen sneered. "No, *what?*

The farmer hated insolence from youth and raised his voice sharply in anger. "OLD DOGS. *KNOW WHY?*"

Glen puffed himself up against this *old man*, grabbing his shirt and leaning close. "*NO WHY?*"

"Because we were taught and saw so much in such a short period of time that we felt truly old. And we became mean and ornery just like old dogs get. I was taught one hundred and twelve ways to kill a man... with my *bare* hands, and if you don't take *your* hand off my *ironed* shirt, you will learn just one of them, *first* hand. *Don't let your age fool you.*"

Glen's stare flickered for just an instant. *His shirt is ironed. What stupid, lonely farmer cares to iron his shirt?* Eye to eye, Glen wasn't even sure why he backed down, but he let him go, and stepped back a few feet. "O.K., so I'll just come back with some more officers."

The man leaned forward. Fierce death danced in his fiery green eyes. It bordered on the maniacal. But he continued with the same paced, harsh tone, "Please do. Please do that. I would love to *spank* you in front of them. Then, since you caused me so much trouble, I'll take up the investigation *myself.* I don't think it would be hard for a man of my talents to prove YOU are the murderer. *You idiot.* Next time, check the other person's credentials before you go shoving your big, fat, ugly face around... GO AHEAD. *PLEASE MAKE*

SACRIFICIAL WOOD

A MOVE TOWARD ME. I'm licensed to kill, *any* time, *any* place, *forever!*"

Glen tried to challenge him a different way. "Well, I have nothing to lose now, because of what you said."

"No. You have time to lose. I don't want to be bothered with you. You go about your pitiful little life and let me finish mine in peace." The old man raised his hand and shuffled his fingers at the boy to leave.

Glen scoffed at him. "You don't have a very strong sense of justice then, do you? You're not much different than me."

That death glare came back in the old man. "Oh, much different. And, I have a *very* strong sense of justice. The true justice waiting on you is not supposed to be delivered by me. There's another who's right it is, and only *he* can measure it out to you in full."

Glen scoffed. "I don't believe in *God*, old man. We're all just dust."

"Yeah, well, you'll believe in the one He appoints to deliver it to you."

Glen scoffed even more, "HA, that runt?"

The farmer decided he was done with him. "You're boring me. Get out of my house. Get off my land, *NOW.* Or I'll save Vaughn the trouble."

Glen headed for the door and called back, "Don't sleep too soundly, OLD DOG."

"I told you. Please do, young fool, anytime, ANY TIME. Wake, sleep, makes no difference to me. You'll still be *dead.*"

DARRYL MARKOWITZ

Glen heard a swooshing sound, and felt something sting his ear, then heard something hitting the doorpost. "HA, what's the matter *young fool,* didn't you see the knife I had up my sleeve? Sorry about *just* the nick on your ear. I'm a little rusty!"

CHAPTER TWELVE
The Train to Salvation

"Like all things glowing, all things dark and magnificent come full-circle." GrrraGagag spoke it into the orb for no one to hear. He laughed because of his special gift. It made waiting more fun, knowing what he waited for.

The man Vaughn had been driven to was only a distant acquaintance of the former farmer, and wasn't inclined to do anything but business. After three days, Vaughn left on foot. He still wasn't convinced he was far enough away from home, and decided to put another hundred miles between him and his *former* hometown before trying to hitch a ride. So, after walking the whole day, Vaughn looked for a place to camp for the night.

"Well Spot. That last farmer wasn't very helpful, was he? But the one before him saved us at least a week of travel. So, a little walking won't be bad. I figure I've come about three hundred miles now. Only about a thousand seven-hundred left. Let's camp in those woods tonight. Looks like we're gonna get some snow."

DARRYL MARKOWITZ

Spot arfed and panted. Vaughn was beginning to detect different patterns to his arfing, barking, ruffing and panting. *I wonder.* Spot picked his head up closer to Vaughn as they walked along the country roadside. "Good Spot, good boy." Vaughn rubbed his head. More panting, panting of delight. "I'm happy to be with you, too."

They crossed over into the woods, made a fire from dried wood Spot helped gather, ate some canned goods Vaughn bought from the last farmer, set up camp, and went to sleep. Or rather, Vaughn *tried* to sleep.

Early in the morning, Vaughn stretched, shrugging off the terrible dreams. He wished he would dream of Stephanie with him and not someone else. He didn't understand why he kept dreaming of other girls. But being in the country had a goodness all its own, and he soaked it in like a dry sponge. After a bad dream, he would lay in his sleeping bag and take in all the country scents, and hear the country sounds. It eased him back to a peaceful sleep. He wished Stephanie would visit him in his dreams, maybe like the time she came to him in the hospital. He poked his head out of the tent flap with pleasant surprise.

"Oh my, Spot, look at *this!* Our whole tent is covered in snow! We'll have to dig our way out." Normally, one would think being snowed in was a problem, but Vaughn relished in overcoming whatever nature decided to throw his way.

Spot seemed to enjoy the upcoming challenge, too. There was extra exuberance in his panting. The more Vaughn observed him, the more he felt Spot had... a personality! *Or is it just me wanting... Oh, get a grip! I'm just lonely.*

SACRIFICIAL WOOD

"Here boy, have a piece of beef." Vaughn had made quick stops in little towns. He bought a whole cooked roast beef at one diner. He knew there would be no problem for him because of the age old rule. *Give no paying customer any reason not to return.* "You know, this snow kept us from getting too cold." Vaughn pushed his way out into the drift. A good two feet had fallen! "Spot, make sure I don't lose a tent peg. There are six, Spot, Siiiiix." Somehow, Vaughn really believed the dog understood and could count. He even imagined he heard six barks. After proudly, successfully breaking camp and trudging through the deep snow for a while, Vaughn made the only practical decision possible when he saw the sign.

"We'd better head for this little town down the road. I guess we've come far enough where, well, we'll always have to be careful, but I think we don't have to avoid people much anymore. I think we'd better rent a room and stay there a while." After two quick barks, Vaughn figured Spot agreed.

Trudging through the snow should have been tiring, yet, neither dog nor boy seemed to lose a step, even with a full pack and knapsack. They played together, talked together, and seemed to have a peculiar oneness together. Spot took a particular liking to running ahead and then crouching down into the snow where he couldn't be seen. When Vaughn got close, he would spring from his hiding place. Vaughn acted surprised each time, which seemed to thrill Spot and cause him to do it all over again. The surprise wasn't all an act. Spot varied the times he sprang. Some were before Vaughn reached him, some right upon him and others after he went by. The dog created suspense! Boy and his dog, or dog and his boy, depending on your perspective.

As they crested the steep hill, Vaughn could see the whole small town down in the valley. Apparently, the heavy snow never made it to the other side of the mountain. A lumber yard was at the close end with stacks of wood setting in organized piles. One main road dissected the little town in half and a rail for trains paralleled it but seemed to head west through some hills while at the other end of town the road veered. There was a small train of five cars parked at the far side which really wasn't that far.

When they reached the train, Vaughn leaned over Spot and tapped on a boxcar. "Here we are, Spot. Hey, look, it's a *train*."

When Spot arfed, Vaughn was sure Spot now knew what a train was. Vaughn crossed back to the road and as they walked parallel to the tracks, Vaughn saw many boxes piled at the train's side between the road and the train.

"Look at all those boxes. Hmmm, why are they all just piled up all over the place?"

A heavy set, balding man in overalls, and heavy, dark-brown sweater stood between stacks of them and the train. His remaining straight, black hair was flying in all directions, blown around by the wind.

Vaughn smiled as he met the man. "Excuse me, Sir. Cold morning, heh?"

The man squinted at him. "No need to tell me about it. I've been up before the sun." His thick, black eyebrows lifted to emphasize the point, as if to say, *This* boy *wouldn't know anything about rising so early.*

"Huh, I thought farmers were the only ones who did that?"

The man reappraised this *boy*, showing a bit of surprise. "That what you are, a farm boy?"

Vaughn squared his shoulders and Spot held his head up, squaring himself, too. "I'm a young man, Sir. I travel from farm to farm working."

The man squinted at him again. "Well, not many farms left in these parts for you to work. Most of 'em died off here cause too small, now. So the government took 'em over but it's not the same. All fancy, mechanized, run mostly by *prisoners*. I'd stay away from 'em, if I was you."

Vaughn acted knowledgeable. "Ahhh, so I've heard. Guess I'll have to find work around town."

The man leaned forward at hearing *that*, speaking distinctly as if Vaughn had a hearing problem. "There's plenty of it right *here*, if you're willing. What ya think I been doin' all mornin'?"

Vaughn played ignorant. He had seen the man working as he came down the hill. He shrugged his shoulders. "Sir?"

Half imploring, half accusing, he informed him. "All this cargo needs loadin', unloadin', loadin'…" His hands were waving in a continuous rolling motion, and with them, his eyebrows lifted, implying the offer.

"Sir, are you *really* allowed to offer me work?"

The man guffawed. "You think I'm *hired* to do this? This is *my* train! But I'm the only one to do it!"

Now Vaughn was truly surprised. "But… but where are your workers?"

That squint returned. "You're not from 'round here, are you *boy*?"

"I'm from a ways away. No rails there."

The man put his hands on his hips. "Ahh, I see. Well, in these parts there are a lot of folks descended from the Southerners come up from the Great Religious War. Didn't want to be ruled by religion. The government pays 'em because somewhere back in history the gov promised 'em somethin' but then tried cheat'n 'em out o' somethin'. To keep from all the riots, they been payin' ever since the Great War. They helped fight it, ya know. Hell, that's how the gov got 'em to come up from the South. They promised to pay 'em for bein' mistreated. Now, almost a hundred years later, we're still payin.'"

Vaughn honestly didn't know. That must have been this year's history lesson. "I didn't know."

The man straightened with a hint of incredulity. "Didn't you learn nothin' in that gov school? Before you graduate, you're supposed to know these things."

Vaughn blushed because of the man's tone. When he saw *that*, he squinted at Vaughn more intensely, so Vaughn looked down. "Hmmm, I guess I missed that lesson. But what does that have to do with no workers?"

The owner shook his head, twisting his mouth in disbelief. "Why work when the gov gives you money for nothin'?"

Vaughn still didn't understand. "To get more money?"

SACRIFICIAL WOOD

The frustrated man threw out his hands wide, leaning in toward Vaughn. "They feels like they're *owed* everything. They gets *insulted* if you offers 'em work! Even if you *double* the standard pay! 'What you think I am?' They say. 'You're not my *master*.' It's all crazy. Somethin' to do with the way the Southerners treated the nonbelievers, but we're *not them!* But the gov doesn't even allow us to speak agains' it. Then, ya goes inta tha bars an' they crap agains' me callin' me a rich man and a slaver, just because I got this damn train to run an' I got a little money to pay 'em."

The man kept getting redder with every word. "But I don't think I'll have this much longer, cause if I don' get these supplies picked up and delivered, the gov'll take my train and put the convicts to work. Ha, then they'll put me in jail for not workin', and I'll end up bein' a convict workin' to load my own train! Ha, I guess it don't make much dif if I complain or not. I don't like to complain! *Politics.*" He spat sideways and stretched out his thick arms in a helpless gesture at the boxes. His eyes waited for Vaughn's response.

"Sounds like yer doin' a fair job complainin' now."

He threw his hands down at Vaughn, "Ehh, just runnin' my mouth to a stranger. Hey, you don't look growed yet. You sure you're…"

Vaughn cut him off. "Sir, where are you headed?"

"Supposed to head all the way to the West Coast, where the Great City at. You knows, it's warm there? Not like here. The ocean keeps it that way."

Vaughn hid his delight. "Well, I guess one direction is as good as the next. How 'bout I work for you an' you pay me regular wages."

The wily man decided to test him. "You look like a *boy* to me."

Vaughn narrowed his eyes at the man, placed his hands on his hips and leaned forward. "Tell you what, *if I do a boy's work, pay me like a boy.* There's no work else for me. Besides, I *love* hard work."

At hearing *that*, the man seemed, for the moment, to forget the point of the conversation as he pointed and shook his big forefinger in Vaughn's face. "You know, that's another thing, I loves it too. And I'm never insulted that I have to do it. I'd rather work at half the money and earn my keep than take a hand out, even *if* my father was wronged by someone." The big finger dropped and he turned his back waving Vaughn to follow. "Here, let me show you what needs be done."

Vaughn's joy mixed with the humorous way that he perceived this man. There was somethin' down right funny about how the train owner expressed himself. His thick eyebrows kept bouncing up and down while the man vehemently expressed his views. He complained, but not to make you feel sorry for him, but to make a sensible point. He made himself seem like a victim, but accepted and took responsibility for the situation. Vaughn could only smile with fondness at the man's good nature, and accept his offer. He followed him, giving a one word answer. "Great."

SACRIFICIAL WOOD

After showing Vaughn what to do, he went back to his work as before, expecting the boy to do as he was shown. But Vaughn always thought for himself how to work efficiently and solve problems. To do that, he needed to take a bit of time. When the man looked up and saw him idle, he came over and raised those eyebrows in one huge question.

Vaughn answered them with his own question, "O.K. you need to have this loaded pretty quickly. How much is my first day's pay?"

Flummoxed, the man growled, "You haven't even done a stitch of work, yet, and you're already trying to haggle? I'll give you six dol. Why?"

Vaughn replied to him as if he were speaking to a lifelong friend. "Should be enough. Advance it to me. I'll be back at noon!"

This time those eyebrows twisted, moving in some inconceivable fashion. Vaughn had to force himself not to laugh.

"Boy, do I look like a fool?" he bellowed, and Spot gave answer with two arfs! Vaughn chose not to translate at this time.

"No. That's why you'll do it! I'll leave my dog here with you. Spot, stay with this man. I have business to tend to." Spot looked up at his master like he was being punished for telling the truth or at least Vaughn imagined so.

The man leveled his eyes into Vaughn's with seriousness now, "What you got in mind, boy?"

"Helpin' you and helpin' myself. We'll have all this loaded by night."

DARRYL MARKOWITZ

The big man straightened, eying him up and down. Vaughn was half the man's size.

"I'll give you the money jus' to see what on earth you're dreamin' of." He fished out a raggedy wallet from under his sweater, pulled out the money, and handed it to him.

"O.K." And Vaughn hurried off mumbling to himself, looking inside each car as he left. *It's no good lifting each box separately. I can't believe that's the way he does it. There's a lumber mill back up the road. They got loaders. They got dollies. But their business is slow, now. I'll rent them from them.*

When the man saw him come back an hour later, his mouth dropped open and his cigar butt fell to the ground. Vaughn was driving a front-end loader with two dollies stacked on its tines.

"*Boy*, where on Earth…"

Vaughn again said, with an, *I've known you all my life tone*, while waving his arm behind him, "Just up the road a ways. You got any empty crates you don't need?"

"Yeah, a slew taken' up the back car. Lef' over from those who unpack 'em an' don't want the crates. I can't leave 'em so I take 'em out an' dump 'em."

"Well, the lumber yard'll pay you a dol for each."

The man's mouth dropped open again, but the cigar had already fallen out. "You're kiddin'?"

Vaughn answered with silence.

"You're not… I got good twenty dol worth back there."

"Well, when I take this machine back, we'll load some of 'em onto it. You're a big man. You can load a dolly with some and come along. Then, we'll walk that dolly back and one more trip by both of us with the dollies should do it! The extra trips'll be worth it."

The man put his hands on his hips. He caught the jibe about him being a big man. "Where'd you learn all this, boy?"

"I told you, I'm a farm hand. This fork lift is nothin' to handle. The rest is just common sense 'bout how things work with machines an' people!"

"Well, I'll be a wet polecat. And I thought ya was dumb."

Fortunately, the boxes hadn't been stacked flat on the ground. Some were on pallets and others on top of a couple of boards. Vaughn smiled, and set to scooping up the first stack of boxes onto the forks. He hoisted them up to one of the cars, then climbed up and helped the man stack them onto the dollies, which they wheeled throughout the boxcar. Well before evening they had the whole train loaded. Vaughn thought to himself, *Machines* are *good for some things like lifting a lot.*

After they made the last trip to the lumber yard with the crates, the lumberman came up to them. "Twenty dol for twenty crates, like I said." The blond, middle-aged lumberman's powerful voice boomed.

The train owner took it and without looking, divided it, and promptly shoved one portion into Vaughn's hand. "*Here.*"

Vaughn's shock came with his question, or vice versa. "What's this?"

The owner squinted a serious expression. "Boy, I'm no *cheat.*"

Vaughn matched the man's intensity with an equal look of innocence. "You're no cheat. You don't owe me this. I made an investment in renting the machinery. He gave me back my six dol plus two because the crates are worth a lot more to him than the eight and the twenty, because the crates made of hard wood."

But the trainman was as matter of fact as any could be and wasn't hearing anything else. "Your business is *your* business, but me givin' you this is *my* business. I want you to have another six! Then you an' your dog come on up front car with me an' ride."

Vaughn shook his head, taking the money with a polite nod. He was further surprised that, indeed, the man had given him exactly ten plus exactly six. *How'd he do that? He never looked to count it out. Twenty-four dol in one day. I can't believe it.* The farmers paid him three per day, and he thought that was a lot. "Thank you, Sir."

Then the weeks began to roll on. Along the way, the train owner taught Vaughn about the towns, the countryside, and the different people. They stopped at every town along the rail and Vaughn repeated what he had done before. He made deals with the lumberman. The train owner didn't have to throw away any more crates. He even picked up some crates he had previously dumped. Having access to loaders when he needed them changed his whole demeanor. Sometimes the lumbermen, themselves, came out to help, and afterward, they sat around all swapping stories. The owner confessed he hadn't been able to do *that* in many years. Sitting around was unthinkable. Vaughn teased him about it, saying, "If it wasn't for me sitting around thinking that first day, you wouldn't be sitting around now!"

His fondness for Vaughn was evident. The train owner made more money in their next nine hundred miles than he had made in any of his previous round trips. Having a train to ride across country, and earning money, too, was more than Vaughn had imagined possible. *Things are finally working out. I can hardly believe this.* But there was something that kept playing on his mind. The trainman kept repeating an old saying to Vaughn. "Somewheres boy, there's this old saying taught to me. Well, I don't remember when, but it's real old, see? It goes somethin' like this, *'We receive good, and shall we not receive evil?'*" But when Vaughn asked him what it meant, all he would say was, "You'll see, boy. You're young, yet."

All along the way, Vaughn wished they could move even faster than they were. Some stops took days, not because their loading took a long time, but because the customers were used to the train owner spending days at their stop, and they didn't have everything ready. Those accepting delivery were also surprised at the speed at which their supplies were unloaded. Vaughn cautioned everyone along the way, that from now on, they needed to be more punctual, so that everyone could receive their goods in a more timely fashion. Looks of astonishment and respect were common in return. The train owner could only shake his head at the boy from being so deeply pleased with him.

Vaughn and Spot relished the sights of the countryside as it whisked by the train. Leafless tree covered hills, huge flat farm fields, and pine woods that stretched in every direction, all these were delightful, fascinating sights. It was all so beautiful. Through it all, winter wove its common thread of cold, white sleep, but Vaughn knew winter was actually an active time for trees. Their roots spread deeper underground in search of unfrozen water.

Every now and then, when Vaughn opened the window, Spot would stick his head out and his ears would get caught in the wind and flap like wings. Vaughn thought it was the funniest sight, but it was too cold to keep the window open for long.

They rode west for hundreds and hundreds of miles through snow covered countryside, stopping at each and every small town and city, until, two months later, the weather began to become strangely warmer, even though there was still about a month left to winter.

Unfortunately, when they were just getting close to reaching the Great City, the man grabbed his belly, started to moan and breathe heavy and sweat profusely. Vaughn had to drive the train himself, which he had learned from watching. Fortunately, the next town had a sizable hospital, and Vaughn helped the big man up to the emergency department. He was quite surprised how strong Vaughn was. After the doctors checked him out, Vaughn asked of his condition.

"Is he going to be all right, Doctor?"

He was a relatively young, tall, skinny man with big glasses and a square jaw, well shaved face, and blond hair.

"I don't know. It's too early to tell. I think it's just his gall bladder. Wrong food. But we have to do more tests."

"Can I see him?"

The doctor smiled a kindly large smile, putting his hand on Vaughn's back. "Sure. Go right in. Is he your father?"

Vaughn shook his head. "My boss."

The doctor seemed to find that interesting.

The trainman hadn't lost his zestful expression. "Damn boy, we were doin' so good. Almost all the way cross country an' *this* had to happen. See, it's like I told you." He shook his finger in Vaughn's face. "We receive good, and shall we not receive evil?"

Vaughn replied, "Well, I'm sticken' with you. A couple of days and we'll be on our way. We're way ahead of schedule now, anyway. I'll take care of the train and see to the loads here. Don't worry about it."

The man had grown used to Vaughn's comforting smile and couldn't help developing a strong affection for the boy. "Yeah, you're right. We've made good time. So, what ya goin' ta do in the meantime, after yer done with the train?"

"Work for the hospital pushing patients around!"

Those eyebrows went up this time in astonishment. "Damn boy. *You ever rest?*"

It was Vaughn's turn to be matter of fact. "Young men shouldn't rest. *They should work.* Take care of Spot for me in your room. I can't have him go 'round with me. I'll stop by from time to time to walk him."

"Well, I dun know…" he hesitated, thinking.

"I already got the Doc's O.K., as long as he doesn't bark and stays out of sight of the black-haired nurse. The Doc said she'd have his head if she found out he said it was O.K." Vaughn smiled his broad smile.

"Damn boy, you're somethin' else."

"Yeah, yeah." Vaughn walked off shrugging his arms as if to put the compliment behind him. He ran into the Doc when he left the room.

"So Doc, I'm gonna push patients while you fix my boss."

The doc chirped, patting him on the back. "Good for you."

"Hey, you got a great job, being a doctor."

But the doctor turned and complained! "GREAT? HA… I work seventeen hours a day. *I have no life*. I went to school half my life to work the other half away. Now I'm stuck. My wife left me because I'm never home. If it wasn't for the fact that doctors are needed so badly and that I do help people, I think I'd go push patients for just eight hours a day!"

"Gee, I didn't know." Vaughn was getting used to being surprised. It was getting more and more normal to hear or see something shocking than not.

The train wasn't expected so early, so Vaughn started working at the hospital, while everyone got their loads to bring to the station. In half a day, he had already pushed more patients to different parts of the hospital than he could remember.

All of a sudden, he felt himself being grabbed, pulled into an elevator and slammed against the back of the wall! Several other patient transporters piled in as well.

SACRIFICIAL WOOD

"*Hey, boy*, can you please tell me what you think you're doin'?" A tall transporter asked him while shoving him again.

Confused, Vaughn said, "Huh? I've been pushing patients all morning." Vaughn couldn't understand what was going on, but he knew he couldn't show weakness or fear. Anyway, the injustice angered him. He didn't believe in fear. "HEY, what you all grabbin' me like this for?"

The tall, skinny, brown-haired young man pinned Vaughn harder. "Because *boy*, look at us. Do you see us pushin' fifteen patients an hour?"

Vaughn bit back. "No, actually, I see you mostly standing around talking and flirting."

"Hey boy, *lose the attitude*."

Another made the patent accusation. "Hey, I bet he's a master's boy. That's what he is."

Vaughn answered the absurdity. "Now how could I be *that* when I'm working just like you for the man?"

"Those damned doctors, all rich, they got money to burn. Give us these stinkin' jobs then complain we don't get their patients to them fast enough."

And another chimed in with his well thought out position. "Hey, yeah, why don't they pay us more, then they…"

Vaughn's anger began to heat. "Then you would *still* do the same damned thing! It's your *attitude,* and if you, and any of the *rest* of you don't keep your hands off me, *you'll* be the patients. I'm not taking your *crap*." Darkness began forming in Vaughn's eyes. A powerful feeling radiated outward. He could see the man holding him begin to flinch, almost shiver.

DARRYL MARKOWITZ

"Well, well, listen to the little man."

All Vaughn could feel was righteous indignation and he felt strength well-up inside of him. If the man didn't soon let him go, Vaughn would fulfill his promise. "Look into my eyes and see how *little* I am," he dared them, and the rest backed off while the man let him go.

"Ha, O.K., O.K., we see. You're the man. Go and push patients. Go. You're not here but for a couple days anyway."

Vaughn's disgust sent him searching for someone sensible to talk to. "Hi, looks like you got a lot of patients to nurse."

Her blond hair was put into a big ponytail in back. Her young, tired, blue eyes shined. "Yeah, too many for us to care for properly, and the hours are too long, too. I'm always exhausted. I mean, the pay is good, and I love helping people, but what about *my* life? We don't make the money doctors make, but we work just as hard. You've seen all I've been doing today. Then we have to put up with them yelling at us, sometimes patients or relatives not being nice, *never* getting our patients on time. I should quit and just push patients for eight hours!"

Vaughn sighed long and deep. "Why don't you have two kinds of nurses, one to handle the advanced stuff and the other to handle less advanced stuff… but pay them less. But since the training is less, it would be easier to become a nurse, and more people would want to do it. This way your load is lightened, patient care improves, nerves are less strained, and there's fewer problems for doctors. Let the doctors take a small pay cut and hire an extra doctor so they work more normal hours?"

The pretty nurse turned and faced him square. Her blue eyes developed a sparkle. "We used to have that for the nurses years ago, and it worked pretty well. But they cut costs to improve the budget."

Vaughn looked dubious, but he knew he was just a boy and probably didn't have the wisdom of all those great minds who ran hospitals and things. "And it helped?"

"Only the first year on paper."

Vaughn raised his eyebrows. *What the heck, why not make the suggestion?* he thought. "I would fire all your transporters! Give them two weeks' notice. Hold interviews in the second week and lay out the guidelines. Make the new salary a dol higher but you'll not tolerate laziness. Appoint a quality control person over the transport. Give him a bonus if he keeps patients flowing on schedule. Give him a sum to award to those he's in charge of if they do their job well."

The nurse was truly intrigued. "That makes too much sense. I'll run it by our director. Thank you, young man. You know, you're quite handsome… and you blush! There are a number of nurses here…"

Vaughn cursed to himself. He needed to do something about his blushing all the time. "Ahh, I'm leaving in a couple days."

She truly looked disappointed, although she'd only known him a short time. Vaughn couldn't figure out her sudden fondness. She continued, "Oh, well, you could have a good job and life right here. There's plenty of work at the hospital. We could even train you on the job for a lot of different things. Get you a government certification, too!"

Vaughn noted that once again he was shocked. He wondered, *Am I just ignorant, or just running into a lot of very unusual people. Government certification!* And he had just been locked away in the State Farm for being a burden on society. He couldn't quite fathom how he had access to all this now. "Wow, I didn't know that. I'll think about it."

Then he thought about how nobody, whatever job they had, was happy with what they were doing except him! That made everything seem absurd. He was the only one that really legally wasn't allowed to work because he was too young! Work that was precious to all his future plans and hopes.

Why are people so sickeningly stupid and jealous? Don't they know everyone is better off if they all just work hard and do the right thing and help each other? He sighed again until his thoughts were interrupted. But sometimes, having our thoughts disturbed can be a good thing.

"Hey, young man, thanks for stacking up those boxes in the hall corner, it made picking them up much easier." One of the maintenance people called out as Vaughn came to the elevator.

Vaughn quickly responded. "Yeah, well, no sweat. I did it while I was waiting."

A nurse came up behind him and pinched the back of his neck. "Hey, cutie, thanks for putting the pillows under my patients' heads and pulling them up to the head of the bed. You saved me the trouble."

Vaughn turned and smiled. "Yeah, well, it only took a second between transporting patients."

"Excuse me, young man. I would like to thank you for the way you made my wife laugh. She wasn't feeling well, but you really brightened her spirits."

"Yeah, well, I just did it while I was pushing her back to her room."

All of a sudden, Vaughn became mystified. This seemed like more than coincidence. He just couldn't figure out exactly what it all meant.

As he headed up at the end of his day to go get Spot, he ran *again* into the transporters flirting with another woman.

"Hey, baby, you be *fine*. Don't you need a *real* man tonight?"

She giggled a stupid giggle.

Another young man edged in. "Ahh, don't listen to him. He wouldn't know what to do with a woman."

She giggled another *stupid* giggle.

As Vaughn watched this unfold, something irked him and the young men saw it. Must have been Vaughn's sneer.

"Hey *boy*, what you be in our business for? Go find your own woman… *if you can*." The man mocked with a threatening, puffed up tone. The other men laughed.

That was it. *I'm not being their patsy for them to try to prove their false manhood.* The darkness flared in Vaughn's eyes again, perhaps even more so than the situation deserved. But these people seemed to stir Vaughn's feelings on so many levels that he couldn't keep track. He rushed at the tall man, grabbed him by the shirt, lifted him up, slammed him against the wall beside the elevator, and pinned him there. The man's fear, along with the impact, took his breath away. But before he could react, Vaughn warned him.

"Go ahead, move a muscle. Even *piss* in your pants and *I'll snap you in half!*" The others froze. Vaughn didn't even know what he was doing, so he just decided to watch himself do it. But he was aware that he felt tremendous pain in his heart. And a faint acknowledgement, almost undetectable, *You want to kill him!*

"What. What you want?" came the fearful reply. The man could sense something otherworldly about Vaughn. He could feel the darkness, even if he couldn't see it.

Vaughn was feeling *too* much. Almost like being torn in different directions. But his words came from yet another place. "Tell me the answer to my questions, and I'll let you go!"

"Sure, sure."

"Being a *real* man, is it defined by how well you just *use* a woman, or by how well you truly care for her?" Dismay clearly showed on all the men that had now gathered around. The woman had a *stupid* look on her face. "I mean, is being a man defined by how well you can turn a woman into a *slut?*" He turned his head, glaring at the stupid-looking young woman whose face changed instantly at hearing his words.

Righteous anger boiled inside Vaughn, but definitely something else too, something out of place, yet somehow not out of place, as he pulled the man away from the wall and slammed him hard back against it, yelling at him. "I don't hear an answer." An image of himself and Tracy wrestling against the demon flashed in his mind, no, his heart. Then he felt Glen's presence within the man he had pinned against the wall. Though his mind didn't quite make the connection, his anger did. Fear and inability to answer Vaughn's question, or was it inability to answer that caused his fear, froze him in silence.

One of his friends tried to answer for him. "Hey, it's all that, my brotha."

Vaughn tightened his grip on the man he had pinned and turned his head toward the other young, stocky man. "First of all, when did we become *brothers?* That's not the way you treated me before. Second, you can't both truly care for a woman and turn her into a *slut*." He slammed the man again into the wall. "Explain what you mean!" he said in a biting voice.

Vaughn realized he was definitely losing control of himself. The urge to kill the man he held became quite apparent, even demanding. He didn't know where this was going and seemed powerless to take another course. More than that, a good part of him didn't want to. Maybe it was killing Gary that changed him. Maybe it was almost being beaten to death. Maybe it was seeing all these low-life men have all their women when Vaughn couldn't have the one woman he rightfully should have. Maybe it was revenge for Tracy, for Stephanie, against *every* scoundrel on Earth! Maybe it was all this, or perhaps none. *But I know I'm right in feeling what I'm feeling!*

Another man finally came to the rescue. "Hey. My br… Hey, you're right. It's not right to dog a woman. We just be playin'. That's all."

Vaughn turned to him, his anger growing even stronger, darker. All could see and feel it now, as the hall in front of the elevators seemed to hum with power. More people gathered to watch. A sense of something special came over the crowd. More and more these were becoming troubled, mysterious times. Vaughn raised the man off his feet again, still pinning him, and narrowed his eyes at the last man who spoke. "Tell me, is *playing* at turning a woman into a *slut* funny?"

The man sensed he had better be honest. *There's something wrong with this boy. I'd better go along.* He hung his head and confessed. "No man. You're right on. It's not funny. It's really not right at all. We just never thought about it like that, ya know. It's just the way we used to doin' things. Hey, we're in a hospital, remember?"

Finally, a distinction between past and present. *I'm in a hospital. I shouldn't be acting this way.* Vaughn dropped the man, and he fell to the floor, shaking. Glaring at the man who spoke, Vaughn said, "Never thought about it before, huh? Then I suggest you *start* thinking about the right way to act. It could save your life!" Vaughn shot the stupid woman a fierce glare, then walked over to the elevator and pushed the up button.

By then, several nurses, a doctor, patients, and assorted others had gathered to watch. When they saw it was over, two of the nurses began to clap. The doctor nodded his head. Other women grumbled he was crazy and shot the nurses dirty looks. They held their heads up anyway.

The transporters grouped together, having retrieved their fallen comrade. They seemed caught between wanting to rush Vaughn or letting him go. The rest of the onlookers seemed in suspended animation. The bell dinged and the up light lit. Vaughn gave a polite nod to the crowd and boarded the elevator to go get Spot for his walk. Once he was alone, he shook his head at himself, *Now what did that accomplish? What's happening to me? Oh God, what's happening?* Tears came into his eyes as he whispered remorsefully to himself, *I could have killed him!*

When Spot saw his master, he rushed up to him. Feeling his faithful dog's affection and rubbing his head seemed to banish the immediate past. And then there was peace while Vaughn walked his dog. Spot was overjoyed to see him and Vaughn found it irresistible. But although Vaughn loved his dog, after checking on the train, he was glad to finally drop him back off with the train owner and enter his own little hospital room for the night's sleep.

The end of the hospital day left Vaughn more than a little wondering. He often sensed evil attacking him, but when all those compliments came from nurses, patients, and the rest, one after another, it was the first time he sensed good actively approaching him from the outside as if part of some great decree. *Or, perhaps it's just the natural result of the way I did things.* And then there were his strange, angry actions, being overcome by some strong power. As he inspected it, he wondered whether he had let evil overcome him. But then he thought about the meaning of his actions and could find no fault at all in it. *And what about those who clapped after I did it? But how could it be good what I did?* It was all too much to study on now. All he could think about was going to sleep in the room provided him.

Oh, the end of the day… Mmm, feels so good just to be off my feet and lie down. I could make a life for Stephanie and me, right here. I hope she's alright. Why did she scream? Ehh, I think she can take care of herself. What's a faithwalker? As Vaughn began to fade into sleep he realized, *Some of those nurses are* really *cute.*

Vaughn sank into the kind of deep, oblivious sleep that comes after really hard work. But sometime in the night he felt something and woke up. "Huh?"

He heard a soft, alluring, feminine voice whisper to him. "Just lie still, I won't bite. I heard you were sleeping in this little room." She had her naked breasts pressed up against his side, and her bare leg thrown over his legs. Her right hand was on his chest, softly running between it and his stomach. Still groggy, the sensation intensified from his lack of alertness, as the body seems to wake before the mind.

Oh God, she feels so *good! No! What does it mean? Get up quick, before…* Somehow, he didn't know quite how, he rolled over the top of her and shot up out of bed, standing up.

Shocked, she couldn't understand because she knew he was ready for her. "Hey, I told you I won't bite. Don't you like women? I don't get out much with working so hard."

Vaughn shook his head when he realized just how fully she'd gotten to him. It hurt. Even though it was dark in the room, there was enough light filtering in through the cracks around the door to tell she was very pretty and naked. To sense her voluptuous femininity hungering after him made him ache even more. He could see her breasts quickly rise and fall with her breathing. She was… staring at him, then into his eyes.

"I'm sorry, it's just that…well… it has to mean something to me before I do that."

She looked at him quizzically. His eyes were accommodating to the darkness, and his vision became sharper, which wasn't necessarily a good thing.

"Mean something? Like what? It feels good. We all need that. That's what it means." She sat up and arched her back, baring her fullness to him as she breathed deeply. The room seemed to shimmer from her natural power. Her body screamed at him to embrace it. Her scent seemed like a drug that couldn't be inhaled enough.

"I know. But afterward, after we've *felt good*, what do we do with the person in the body, after the body has gotten its satisfaction?"

"After? I guess I'm always too tired to think of that. I guess if we really like each other, then we make each other happy."

"And if we don't, wouldn't it bother you that we…"

"I don't think so, because we weren't expecting anything."

"Well, I'm sorry. But I just don't know what to do with *my* person while I'm making love, no, having sex with someone I don't really know. Even if I did like you, and I do, it would be very uncomfortable to me, even if my body would like it. I'm more than just a body."

She couldn't believe what she was hearing, and from a *man*. A very handsome man. She felt something she never felt before, but she couldn't love someone *that* quickly, she told herself. But it really felt like love. In a full, deep feminine voice she responded. "You know, you're really very special. None of the doctors even act like you. You have real class. Maybe we could just lie together and hold each other…"

Vaughn knew he shouldn't even entertain that thought, so he quickly answered before he changed his mind. "No, I don't think so, because I'm not strong enough to resist such a warm, pretty, sweet woman like you." His smile took her breath away, because she could sense the decency and love in it. Not love per se for her, but love for love's sake. He was a truly good person, and that made her long for him even more. She slowly stood, and, silhouetted by the dim light entering from around the door, stretched, moaned, and slipped her dress back on.

As she eased from the room, she cooed her last response. "Oh my, you just make me want you all the more. O.K. It's just a shame to waste the night. Good night."

"Good night," Vaughn replied, and as soon as she left, he doubled over on his bed in agony. *Oh God, hot…HOT…gee. Stephanie, let me dream of* you *tonight, please.* Thankfully, he couldn't have stayed awake even if he wanted to. If the hard work he'd done hadn't exhausted him and drug him into deep sleep, he could see what just happened keeping him awake all night.

Unfortunately, though, this night continued as the nights of the past two months, with every girl in his dreams *but* Stephanie. They particularly tormented him this night because the nurse had stoked the fires. He could still smell her sweetness, feel her feminine presence beside him, and feel her feminine hand running over his body. All that combined with whichever woman entered his dreams. If it was possible to lose one's mind to desire in a dream, this was certainly the night.

☙

Another miserable night came to Stephanie. She couldn't remember how long it had been since she had normal sleep. For her, always the same dreams of either Gary or Ralph, or others, but *never* Vaughn. And part of her always relished in it, enough to suck her into a seeming vortex, while some other, lonely, desperate part of her watched from a helpless distance, feeling intensely more alienated. And every morning she rose up and drove it all away from her, remembering Arlupo's lessons. But even for the *faithwalker*, there was a breaking point.

She awoke again in her familiar night sweat, with the same sick feeling and the same taste of left over lust pounding within her. But this time, she knew she couldn't take another night of it. Something snapped inside of her. Anger bolted her upright and out of bed. That anger kept her from crying. She had to hold on just a little longer.

Damn it! I am sick *of all these dreams. Well,* damn *them to hell!*

She threw off her nightshirt and stormed into the shower. Although she wasn't quite aware when or how, her sense of newness had slipped away some time ago, and with that loss the joy of washing had also vanished. When she had finished her perfunctory shower, she went to her closet. She knew what she wanted, angrily sliding dress after dress to one side. *Where is it? Where…WHERE…* She yanked it off the hanger, instantly feeling the comfort of the blessing within it. It seemed like a long while since she'd worn it last. She hugged it tightly to herself, remembering. She realized that somehow she'd been drawn away from this beautiful feeling. *I know why. I know how. DAMN IT! I've been living right, I shouldn't feel…* Tears began to roll down her cheeks. *Why haven't my prayers worked?* She began to sob and shake uncontrollably, and that began to scare her. And that made her angrier. *I have to hold on.* She threw on her holy dress. Then she flung open her lodge door with a bang, and down the main road she marched. *Faithwalker. What good is it?*

"Miss Stephanie, I heard the door slam. Are you all right?" an elder lady queried, looking very concerned.

"Fine," Stephanie quipped, briskly walking in the chilly night air. *I can't stand all these feelings.*

The elderly lady's long, silver hair trailed behind her as she ran to catch her. "Where are you going?"

"To the Sacred Room!" she snapped, not wanting to be disturbed.

"But…"

She left her behind as she couldn't keep up. Stephanie's angry mumbles filled the still night air without her realizing it.

"Miss Stephanie, where are you off to in such a huff?" an elder man came out from a diagonal direction expressing concern.

SACRIFICIAL WOOD

Frustrated, she threw her arms out as she kept up her pace, "Wow, I didn't know so many people would be up in the middle of the night."

Hearing her tone, feeling her condition deeply worried him. "There have to be those that pray through the night. There is continuous prayer among our people. You know that."

"I don't know what I know!" she snapped, but after a pause, she retracted. "No. I know. I'm going to the Sacred Room." *Will they PLEASE leave me ALONE.* She made sure she didn't speak that thought aloud. She had to hold on. Tears once again rolled from her eyes but the darkness hid them.

"But then the whole town must…"

She cut him off, scolding him. "NO. This is *private*."

"But…"

Rather than have the man struggling beside her as she marched on, Stephanie stopped to face him. *I have no time for this. But I shouldn't have yelled at him. Oh God, what's wrong with me?* She took a deep breath, trying to control her emotions so she could speak. A lot of feeling poured out anyway. "Kind Sir, no one has the right to stand between another and the Light or the Tree of Life. Am I right?"

Her tone's desperation froze him. Her tears hurt him. "You speak truth." He bowed with a short bow of his head, not knowing how to deal with such frustration, such pain, such…

Stephanie's lip quivered. "Then please, let this be between me, God, and the Tree," she begged. It was the last sentence she knew she could speak without losing control. She had to get to the Tree of Life.

He spoke devotedly. "As you wish, my Lady." He bowed again, but more fully this time and with deep respect and love.

It captured Stephanie's attention that an elder should act and speak to her so. She couldn't help politely scoffing at herself being addressed so. "Ha, that sounds *royal*."

Hearing her self-deprecating tone, he picked his head up, smiling appreciatively. "Only true royalty could speak with such faith and strength as you just have!"

"You don't understand, this is just… private."

She left him there and entered the Sacred Lodge from an outside door. She closed the door behind her and locked it, then looked at all the other doors, and they immediately locked, as well! When she turned around, the sight of the Tree of Life undid her. *Oh Treeee…* She worried her legs wouldn't have the strength to carry her over. The next thing she knew, she fell down under the Tree as before, leaning on the brass bench, weeping. She let all her feelings loose.

"Oh Tree, I AM SICK. *I'm scared.* I'm losing myself. Help me. SICK FROM THE DREAMS I'M HAVING. I CAN'T GO ON LIKE THIS. NOT ONLY AM I EXHAUSTED ALL DAY, I FEEL…JUST *SICK*. FOR WEEKS NOW, *I CAN'T TAKE IT ANY MORE.*

"Oh, I'm sorry for yelling at you. Wait a minute, you're not a person. But, no… you're what makes *us* all real persons. I'm sorry, my mind is so foggy. You're much more than these eyes see."

She paused. She began to question and listen for answers. The answers came in silence, but she heard them.

⚜ SACRIFICIAL WOOD ⚜

"What can I do? What? Why does it trouble me so? Because these dreams are terrible. Why? Because they're the *death* from my past. Oh, if it was just the past then why worry about it? No, it's past death trying to *force* itself to be *present* within me. That's why I *hate* it so. OH TREE, I can't let this destroy me. But I'm only mortal. If this keeps up, my strength will eventually fail. It almost has. I'll be crushed, if from nothing more than lack of real sleep and rest, but also by having that *sickness* force its way back into me. Oh Tree, it's not the desire I want in me. I just want Vaughn. But *that* desire *is* a part of real life. Oh Tree, it's being used against me, just like it was in my past."

Stephanie shuddered at the thought. The mere thinking of her past lewdness almost made it feel real in her, as feelings from her dreams instantly invaded her. The line between her nightmares and reality seemed to blur. But when the Tree of Life asked her pointedly is it in her at this very moment, the fact that the Tree was asking it caused her to focus on reality.

"No, it's not in me, now. Yes, that is *why* I WANT THE DREAMS TO STOP. *Please help me.* I've prayed, but..."

Stephanie began to cry like a baby. She couldn't bring herself to ask why her prayers hadn't been answered. She felt forsaken, helpless, yet knew the Tree of Life would not do so. She wailed for some time, helpless to stop. The pain and humiliation of the nightmares drove her cries, breaking her heart, seeing the depravity in a depth she had never seen before, seeing her every passion, her every sensation to its finest detail and sacredness given to the meaningless, derisive black hole that was Gary and the others. Her failing strength drove her wailing even further, and became a strength of its own. The possibility of losing all the goodness she loved pushed her even deeper as that goodness felt all the pain of it.

But slowly, her sobs began to space out. Then only whimpers. After a while, that was it. She had given her all. She felt herself helplessly suspended in the unknown, unable to take any direction at all. The Tree of Life asked another silent why.

"*Why weep?*" She picked her head up. "Because the life, the goodness you have placed in me HATES that evil." She paused and thought for a moment. "Well…that means, of course, how stupid of me, you hate the evil. I'm sorry, I didn't have to yell. You hate it… How much? Well, because you understand more deeply, you hate it even more than I do. Oh, right, but it's happening to me, not you. That does make a difference. Right. So I do have a right to really *hate* it. Oh, thank you. I have a right to pray as I have. Well, I still don't think I should yell at you."

The Tree showered her with a refreshing coolness in acceptance of her being. "What should I do? What? Where does this evil come from? Hmm, I don't… wait a minute, evil can't understand good, but goodness can understand both good and evil for what they truly are. Oh Tree, help me understand, help me so I can know what to do. Show me from where this evil comes."

She was expecting to be shown some dark secret within herself, something she might yet still be guilty for, but… The Tree became a golden vision as before, as when Stephanie saw Vaughn through its golden light. That golden light lit up the room and shined through all the windows and the glass above. Now she saw a *demon* floating before something blue, and within the blue was a dead forest. The Tree of Life adjusted the focus as she concentrated. Fire burned inside Stephanie. She felt cheated.

"You little *bastard!* I *recognize* you. But… but, you look, somehow different from before. Hmm, bigger, even *uglier*, darker. Hmmm you're even uglier than your friend who tried to eat me. Hey, where is he? Hmmm, what are you doing now? What is that you're looking through? What is the *dead forest?* VAUGHN!"

The vision split in half showing both the demon and his actions and the tree that became Vaughn.

"Oh Vaughn, do it again to me." Vaughn bolted sitting up, his sleeping bag fell from around his shoulders and he was soaking wet.

"AAAAAAAhhhh, NO, I *hate* these dreams. Do it *again*? What *crap*. I never did it the first time. I miss you so much Stephanie." He grabbed his head, pulling his hair hard. He wanted the pain to ground him, to keep him from losing his mind. He wanted to run. *But where?* Vaguely knowing he was in the hospital, kept him from screaming in agony. He collapsed into his pillow to muffle his bitter cries, cries not only of furious desire, but excruciating loneliness, and an even deeper fear that he might lose himself, lose all the goodness he had fought so hard to be.

Tears instantly flooded Stephanie while raising her hand to her mouth. She remembered the first wretched dream she had and how it made her doubt him. Seeing him now, feeling his insides, she knew he was true. She knew his suffering. She called through the vision to him. "Oh Vaughn, I know you didn't. I know you're true." But she realized she couldn't communicate that way. He was in the demon's orb, not hers. She saw the demon's dark gray arm extending into the blue orb and reappearing over Vaughn's head. *So that's really what that is!* "DAMN! That *demon* is doing the same thing to you as he must be doing to me. Oh Tree, what can we do?"

The Tree of Life brightened with a soft glow around its edges that felt like velvet as it shined upon Stephanie. She felt as if she were floating on a cloud.

"Oohhhh Treeeeee, soooo sweeeeet, so gooooooooooood, so beautiful. I will. *I will.* Let me sleep here tonight under you and we shall put *an end to all this torment.* Yes, I will focus…"

She curled up under the Tree, and the Tree of Life wrapped her in its soft glow, warming her, comforting her, relaxing her, draining away all her stress and frustration. *Everything just works right.* Time seemed to disappear. She focused as sleep came fast for her. *Vaughn, Vaughn, Vaughn, Vaughn, Vau…*

"Yes, oh yes, yes my love, I am here, here with you."

"Stephanie? Oh, thank God it's you and not… ahhh, the others."

She took him in her arms and they laid down face to face on the warm green grass. Their eyes sparkled together. "Don't be ashamed. I know about the others in your dreams! It happened to me, too. Evil is attacking us my love. We have to fight it together. Tonight!"

Her words spoke to his deepest dreams for them both, to fight evil together. In this dreamworld, these feelings were more real, more powerful than they ever had been. "Oh Stephanie." He squeezed her in his strong arms so tightly that she moaned with terrible longing, the longing for his soul and his strength to be one with hers. All her pent up desire loosed. Reflexively, she pressed up as tightly as she could to him as her every fiber sought to be closer, seeking union.

She grabbed his head full of thick, curly hair in both hands, breathing her words out heavily, "Make love to me, Vaughn."

Oh God, more than anything I want to. I don't know if I have the strength to fight this like I just did with the nurse. This is Stephanie. But Vaughn fought back the consuming urge anyway, pulling his head back to look in her eyes. He could see she needed him, wanted him *now*. All of him. As he stared into her eyes each became a part of the other's feelings, and he knew her terrible desperation. She also knew his. She sensed his desire had been greatly provoked, and could tell some other woman must have somehow stirred him up. Her pain tortured him, her desire added even more to his own. Before he was overcome, he rushed to speak. "Stephanie? But, but, oh no, is this going to be another nightmare? I can't. I explained." But he couldn't seem to let her go from his tight embrace.

Stephanie forced herself to control her panting so she could tell him, make him understand. She ran her fingers through his hair, "Dear Vaughn. This is a dream. We're allowed to dream of each other. Vaughn, *my only love*, there is no sin in that. If anything, it's a blessing to our love because our dream will be our hope of the future."

Her words saturated him as he gasped with the possibility. "Oh Stephanie, can we *really*?"

She gave him coy smiling eyes. "Don't you dream of me, Vaughn?"

"Oh *yes*, I mean, in my waking moments, you're all I think about when it comes to women. Yes, I'll make love to you my darling bride to be.

They kissed, they caressed, they squeezed and most of all, they looked each other in the eye. Though they had never beheld each other's nakedness, and curiosity should have gotten the better of them, it was the eyes that captured their love and passion in this dream. They lovingly disrobed each other, felt their naked flesh against each other, but the meaning of the feeling became the dreams central experience, expanding within their hearts and minds, knowing one another. Their flesh became a conduit for unlimited expression of their hearts, and within that common expression they found themselves as one.

As soon as their passions were sated, Stephanie hurried to speak. "Vaughn, listen to me, when the evil presence comes to us, we must join our perceptions, our intuitions, our very concentration into one. All reality is connected. We follow the evil's connection back to its source!"

He laughed with unbounded joy. "We're already one! We've never been more so. How do we follow it back to its source?"

"Through feeling, Vaughn. We'll draw on each other's insight as one. We can feel each other."

"That we can. Then what?"

"I don't know! But Goodness knows. We must trust in the goodness God has placed in us, and His Goodness that supports us, to give *their* natural reaction and answer to the evil. It can't be our answer. We must not try to embellish it, nor diminish it. It must be exactly as it is and we must be one together with it."

"Oh sweet Stephanie, you are so much more beautiful than I remember. I love you so much. We're already one in wonderful goodness. I was so worried because you screamed."

"And I love you, dear Vaughn, but what caused me to scream so terribly, almost horribly killed me, it's coming after us both! There, THERE, do you feel it?"

As soon as he heard her describe how she almost died, a deep anger, a deep blackness fell over him, and the deeper he sensed her extra goodness, the angrier he got. And then another kind of blackness drifted in, a sickening darkness wafted through like a fog and touched them. The connection was made. Vaughn squinted his eyes, pressing his lips together with determination as he tingled from head to toes. Stephanie felt him, an instant deep blackness, blacker than the evil darkness, shrouding Vaughn. "YES my love. Let us join our hearts and minds into one to *fight* this evil as one. *Together*."

They clung tighter to each other than they ever had before, burying their heads into each other's necks and shoulders. Nothing was real to them except their common concentration.

Vaughn recognized that evil presence. It was the evil that was in his parents. It was the evil at the school. It was the evil at the State Farm. It was the evil of Gary. It was the evil that was even somewhere still hidden in him that he fought continuously. It was the evil that fought to destroy them both, and to keep them apart. Furious rage boiled inside him.

She felt it all in her heart. Her tears wet them both, knowing his rage, being thankful for it, feeling protection through it, she clung to him even tighter. Once again the *faithwalker* let herself completely go, to prove her love, yet again, yielding to the fullness of Love and Goodness. He felt her do so, never having felt such a depth before. He wanted to follow her to that depth, but feeling Love's utter preciousness inspired his rage to protect it, rather than follow it. He yielded to the will of his rage as Justice became his sole focus. Deep, dark blackness swirled in harmony with brilliant, golden, fiery light.

CHAPTER THIRTEEN
Knowledge

After three years, their eldest son returned, falling at their feet, weeping, "Forgive me, Father, Mother. I could not find her. I failed."

The King and Queen took each other's hands. Queen Yinauqua nodded to her husband to speak. "What evil have you done while you were away, my son?"

He picked his head up, looking into his father's eyes. "None Sir. I have kept our honor and taught many of the ways of the Tree of Life. Many have listened."

The Queen could not refrain a tear in her eye, "I am very proud of you. Far from failing, you have made the loss of your sister meaningful!"

Her words eased his pain, but he felt it wrong to feel reprieve, "I do not wish to be comforted."

The King spoke tenderly. "My son, do you then wish to make our loss meaningless and compound it by murdering yourself?"

"But isn't it wrong to feel comforted? She is still lost to us."

"It's more wrong to lose yourself for any reason. When we cannot take comfort in meaningful life, we suffer the greatest loss of all. Do you not think your sister is acting, even at this very moment, as you have while you were away?"

He began to tingle at his father's words. Tears ran down his cheeks as his heart suddenly seemed to touch upon his sister's spirit in common knowledge. He whispered to his parents. "It is so."

Master ScrabaGag aimlessly danced in front of his blue orb enjoying himself. He was now often seen happily bouncing through the ethereal halls, much to the irritation of the High Council. He made sure he bounced more whenever he went by them. "You need to learn how to be happy," he would tell them. They looked like they wanted to consume him on the spot, which made the experience all the more delightful. He simultaneously studied the orb vision, worked his arm about within it, and thought about his circumstances.

Everything's going so sweetly. My own orb. My own room. Even my own secret room. I know how to get in and out now. Nothing can be withheld from me. If not this night, then the next should finally push the girl over the edge. She's lasted a lot longer than I thought she would. I wonder what I'll be able to do with her after that. Master ScrabaGag had a special fondness for Stephanie. After all, if it wasn't for her, he wouldn't be SRABAGAG. *Hmm, odd how she's ended up in his dream. The orb watch must have faltered. It gave me no warning* at all. *Nevertheless, this is opportunity. Something new to take*

◈ SACRIFICIAL WOOD ◈

advantage of. Hmm, why isn't her image responding to my manipulation?

There are all kinds of things Master ScrabaGag wanted to have her do. Then, as it hit him, he realized the image wasn't an image at all! *It's the girl!*

"MY EYE…" ScrabaGag whirled away from the orb, but it was too late. Fire that was hidden by a deep blackness he'd never seen before suddenly burst upon him. Images of what he'd done to his former Master flashed in his bulbous mind. GrrraGagag leapt inside him for joy. ScrabaGag would have none of it, instantly scolding himself. "*Q*uiet, you *idiot*, do you want the High Council to hear you? Salve. GrrraGagag mentioned a black salve, oil, by this orb." He blindly felt around the orb's edges till he found the compartment. "Oh, here. My poorrrr, precious Eyeeee. Ahhh, feels betterrrrrr. If I had been *stupid* enough to give this to GrrraGagag... Something is wrong with the orb. It shouldn't have been able to do that. I'm sure there must be safeties to prevent such things. I don't remember reading of them, though. That girl really has some *zing* in her. Oh, she's so *tasty*. But not yet. How did she get into his dream? Oh well, I better lay off this procedure for a while until I figure out what went wrong. I can't afford to have my *Eye* hurt. My pooooooorrrrrrrrr Eyyyyyeeeeeeeee… feels better GrrraGagag. As always, you're too quick to underestimate me. *That's why I ate you.* Wow, she's becoming exceedingly tastier by the moment, *Isn't she Master GrrraGagag?* Perhaps, when I eat her, you'll be able to taste me tasting her? I'll have to be very careful, though, can't take her for granted."

A very black demon burst into his new ethereal room. It was his Sire, High Councilor Premion, who came rushing hopefully up to him. But as soon as he burst in, ScrabaGag had whirled away, using his ethereal power to instantly clean the black oil from his Great Eye.

"What was all that racket?" Premion asked, as he tried to get in front of ScrabaGag to inspect him more closely.

ScrabaGag finally turned to him with an innocent Eye, "Sir? Sire? High Councilor?" ScrabaGag bounced up and down a little. "Happy to have you visit!"

"The whole Council felt a terrible pain, an invasion, something *holy* invaded our realm. *And it came from your outpost.*"

ScrabaGag put on sincerity. "Oh, well, I've been briefing you on all my exploits, Sir High Councilor, Your Darkness. Surely one such as you knows all about it."

The High Councilor backed up a bit, sneering. *Does he think I would lower myself to read one letter of what* he *writes?* "What are you trying to pull, *Scraback?*" He liked calling him by his former *underling* name because he knew ScrabaGag hated it. He closed in, lowering his Great Eye over him, expecting to force the truth from him, disdaining himself for previously backing up.

ScrabaGag made his decision on the spot. *That's it. He's disrespected me for the last time. These old demons think they know everything. I will eat him for his arrogance.* "Oh, forgive me, High Councilor. I wanted it to be a surprise. That's why I didn't put that part in the report."

The High Councilor saw ScrabaGag's fatal mistake and pounced with glee, "YOU KNOW I CAN'T BE HELD

❖ SACRIFICIAL WOOD ❖

RESPONSIBLE IF YOU DON'T PUT IT *ALL* IN YOUR REPORT."

"Sir?" ScrabaGag questioned as if ignorant.

"The rules, you *ignorant idiot*. You might have had me if you knew the rules. *Show me what you hid from me or I'll eat you on this very spot and take your orb for myself. I'm making a collection!*" The greed in his Eye, the anticipation was unmistakable.

ScrabaGag tried to stop his shimmering to hide his expectations. He imagined how he felt when GrrraGagag had threatened him and he put on that appearance. "Yes Sir, oh yesssss SSSSSir, pleeeease, don't eat me. Here, look here at this treeeeeeeee, but Sir, BE CAREFUL ABOUT…" ScrabaGag got up real close to impress the point, but the High Councilor snapped his tail at him and sent ScrabaGag hurtling away before he could warn him. He couldn't stand ScrabaGag anywhere near him, and ScrabaGag knew it.

"YOU IDIOT. YOU TELL MEEEEE TO BE CAREFUL?" The High Councilor thought to himself, *Idiot, how did he ever eat my friend, GrrraGagag? Let me see… ahhh, oh, him, yes, I briefly remember reviewing his case. Insignificant, too young, too unremarkable to be important. Ahhh, a beginners trick, Scraback probably thought messing with his dreams was some advanced methodology. Idiot novice.* "How could *YOU* possibly have eaten GrrraGagag?"

ScrabaGag inched closer and closer, slowly irritating the High Councilor again. "Sir, when you try to invade his dream, pleeeease be careful, *or you'll hurt your eye like I did!*"

The High Councilor couldn't restrain himself. That buffoon was just too funny. He barreled out his laughter till his Great Eye teared. "How in the ethereal plane could you ever do *that*? You fool. OH DARKNESSS, let me show this fool." *There he is, hmmm, he's dreaming of a girl. Ha, let's twist it.*

A thick black fog engulfed them. "Oh God, Vaughn!"

"I feel it, too. Different. Oh GOD, So *VERY* EVIL." The evil presence they recognized right away, but what they also recognized was that *this* evil presence was intensely more evil than the previous, and much more powerful in force. Contrasted with the victory they thought they had just won, their letdown made them feel even more smothered, even inconsequential. What other strength could they possibly throw at this thing?

But it was Vaughn who tore free first, squeezing Stephanie resolutely. "I will *not* fail you*, no matter what."* Vaughn vowed it, as surely as any knight had ever vowed a sacred oath. After feeling how utterly precious she was, how goodness had become so very tenderly refined in Stephanie, his commitment had reached levels of power he never knew possible. With the memory of his recent failures all too fresh, there was no question now, that he would suffer anything to protect her, no matter what.

They both held each other with an intensity and focus of concentration they had never known, each one's feelings again becoming a part of the other. Her goodness. His goodness. Then, one goodness…feelings revolving around as every part of a circle leads to the next part. Her love, his justice, their common understanding and virtues, oneness. Love and justice doing the beautiful dance of Life together, and they now lived at its epicenter.

They quickly covered the familiar ground of their previous joining and then somehow exceeded it. He was aware that she was experiencing him and she was aware that he was experiencing her and this repeated infinitely until the boundaries distinguishing two separate individuals dissolved. Now their unity focused in singular, agreeable feeling and thought and a tremendous light shined in their center. A tremendous blackness shrouded the mystery.

"Hmm, what are they talking about?" the High Councilor asked, trying to figure out something strange inside the blue orb. The girl wasn't responding to his forceful manipulation. The High Councilor's tail kept rapping on the blue orb's glow, trying to jar loose the malfunction. "Confounded contraption! It's too old! I've been saying we should modernize!"

ScrabaGag eased up close again when he heard the Councilor's grumbling, but he was careful not to look into the orb, but rather in the reflection in the High Councilor's Eye. *Watch him. Watch,* he told himself. Then at just the right time, he reached out with his arm and *tugged* on the High Councilor. "MASTER, BE CAREFUL"

Totally repulsed, *enraged,* the High Councilor slashed ScrabaGag even harder with his tail, sending him flying again, but ScrabaGag bounced off the wall rejoicing.

"*IDIOT, NEVER TUG ON MY EYE LIKE THAT AGAIN.*"

ScrabaGag had grabbed the lower Eye lip and tugged hard. Harder than what he had done to his former Master. It made the High Councilor's Great Eye tear, and the High Councilor strained to regain his focus, as well as his dignity from the disgusting insult. *He touched my Eye. He* touched *my Eye. Oh Darkness, I'll have to wash it when I'm done. Let me hurry and get this over with.* "Let me see, where was I? Oh, yes, what were they talking about? If I can't get her image to respond, well, then let me change the woman in his dream. Maybe that'll work. He's too happy with her anyway. What? *What is this? Why isn't she changing?*"

"Through our prayers, my love," Stephanie whispered.

"Through our prayers, *together*," Vaughn made the oath and as one they prayed.

"Oh LIGHT, we give ourselves to Your will. We cannot bear up against such a great force of evil." Never had Vaughn felt so consumed by impending Justice. It was as if he lost his whole identity to it. Stephanie's love now moved her into Life and she gave her whole identity over to that virtue of Goodness, feeling its busting energy, its desire to grow outward in wonderful, eternal meaning. The power was so great, it was as if she could feel the oneness of *all* life on Earth. *These were the feelings I touched on at my shelter,* she realized. *The very beginning of my awareness.* When he became aware of her depths, Vaughn instantly joined in her rejoicing, and this time Justice drew power from the meaning of Life, that it shouldn't be violated, validating Justice's very essence. At the same time, Life also felt validated by Justice, knowing itself to be pure, which only

SACRIFICIAL WOOD

increased the joy. The fireball surrounding them was as a great burning sun, and the cloud that hid it, was as the great dark nebulae that hide the birth of many stars from prying eyes.

"Scraback, what is going on?"

The cloud drew close to emerging from the orb. ScrabaGag saw its reflection in his Master's Great Eye. He was instantly fascinated. *Last time it wasn't a cloud, just deep black light.* This time he actually was able to study the phenomena. But he knew what to expect. The cloud focused upon his Master's eye and ScrabaGag knew there was no escape. Suddenly, like a supernova, a ball of bright golden fire erupted from the cloud and streamed straight through the orb. Premion reflexively changed the orb image back into Vaughn's tree. But the fire only instantly intensified, striking his Eye dead center. *"MY EYE!"* he howled. He growled. He screamed in searing pain. He begged! *"THE OIL, THE OIL!"*

ScrabaGag smiled from one side of his Great Eye to the other, as he saw the reflection in the High Councilor's Eye light up so bright he had to even turn away from it. He was sure that the *glow* this time was even much stronger.

"What oil, Sir?" ScrabaGag said timidly as he inched closer, watching…watching…closely. This was a High Councilor, his sire.

"*Scraback*, YOU *IDIOT*, RIGHT BESIDE THE ORB"

But ScrabaGag had moved it away so when his Master's very long tail groped there… ScrabaGag began extending himself slowly, carefully upward, uncoiling. He still maintained his fearful tone, "What's the matter your darknessssssssssss?"

"NEVER *MIND*, JUST GIVE ME THAT BLACK OIL NEXT TO THE BLUE ORB...somewhere..."

ScrabaGag's tail had snuck in, grabbed the box of Sacred Black Oil and was now gleefully holding it ever just out of Premion's reach. "Here, Master, let me help you over to it," came his kind words.

"NO, *NO, STAY AWAY FROM ME.*"

ScrabaGag was now fully extended and towering over the High Councilor. He knew he was helpless. *Ha, that much glow might even sting the Father.*

"Why, Your Darkness, if I didn't know better, me being an IDIOT, I would SWEAR, that you were SCARED of me. Why would you be scared of meeeeee? Let me help you."

"*NO...NO...STAY AWAY...*"

And then, the most disgusting insult possible to a High Councilor, ScrabaGag let his Eye drool upon him. When he felt it, he tried to blindly float away, but ScrabaGag focused his ethereal power and froze him in place. To counter it, Premion needed his own Great Eye to work, or at least not to have a sizable *glow* stuck inside it. He was helpless. The reality of being in the helpless grip of the *Buffoon*, waiting to be eaten was more than he could bear. He began to blubber.

Should I play with him a while longer? No! The results are what's most important here.

Some lessons learned about the true nature of reality are hard for some, but delightful for others. The High Councilor's last thoughts were of the utter disgust and humiliation he felt at being sucked into this underling's Eye, that everything he was would belong to *him,* his offspring.

ScrabaGag instantly felt the tremendous surge of power. "OOOOHHHHH, YESSSSSSSSSSSSSSSSSS, *those two weren't the only ones having pleasure this night.* He's far more tasty than, GrrraGagag...OHHHHHH YESSSSSSSSSSSSSSSSSSSSSSSSSS, I FEEEEEL, POWERFUL. BLACK. YES. I AM NOW HIGH COUN-CILOR SCRABAGAG." He belched out a fowl tasting glow that fled into the blue orb and disappeared.

High Councilor ScrabaGag didn't know how long he rolled in midair. This meal was at least as sizable a difference as when he ate his first Master. When he finally was able to inspect himself, he was black! Black through and through. And even larger than before. He looked like a High Councilor. But what he learned astonished him. *Fascinating. He hadn't a clue as to GrrraGagag's plans. Not a single clue! How could he not know the Earth is already being transformed?* He searched his first master for the answer. *My darkness. You sly demon. If you were able to do that, how come you didn't suspect I did? HA. You thought I was too stupid. Let me see what other orb knowledge you have. How were you able to get to the High Councilors' orbs? Oh my, you spent time with all of them when you were an underling! My, my, you've been planning for a* very *long time. Thank you so much!* I'm grateful! *Remember what you told me about* that? *But how did you know way back then that this day would come? Prophecy? YOU? In a way, you're more valuable than the High Councilor I just ate. Wait. How come you didn't* know about me? I don't show up in your prophetic knowledge! Now why is that? Ha, you thought it was because I was too stupid. But then why is it really? Hmm…*

Once again ScrabaGag found himself before the High Council, *minus one*. He told them his name, but for some reason, they didn't believe him. Another round of questions barraged him.

"All right you… what's your name?"

"*HIGH COUNCILOR SCRABAGAG.*"

The other Councilor laughed. "Insult us one more time and we'll…"

ScrabaGag wasn't hearing any more sneering jeering at him. There was no more need to play the fool. "Then look at my blackness if you don't believe me, *or break the Father's rules if you dare!*"

"He's smart, High Councilor," the First said, enjoying the gibe.

"I hardly think so, High Councilor," said Second. Both had their inky black tails folded in their arms, but Second's tail tapped repeatedly in frustration. He didn't want *this* demon to be Third next to him.

"But he has the blackness," First countered, enjoying Second's frustration.

"*Where is the High Councilor?*" Second decided to cut to the point.

"I ate him." ScrabaGag folded his tail in *his* arm as the others.

"*YOU* ate him?" Second, derided.

SACRIFICIAL WOOD

"*I* ate him." ScrabaGag glared back, a reaction that surprised them both. He wasn't timid any more.

"He ate him." Said the First High Councilor convinced by his blackness.

"Why is everyone repeating it? Am I deaf?" Second, complained.

High Councilor ScrabaGag had enough of their derision. "I ATE HIM. NOW, BESTOW UPON ME MY RIGHT!"

"Right? Ha! What right? You're still an *underling*," First said. He didn't like the way this flunky demanded *rights!*

ScrabaGag squinted his very black Eye at him, "MY first job as an underling was to condense all the Father's *supreme* rules into a less cumbersome language. I know *all* the rules! Would you like me to quote them to you line by line, by numbered paragraph and numbered line?"

"What's he talking about?" Second, asked. "Numbered lines?"

First was astonished. "There are no numbers…" First began to say.

Interrupting him, ScrabaGag proclaimed, "There *are* NOW. *I* put them there, and the Father Himself *approved*. Now, bestow upon me the Sacred Oil of Black Knowledge, that I may know the Inner Secrets, or I *will* call for a hearing before the Father Himself."

Second couldn't stand it anymore, "We've had enough of your insolence. We will consume you *now*. Help me consume him, First. We shall split him evenly!"

※ DARRYL MARKOWITZ ※

A thunderous roar split the Ether followed by a blackness that made all others around seem only gray as they all shrieked in ethereal pain. Then a voice with the same quality threatened to consume each of their very essences. "You all serve my purpose. You will all follow *my* rules." And that was all the voice spoke. But it was all that was needed.

"YES FATHER, WE HEAR AND OBEY," First promised.

"YES, YES," Second quickly asserted.

"YES, YES," ScrabaGag agreed wholeheartedly. "I LIVE TO SERVE YOU, MY FATHER, WITH MY NEW BLACKNESS GIVEN TO ME BY YOUR GRACE *THROUGH THE NEW OIL OF BLACK KNOWLEDGE.*"

The first two High Councilors quickly disappeared and reappeared, each holding an ebony horn. They proclaimed together, "We pour the Sacred Black Oil of Black Knowledge upon you. We are three again, united into one Blackness by this Oil of the Blackest Knowledge."

The horns together poured the thick, rancid, black oil upon High Councilor ScrabaGag's bulbous head, and it promptly absorbed, spreading an even darker darkness throughout his form. A few seconds later, he felt its effects and promptly left the High Council ethereal chamber! He owed them nothing!

Oh my blackness, those idiots, complete idiots. It's all so clear to me now. But their arrogance has kept them from seeing it. Kept the meaning of these events from their black eyes… But I know it! They have no right to be High Councilors. How could they think that simply ignoring the glowing trees would discontinue their

SACRIFICIAL WOOD

part in reality? All reality is connected. Just because the people were isolated, they're still connected to things that are connected to things that… all reality connects. They should have been destroyed a long time ago. If it wasn't for them, that girl wouldn't have been able to put the glow in their eyes." He paused when he realized what he'd just thought. He howled in laughter.

"*Their own* stupidity *has given me their greatness. GrrraGagag was right, I think more than he even realized. But I think the Father does know what has been going on.* YES, that is why He has blessed me to prevail and become great. He wants me to straighten up this mess. And now, with all this extra blackness, all this wonderful knowledge I now have, I'll be able to rise to the… I'll be able to be the First, closest to the Father. Those Appendaho must be destroyed, and the girl and boy. Then I'll begin a review of all that these idiots have classified as non-essential, and I'll rid the Earth of all such as those two. Then, finally, our dream shall be realized, and we shall have peace. I can't wait to have my own offspring. Wait! I now have that right. Now that I'm so much more powerful, and I know about the girl's powers, I can eat her any time I want. His eye began to drool as he thought about the kind of offspring he could spawn using her.

CHAPTER FOURTEEN
Time Of The End

"Shall we mourn for Yana?" asked their eldest son.

"What is the purpose of mourning?" asked Queen Yinauqua.

He looked down at his shoes, knowing. He wanted to say, to send the dead away with good feeling. But he knew that was a lie. "To comfort the living."

"Then let us do so, my wise son. Gather the tribe and we shall tell stories this night of your beloved sister, our daughter." Yinauqua turned to her husband who nodded approval, already deeply thinking which story he would tell.

The elderly man and woman woke their leader, telling him about Stephanie. But he told them that was her businesses and that they would have to control their concern. "It's not our way to hamper another's freedom." But the night turned to day, and at noon, people began to worry. "What if the prophecy was true and the *faithwalker* died?" But another countered with, "Our people are still around. Besides, no one is sure whether that's really prophecy or just part of the legend."

SACRIFICIAL WOOD

No one in their known history had spent so much time alone with the Tree of Life. All the windows to the lodge were closed so no one could peak, and no one felt right about actually entering. One even thought of climbing the roof and peering down from the open area over the Tree of Life, but that was rejected by the rest as meddling.

"She's been in there all morning Father, and I'm told most of the night. She hasn't been doing well at all lately. Even her schoolwork has suffered. Tradition requires a caretaker to enter…" The graveness of her emotion conveyed so much more than her words. She had watched her most precious friend slowly slide into a grayness, a dullness, and no matter how hard Arlupo tried, she couldn't pull her out.

Arlupo's father looked and sounded tired. He had fallen asleep in his winged-back chair in his study and never made it to bed that night, and here, now, were all these people. He sighed what he felt was the deepest, most difficult sigh of his life because all these feelings and thoughts that even his daughter had, he'd been having them, too, including climbing up on the roof! But he was the Leader so he said what he knew was right, was real, no matter the pain. "Win or lose, the battle is hers alone to fight. If we interfere, she loses along with everyone else. She *must* be able to stand on her own. You were right all along, Arlupo. Prophecy and legend have come to the present and become one. We *cannot* hinder it by our traditions. Tradition was meant to serve, not to be master. When it becomes master, it's no longer true!"

The elder standing next to him nodded to them both. "He speaks truth."

"Yes, Father speaks truth. But why does prophecy end with Stephanie?"

"Because she may win or lose!"

Arlupo's painful look spread to her father and the elder. Her demeanor just changed noticeably. Her father thought she suddenly looked pale. For a moment, her eyes had gone distant. They thought they heard her whisper a denial under her breath. *No! Not now! She's not ready. Why now? I don't want it to be now. Oh Light! Not now. Please!* There was a pause, a heaviness, but Arlupo turned resolutely to the elder. "Explain to the others, our time has come."

The elder looked shocked. He knew the legendary meaning of *that* phrase, but not quite sure if he should follow her decree. Arlupo turned resolutely around and left, heading for the Sacred Lodge from the outside! For some reason, everyone felt compelled to follow her, even her father. Then a door to the Sacred Lodge swung open. Arlupo's heart jumped. Her eyes grew large as she examined Stephanie's disheveled appearance. But it was her face that she desperately searched.

Stephanie's hair was all a muss. Her beautiful royal dress had sacred dirt all over it. Her face looked oily and dirty. Yet, for all that, Arlupo also noted she had a definite spring to her step, and a pep to her voice that she hadn't seen for a long while. But most of all, though dirty, her face was full of light. Stephanie squinted at the brightness of the sunshine. "Oh, my. Wow, what time is it?"

SACRIFICIAL WOOD

"It's high-noon, my daughter." Her father spoke with a single eyebrow raised in question.

She smiled deeply, broadly. The warmth of it instantly cheered them all, relieved them that she was once again herself. She loved that look her father gave her. It asked the question, but all the time said it was up to her to offer what she wanted to tell. Stephanie became self-conscious of her appearance, and that she needed a *bath*. "Oh! I'm so sorry. I look a mess."

Her sister comforted her. "It's all right, Stephanie, we cannot come between you and the…"

"Tree of Life. I know, Arry. But I still feel sorry. In fact, I feel *very* sorry for how I've been acting lately."

Then, in spite of her outward appearance, her best friend noted just how relaxed and refreshed Stephanie really was. "You look well rested. I'm so glad to see this. I was beginning to really worry about you." It was an odd mix of emotions for Arlupo.

Stephanie peered into her face and frankly confessed. "I was at my limit. I had to do something or I wouldn't have made it. So I went to the Tree, and the Tree helped me to confront the demon."

Immediately, those who heard her words began to Ohoo and Ahhh.

Stephanie could not restrain her annoyance. "WHAT? What's all this Ahhhhing about?"

Her father put his arm around her shoulders, squeezed her, and kissed the side of her head as they walked back to her quarters. His frank words were meant to educate, as much as comfort. "You are a *faithwalker*. What you do is as natural to you as walking is. Remember, Stephanie, to always keep it so. *No matter how it seems to others.* The moment it seems otherwise, *you will fail.*"

Stephanie scrunched her eyebrows together. "I hadn't really thought about it like that."

He smiled that broad, accepting smile again with that glint in his eye that said that every day he saw her was brighter than the day before. It made her feel like she was three years old, and she loved it.

"Consider it like this, suppose one day you just knew you had to get from one place to another right away, and without thinking, you stepped out onto a lake and began to walk across the water to the other side, because that was the shortest distance. As you walk naturally in your faith, others begin to call out to you what a strange thing you're doing. Then you look at yourself."

Stephanie broke in with instant understanding, "Ahhhhh, ooooops, and sink. Because my regular mind takes over, or I absorbed the regular mind of the people to whom it's unnatural, and I believed their mind because, well, faithwalking is rare. But *rare* doesn't make it unnatural. That's the people's mistake. That's *why* faithwalking is so rare. Because it's rare, they think it's unnatural, and because they think it's unnatural, it's rare. Sort of like a self-fulfilling prophecy. But also, I think that to *faithwalk* requires me to be within the flow of greater meaning. When the people called out, they refocus my attention on my limited mind from which this power does not come. *Faithwalking* is not done alone by oneself, but as part of the greater whole. It's experiencing yourself fully as a conscious entity, and all else in relation to the underlying Consciousness from which things manifest. In this way, meaning connects to meaning and I simply walk with it! So, for instance, if I wanted to walk on water, I don't see water as water, but I see the meaning that makes water to be water. Then I simply ask that meaning to support me because I have a good reason for it to do so. While the physical properties of water are confined to the laws of physics, the meaning that makes it into water is not confined at all. So then my physical aspects, as well as the water's sorta meet somewhere in the middle as *conscious will* makes them to cooperate. Well, I never actually tried this. But I think that's the way it would work! Or, ahhh, at least *one* possible way it works… I think there's actually several! Now that I think about it! But I'm not sure, yet!"

When Stephanie finally stopped, she suddenly realized how carried away she'd gotten, and, surprisingly, how much she understood. But she also saw that her words were making her father's eyes dart around, and for some reason, she felt embarrassed.

"That sounds, ahhh, correct, dear daughter."

Stephanie questioned him. "Sounds? You're not sure?"

"I am *sure* it *sounds* correct. But remember, you're walking where I have not. But all reality, all truth is connected, and that's why we have the capacity to understand the things of truth that are even beyond our walk." He looked at her and his eyes watered. "Dear daughter, I have to tell you now what we haven't been able tell you, because you weren't ready. Our time is at an end!" He had finally come to accept Arlupo's word completely at face value. He had noticed her patiently, frustratingly, painfully waiting for someone to acknowledge her earlier request. The elder looked from him, to Arlupo and back again, still not wanting to accept it. He seemed frozen there.

Stephanie had just recovered her strength. She didn't want to hear yet another gut wrenching proclamation. The intensity of her reaction even surprised her, as if somehow she knew he spoke truly. "WHAT ARE YOU TALKING ABOUT? NOOO!"

But her sister, walking on her other side, calmly backed her father up. "Reality is what it is, Stephie."

Stephanie's fingers gripped Arlupo's arm as they walked. "Arry, *what are you talking about?*" It was the first time she felt anger toward Arlupo or any of them.

Arry helplessly turned her head toward her but protested. "I tried to tell you a little… before. All our prophecy stops with you and Vaughn!"

Stephanie came to an abrupt halt, shaking free from her father's arm. As they turned to face her, she threw her arms out and leaned forward. "WHAT ARE YOU TALKING ABOUT?"

Arlupo and her father looked at each other, and then back to Stephanie. "Whether you like it or not Sister, you really *are* a legend and a prophecy combined. Our prophecies, and the conclusion of our legends all end with your beginning!" It was stated so as a matter of fact. There could be no argument with it.

SACRIFICIAL WOOD

"I just don't understand. I think you're all getting carried away!"

Her father sighed and his words strained, something very uncommon for him, "Dear daughter, it means that we know of your coming, what you are supposed to be. But we have no legend, no prophecy that tells us any details of your life beyond that you are the legend to come, and our time is at an end."

There it was again, *no argument.* It was a fact of nature as certain as the sun setting every day. It was ridiculous to her. This was her *family,* her *real* family. In fact, she'd forgotten all about her biological father, Jean, and even Lana.

"NO! Just because…" Then she cut herself off when the full meaning of the message finally hit her. "There's no more mention of *your* people beyond…?" She couldn't complete the thought. True, she'd worried about how the Appendaho would survive *generations from now,* but all this had the feeling of… Stephanie's stare bore deeply into Arlupo, who had tears in her eyes.

"None dear Stephie… none." her voice trailed off.

The *faithwalker* walks in the meaning of the whole. When Stephanie perceived the whole with a hole in it where the Appendaho used to live…

"NO! *That does not mean…*"

Her father's unarguable honesty rang through his words as he interrupted her. "It means, dear daughter, that the future is in your hands to create between you and the Light's will."

Fire entered her eyes and Arlupo and her father saw it, and looked at each other. Stephanie's determination was clear. "Then I will *not* let your people end. NO!"

But her father's eyes brought the unquestionable truth back into her soul. "I don't think that *that* is within your power."

It stifled her, making her feel helpless. But this was no longer the helplessness of a three-year-old. It was as the helplessness of a new adult unable to meet the demands of reality. Tears fell off her face to the ground.

Arlupo wasn't doing any better, but told her beloved sister. "Please don't cry, Stephie."

"But I love you all, so much. And you're giving me the feeling that the end isn't even in ten years, or five…" She looked at their expressions to try to read the timing, but… "I couldn't bear…"

Her friend challenged her with a stern tone. "Would *failing* us after we're gone make it more *meaningful?*"

Stephanie had never heard Arlupo address her in that voice. Stephanie flushed under the accusation. She didn't understand. "WHAT?"

"If you don't accept the goodness you've been given the opportunity to live by, no matter how painful, then all that you love with us shall have been in *vain. Meaningless!*"

Vain, meaningless, those hated words stung the *faithwalker*. She could even feel the pain of it on her skin. *But what is she talking about? With life there are* always *possibilities. I'll find a way. They said they couldn't tell what I will do. I'll find a way to save them. Why should I wait 'til after they're gone? I'm *not going to fail them* now. *I'll begin studying the problem right away. But how can they simply just end?*

"But…" Stephanie fought the mountain crushing her.

"In this case, dear daughter, there are no buts."

His other daughter backed him up. "There are no buts, Stephie."

"But…"

But just then, an out of breath man came running up to their leader. "Sir, we have warning, there are many that approach us from the North, South, and East."

Stephanie's eyes widened, her mind not understanding what her heart knew, but it pounded with the meaning of it.

"My daughter, take Stephanie to the Sacred Cave we visited. She mustn't come out for any reason, or all is in vain."

Arlupo looked solemnly at her father. "I'll *chain* her down if I have to!"

But he gently scolded her. "No, my dear daughter. It just can't be so with our people. No matter how painful, you must *not* restrain her." Terrible realization at the enormity facing Stephanie became apparent to them. She was about to lose almost *everything* around her that she held dear.

Stephanie spoke what Arlupo also thought. "Oh my God. It's just like our bond, except that now…" She couldn't finish the thought with spoken words. Her mind still hadn't formed them yet. Rather, it refused to form them. It was starting to go blank. A final rebellion against the inevitable.

"No matter how painful, the bond was your choice, dear daughter. It was *true* love. Love for God, love for yourself, love for us all because you wanted only *pure* goodness. We are honored. We have fulfilled our purpose. We are needed no more! In a few years we would have ceased to exist anyway. But *you* are free."

Stephanie saw an opening and grabbed for it. "But, you were sending your young…"

"I've learned enough of this world to know that it wouldn't have worked! The world, I think, is too tricky for us to live in. But *you* fought through the evil, the confusion, to come to the Light. But we aren't so prepared, I think, as you! I think it may be better for us this way. Even if we could withstand the world, surely our remaining children…"

But Stephanie quickly rejected her terrible, pounding insight of impending doom in favor of a safer ignorance, "WHAT WAY? *What are you talking about?*"

So Arry informed her. "The last prophecy. But remember, by your living, we all live inside of you. You are the beginning of prophecy, now."

Stephanie began to whine. "Oh God. I don't understand."

But Arlupo swallowed her own tears with determination and cut her off. "Please come with me, my sister. If you don't come now, everything will have been for *nothing*."

"But why must *I* hide?"

In response, Arry took Stephanie's cheeks in her hands as if holding the most precious and poured herself into her eyes. "Will you trust me, my sister? I am the last prophetess of our people."

Her father felt her words shower over him like a great presence. It was the presence that had always been with her, but was withheld from his full sight until now. "My daughter, I suspected!"

Stephanie's face was a large question. "Arry?"

Arlupo looked away, ashamed, because of her knowledge, and because she withheld her secret 'til now. "Yes, it's true." Then she peered into her beloved best friend's eyes with urging. "And I am telling you, if you do *not* come with me *now*, not only will *you* die, and the rest, but Lana and Jean too!"

Stephanie threw her hands to her face. She still couldn't believe the Appendaho were going to die, but… "Oh my God, I'd forgotten about them." Stephanie felt shame at how long it had been since she'd seen Lana, but with all that had been happening…

But Arlupo wasn't done. She knew she had to make *sure* Stephanie wouldn't fail, no matter what! "And Vaughn will suffer terribly. Without you, he will *not* be able to overcome the evil *he* must face."

Stephanie began moving toward the plum field where the path to the cave began, even before her mind had fully conceded. "I'm going. But I still don't understand. Prophetess?"

Arlupo spoke as they hurried. "Jean knows. I told her."

"You did?"

"Because she needed me to tell her, and now you needed me to tell you. It's not a gift to tell people of. Because then they look upon that person too much instead of the God who gives the prophecy. It's not for us to be questioned of the future. We only give what we are given to give. Prophetesses and prophets do not make the future."

"But what does it *mean* that you say I'm the beginning of prophecy?" *I need to understand this,* now!

The scenery was now rushing by like a blur, as the girls were half running into the plum orchard. The birds fluttered from their mid-day rest.

"When a tree grows from seed, that seed's life is the beginning of all that follows from it. A prophet is merely one who is informed of a small part of what the tree will grow into, and a tiny bit of what weather it will face, and the possibilities created by these interactions. All I know is that seed is *You,* and the kind of tree you may become. But it is *your choice* what you will be. That *choice* happens to be the center from which all other reality will revolve! Prophecy, therefore, begins again with *you!*"

Stephanie couldn't conceive of it. *My choice…the center… from which . . . did she say ALL?*

"Here, we're almost at the path to the cave. Just in time. I don't think we were seen. We must *not* be seen."

Was that fear in her voice? Stephanie remembered the barren rocky path and they scrambled up its hidden, winding, narrow length like mountain goats. *This is probably all just going to blow over.* Finally, they reached the cave, and Stephanie instantly became aware of a greater presence there.

"Oh, I remember the feeling of being in here. It feels sacred. Look, we can see down on the village from here. Let's watch."

Arlupo hesitated as they stood in the shadow of the cave's mouth. "Maybe we shouldn't."

Stephanie immediately protested. "Arry, how can we not watch? I still think you're being way too dramatic about all this."

"If you want us to watch, my sister, we will watch. But all things have consequences, even little things, and you must bear it. Please Stephie, bear even this for our love's sake?"

Stephanie couldn't figure out the intense look on Arlupo's face. It was telling her something she couldn't understand. At least that was what her mind was telling herself, as she frustratingly answered while turning away from Arlupo, "WHAT ARE YOU TALKING… OH my God, what are they doing down there?"

"We are the Special Harmony Forces Unit, certified by the government to bring back strong natural life to our country, as it should be. Men and women have specific roles they should fulfill, or our country cannot be strong. We have been informed that your people are sending many into our schools, and are spreading your corrupt ways to the people."

Stephanie gasped in recognition.

"OH MY GOD, THAT'S MY *FATHER*!"

Arlupo responded dryly. "I suppose we should have gone back and visited. He's the man through whom you entered this world, yes." And then she turned warmly to Stephanie, and at her last word, affectionately pushed her finger into Stephanie's chest. "The man where God took of some of the goodness that was in him, to make *you*."

Stephanie abruptly revolted. "GOODNESS!" Stephanie was appalled, because she couldn't see *any* goodness in him. She went back to watching below. Her natural father was shouting orders and pointing to a tall, black-haired, handsome young man that looked to be Appendaho. He wore a faded brown tunic with brown pants, which was the usual modest male Appendaho attire.

"Everyone must line up and be counted. You see him? Jargono is of your people. He's told us all about you and your *ways*. Don't try to hide from us, or…"

Arlupo's bitter reaction lashed out. "Jargono, how could you!" Her bitter sneer of surprise told Stephanie that this was clearly not seen by the prophetess.

"I don't recognize him, Arry."

"He was the first to be sent to school. We all looked up to him. But because he was the first, and older, we had little contact."

"But didn't he come back with reports?"

"At first, yes, but then less and less."

Stephanie began to see their foolish negligence. "But didn't you realize?"

Her sister shot her a glance and reminded her. "Stephie, we do *not* force our will upon others."

Stephanie also sneered at what was happening below. "I see by the woman hanging at his side that he's abandoned your people's ways."

Arlupo's heart pounded as she watched her father speak to the traitor.

"Jargono, what have you done?"

But Jargono's speech condescended to his leader. "Don't take that tone with me, *old man*. You're not *fit* to be my superior."

The Appendaho leader threw open his arms, his visage obviously pained and surprised. "When was I ever? Truth…"

Jargono spitefully cut him off. "Is only what YOU say it is. I don't believe your lies anymore. They were hard for me to accept from the beginning. You have everyone brainwashed. Well, *not me*. Where is your daughter?" It wasn't a question, but an order.

He answered calmly. "She's gone. You know she's a student."

"We've already rounded up all the others. She wasn't there."

The students were shoved forward and they rejoined their families.

"Oh God, what have you done?"

But Stephanie's father's impatience interrupted them, and Jargono didn't get to answer. "All right, I've heard enough family squabbling. As the commander of this operation, I ORDER you all to come back with me. Your men and women will be separated, and we'll *attempt* to re-educate you. You can no longer exist as a people, because your relations are a bad influence on each other and us."

A polite feminine voice gave the reply to his order. It was the Appendaho leader's wife. "I would like to speak to your commander. I think…"

"Who is this *woman* who speaks out of turn? You people are *ignorant*. You let your *women* lead you, run your affairs…"

Her husband narrowed his eyes at him, not at all liking his tone of address at his wife, "That *woman* would be my wife, and leader of our people *with me*. We, our men and women, are all *equal*, but not the *same*. They follow their true nature always, as do the men their own."

Stephanie's dad walked up to the short woman so that he towered over her, but she continued to hold her head up. "So you're the lying bitch who sent that snake of a daughter into my home to try to deceive me and steal my children. And where is Stephanie? I demand you bring her NOW! Where is that bowing snake of a daughter? In fact, *woman*, bow to me *now*."

She kept her calm, along with her dignity. "Our women do not bow to men, or anyone in that way."

"Well, your *daughter* does. Where are you hiding them? I demand you produce them now, or we'll…"

Stephanie's hand went to her mouth. Guilt began to suffocate her, and her heart began to pain in ways she never knew possible. "Oh God, it's because of *me!* I brought them here! If it wasn't for me…"

Arlupo spoke through clenched teeth. "No Stephanie. Jargono just used you as an occasion to stir up your father to do this. But even if you hadn't come, I am sure he would have found another way."

"Oh God, I've been nothing but a pawn in a much larger picture."

☙

When he woke from that dream that was more than a dream, he could barely contain himself from immediately heading toward the Great City on his own. He shook himself, hardly believing how good he felt. To go so quickly from nearly losing his mind in torment, to such a sense of relief and satisfaction, gave him pause to greatly wonder. *I'll have to remember this for the next time, when things get so miserable. Oh, I can't wait to hold her for real.*

But being still a hundred miles away, he knew the train was best. Besides, he wouldn't abandon the train owner, because not only did he give him his word to stay on 'til they reached the Great City, he'd also developed a deep fondness for him. Yet, Stephanie's presence lingered in his mind, his heart, and even his senses.

It was more than a dream. In between battling demons, all night they made tireless love. But the oneness of that love, even now, became completely a defining characteristic of his very essence. *A dream has completely changed my life. I never knew how wonderful... We beat that evil! Together! I knew we're supposed to be together. Even the farmer knew it. Our dream is like a sign that we're supposed to beat the evil invading the world... Together.* He quickly found a shower, washed up, brushed his teeth, got Spot, and took him for a walk. Vaughn noticed Spot was getting use to the train owner. They seemed to be developing an understanding. Vaughn chuckled at it.

After Spot's walk, they went straight for the train. Vaughn unloaded and loaded the entire cargos by himself, and was done by noon. He returned right away to the train owner's room just after lunch. Seeing the man's empty food tray, Vaughn's stomach gnawed and he realized he hadn't eaten anything, yet. *Ehhh, there's time for eating later.* Vaughn was hoping they could leave soon.

The man gleefully eyed Vaughn. "Well, young man, you ready to head back to the train? I might even be able to help you load her up."

Vaughn was overjoyed. "Already done! You bet I'm ready."

Those eyebrows rose in surprise. He studied Vaughn a moment. *There's somethin' distinctly different 'bout the boy this mornin'... but what?* "I heard you made quite a stir all over the hospital? You really are somethin'."

Vaughn waved his hands side to side to hush him, "Yeah, yeah."

There was only one more stop before the Great City. The man hung his head, telling Vaughn he'd made enough money, already, to keep going for a year. And with the deals being in place, he felt he would continue to prosper. But Vaughn wanted things to be equal between them. "Ehh, we were just fortunate to find the right things at the right time. But I can't thank you enough for all that you taught me. You didn't have to do that. I was afraid I'd wear you out with all my questions."

The train owner's lessons were invaluable. Since he traveled across the country, Vaughn was sure he knew the real truth of things. It was a lot different than what school taught him. It turned out that the government was in an elaborate dance to balance several different people's avarice. The deals were complicated, cumbersome, and fraught with conflict. Vaughn wondered and asked if that was why they tried to keep kids out of the regular work force, one less competitive group.

SACRIFICIAL WOOD

The big man raised an eyebrow at him. "Hadn't thought of that my boy, but it sounds like it could be true, that is if kids could really do adult work." Vaughn squinted at him with a wry smile, and he squinted back.

The train owner figured this Jargon thing might actually be a blessing in disguise for the government, because he owed nobody anything. He was somehow mysteriously powerful, but also popular with almost everyone. Putting him up at the top as a sort of figure head would change nothing for the government, except get them out of some major troubles. They wouldn't have to owe anyone anything anymore because supposedly they weren't in charge. They could even use force against those groups who pushed too hard, since the force would be coming from Jargon and not them. At least, that was the quiet gossip the owner heard.

It turned out there was one thing that unified the country even more than their growing fears of outsiders, other countries, and strangers in general… people blowing up from the inside out. One town, being sure it was from some new disease, refused to let the train stop. They were so scared they refused the money he offered to let him pass! It might spread the disease. He had to convince them to at least let him go through, since others depended upon it, but he had to rush through at top speed. That was fine by Vaughn. Sometimes people's fears can be put to good use.

Since Jargon promised to find the answer to the terror, it made him even more popular. *If I could somehow meet him, maybe we could work together to put an end to it.* But when

Vaughn questioned about Jargon, the owner leveled his eyes at him. "There's somethin' 'bout 'im, I don' know. He's *too smooth*. Everythin' he says, people love almost automatically." Vaughn wanted to know if that was a bad thing. "The truth don't often win popularity contests. It's far easier to tell people what they want to hear." Vaughn wondered if there was hope of ever having a true country. "Got me, boy, I'm just tryin' to survive this one!"

When they reached the Great City two days later, it would be grossly understated that Vaughn was sad to be departing his mentor. The train owner and the old farmer were quite different people, but he loved them both intensely. It made Vaughn wonder, *Is this how life is really meant to be? So many different great people in the world, and we can love them all so intensely? I mean, if the world were made up of all* real *people…* Vaughn's thoughts were interrupted when the man pointed directly ahead.

"Well, there's the Great city. I stop several times in her. But we'll say our goodbyes at this first one, before we really enter. After we unload, we'll be done." He paused, leaning back from the train's control panel. Without looking at Vaughn, he began to speak again. "I been thinkin'. How would you like to be my partner? We could ride back and forth 'cross this whole country together. I'll get you certified gov papers. Hell, I'd even think about gettin' you your own private box car to live in! This way, if you take a fancy to someone, you'll have…"

Vaughn just couldn't get used to the surprise. His heart opened at the man's generous offer. "You're kidding!"

SACRIFICIAL WOOD

The man's silence told him his seriousness. It actually meant a lot more than that. He couldn't look at Vaughn, because he didn't want to show just how great a fondness he had for him. It was something he hadn't felt for anyone in a very long time.

"You're not. I'm, wow, I'm just a crate mover, that's all."

The big man laughed a full belly laugh, and this time turned to Vaughn eye to eye. "You kept me from goin' under. *You* boy, are worth *five* of the regular men around."

"Well, I figured I'd see the Great City first. When will you be back?"

"Three months, I figure, now we got everything situated, and I hope to see you *right here*," and he slapped the train panel in front of him.

"Maybe I'll see you then."

The kindly man studied Vaughn. "O.K. None of my business, but I think there's more to you than you say." Then the man scrutinized him even more deeply, watching for any reaction.

Vaughn changed the subject. "Hey, I heard there was a strange people living in the Western Mountains, just east of the city. Know where they're at?"

"Hmm, I heard there were some ancient people. Always kept to themselves, though. We ship some of their goats back East every now and then, right from this very stop. I even met their leader. He'd be the one with the goats all the time! You believe that? I never would have suspected he was their leader, but one day an old fella came up and addressed him as, Sir, so I asked him. "Oh, I sort of run everything," he says. We looked each other in the eye, then. I don' know.

"What?"

"I get feelings about men when I shake their hands and look 'em in the eye. He just seemed to *know* life, that's all. I don't know how else to put it. I says to him, 'My train might not be mine too much longer.' He actually got all concerned and started asking all kind of questions, particular like. Then he says, 'Well, before you end up in jail, come settle with us! We have more than just goats. We have chickens, too!' I just rolled out laughing, and so did he.

"If you head back down the tracks away from the city, you'll see the hills to each side. They're to the northern side. They're supposed to be real hard to find, because the hills confuse you, 'cause there's so many different ways to wind through 'em. From there, I don' know. But I'd be careful asking around about them. People are strange in these parts, what with all the universities. The government is scared of new or different things getting hold of the young people, so they watch pretty close. Has the whole city on edge, even as big as it is. Also, the border isn't far from here, just south a ways, with all those guards. The military port on the other side of the Great City always has soldiers comin' and goin', too. It's an odd mix."

Vaughn tried to picture it, but he was too inexperienced to do so.

"Thank you, Sir. I won't forget your kindness or your offer."

SACRIFICIAL WOOD

Vaughn unloaded his last load, and the man gave him fifty extra dol! He knew better than to protest, so he just walked up to the big man, wrapped his arms around him, and hugged him like a father. To his surprise, the man hugged him back.

"Be well, Vaughn. Remember, if we receive good..."

"I know, shall we not also receive evil. I know it better than you might think, Sir."

"I don't doubt that for an instant. If you ever need anything, just ask. And if your dog ever sires pups, I want one!"

Spot danced around the man than jumped up on him and got his final head rub. Vaughn quickly glanced away. He thought he saw a tear in the big man's eye.

Back the way the train had come, he could see the mountains. According to the train owner, they were a good ten miles away. The land up 'til then was open and dry, so Vaughn decided he wouldn't camp till he reached cover.

"We're in for a long walk, Spot. Oh God, I've lost track of time. It's taken about two months to cross the country. But really, I wouldn't have traded it for anything. I think, for some reason, I needed to experience this, for myself, even somehow for Stephanie. Let's see. She left just before school started. We're nearing the end of winter. It's been at least half a year since I *really* held her in my arms. Hopefully, three months has been time enough for people to worry about other things than me. But I just still feel like, I don't know, I haven't heard the last of it."

Spot kept turning around, stopping, looking across the land, but when Vaughn turned, he saw nothing. Spot growled.

"What is it boy?"

He growled even louder and ruffed deeply. There were some parked cars along a distant roadside, but Vaughn couldn't make anything out.

"I don't see anything, just people on the road. Hush now, or you'll draw attention to us."

Spot hung his head low, but kept glancing around, making muffled sounds every so often. If it was possible to ascribe human feelings to a dog, one would say that Spot was passionate about Vaughn. He would do anything to protect his master, and that was clear. He whined.

Vaughn looked at his pitiful pet, rubbed his head and remembered the dear old farmer's advice. "Dog sense, that's what your old master said, dog sense that I don't have."

"Hey Spot." Vaughn pointed up the road. In the dimming evening light, a giant neon sign became visible, *U for the Night*. As they strolled, Vaughn suddenly found himself longing for a bath and a real bed.

U for the Night hotel. He had never heard of such a thing. *What if someone wanted to stay more than one night?* The man at the admitting counter eyed Vaughn suspiciously, until he plunked down the money. Then he charged him an extra fee for his dog, but Vaughn didn't care. He had earned himself hundreds of dol and knew that any time he wanted to make more, he could.

After eating average tasting chicken and potatoes in the small hotel diner, part of which he shared with Spot, they both wearily plodded up to their single room. The first thing Vaughn did was strip off his clothes, shower, and brush his

SACRIFICIAL WOOD

teeth. Then he headed for the bed. Spot laid down between the bed and the door.

"Oh sweet bed, and sweet sleep." But Spot started growling again.

"Shhhh, you'll wake everyone, get us thrown out."

He growled even louder.

"It's O.K., it's O.K." But Spot was unusually insistent. The hairs on his back bristled.

Vaughn had that sick feeling he had when he explained to the farmer why he thought he was being followed. Spot obviously sensed something, too. Vaughn's eyes darkened as he fell asleep. But it wasn't dreams of women that troubled him.

Just before sunrise, they were up. The bed wasn't as good a sleep as Vaughn anticipated. Something about how the old springs bunched up in all the wrong places, but by the time that's discovered, you're too tired to do any more than keep shifting around. The chilly morning air perked his awareness as he and Spot walked each other. Yes. Walked each other, for the dog had almost developed an air of being in charge of the boy.

After eating, Vaughn washed and brushed his teeth. *Maybe I should get Spot a doggy toothbrush. Do they make such things?* "Would you like a toothbrush Spot?" Spot calked his head oddly.

At the little store next to the hotel, Vaughn purchased some food. *Doggy toothbrush, I wonder.* Vaughn still couldn't get over how fantastic he felt at having his own, his very own earned money. Not just a few dol, but enough for some time. *I can be responsible now. No, I AM responsible now. YES! Oh Stephanie, I am responsible now.* Vaughn hearkened back to their big fight under the oak tree before everything turned bad. She'd desperately wanted him to make love to her. But he'd rightfully argued that to really love her, he had to be truly responsible for her first. He wouldn't dishonor her with anything less. *But now I am responsible. I can take care of both of us. The only problem left is, who in the world would marry just a couple of kids! Do we even need a stupid ceremony to be truly married? What about children? We're too young for that. But, we're not too young to make love. But...*

No canine toothbrush, but there was dog food. Spot recognized it, of course, because of the pictures of the dogs on the bags. Vaughn even thought Spot was particularly attracted to the poodle image.

After another three hours of walking, he found himself at the foot of the Western Hills that Stephanie had sent him to. However, she'd placed an image of the village in his mind, but not how to get there. After entering the wooded hills in early afternoon via the only road that went through, a fork split left off the main blacktopped road only a mile in. The main fork continued as the same broad blacktopped road, and disappeared around a mountain. The smaller fork was unmarked, and oddly, the road was made of stone. It too, disappeared around another mountain.

Vaughn took the stone road that wound around one hill, and then there were no more stones. Dirt roads spread out in several directions, weaving through low wooded hills.

Vaughn stopped, breathing slowly. *Which way?* There was a thickness, a richness in the cooler hill breezes. Excitement

SACRIFICIAL WOOD

grew. *So close now, but which way? I think it would be up to God whether and when we had children. Of course, there are ways to keep from having them. I* certainly *don't believe in abortion. Best to prevent pregnancy to start with. But is that even right?* Vaughn studied the diverging paths. *Which way?*

There comes a time in life, seemingly foisted upon us all, when a decision must be made, where even indecision is a choice. And we can't go back. Those who procrastinate have decided to stagnate, and they pay for that as well. Either way, our lives are irrevocably different from then on. Usually, these crossroads appear at the onset of true adulthood.

Spot walked up a path for a few steps. He had always either walked a step behind or beside Vaughn. Then he came back and sat in front of him, looking into his eyes, and then kept repeating this behavior until, finally, Vaughn decided to follow him. "Go ahead Spot, your first big assignment. I don't know which way to go. Find me the people that live here. Stephanie, my love, is with them."

Spot's ears perked, and he sat up straighter. He went and sniffed the ground again, just to make sure, then darted off. Several times he had to double back because his master wasn't keeping up. There were advantages to having four legs. But then, after a good while of weaving through the hills and ignoring many other paths, Spot stopped cold. The dog slowly came back, sitting down again in front of Vaughn, but this time he didn't move.

Vaughn stared at him. There seemed to be sadness in his doggy eyes. Something jerked Vaughn's heart to skip a beat.

Strangely, tears welled up with what his mind, yet, had no inkling to understand. He'd never experienced such a thing. Then a greater feeling swept over him. It was as if the very spirit of life itself had passed by him in sorrow. He could see it in Spot. Vaughn's eyes darkened. "Spot, lead on." Spot hesitated, and Vaughn just stared at him. The dog reluctantly got up and led the way.

Around the next hill the smell of death drifted into his nose as well. He looked up through the trees, and there were large black birds soaring up and down just over the next hill. He'd never seen buzzards except in movies for science class. But Spot knew full well what lay ahead. He stopped and sat on his haunches and whined and howled.

Vaughn studied him. He'd seen this animal behavior somewhere before, some movie, but he couldn't remember. It felt like Spot was mourning the dead. Vaughn sighed.

"C'mon, Spot, let's go see what's going on, probably some dead animal."

CHAPTER FIFTEEN
Another Vision

"Father, why must there be mortal life?" Yana's teary twelve-year old eyes begged for solace, as she held her dead cat who had been with her from the beginning.

He picked her up, while she still held the dead corpse, and set her on his knee. He stroked her hair. "This life, you have now, is my chance to know you. I cannot think of anything more precious."

"But Father, you didn't answer my question."

"Yes I did. For when I'm gone, or you're gone, it's this preciousness that we'll treasure... more than the loss."

"No Father. You still didn't answer my question."

Of all his children, because of her natural tenacity to dig deeper... "The answer to your question is found in understanding the meaning of the treasure of your life. And it is an answer we never tell another. You must find that for yourself, from the inside out."

She buried her head into his chest, stroking her cat's fur, remembering all their precious time together.

When Mafferan finished the memory, tears were in all eyes.

Up around the next hill, the path became a stone road that lead into a valley. In the distance stood a village square made out of stone with stone benches. Big black birds covered the ground, along with rats and other animals.

Spot bolted in anger, growling fiercely, madly rushing back and forth, until no animal or bird was near. Vaughn, still too far away to see clearly, stopped to take an undershirt out of his sack and tie it around his face. Every step closer brought his heart to pound more, yet, he kept rejecting what he saw. And now there seemed to be an impenetrable presence that withstood his advance, so he fell on his knees to the ground, still some thirty feet from the nearest corpse.

"Oh God, what has happened here?" he cried while shaking his head. Spot sat in front of a line of corpses, watching his master. When he saw he wasn't coming, he barked, almost scolding him to get up.

Something felt odd under Vaughn's feet as he drew near. Spent shell casings littered the ground. Vaughn's eyes darkened more, but grief already claimed most of his heart, competing with the anger that beckoned him. He'd never seen so many dead people before, least of all murdered in such a brutal, bloody fashion. And here there lay nearly one hundred. Walking closer to the bodies revealed that many of their eyes had been pecked out, some bellies torn open, and parts of their faces eaten away. But many were still fairly intact, though bloated from being long dead. Grabbing his chest in horrible realization, but before he could pass out, Vaughn frantically ran amongst the corpses.

❧ SACRIFICIAL WOOD ❧

Red hair, she has red hair. Smells, oh God. Black hair, black hair, more black hair. Not here. Oh God, where is she? Vaughn spun all the way around, knowing, without even comparing the image in his mind, that this *was* Stephanie's village. *We receive good, and shall we not receive evil?* It kept echoing in his mind but it never dawned on him *how much* evil there possibly could be . . . until now.

Once again, an odd mix of emotions, relief that Stephanie didn't lay dead, grief that all these people did. Turning to survey the greater scene, talking to Spot and himself, he realized that he *needed* to talk... so he just spoke out loud, "All the buildings are burned. She could be inside. If she is, it won't make any difference now. This just happened within a few days. How could they just *leave* them like this?"

Now grief, itself, began to seek answer. No, to *demand* understanding of the answer that could move beyond the unknown forces that produced such depravity. And that feeling refused to be cowed, as it called beyond any *human* feeling for compassion or any attempt to explain or even desire to understand how another human being could perpetrate such callous evil.

Only one answer cried to be received. Only one answer was sought. Some unnamable power began to inundate Vaughn's heart, spreading throughout his being. Never before had he felt such an intense darkening overcome him, but he couldn't reject it, just as he couldn't stop himself at the hospital when he grabbed that vulgar man. He wasn't sure he wanted to reject it, then. In fact, he was sure he wanted to accept it now.

Yet, another distant part of him did question if that was what he wanted to be, but there wasn't time to consider it now. Not now. Not here. Perhaps not ever. Standing amidst these corpses, Vaughn knew that from this point on, the very fabric of his person had forever altered, and whatever possession of boyhood he had, now surrendered its innocence, its tenderness. Spot began a mournful song of whines and howls. Somewhere in the distance, other animals joined in.

Yet, now that Vaughn's character had been newly determined, a certain freedom returned to his heart, again. Fighting back tears to no avail, he sobbed to Spot, "I know boy... I cry, too." Vaughn bowed his head, listening to the chorus of the animals' mourning reverberating through the hills. *It sounds sacred!* And he added his tears, also, to life's offering.

And then the tears moved on. As he wiped them from his face, and stood up straighter, anger spoke through him. "We have to bury these people."

Memories. Memories of how he'd been brutalized and lay for so long suspended in hell, near death, came before his eyes. Then, as he looked upon the corpses, the images Stephanie had given him of these beautiful living people flashed upon him. Memories of how his parents betrayed him, of how Stephanie was almost brutalized, these then jumped into his inner vision. He kept hearing a single word, *INJUSTICE.* "Even in their death, they just look special. At peace, really."

Men, women, and children, all dead together. The realization that neither he, nor Stephanie, nor these innocent people deserved the treatment they received in this world stuck in his throat. *This world is a very* sick, wretched *place*. Vaughn's eyes darkened more deeply. A man's calm voice from behind him startled him. Spot looked as surprised as his master as they whirled around together. As they did so, in the back of Vaughn's mind, he thought it odd that anyone could sneak up on Spot.

"Hello, young man." A tall, elderly man with gray hair stood in blue overalls. Spot sat quietly at Vaughn's side while Vaughn stumbled for words.

"Huh? Oh, hello, Sir. I didn't see any one here. What happened here?"

The man leveled his eyes deeply into Vaughn's, and as Vaughn looked into them, it was as if he got lost in some huge picture. The man's voice brought his attention back.

"Misunderstanding? Ignorance? *Evil?* Take your pick. Take them all."

That answer sent a wave through Vaughn and the darkness fought with his grief for even greater dominance. Vaughn focused on the strong, elderly man with the very square jaw, and piercing brown eyes. The man's tone was so casual. It disturbed Vaughn greatly, and he couldn't help but square off against the elderly man, speaking sharply.

"This is not just a *misunderstanding*. You don't do this to a peaceful people from *misunderstanding!* The soul would reject such action for just misunderstanding or ignorance. *Ignorance* cannot excuse this. This is beyond just evil, if there is such a word. This is treacherous, sadistic, insane evil. Are there any tools around?"

"I saw a pick and shovel in the field over there, but I wouldn't bother."

Vaughn saw him point past the other side of the square, but Vaughn was beside himself with anger, now. He didn't want to be disrespectful, but…"WHAT? As aged as you look, how can you say such a thing?"

The man kept his casual tone. "Don't get me wrong. I think the bodies should be buried. But the people who did this come and check to make sure no one disturbs the corpses. They have forbidden them to be buried. They even slaughtered all the farm animals and just left them to rot!"

Vaughn's eyes burned with blackness. "To *hell* with them!"

The man remained the same. "They're from the government."

The blackness seemed to enshroud Vaughn, vibrate from him. "Then *to hell* with this damned government. I will bury them myself. SPOT." Spot left off inspecting the corpses, immediately running up to his master. He'd never heard such an important tone. He panted, waiting for instruction, his ears raised, head pointing up.

"Spot, warn me if anyone comes close and then we'll hide." Vaughn motioned back toward the entryway to the valley. Spot ruffed once, and bolted back up the road out of sight. "You best be on your way, Sir. No sense in you being in danger." Vaughn turned abruptly away from the old man. He needed to find something to transport the bodies out to the field, but then something came over him, and he turned around again. He looked past the old man. *No*, he thought to himself. *I'm going to bury them on* this *side of the square from where I entered, so whoever comes here will be greeted first by their graves.*

The old man answered Vaughn's suggestion to leave. "No, I'll look for some tools for myself, too. Your dog'll warn us."

Vaughn turned away again from the man to walk among the corpses. As his eyes searched them, he threw open his arms as if asking why, at the same time wanting to comfort that which was out of his reach. Every peaceful face stabbed him in the heart, enflaming him more. Tears streamed down his face as he beheld the slaughtered children. He could see the little girl from his vision, like a ghost haunting him, calling to him, *save me, save me…* There was no controlling the power that had taken him over. Feeling as if he would burst he vowed, "*What kind of people murder innocent women and children? I swear to God, if it is in my power, I will AVENGE these people.*"

The man walked up beside him into the midst of the carnage and still spoke with that same controlled voice. "Young man, you're but a boy and you don't even know these people. Why would you say such a foolish thing?"

Vaughn whirled around on him with biting words, but he kept from yelling. He hated yelling. "Know them? Can't you *feel* them? Can't you *feel* their lives crying from the blood soaked ground? I don't understand you."

The man avoided Vaughn's dark glare and continued to speak calmly. "What do you mean?"

Vaughn's eyes widened in disbelief. "We're all human beings. We don't have to know each other personally to feel deeply for each other's lives. It's *sick* not to feel deeply. We may be different leaves, but we're all from the same tree, share the same sap, travel far enough back, and we all have the same root. Love is the same for me as for the stranger I never met before today. True love just is." He pointed at the corpses. "It was the same for them. Evil will always be evil, and good always be good, no matter the people. The differences in our languages and cultures are small in comparison to what we fundamentally share."

The old man seemed drawn into Vaughn's eyes, past the blackness, but he still maintained his aloofness. "Hmm, you're just a youth. How would you know such things?"

Fire burned deeply within Vaughn, and its bright light burst through the black fire in his eyes. "I know it from the inside out. When any human being truly knows what he is inside, he knows what good and evil is in everyone. Not the fine details, mind you, but you know enough to come to understand any of them."

The old man's eyebrow rose. "I know enough? Are you talking about me now?"

He caused Vaughn to calm and pause at the oddity of his question. *How odd that he uses the very same words I do.* Once, it seemed so long ago, Vaughn was sent to a psychologist who used those very words in just that way. From then on, Vaughn used them often when catching people saying 'you' instead of 'I.' Vaughn moved off and the old man followed beside him towards the tools.

"I'm talking about me, and anyone else who makes the search inside themselves."

The old man scoffed. "Isn't that arrogant? People live in their own little worlds."

And that sent Vaughn's temper to drive words from his mouth as light and blackness seemed to swirl together. Vaughn abruptly stopped, turning towards the man.

"What? To say that I've taken seriously my responsibility to know myself, and that it bore me understanding? You call *that* arrogance? Do you think people could have done such evil if they truly knew themselves? Those murderers were *arrogant*. One day they're going to want the same mercy they denied from these people! Then they'll realize their world wasn't so *different* after all." *Own little worlds, huh, what crap!*

Vaughn whirled away from the man and picked up a shovel and a pick. There was a wheelbarrow a little ways away. He put the tools in, along with an extra shovel for the man, and headed back to bury the bodies. The old man held his peace.

But all of a sudden more poured forth from Vaughn.

"And what *fool* would say that such a search to know oneself could *not* bear meaningful fruit? To say such a *stupid* thing would take away all hope of any real knowledge or happiness. If you first can't have real knowledge about yourself, about the life you use inside your very self, your person, then you have *nothing!* You're just a ball of mud waiting to rot. Actually, *worse* than mud. You become a self-destruction."

Vaughn pointed to the corpses he was again approaching. "But these people had meaning, *have* meaning. I can see it even from the expression of their corpses. ARROGANCE?

That's what people do. I've seen it all too much, and I'm *sick of it*. When people feel ashamed because they come in contact with someone who's found the goodness the people *should have* found, but they didn't search for, or care to search for, they feel weak, small, and pitiful. So to make up for their own short-comings, they call us names, to try to make themselves feel big. Well, I'll tell you, I'm *sick* of feeling sorry for those wretched people. To *hell* with them!" Once again the blackness closed into his eyes.

The man calmly observed. "You're very angry."

And that sent Vaughn into a rage as the power once again took him over. "How could I *NOT BE*? LOOK AROUND. LOOK WHAT DID THIS. IT'S A PEOPLE WHO HAVE COMPLETELY TURNED THEIR BACK ON ANY FORM OF TRUTH AND WILL FIGHT TO PROTECT THEIR VILE WAYS." Panting from his raging, he picked up the first corpse and placed it in the barrow. Somehow that calmed him, as if it was disrespectful to yell while handling them. "Only that kind of sickness could do this."

As Vaughn pushed the first corpse to where he planned to bury them, the old man continued to press him. "Will you fault the whole country?"

Once again the blackness spoke in its power through Vaughn, "Show me who opposes it. *Show me*. How long have these been lying here and not buried? When do a people stand up against evil? All reality is connected. Good at one end, and evil at the other. When you don't stand up for good, no matter what, you slip further toward evil. That's the way I see it."

SACRIFICIAL WOOD

The old man rubbed his chin. "Many have children of their own to protect and fear losing them if they protest."

Vaughn bristled at the statement. "Yeah? And who protects their conscience from THIS?" He pointed at the body he pushed out to the field. "The people who did *this* were once children of people who did not stand up against evil!"

"You must have had wonderful parents, then."

His statement paused Vaughn, again. Vaughn looked away, suddenly not so sure anymore. "It doesn't always work that way. But generally, the apple doesn't fall too far from the tree."

"Ahh, sounds like a very old, wise saying."

"Nah, just some common farmer knowledge. But good people have a choice. They can be driven underground and live like moles, if one can call that living, or they can stand upon two feet, hold their heads up and live true, no matter what. Underground, their children will learn to be moles, because that's all they'll know. Then they'll rebel against the so-called truth their mole parents claimed to be using to protect them. Evil is supposed to be driven underground. *Not truth, not goodness.*"

"Now that does sound like ancient wisdom."

"Nah, I don't know. It's from the last book in a series, *The Art of Fighting*. I sorta added a bit. The book doesn't really say which way is best, just how it is in each circumstance. I think the author wanted people to think for themselves as to what's best. It's rule nineteen, from *Advanced Future*: 'Moles never see the light of day. If you can take pleasure in their life, you may be able to survive. Yet, when they multiply, the gardener hunts them, so is the fight between good and evil, which can be the mole and which can be the gardener.'"

The old man leveled his gaze into Vaughn, seeming strangely pleased at Vaughn's words. "I must say, young man, I can't fight your wisdom. You're definitely a thinker. If you ran for government, I would…"

Vaughn threw up a hand to cut him off. "Yeah, yeah, I know, vouch for me. But the problem is much bigger than government. It's this whole damned country. Its culture has degraded to crap. They endorse these things, actively or passively, they're *guilty*." Upon the word, guilty, Vaughn's swing of the pick struck into the ground.

The old man took a shovel from the barrow and leaned on it, watching Vaughn. "Then what's your solution, young man?"

Vaughn replied while breaking up the surface ground of the first grave so he could shovel it out.

"All reality is connected. There are other countries. They must know of this, or I'll find a way to tell them!"

The man's eyebrows went up as if surprised. "And then what?"

Vaughn answered in a matter of fact tone. "Then we go to war! Yeah, that's right, *war*, and kick the crap out of this country. It doesn't even deserve to exist. *That's how you deal with a cultural disease*. All reality is connected. If the other countries don't take justice in hand, then they, too, become corrupt, just as the people here ignored evil in their midst and, therefore, sided with it."

SACRIFICIAL WOOD

It was clear the old man was truly astonished at the youth's thinking. "You would put the whole world to war just for a *moral question?*"

Vaughn buried the pick point into the ground and took a shovel from the barrow. As he turned back to the grave, he answered, pointing again to the dead body. "*This* isn't just a moral question. *This* is trampling on the basic essence that makes us even capable of *any* morality at all. Yes, I'd bring war for such atrocities, and I'd be justified in doing so, and *slaughtering* every complicit person I could find!"

Vaughn never knew himself to say, or even think such things. To say he was as much a spectator as the old man is greatly understated. At the same time, there was no doubt at all in his heart that he was right. The power he felt, he realized, must be coming from his heart. It wasn't the power of love, though, and he had a disturbing feeling about that. All his progress and strength came from his understanding and his connection to Life and Love. But what puzzled him even more, was why neither aspect of the Light was rejecting what he was saying. What he was saying was indeed severe. *I need to understand this other power in me... I think it can be a little tricky... scary.*

The old man continued the debate. "But this country is no threat to others. They're weak."

Vaughn threw up his hand again in disgust. Normally, he would have shown respect to an old man, but he kept provoking Vaughn. "*Please* spare me. NO THREAT? Tell me, if you live down river from me and I start dumping poison in that river, but I drink from above, does it matter that I've done it within my own borders? It's the same thing. Immorality doesn't stay confined any more than a contaminated river. Water circulates the whole world over. So do ways of life and death. You're a *fool* if you don't pay attention to people dumping poison up river in their own land. The problem is, we have too many cowardly, spineless, selfish people that would sacrifice their children's future just to avoid the sacrifice love requires of them in the present. And they expect their children to respect them for that? Do they think we're *idiots* just because we're *young?*" The darkness in Vaughn's eyes became so deep, it shined like a black jewel.

The old man tried to change direction. "So, *you're* just a child."

But Vaughn looked unwavering with all his heart and strength into the man's piercing, rich-brown eyes. "Close enough. I swear by God, I will seek to avenge these people!"

The old man straightened as he felt the intensity of his oath. "What if no country will heed?"

"Then I suppose it's time to ask God to end this world! It doesn't deserve to stand!"

The man attempted to scoff, again. "Who are *you* to judge?"

But Vaughn had realization pouring into him the whole time, and seemed to have received answer to the question even before it was asked. "I only make the prayer. God is the one who decides what to answer!"

SACRIFICIAL WOOD

The old man's eyes widened as he leaned forward on his shovel. "Hmm, I'm afraid that if *you* made that prayer, God might just answer it!"

Vaughn stared at the gray-haired old man not at all knowing what to make of him. *How can he be so unsympathetic and now be complimenting me so much? It doesn't make sense.* Vaughn answered him. "We'll see. There are many other countries to visit first." *I just have to figure out how to get there. Oh, where's my head gone? First things first, Vaughn, you're still at the bottom. You're already trying to climb to the very top.*

After all that, both set about burying in silence. With every dig, scrape, and pull, Vaughn could hear the words he'd spoken sink a little deeper. He buried those who'd laid close to each other in a common grave together, assuming they were family. It was obvious their last action in this world was to cling together. In all, there were only around thirty graves to dig.

As they finished shaping the last mound, the red sun lowered peacefully into the West. Earlier, during a break from burying, Vaughn had made a cross from some old boards and nails. Now, he took his axe and drove the cross into the ground at the front of the gravesite. The length of its shadow stretched off toward the entry into the valley. "Let this be a sign of my oath between us."

The softened sunlight upon the fresh graves seemed, in itself, to be a prayer of peace. Vaughn and the old man turned to watch the sunset. It shined straight down the main road to and from the square where their daily lives had all joined. Vaughn wondered what kind of life they had, as his tears flowed once more. Seeing the sun shining straight through the village and falling directly onto their resting place confirmed to him he'd chosen correctly. *This is where they were supposed to be buried.*

In Vaughn's experience of working with others, he found that one learns a lot about another person just by working with them. Even if no words are exchanged, just the way they approach their work, the way they handle the stress of it, plan their next move, silently communicates meaning. What Vaughn learned about this old man didn't at all make sense when compared to his speeches.

Vaughn couldn't help having a deep respect for him. Yet, he couldn't help disliking him. It didn't make sense.

Vaughn addressed him with mixed emotions. "That was the last one. You're the aged one. Do you have any words to say over their graves?"

The old man paused and seemed to choke. As he did so, Vaughn's stare tried in vain to penetrate him, to see what his true nature was.

"I'm afraid I'm speechless. Your youthful wisdom has made *me* feel young and ignorant. Please, go ahead."

Vaughn's sudden flush revealed his embarrassment, but he was deeply touched as well. Nodding respectfully, he turned away and put their tools in the wheelbarrow. Then, with his back turned to the old man, he rested his hands on the barrow in silent prayer. When Vaughn finally turned toward the graves, the red, half setting sun shined on his back, casting his shadow over the graveyard.

❖ SACRIFICIAL WOOD ❖

Vaughn raised both hands to heaven, praying, "Oh Lord of Light, BEHOLD THIS DAY THESE GRAVES. GRANT ME THE POWER TO AVENGE THIS EVIL." Vaughn then walked away in silence.

The old man seemed shocked and found himself following the boy. The young man kept surprising him by doing things he hadn't anticipated. He hadn't expected to chase after him either, and that he would be pursuing him more for himself than to help the boy!

"That's it young man?"

Vaughn answered him while walking toward the village. "What else could do them any greater honor? Anything less would be a dishonor. Let me now explore this place."

The old man didn't know what to say. He understood the truth of the saying, but he didn't want the conversation to end. So he found the best way to continue.

"Why?"

"To learn, to understand."

Vaughn walked past burned out buildings, burned orchards, and charred hillsides, swinging through each in a broad circle, as the old man walked silently beside him in the evening light, watching and listening closely. The birds that used to call out their evening songs of thanksgiving were all gone. When Vaughn reached the place where he began, he had also reached his conclusion.

"These people were peaceful shepherds, and orchard tenders. The bastards even burnt good fruit trees, but I can tell what they had here. They were peach, plum, cheery, and apples. Oh God, those orchards were tended, really tended. I don't even know how old they were."

Then he returned to the village and came upon the place where the Sacred Lodge had been. Stepping inside the broken down frame, his feet crunched upon inches of shattered glass. Feelings overwhelmed him as his eyes widened. "What was this room?"

The old man found his footing again. "What room? It's all burnt to the ground."

"Yes, but look at that huge brass urn. How beautiful the carvings."

Carvings of trees with various birds flying between them, and squirrels running among them, encircled the urn.

"What, young man? What is it?"

Vaughn had put his hand upon the brass urn, and kept it there, absorbing even more feeling from it. Then, he turned his head toward the old man and spoke from a hunch. "Put your hand on it."

"I'm sorry, but I don't want to. What do you feel?"

Vaughn again tried to penetrate the old man, but couldn't. Vaughn had never before met anyone whom he couldn't see to their insides. Even the old farmers he had worked for, he could see into them. Confused, Vaughn redirected his attention back to the urn and the feelings coursing from it. Still touching it, he spoke as if from a distance. "Holiness! What kind of tree was in you? Oh God, what has happened here?" Vaughn stared at the pile of ashes at its center.

SACRIFICIAL WOOD

The old man's eyes widened, and out of the corner of Vaughn's eye he saw him rubbing his chin, studying Vaughn intensely. When he stopped rubbing, he spoke. "I heard there was some kind of special cave up there." He pointed upward to a hillside.

Vaughn didn't want to stop running his hands over the brass carvings as he squatted in front of it. All the shapes seemed to curve at just the right points, have just the right thickness. Finally, he straightened up, looking to where the old man pointed, but the shadows were too dark as the sun was now completely set. He strained to see a cave, and considered how he might reach it.

Staring upward, he spoke. "Tomorrow, I'll go see it. I better set up camp for the night. You know, I could have lived here in peace, I think, with these people." As Vaughn pictured what kind of beautiful life he might have had here, his heart melted. He turned back towards the man to share his softer thoughts, but... "Sir….. Sir? Huh, he disappeared." Noticing Spot had returned, Vaughn directed him. "Come on Spot. Did you see where that strange man went?" Spot began his mournful song again. *Where could he have gone that quickly?* Vaughn shook his head.

There was a wild hill to the right of where they entered the valley, and because it was not tended, it was not burned down. Vaughn decided he wanted to camp amidst life, not death. Passing by many discarded torches in the village square, he assumed they were left by the murderers. Realization came that they had premeditated what they did, otherwise why bring so many torches! He couldn't get over it. *Why destroy this peaceful people? Why hate them so much as to plan such a terrible destruction?*

Shaking his head, he shifted his pack onto his back and his knapsack to the other shoulder. He begrudgingly picked up a couple of torches. *If I didn't need you, I wouldn't touch you at all.* But Vaughn was exhausted and expediency was best now. Lighting one so he could find his way to the green hill, he stuck the other between his sack strap and his back. He stopped for a moment of silence as he passed the burial site. The dancing torch light seemed like life playing over the fresh graves, and the sound of its burning like a prayer or mysterious conversation.

At the top of the green hill, he first made a fire pit and a fire then smothered the torch. From the campfire light, he set up his tent. Then he buried potatoes under the coals and slowly roasted spiced meat on a stick propped over the now low fire. The beautiful aroma had Spot drooling. As they waited upon the food, Vaughn slipped into meditation while staring at the glowing coals. There had been so many internal events that needed attention… that needed to be understood.

Flames suddenly exploded. They grew and grew. They divided. Vaughn gasped. The little brown-haired girl from his heart vision walked out from the midst of the flames. She knelt down, kissing his cheek, taking him by the hand, leading him into the fire. He felt part of himself run away, but at the same time, her heart was his to fully follow.

A village. Creatures. Half-human, half-demon. Other humans . . . worshiping their crude offspring. The monsters

SACRIFICIAL WOOD

howled in glee. Suddenly, the flames showed other villages the monsters invaded, the women were ravished, the men and boys slaughtered, and the little girls were taken captive.

Suddenly, a thousand, and thousands-of-thousands of little girls weeping. Vaughn could distinctly see them all, feel each of their fears, their hopelessness, and their cries, *"Save us....save us..."*

Suddenly, he was in a room from long, long ago. An ancient king sat on his throne. A holy man threw his staff down, and it became a serpent. Unholy men threw theirs down and they, too, became serpents. The holy serpent ate up the other serpents. The holy man took his serpent by the tail, and it became his staff once again.

Vaughn noticed the little girl was still holding his hand. When she led him back through the flames, he was surrounded by the thousands upon thousands of little girls, clutching at him, pressing upon him, every touch multiplying their pains within him. He felt he would die from their pain, from their fear.

When Spot couldn't stand the wait any longer, he began to nudge Vaughn for food. As Vaughn came to himself, his grief doubled him over with weeping. "No, no, no... too much, *too much...*" He kept repeating it, he didn't know for how long, except that he still seemed to be experiencing, in some impossible fashion, every little girl one by one, until Spot's licking him in the face brought him fully back to reality. *But I haven't even rescued the first little girl yet. Why was I shown all these others? Why was I shown any of it? What does it mean? Oh*

God, help me. Oh God, what do you want me to do? But there was no answer, and no comfort. Vaughn was sure of only one thing… his loneliness. Camping above the graves of the holy people he just buried only intensified the feeling.

The potatoes were perfectly soft, and the meat crisp on the outside, accentuating its flavor. Spot enjoyed the meal, but Vaughn had lost his taste for food, but he ate anyway, he had to. He crawled into his sleeping bag without even washing up. It was the deadest, numbest sleep he'd ever had.

CHAPTER SIXTEEN
Find the Truth

"Father, one of the girls from the other villages..." Yana began.

Yinauqua interrupted. "Are you supposed to play with outsiders?"

"My cat ran away. I had to find her."

"What did the other little girl say?" asked King Mafferan

"That there are many Gods. One for the Earth, one for the Sky..."

"Is the Sky more powerful than the Earth?" asked Queen Yinauqua.

"Well, the Earth often stops the sky from moving. I mean it stops the wind. So...no. But, sometimes the great wind or the water from the sky moves the Earth, so...the Earth isn't more powerful either.

"Which are you made out of?" asked the King.

"Well... I'm definitely made from the Earth...but... I breathe the air of the sky...so...I think both.

"Which is the most important part of you?" asked the Queen.

"Oh, that's easy for me." She laughed. "That I can think! Well…and feel."

The King and Queen took each other's hands and placed their other hands on their daughter's shoulders, speaking together, "Then it might be wise to worship the God whose thoughts and feelings are most pleasing to you."

After a moment, and with a smile directed into her parents' eyes, she said, "HA! I already do."

Just before sunrise, Vaughn hiked all the way over to a spring he saw yesterday coming down between two hillsides from the north. The spicy meat had made them both exceedingly thirsty. This spring was the kind that came from deep within the Earth. It proved to be safe and tasted sweet. Besides, there were ancient stones set up under a portion of its flow in such a way as to make it easy to collect water, which would only be done for a drinking station.

Vaughn had packed up and brought his stuff with him. He kept the dry, sweet cakes within reach for easy access. Of course these, too, he shared with Spot for breakfast when they reached the water. When Vaughn had bought them, he'd been looking forward to the delicacies, but he still hadn't regained his taste for enjoying food, and so only ate because of need. Spot finished his in one bite, and then proceeded to lick his master's fingers clean.

Vaughn stripped his clothes and bathed in a deepened stone area further down, and then brushed his teeth. Its well-kept bottom was free from silt, and he realized this was something the people had to have given continual maintenance.

Though cold, it was invigorating. Something about being in the water began to rejuvenate his spirit. He was glad to be clean from the smell of death, even if his latest vision still lingered all through him. *One thing at a time,* he told himself. *Focus on what must be done now. Stephanie is alive. She has to be. I can't imagine…*

He took the clothes he'd worn yesterday from a dirty clothing bag and washed them as well, then hung them on the branches. Then he sniffed in Spot's direction and wrinkled his nose.

"Spot. C'mere boy. That's it, that's it." When Spot got close enough to the edge of the pool, Vaughn grabbed him and pulled him in! There was nothing Spot could do, as Vaughn used the last of the bar of soap on him. Then Vaughn pushed him out of the cistern, with Spot immediately shaking the water from himself. Sulking, he stared at Vaughn for a moment, and then walked off a ways to lie down with a doggy sigh.

Vaughn reluctantly decided to rest that morning, feeling his body greatly in need. The sound of the spring soothed him, aiding in contemplation. Definitely time well spent. But in the back of his mind, he dreaded having any more visions. Powerful forces stirred inside him at deeper levels than he was able to understand. This worried Vaughn, because he knew a person is vulnerable to evil when they don't understand themselves.

What overcame me at the hospital? Could I have really killed him? What overcame me while talking to that strange man? They were similar feelings. Not Love, not Life. Then what? The feeling to do what's right! To right wrong. Without compassion, without pity? When do those feelings stop, and only Justice reigns? But isn't true Justice, Love and Life all One? Don't they have to be? If Love isn't Just, then it's not Love. And if Justice isn't for the sake of protecting Life and Love, then how is it Justice? Without one, the others can't be what they truly are. Administering Justice must be a form of Love. But why doesn't it feel so? Something felt off at the hospital. I'm just not sure about talking to the old man. I know I was completely right when fighting the demon with Stephanie, and with Tracy. Vaughn sighed. He wasn't used to not getting satisfactory answers. *It just means I have to keep searching. I know* the answers are there. *Maybe I'm just not prepared for them, yet.*

Around noon Vaughn and Spot regained their energy. Vaughn couldn't see a way up to the cave the old man mentioned, so he deduced it had to be reached from some circuitous route. If it was a 'special' cave, it was probably part of the same ancient construction as this spring, because caves were ancient dwelling places. That meant, whoever lived there had to come down to the spring for water. That meant, there had to be a route they took to the very place they now rested at. He reasoned, *If I could retrace their steps, I could find the cave. Hmmm, they built this spring formation here, not further up or down. Something about this area's proximity is important.*

◈ SACRIFICIAL WOOD ◈

Vaughn began to explore in widening circles from that area. He passed an outcropping of rocks that he knew was part of the southwestern spine of the mountains that had the cave. About an hour later, he returned to the spring for some fresh water, and to contemplate. *The way up to the cave would be hidden. The closest place the mountains descend is from that outcropping I just passed. It's got to be there, somewhere.* "Spot. Help me find the path."

Spot seemed to have gotten over his upset about the bath. They went back to the outcropping, and Vaughn kept walking around it but didn't see anything promising.

"Well Spot, I guess…" But Spot disappeared. So he yelled for him. "SPOT, SPOT." Spot reappeared, almost in front of his eyes, as if he came out of the very mountain itself. "Spot, where on Earth did you go, or, ahhh, come from?"

Spot disappeared again, right before his eyes, into the mountain. Vaughn stepped closer to where Spot was doing his magic act, and leaned down around a white boulder. An opening! The back wall was the same color as the boulder in front, making it impossible to discern the depth difference. Vaughn pushed his head and left shoulder into the wider, lower part of a vertical crack and Spot promptly took advantage, licking and slobbering on his face. "Agggggggh… Spot!" Vaughn pulled back quickly, banging his head with a yell on the curving boulder wall. Spot eased out, put his head down on his front paws, and raised his guilty eyes, but Vaughn squinted at him while rubbing his head. Somehow, Spot didn't look *that* guilty. "Hmmm, I guess this is pay back for the bath

I gave you?" he said, still rubbing his bumped head. Spot's eyes looked away with a true look of guilt. Vaughn shook his head and then squeezed through the curving crack, emerging onto an ancient path covered in decaying, loose rock, and dust. As he looked up the path, there was no question someone had trodden it recently.

"Spot. Stay!" Vaughn didn't want him running ahead and obliterating any trail signs. Thanking God for the old farmer sharing his tracking knowledge, he gazed ahead at the overall panorama of the trail and could tell where its pattern was distinctly disturbed. Focusing on a few of those areas, he noted their positional relationship to each other. He then moved towards them without taking his eyes away. He knew the closer he got, the less obvious they would become.

Trail signs in rock were the hardest to discern, but it wasn't the rock that interested him as much as the dust underneath the loose jagged shards. He knelt beside the first disturbance, and pushed aside the top stones. Nothing was in the dust underneath. He checked several other areas until he found where a foot had squeezed between a thinner rock layer and the dust below. It was a man's shoe. From that position, he eyed the path ahead, and tracked that particular set of footprints. After inspecting quite a few, he realized, whoever made that track was alone. His disturbances in the general rocky pattern interwove through at least two previous disturbances. He knew they were previous, because when they overlapped, his print covered the others. Also, his track edges were sharper, so there had to be a significant time difference. "Spot!" Spot came

SACRIFICIAL WOOD

running, and Vaughn motioned him to sniff the man's print and then to stay. But as Spot sniffed, he growled a low growl.

Vaughn looked at him and wondered. It was an angry growl of recognition.

Vaughn wasn't just trying to find the cave. He felt the story behind these prints important to understand. The trail was ancient and secret, otherwise it would've been regularly traveled. There was no sign the man returned this way. Further inspection eventually revealed two sets of women's tracks going, and only one coming back, but prior to the man's tracks.

Vaughn sat for a while on a dark gray boulder, watching the path, and Spot came up, sitting at his feet. He started growling when he saw little furry animals come out between some of the rocks, routing in between their spaces for fallen seeds. Birds came down and did the same. Vaughn nodded his head in understanding as he looked over the landscape. Spot put his head into his master's lap, and Vaughn began absently stroking it. "Spot. These little animals and birds would eventually erase any trail signs. I don't think the signs would last more than a week. Two women went up, but only one came down. The man followed, probably no more than a day later, and he never came down." Then Vaughn realized, or hoped, that one of the women's tracks had to be Stephanie's. *She wasn't slaughtered with the others.* Spot had never seen Stephanie, but he had sniffed everybody he buried. So Vaughn took him over to each set of woman's tracks. "Spot. *Sniff.*" One of the ones going up was new to Spot as he sniffed intently.

But when Spot sniffed the set that came back he immediately whined with mourning.

Vaughn's eyes teared as he stared at Spot, speaking softly. "Two women went up to a special, ancient cave. This native woman knew of it, and took Stephanie. Normally, people would go up together and return together. But why would the native girl leave Stephanie behind?" Tears rolled off his cheeks as a picture began to form of the happenings. "You only leave someone behind if you know of the danger. I bet she took Stephanie up there to protect her. They would have had some forewarning of such a large invasion. But why leave at all? Why not escape together?"

Vaughn hesitated, as the thought was hard to receive, but the truth crystallized anyway. "It must have been that her absence would cause trouble, so she returned to give her life to protect her friend." Vaughn buried his face in his hands and wept. Memories of all the dead women flashed in his mind, as he wondered which loving, brave soul gave her life for his beloved. He felt his oath of vengeance burn hotter. *Hatred! HATRED! Am I wrong to hate so?*

Spot stood up, leaning against his master. Vaughn picked his head up discovering even more. "But Spot, you didn't howl when you sniffed the man's tracks! No. You *growled*. He's still alive!" Vaughn jumped up while talking to Spot, carefully climbing up the mountain path. "Stephanie went up and later a man, but neither came down. He must have been native as well, because I don't believe Stephanie's friend would betray the cave to the strangers. But if the woman returned during the trouble, that'd mean the man went up after. Why would he go up, and what kept him from being killed while the woman couldn't keep herself from being killed? And why did you growl when you sniffed his tracks?"

Vaughn stared at Spot... wondering. "You must have smelled the invaders' scents as well. If he was among *them*... Oh God..." Vaughn felt the need to hurry, now, but forced himself to be careful. There might yet be more valuable knowledge hidden on the trail, and he didn't want to miss it. Just three days ago, Stephanie had come to him in his dream. *I'm too close to lose her. I* can't *lose her.*

&

Arlupo couldn't get around the fact that they were looking for her and she knew there was no way she could conceal her identity. She knew if she stayed with Stephanie in the cave, or anywhere else for that matter, she would be endangering her life.

As they stood watching the horror unfold, Arlupo spoke in a soft, trembling voice. "I'm sorry, Stephie. I have to go down there."

Stephanie felt her heart skip. "WHAT? NO."

Arlupo turned her head to her, pleading, "I have to. If I don't, they'll come looking, then they'll find you. You can no longer hide what you are from your father, Stephie, and we can no longer hide either."

"NO! You said this cave is secret. Let's just go to the back of the cave. There's nothing we can do right now."

"It's too late for that now. Besides, it's better we did watch. Jargono knows of the path we took, I'm sure of it. Because one day, when we were playing in the orchard, he disappeared, and one of the elders brought him back scolding him not to ever go up there. I never thought anything of it until now. We've already seen what's happening. Seeing requires the response I must do." They turned together to look below.

"Your *people* are not allowed to resist *by government order*. If you don't tell me where they are, now, I'll begin *executing* you."

Arlupo's father held his head up, squared his shoulders, and spoke clearly. "It makes no difference to us about that. We wouldn't go with you. These are our sacred lands. We've been here when many of your governments have come and gone. Before you even called yourself a country, we've been the same since ancient times. Your education is meaningless to us. We only sent our children to you to learn of you, *not to follow you*."

He officially responded back. "You're men. You have your choice, fine. But under our new law, the women have no choice. They will come with us regardless." His sneer and delight mingled together grotesquely.

The leader's wife spoke again in that same, calm, polite voice. "We will not go with you." But her strength and calmness only stoked his fury, and he reached out, grabbing her arm.

"YOU WILL GO WITH US IF I SAY!"

He was unaware of the invisible fire guarding her from such contact. Definitely not a good idea to put a hand on a holy woman. He screamed, as if suddenly struck by terrible pain. He reflexively released her arm, holding out his hand that had grabbed her, and he grasped his wrist with the other hand.

Her husband calmly spoke. "You may not put your hand upon our women."

The man continued to scream in agony and Stephanie smiled, and tugged Arlupo's arm for emphasis. "HA!" Stephanie knew it was foolish to worry about the Appendaho being destroyed. They could take care of themselves!

"IT BURNS, AHHHH, IT BURNS!" He was still holding the wrist of the burnt hand while doubled over in pain.

Jargono came up to him and calmly held out a small, black bottle. "Take some of this oil and spread it upon your hand and the burning will cease." Then Jargono opened it, pouring out some thick, very black oil. Fred gingerly rubbed it all over and it promptly nullified the burning.

"Oh, thank you, Jargono. Is this from your people's medicine?"

Jargono scowled. "They know nothing of this power."

Something wasn't right. No. More than that, something was *very wrong*. Ever since Stephanie saw Jargono, the hairs on the back of her neck stood up. But when she saw that black oil, goose bumps raised all over her, making all her skin crawl. She sensed something she didn't understand, but the feeling reminded her of the terrible evil she encountered when facing the demons. She knew its intent! She knew its power! Realization again opened Stephanie's eyes, but this time she couldn't avoid it, and the realization gave voice to itself.

"Arlupo, they're…they're… going to die." As Stephanie heard the revelation come from her own mouth, its sound shook her to her core. Arlupo gave a gasping breath, as she desperately grasped for strength to do what needed to be done *now*. She'd already seen it in her prophetic visions. Now, all she had to do was live it.

"Please don't weep, my sister. I must go *now*." Arlupo began walking out of the cave entrance, but Stephanie instantly…

"NO, I WON'T LET YOU!" Springing onto her friend, Stephanie grabbed her arms in vice-like fingers, dragging her back in. Arlupo twisted vigorously, struggling just as much, if not more, with the hollowness inside her. Then, when she almost freed herself, Stephanie threw her arms around her waist, and pulled her to the cave floor. Once down, Arlupo stopped resisting and Stephanie pinned her to the cave floor, sitting on top of her.

Arlupo became docile, with tears running down her cheeks as she whispered, "You *must* let go of me, Stephie. You *must*."

Stephanie leaned forward, putting both hands on Arlupo's shoulders so she couldn't rise. She pinned her harder. "NO. I WON'T. *NEVER!*"

Arlupo began to bawl. Stephanie was making this even harder for her. Arlupo spoke through her sobbing. "I can't fight you. You're holding me against my will."

Fire blazed in Stephanie's eyes as her burning love for her friend and her people consumed her. Her mind and heart were united into one purpose, and that purpose was quickly manifesting itself in the outside sky in Stephanie's conception of brute power.

"I have an idea. I'm a *faithwalker*. You said there's no limit to my powers. Look at the sky, it clouds already. I'll... I'll call down lightening and *destroy them!*"

Arlupo halted her weeping as fear took its place. She could see Stephanie changing before her very eyes, and could feel the terrible power emanating from her. Worse, she could feel her best friend's soul teetering on the edge of death. Arlupo spoke soberly. "To what end? And the next people?"

Stephanie began to look crazed. *"I'll destroy them, too."*

Arlupo's eyes grew wide as her heart pounded. "And the *next*? Do you *hear* yourself?"

Thunder crashed outside as flashes of light streaked across the sky and illuminated the cave opening where they were. The lightening waited upon Stephanie to direct it. "They have no *right* to live."

Arlupo locked her eyes into Stephanie's with all of her will. "It's one thing to confront a singular threat, my sister, but this threat is not singular. It's from the whole way of life of an *ignorant* people. For such things, only God may judge truly."

"But..."

"What if this had happened in an earlier time, with different people, and instead of you here with me, you were down there on Jargono's arm, say, two years ago!" Her words slammed into Stephanie, taking her breath away, as images of herself two years back danced before her eyes. She let go of Arlupo's shoulders.

"Oh God." *That could've been me!*

"Or what if that girl on his arm was your own mother when she was young?"

Stephanie grabbed her head, putting her hands over her ears. She shook her head as she growled, *I don't want to hear this.* She shook all over. With so much power coursing through her, the sudden doubt of intention felt as if it would rip her apart, as well as her conflicting emotions. Arlupo could feel it, but the alternative was worse. She reached up, squeezing Stephanie's arms to give her focus.

"Your mass destruction has effects you know nothing about. I have no doubt you could do it, but when you would find out the harm you also caused, I think it would tear you apart, because it would give evil the chance it seeks to conquer you, to twist you unmercifully, because *you* didn't have mercy when you should have! My dear Stephanie, any time we kill anyone, somehow, someway, we come to know about their lives and the consequences of killing them, even when justified! That's why, *if* you destroy, it must only be *through* you, not *by* you. If Life's natural course is to destroy *through* you, then to try to hinder Life's course would bring a similar harm to you, as would killing when you should not." Arlupo paused to give Stephanie time to think.

"Does the Light now desire to destroy *through* you?" Arlupo pointed the question, leveling her eyes deeply into Stephanie's, watching as that arrow struck her friend in the heart. Stephanie's strength in holding her best friend faded away into weeping tears that fell on Arry, tears that answered the question.

SACRIFICIAL WOOD

"*Oh God, NO!* But the clouds, they gather anyway." She pointed behind her, outside, at the dark, roiling clouds, crackling with energy, and rumbling like a growling animal.

But Arry had answer to that. "And you are able to walk *anyway*. That doesn't mean you have always walked because God led you to!"

The truth couldn't be fought. The answer was too perfect to contradict, and Arlupo knew it. She put her hand to Stephanie's cheek, who was still sitting atop her. "I must go, my *beloved* sister. But if you truly love me, as I love you, you'll let me go."

Then another realization hit Stephie as her hands preciously embraced the hand that held her cheek.

"THE BOX. *You* haven't opened the box, yet. None of you have. Something's wrong. You have to open the box… NOW."

Arlupo remembered how her father had chastised her and made her remember their sacred promise. She searched herself to see if indeed her sister was right, that *now* was the time.

"I can't. It's not the right time."

But Stephanie knew it had to be. There was no alternative. "BUT THERE WON'T BE ANOTHER TIME FOR YOU. *You* said prophecy said…"

Arlupo was calm. Oddly calm. "That we would know when the right time is to open the box. Prophecy never said we would open it!"

Stephanie bit back at her sister. "*That's ridiculous.* There won't be anyone left to open it if you don't *now*. Maybe there's something in there that could save you. This has to be the right time. DON'T YOU SEE THAT?" Stephanie scolded her.

Arlupo sighed. "No, dear sister. I'm sorry. I do not. Once upon a time, I thought as you do now. But I learned better. The knowledge of when to open the box comes from the box itself, not from the prophecy! We haven't lived faithfully for all these years to break our promise now. Would you want that to be so?"

Stephanie leaned back with her head wagging as she felt her powerful realization that the box should be opened fade, like a mist the wind drives away. Arlupo's life began to flash before Stephanie's eyes, their dear friendship and more, as well as the lives of all the dear Appendaho people, her family. Stephanie pleaded like a baby, her hands covering her face. "Oh God, NO! I don't understand…I don't understand…!"

Arlupo, still on her back, felt Stephanie's tears falling on her and her own tears making it hard to see her. "I know. But if you don't let me go…"

Stephanie leaned forward cupping Arry's cheek with her hand, "Pleeeease, how can I let you go to your death? Don't ask me to do that. Pleeeease. Don't you love me?"

Arry took Stephanie's cheek in her hand, again, "Of *course* I do… *More than anything!* That's why I go down there to save you. It's a sacrifice I gladly make."

Sacrifice, I hate *that word.* "But if you go down there and die with all the rest, I'll have *nothing*. I couldn't live like that. I'll be *nothing* without you."

Her words shot through Arlupo, because she knew they weren't true, but she had to make her sister see that for herself. Arlupo spoke sternly. "That's not true, and you know it. You're

SACRIFICIAL WOOD

just trying to avoid the pain that love requires of you, if you want your love to be true. Will you love me truly, Stephanie, and let me *choose* as *I* see fit?"

"Then I might as well go with you!"

"If you want to throw away all that we've given you, that *is* your choice. I repeat, dear Stephanie, will you love me *truly* and let me choose as *I* see fit? I will not restrain you if you wish to come with me! It's not our way to infringe upon another's will."

Boxed in. Again, the truth of Arlupo's words could not be challenged. Her question had only one correct response to it. Stabbing pains shot through Stephanie's heart, her gut wrenched, squeezing the air from her lungs as she rolled off Arlupo. No strength, Stephanie could only manage to lie flat on her back, wishing to die herself. The thunder continued to roar angrily and Stephanie drew a deep, gasping breath and then wailed. Her bitter cry seemed to mingle with the thunder and intensify it, as if thunder proceeded from her own mouth.

Arry sat up. Her head was spinning, but she pulled Stephie up to sit beside her. Then she stood up, and took Stephie's hands and pulled her up to stand in front of her. They were both weeping uncontrollably. Love was holding them tightly together, yet love required them to part. Arlupo called with all her might that the Light would give her strength, fearing she may have already delayed too long. She shook off her misery as she must, squared herself and straightened. She looked deeply into her friend's face. Arlupo wanted to remember this remarkable young woman, who improved her life so much, who brought her so much joy.

She spoke softly to Stephanie, as she held out her left hand, palm up. "Place your right hand upon my left. I will place my right upon your left." They stood like that for a long moment each taking in the enormity of meaning. "Now we part together so that our love will always be true."

They slowly eased their hands back from each other, peering through tears into depths beyond this world, hands slowly beginning to slide past each other, then palms, then finger tips. Stephanie collapsed onto the cave floor, as Arlupo crept out of the entrance.

The clouds cleared. Stephanie's muffled sobs echoed in the cave and then, after a long, torturing time, she sensed Arlupo had reached them. Stephanie stood up, peering out the opening.

It was amazing how close the bluff was to the village square. The huge overhang above the recessed cave effectively hid it in its dark shadow. The sound below carried up and seemed to magnify. Arlupo pushed through the crowd of her people and stood between her father and mother, facing Stephanie's father. She spoke calmly as she bowed. "You don't have to look any longer, Sir. I'm here."

His eyes became as daggers, as if he beheld the reason for evil itself standing before him. He leveled his eyes at her mother, and shoved his finger at Arlupo. "You see? I told you she bows."

SACRIFICIAL WOOD

Arlupo met his maniacal eyes with love in hers. "You are the father of the sister I love. Whatever goodness she has gotten from you is worth bowing to. It is part of the Light."

Jargono watched intensely, and warned him, "Don't listen to her words, Sir. She's trying to confuse you."

He hesitated, as if frozen in time. "Yes, right. Your bows mean nothing to me, now. I'll not be tricked by you anymore. Where is Stephanie?"

She looked him straight in the eye without as much as a blink. "Didn't you see her on your way up here?"

His eyes tracked up and to the left as he reflected. "No. She's gone back to the house? Hmm, I hadn't counted on that. That's good. She'll not see what'll happen here. Then I'll *try* to correct the harm you've done to her." He turned back to his men and issued orders. "ALL RIGHT, THESE PEOPLE HAVE ALL CHOSEN TO DIE. BURN THEIR HOUSES, THEIR TREES, *EVERYTHING*. WE DON'T NEED THEIR *FILTH* CONTAMINATING US."

The men looked at each other as his glare intensified. One of them spoke up. "How shall we deliver punishment, Sir?"

"Don't touch them. They're too *filthy* to touch. Just shoot them. Leave their corpses *unburied*, as they don't deserve a proper burial."

Stephanie watched in horror. Clamping her hands over her mouth, her legs collapsed from under her, bringing her to her knees. For a moment, everything seemed to swirl around, but she fought it off.

She saw the men, still a good ten feet from the Appendaho, aim their rifles and pistols. This wasn't even going to be a humane execution. She heard the sounds of the first shots enter her ears, and saw people in the front begin to fall. Her eyes were glued to her mother and father standing straight, arm in arm, looking at each other with Arlupo in between, bowing her head. She saw them knocked to the ground, as the bullets tore into them. They all fell arm in arm.

Stephanie fell completely over, curling up in a ball.

"Oh God, I can't breathe! Oh, oh, oh, let me die! Let me dieee…"

Stephanie felt suspended between this world and an endless no-man's-land, her every fiber dissipating into it. Yet, even though she wasn't looking any more, the suffering below still seemed to have a direct channel into her vision as she beheld and felt every aspect as it happened. She could not turn off her *faithwalking* ability to empathize. Many didn't even die when the bullets struck them, but waited in agony to bleed to death. Within this consuming picture, Stephanie was insignificant. She was lost, and she gave herself over to it, waiting to disappear from existence!

CHAPTER SEVENTEEN
Family

"Dear children. Today's lesson is on sacrifice. Nothing proves love more than true sacrifice."

Yana, their youngest daughter of thirteen asked, "Why do you say so Mother? There is bravery, tender care, showering of gifts and other things that belong to love. Are they not all equal?"

"But only sacrifice says that the one for whom sacrifice is performed is more important than what has been freely given up."

Yana remembered one of the end time prophecies and recited it. "In that day, what will you give to the stranger among you? This day, my children, will I call you into judgment." Is that then the meaning of this prophecy concerning our end?"

"Sacrifice does not bring about a total end, but a beginning of something greater, otherwise it would not make sense to do so. Those who claim to sacrifice, but feel ending greater than beginning, have not truly sacrificed. Those are bitter, loveless people."

"I see. It is the meaning of the prophecy."

"Live, Lady Stephanie!" From behind her, she heard and felt a soft, soothing, feminine voice and couldn't understand how there could be *any* voice in the place where she now was at, in this desolate, lost netherworld. But she couldn't resist it. It cut through her grief with a power that was greater. Stephanie picked up her head of matted and tangled red hair.

Somehow, the voice seemed familiar, pulling at her heart. *But how could that be?* If not, Stephanie would have ignored it in favor of oblivion. *I've never heard anything like it before.* "Huh? Who?" But Stephanie saw no one. *Where did it come from? The cave is so soft. The box, it...* The box glowed a soft silver!

"No. NO! NOOO! It's not for me!" she wept. Its long history with the Appendaho blanketed her conscience, intensifying her loss and her sense of unworthiness. *For thousands of years they kept you. If it wasn't for me, they'd still be here.* "They're supposed to open it, *not me*," she wailed even as the voice came again.

"The box glows for you, dear. The way of truth does not belong to any people, but all sincere people belong to it. I believe that's what you said!" The power of the voice resonated in her heart. She couldn't fight its love. She couldn't fight her truth. "You may not understand this, now, but what happened to your people was actually best. And now it falls to you whether you will honor their lives or not. That box is now *your* choice. Honor or not!"

Damn it! Always truth! Always! Stephanie thought she heard the voice chuckle, but wasn't sure. Begrudgingly, her eyes drifted to the table and then to the box. And she reflected, "Oh what a beautiful voice, though. But where…"

Then a man's voice. "My Queen has always had such a voice. It's your choice. If you don't open it, the others down there will."

Stephanie sat up at the horrible thought of it. "NO, NO…but…I'm not…" Then she saw the paintings vibrate as if they were alive. "You, you, the paintings, oh my God…" Stephanie bowed herself to the paintings.

"Why do you bow so?" came the feminine voice again.

Stephanie couldn't speak as she felt tremendous power all around her.

Then the man's voice, so strong, but so gentle, said, "We never allowed it when we watched over the people. Please, honor us so, now. Do not bow."

Stephanie, still on her knees, looked up at the paintings. "Where are you? I can hear you."

They both answered as one. "We are to you as is meant to be. You were going to say, that you're not our people, and so you can't open the box. But you *are* a beloved daughter to us."

"Oh God, why did this have to happen? *Why?*" Stephanie waited in silence for an answer. "Hello? Hello?" Stephanie couldn't believe it. "*They're gone? Just like that? That was it?*"

But the box began to glow more loudly. Not just brightly, but a calling within the glow, and her attention was diverted.

Oh, the box glows to me? It feels like the glow is glowing to me. Arlupo, OH Arlupo, why? You should be the one, not me.

Oh God, I'm alone again, so alone. Oh no, Lana! I have to… what? Oh God!

Realization of the scope of the previous events fell on her as she suddenly joined two thoughts: Arlupo was a prophetess. She gave her all that money months ago!

She knew! She knew all along! Why didn't you tell me? You couldn't have told me. I wouldn't have heard it. I would have fought you. Oh, we didn't have time for fighting. Time. The box. I don't have time. I can't let them have this box. I promised! I promised I would help protect it! But I didn't know. Maybe I can just hide it. Where? I could never be sure. Oh God, why should I have such a responsibility? I've only known a short time. Time. No time. The box. Oh God, it glows to me.

Stephanie stood up and walked over to the sacred box. The closer she got, the more intense were her perceptions of its communication. It was as her sister had said. The knowledge of when to open it was with the box, not the prophecy. *Ahh, it feels so soft. The glow feels alive…so open…Yes Open.* "Forgive me, I'm not the one who should be doing this."

She put a hand to either side of the old, carved stone box, and her hands glowed silver with it. She instantly felt joined to its deep sacredness and that feeling caused her to pause. *Oh God, I can't just barrel on through this. What are all these new feelings in me?*

What can one say about putting their very hands on something four thousand years old or more? Something glowing with a sacredness that transcends time. Something that was protected by a sacred oath, made by a people unmatched in

⬥ SACRIFICIAL WOOD ⬥

faith and dignity. Stephanie's heart immediately reacted, but once again her mind lagged woefully behind, leaving her to feel as if she were being rended in two. Yet, the very sacredness of the experience, the draw and the embrace of the glow which felt like pure preciousness of being, superimposed a peculiar unity that staved off any fear. The outcome then, resided totally in Stephanie's faith to proceed, regardless of her inability to fathom it.

Oh God, what could be inside you? Why me? I'm nothing but a kid! I don't know Appendaho history. I'm not even Appendaho. What could possibly be so important that no one could see inside you until....me? ME? Why me? How fair is it that all those thousands of years they guarded your secret and none *of them... Oh...I don't have time for this.*

Oh God, you gave me this new will...and I love it so. But I had no *idea that things could still be sooo very hard. How is my little new holy will worthy to open something that thousands of holy people over so many generations protected? How could I possibly be worthy to do this? Oh God...no time. I may have already waited too long.*

It feels like I'm holding in my hands...what? Something sooo sacred that...what? Oh God, it feels like....I'm holding... How could that BE? What does that mean?

A darkness seemed to pass by her, fleeting, but nonetheless ominous. It was enough, though, to change her perspective. *Oh God, I can't let anyone else open it. I gave my word. Oh please, God, let my tears cease so I can at least seeee what I'm doing.*

Reverently, she finally opened the box, and a golden light shined from within, bathing her, entering into her. Her eyes widened as she saw the contents. *Oh God, they never got to know what they protected for so long.* Tears rolled down her face, mingling with the dirt on her cheeks and dropping onto her holy dress that Arlupo had made special for her, tears of longing that they should have seen their mystery unfold. *I've got to hold on.*

Alone. So alone. Opening the box brought to her the terrible loss of Arlupo and all the Appendaho, so much so, her gut wrenched again, driving her breath from her. Caught between such intense grief and the deep sacred power of the box, there was simply no way for Stephanie to bear so many predominant feelings all at the same time. For such rare times in a human being, their mind seeks an escape.

As little girls put voices to their dolls, she spoke her thoughts in an unconscious attempt to fill her bitter loneliness. In fact, this childish role took her completely over, perhaps as an attempt to shield her from reality she could no longer endure, or perhaps the glow simply called her to be that little child. "Ooohhh, *a scroll!*" She was feeling like such a very young child she spoke in their sing-song voice. "Very old, but it doesn't look worn at all, just sorta tannish. But maybe that's the way it always was. Oh what a *beautiful* blue ribbon tying this. Oh, it's got golden fibers and edges. So pretty. There's golden fibers through the scroll, too! Ahh, the scroll glows to *me*. Take it. Oh, it feels sooo soft, love. Open the bow. Ahh, it slides sooo silky. I love silky. Put the ribbon aside. NO! They can't have it! It's *mine?* Put it away, such a beautiful ribbon. I'll tie it around my hair. Then I won't lose it. Until I can find a place to put it."

Stephanie gathered her matted and tangled hair into a large pony tail, and was about to tie the ribbon to it when she thought, *How can I put this special, pretty ribbon on my filthy, messy hair?* Still thinking and feeling as if she were but a mere child, she folded her hands on her lap and bowed her head and her hair began to glow. Moments later the glow faded, and her hair appeared to have been freshly cleaned and brushed. She bowed her head again, and when the golden glow faded again, her hair was into the three braids she wore during the sacred ceremonies. *There! That's good. Hee, hee..* She tied the ribbon to the center of the middle braid. Upon doing so, a wave of spiritual sensation moved through her, settling into her, and her whole world seemed to jolt, snapping her out of her childish orientation. "Wow!" She took a deep breath. Looking into the box, still seeing the golden glow, feeling the ribbon around her hair, confirmed it all to be real. *But it felt like I was…I don't know. Somewhere else?*

She reached for the scroll again but stopped again. She felt dirty. She looked at her dress, her holy dress. It was filthy, too. *Vaughn always had me wash, brush my teeth, even when Mom died. Self-respect.* She bowed her head a third time, and her whole body glowed a soft gold. She didn't need to look at herself or her dress. She felt clean and knew her dress was, also. She straightened. "This deserves to be approached with the utmost respect." She reverently picked the scroll up and unrolled it. Her eyes clouded from instant tears.

"How can this be?" she gasped at the sight of the letter's heading. "This is thousands of years old." If it wasn't for the spiritual voices that spoke to her moments ago, she would have thought it was a trick, or that perhaps Arlupo had placed it there. But she knew none of those things were true, not to mention that her best friend would not have done such a thing.

Dear Stephanie,

Long ago I came upon the two most precious things in this world, besides the Light from which I was born. The Tree of Life and my true mate who became my Queen. I found the Tree alone on top of a dead mountain. The Tree of Life, standing asleep on top of a poison mountain, like a prisoner, as I and my future wife were. As I wept upon the Tree, it sprouted, as did your Tree for you, as you wept the true tears of true grief. The day I married my Queen, we went to the top of the mountain, and the Tree had born a single fruit that glowed to us. We ate from the fruit, and as we ate, the Tree died, and crumbled to ash.

Inside the fruit was a single, beautiful seed, shiny like a black pearl. That same day, we took the seed, and with the whole town, constructed the inner basin of the sacred brass receptacle where the current Tree resided now. That same day we were married, we planted that seed together. On our first night, we slept together in the sacred room you are now in. It was the first time we had been together that way. When we

SACRIFICIAL WOOD

awoke in the morning, the Tree of Life had spouted. Nine months to the day, our first of many children was born to the Tree of Life.

On the day of my beloved's passing away, I wept before the Tree, and it bore another fruit. As I looked upon the Tree, the leaves began to fall off, and the Tree began to sleep, even as my heart felt from my beloved's passing. But we were just the tiniest twig on that Tree, and I did not know the meaning of these things that were happening to the Tree, even though I had been taught a long time and deeply by it. I was again as a helpless child, not knowing, not understanding. Then the fruit began to glow, and the Tree became a vision. The vision I saw was you, dear Stephanie, with red hair, true tears, scars not a few, and true love and faith, my daughter, and I understood that this fruit was to be put away for you. But I knew the fruit would perish. So, knowing through wisdom that the spirit of feminine goodness passes from mother to daughter, I took all the fruit and placed it with my wife's body with a prayer that the spirit of goodness would be passed down to you.

One of our children, a red haired girl, the only one to be born such, had long ago disappeared from us when she was just thirteen. We never knew what happened to her. We were stricken with grief, as we felt for each child as if each was our only child. But I know that you are her descendent.

❖ DARRYL MARKOWITZ ❖

When the Tree showed me your vision, I understood that this was the way the Tree of Life was to return to us that which was lost, so I wept again to the Tree, to God, and to my departed wife, that all had been put at peace, and that our child's life had not been in vain. Then I understood that I should place this seed in the box, and tell you of your ancient history. But as to *what* you are, that will always be your choice, my beloved daughter.

Stephanie couldn't help it. She had to continually brush tears away so she could see to read. But upon reading 'my beloved daughter' the words glowed to her, and she felt the love of those words as surely as…when she heard their voices just earlier. *My God, I'm not just a spiritual daughter! I AM his daughter! Oh my God, Oh GOD. I'm Appendaho! Just like Arlupo and the others, sorta. But why was this written, since they can talk to me anyway?* She desperately wanted to hear from the spirits again. Then she realized, *Silly, when he wrote it, he was mortal. He wouldn't know anything about whether he could talk to anyone. Besides, I love this letter. I* need *this letter!* Then she looked into the box and pulled on a gold chain resting at the bottom. Attached to it was what looked to be a black pearl. *Oh my God! Is this?* She put it on her lap. Seeing nothing else in the box, she continued to read.

You must guard this seed with all your being. I have fastened it to a gold chain, which my wife assures me will be fashionable in your time. Wear

❧ SACRIFICIAL WOOD ❧

it my daughter, next to your heart, where also your beloved mate rests. At the time that you both know is right, do what you know is right with the seed. My daughter, there is no other seed like the one that you now protect. Protect it with your faith. This is not the time of the end for you, my daughter, it is your beginning. Queen Yinauqua, your mother, used the ribbon I tied to the scroll, to tie our lost child's hair. You and your mate shall always be with us through our prayers.

Your beloved father for eternity, *King Mafferan*

Stephanie sat on her knees before the open box. The glow was gone. The letter rested on her lap as she stared into it as if it were another world. Finally, she remembered to breathe. Her hands seemed to have made a decision. They took each braid and bundled them on top of her head. Reaching under the letter she pulled out the necklace, her hands holding up the open chain by its ends, and she saw that, indeed, it was a rather ordinary gold chain for her time. The seed dangled at the bottom in front of her. She bowed her head with a prayer. "My life for you, *no matter what.*" And then she placed the chain around her neck, and let her hair down again. She tucked the chain completely under her dress. Then fright ripped through her as Stephanie realized… "Oh no, the Tree! No! They're going to burn the Tree of Life! NO!" She began to rise, having instantly dedicated herself to protecting the Tree, but was interrupted by the same beautiful feminine voice.

"You must not go down, dear daughter."

Stephanie looked to her right at the painting that was once again vibrating.

"Queen Yinauqua? Mother?"

"Yes, child. The Tree has gone to ash. But no fire of this world could have done it. When you put the seed around your neck, the tree disintegrated. Its form was long in bearing this world, and it was delighted when you came to it."

Once again, more meaning that was too much for her to take in right now. She tended to the present with her question. "Oh my Mother, what should I do?"

The painting's smile seemed to smile at Stephanie. The voice was that of a Mother teaching a beloved daughter strength, "What is in your heart to do? That is what you do. Will you do something for me?"

Stephanie was shocked at the request. What could she do for a spirit? "For you? How could I?"

"Let me hold you, just once, and the pain of missing our child shall be taken away from me."

Stephanie was bewildered. "But, how can you still feel, I mean…"

"Love never stops feeling, never. Step close to my painting, and close your eyes."

Stephanie studied the painting as she drew near it, the letter in her right hand. "Do you really look like that?"

The Queen's voice was jovial. She laughed. "Oh, my husband fancied himself an artist. I'm afraid he over-embellished a bit. I'm really just a plain girl."

SACRIFICIAL WOOD

Stephanie couldn't help breaking into uncontrolled giggles, that broke through her grief as she felt the heart and the mind of this ancient spirit, *her mother*. She could feel the great love she had for her husband. She stepped close, and closed her eyes.

"My daughter." A golden glow formed around Stephanie and entered into her.

"Ooohhh Mother, I can *see you, feel you*. Your hug, oh God, *oh my dear, beloved Mother*."

Stephanie lingered in the feeling, even after she knew her spirit mother had departed. But the voice returned, thankful, but warning. "Thank you, my daughter. Now, do not grieve me. Go to the back of the cave. To the left of the demon in the right rear corner, there is a stone sticking out. Press it and escape for your life. The door will close behind you."

But the thought instantly occurred that Arlupo would have been able to escape with her. Her heart pained her, and she had to ask. "Mother, why didn't you warn us earlier, when we were yet both able to escape together, Arlupo and I?" She didn't mean it to come out quite the way it did, but she couldn't help it.

"Your mortal enemy hunted her, and would have quickly found and destroyed you both. Behold…he approaches. *Go quickly my daughter!*"

With the letter in hand, Stephanie raced to the stone, and pushed it. She fled down a narrow, rocky path, that she could tell hadn't been trodden since ancient times. She went along a narrow ledge with a steep drop, and eventually came out on a neighboring farmer's land on the Appendaho's northern border.

☙

Jargono rarely lost his temper. This had been one of those occasions. He was sure if anything could solve his predicament, the Appendaho's sacred treasure could. He turned to the paintings he had defaced and scoffed. "I heard you had great powers, even like I have. You're nothing but myths. There probably never was a sacred treasure." He whirled around sensing something.

King Mafferan smiled. He looked exactly like the paining. "Like I have."

Jargono peered at him, not understanding. "Pardon me?"

"You said, like you have. But, I came before you, so really, you have powers like I have, not I have powers like you." Mafferan studied his reaction. He had, for some time, been watching him with shame, but meeting face to face, he could feel the tremendous power in the lad.

"Yes, well, I can see you're wild with uncontrolled glow. You *are* a myth! You have no real power. Why are you bothering me?"

"I'm sorry. I didn't mean to. I heard my ancestor's cry for help. I must have been confused. Perhaps a different ancestor called." Mafferan began to fade away.

"Wait. Besides, there are no more ancestors left. Only me."

Mafferan's form returned, and the king glared at him, his eyes turning a black even Jargono had not seen. "And tell me, *why is that?*"

SACRIFICIAL WOOD

Jargono realized he had fallen into a bad position, but he shrugged the meaningless point aside. "It's said you had great love for people, but you chose to hide yourself and your people from the world. What kind of *love* is that?"

The lad is clever. He's trying to flank me and put me where I'm at a disadvantage. Alright, I'll go there. "Some wrongs don't show up until long after they're committed!"

"Then perhaps you can do something right for mankind, now. The Black Death spreads. I don't know how to stop it."

"If you don't, it *will* consume every human being."

Jargono was smug. "Not every, my powers protect me."

"Its powers grow with its numbers. You haven't realized that, yet. The Tree of Life is no more. That increases its powers even more."

Damn. I was afraid of that. He's telling the truth. I know, because lying is offensive to him. I can tell. "You are the wise King Mafferan. Surely, you know how to stop it. Or perhaps you can stop it yourself."

"Man brought this evil into the world. I'm not allowed to interfere with it. If the demons had brought it directly, I would have already stopped it. Tell me, do you know how the Black Death got here?"

I suppose he knows. But I'm not going to dignify him by answering. "What does it matter? It's here. Can you tell me how to control it?"

Mafferan heated. "*Control it?* You don't strike me as foolish." Then he paused, suddenly realizing he was falling for Jargono's ploy. *Clever indeed. He doesn't want to control it.*

He wants it destroyed and is baiting me to tell him how. "No. You aren't foolish at all, are you?" Jargono just stared at him, waiting silently. He knew the *glow* would want him to destroy the Black Death. Mafferan leveled his eyes into him. "You have the power to destroy it!" Now Mafferan waited.

Jargono knew he had to respond. He hated that he had to. *I almost got him to bend to me.* "But I thought you just implied that my powers aren't able to."

"Well, you would have to make a few alterations." Mafferan began to glow brightly.

Unlike the demons, the *glow* didn't bother Jargono as much as its uncontrolled expression disgusted him. Jargono channeled the power of the *glow*, whereas the demons rejected it outright whenever possible. Jargono spoke sarcastically. "I take it by *glowing* all over the place you're trying to tell me I have to become like you?"

"That *is* the only chance you have to truly destroy the Black Death."

I don't believe him. He, in some way, is being clever. I don't have time for this. "What about the sacred treasure?"

Mafferan folded his arms across his chest, speaking dryly. "What about it?"

Jargono stared at him. He felt the tremendous power in Mafferan. He knew there was nothing he could do to this spirit. *At least, not in the Earth realm.* "You're not going to help me?"

"I've offered it to you. You're not going to accept my help?"

SACRIFICIAL WOOD

They both stood and stared at each other. Jargono finally confessed. "I have a way to stop the Black Death. But I wanted to see if there was another."

Mafferan could see it in his eyes. *Oh God on High. If he does that...* Mafferan shook his head. "Jargono, please. You *are* indeed the most powerful human being on the whole planet. Don't do the thing you're already attempting. Far from solving the problem, it will make it *much* worse."

He's pleading with me. Why? "I'm far too busy. Go haunt someone else." Jargono vanished from the cave.

Yinauqua appeared in front of her husband. "If our evil son does what he intends..."

"I know."

"The last time that happened, the only solution was to destroy everything and start over."

"Yes. Our good friend Noah has told the story over and over. It seems he never tires of it."

"With good reason, my husband. There will be no ark to save mankind this time."

Mafferan sighed. He knew Jargono was the only one with enough ability to destroy the Black Death. He also knew he wouldn't listen, and that worse was to come. "I'm sorry, my Queen. Perhaps..."

Yinauqua shook her head. "They can't even possibly be ready or able enough in time to defeat the Black Death, let alone everything else trying to destroy them. They're wonderful souls, but too young and inexperienced. What follows after Jargono completes his plan will destroy even him. The Earth is lost to us, my husband."

"Perhaps. But remember, prophecy no longer belongs to you, my dear. We will just have to wait and see what we cannot now determine."

☙

Jargono was still angry, angry at himself for not foreseeing this possibility. Yet, he remembered being aware that there were possible unexpected consequences, but he was sure he was able to deal with them. *The demons have their own objectives. I have mine. Perhaps* Mafferan *will intervene anyway. If I really can't stop it, and worse happens, he'll have to. He'll do my work for me and I'll take credit for it. No, that's too easy. He'd decline just to spite me. They follow their damned rules.*

Jargono was seething at the demons. He soared above the Dead Forest, over the many dead trees, still searching for the right one. There were precious few possibilities left. He looked at one of those that still had faint glow in it, remembering when he'd tried to convince him to sacrifice. He was sure he had him when he lured the Black Death into the girl. But now, a deep blackness shimmered in the tree, but not the Black Death. It looked worse to him. *Hmm, what has happened to you?* He shook his head. *You should have just accepted the Black Death like I told you to. It would have been better than what you are now.*

He knew now that the Black Death instinctively sought a form it could localize in. After it succeeded, he was sure he could control it, or destroy it if need be.

❧ SACRIFICIAL WOOD ❧

He knew how to lure it. It wanted him the most! All he needed was the right container, or perhaps containers. *Mafferan is right. Its number increases. But if I don't keep experimenting, then I certainly can't find the solution. The solution's importance outweighs increasing their numbers a bit.*

His anger had him touch down at the river bank. Every now and then its black vapors rose in whisps but then disappeared back into the river. "GrrraGagag." He called with more anger than he wanted. *If I can't find a solution, at least I'll destroy you!* "GrrraGagag!" He shouted.

"Well, well," a demon's voice called out of the ether. "To what do I owe this *rude* summoning?"

"You're not GrrraGagag. Who are you?"

"Hmm, making demands of your God?"

"GrrraGagag never talked so foolishly, demon. Who are you?"

"I *am* GrrraGagag but much *more*. Let's just say *I* am privy to all that you two worked out."

Jargono laughed. "I see. You ate the poor sot. Fine. Makes no difference to me."

"Oh, yes. I see now that you know many things about us. I see GrrraGagag taught you a bit, a bit more than I might have, but that's O.K." He waited for Jargono to bend to him.

"I was never told of certain consequences of the Black Oil I was given."

Now it was ScrabaGag's turn to laugh. "Well, you have your objectives and I have mine. You took it and accepted it of your own free will. *As is.* There was no proviso concerning consequences."

"I see. I had a little talk with one of your glowing rivals. Seems he's going to clean up this mess, anyway." Jargono was sure they weren't able to eves drop on such conversations.

"That's wonderful. Have a nice, *short* life…"

"Wait. Why are you hiding from me? You're even more powerful than GrrraGagag. I can tell. Come down, let's chat a while. There may be something I can offer you. I rule the Earthly realm. There's none to match me."

"Yesss. I seeee that. Well, when you're the last standing of your kind, call on me and perhaps I'll make you my pet. I've always wanted a pet human. They say it would be insulting to us, but I think perhaps you might *squeak* past!"

Jargono found the entry point of the demon's voice. He knew ScrabaGag was too smart to risk any more meetings. He focused his mind's energy at the entry point. Bolts of bright blue light shot from his forehead into that point and disappeared.

ScrabaGag's eye stung. He immediately looked away. He rubbed it with his arm and brushed the tears away. *Hmm, it's different from what the girl did to me in the orb and different than what I felt her do to GrrraGagag or the High Councilor. This is bothersome, like an* eyelash *in an eye.* He mocked at Jargono. "Oh please, great king, please don't throw any more of your terrible light bolts into my Great Eye." Then ScrabaGag angered at the insult. He focused through the orb, deciding he would begin consuming Jargono through it. He

❖ SACRIFICIAL WOOD ❖

wanted him to feel what real power was. Then he would ease back and let him live. He was sure Jargono needed to ripen a bit more.

From the entry point, deep blackness opened up and fell over Jargono. He sensed it before he even saw it. He could have vanished before it arrived but that would be running. *He thinks those bolts were the best of my power. A pet!* Jargono stood, smiling. He raised his arms up and a web of finely glowing strands appeared all around him. Each strand glowed brightly blue, but there was no wasted leakage of the precious energy. No wild glare like Mafferan displayed. The blackness was halted.

ScrabaGag's Great Eye jerked backwards with instant Eye ache. *This is new.* He exerted more of his will into consuming Jargono. Jargono felt his web begin to crush and he reinforced it. ScrabaGag jerked back again. Frustration and anger rose in him. He intensified his effort. He was beginning to feel embarrassed. Something he hadn't felt since before he ate GrrraGagag. Jargono collapsed onto one knee. *If I'm to make the Earth truly mine, if I'm* anybody, *I can't let these* vermin *win over me.* He mixed a new ingredient into his web and it shot the same blue bolts into the blackness.

ScrabaGag's Eye began to tear, but if he looked away, he couldn't consume him. The stinging intensified. Anger boiled in him. *I'll ignore the pain.* Focusing through the tears, he let loose his full effort, part of him not wanting to admit that he actually reached for that much power.

Consuming pressure seemed to squeeze the air from Jargono's lungs, even though he didn't breathe here in the

Dead Forest. *I'll die before I let this demon consume me. Then we can battle on the other side of my mortal life! Meet spirit to spirit!* Jargono forgot even his very existence and placed his full essence into the light bolts They now glowed so brightly blue that they looked like blue smudges instead of distinct bolts.

ScrabaGag's Great Eye reflexively twitched. It blinked. His bulbous head jerked involuntarily. The connection was broken. Grudgingly, he rubbed his eye, unaware that just a few seconds longer and Jargono's web would have been broken. *Heaven! I'll have to do something about that awful twitch.*

Jargono smiled with satisfaction. *Hmm, just a few seconds more and he would have had me. HA! Almost doesn't count. I am stronger than him.* Jargono stood up. "You know, demon, after I solve my little problem with your defective black oil and I formally rule the Earth, I'm going to teach everyone about you demons." Jargono's voice became menacing. "And then I'm going to show them how to totally ignore you! *You,* my poor misfits, will lose all connection to the Earth. Then, all you'll have to consume is each other. Eventually, there will only be one of you. But ahhh, since you won't have any connection to the Earth. *You'll be unreal!*"

Jargono's jibe about becoming unreal and severing their connection to the Earth was so amusing that ScrabaGag decided to tell him a bit of what he was dealing with, knowing it would only increase Jargono's frustration and make him tastier down the line. "Poor ignorant *pet*. Let me help you. You don't even know what you're dealing with. The Sacred Black Essence that has escaped your attempts to make your

SACRIFICIAL WOOD

own earthly demon is not really even a demon. No more than your human sperm or egg is really a human before it joins. Just like your biology seeks to join together, the Black Essence seeks a joining between humans and itself. You can't control it. It doesn't even have a mind that you can really influence. Just some basic dear demon feelings. That's all."

Jargono heard what he wanted to hear. He knew it. Once the Black Essence joined, it would have a mind and heart partly of Earth and that was something he knew he *could* control. "Thank you kind demon for telling me what I already knew."

ScrabaGag was pleased to see Jargono's thoughts. "But be warned, Jargono. Once you make your demon, they are insatiable. They will have both demon and human lust." *Telling him the truth now will completely absolve us from any accusations the* glow *may bring against us later. I told him the truth.*

"You're saying the earth demon will want to reproduce."

"I said what I said."

Jargono hadn't considered that possibility. He scoffed to himself. *Hybrids are almost never viable, at least on Earth. Almost never. But even when they are, the offspring are weak and don't last. Besides, why would he tell me the truth?* "Are you telling me the truth, old demon?"

"My pet, demons never have a problem with telling the truth." ScrabaGag closed the entryway and was gone. But he watched him through the dirty blue orb.

༄

Stephanie walked up to the farm house as the sun was fading below the horizon and about to close on the worst and best day of her life. To be entrusted with such responsibility, there were no words to fully express it, but her fingers kept reaching to her chest to make sure the Seed was still there, even though she could feel its spiritual presence between her breasts. *I could feel the Tree of Life even when I wasn't around it. I can't lose this Seed.*

As soon as she had put the necklace on, the Seed to the Tree of Life began… well, communicating. Not always words, mostly in feelings, and by the time she had knocked on the farmhouse door, the Seed and her had become as one, in a way far different than just receiving her new will. The Seed now felt very much a part of her as her own arm, or her own heart, and even the Holy Spirit within her responded to the Seed in the same way. For lack of a better description, it was like *being* a family within herself. The Holy Spirit, her own new will, and the Seed to the Tree of Life all constantly watching and relating to each other. And though all the pain of the terrible events still indiscriminately made her ache all over, it was now in context of a far greater meaning which, for now, Stephanie could only feel around the edges, being far too vast to comprehend.

This farmer had little contact with the Appendaho because the mountain separated them. Stephanie knew she didn't resemble the Appendaho and reasoned she would have no trouble. She told them she got mad at her father and ran away into the country but now decided to return home. They offered to drive her back, but Stephanie insisted on paying for the help. The oldest son would have been glad regardless. *Farmers are beautiful people.*

SACRIFICIAL WOOD

It was dark when Stephanie ran up the long sidewalk and threw open the front door, out of breath, thankful she was able to make it home so quickly. Now all she could think about was rescuing what she had left of a family from a fate worse than death. She had thought about it all the way home. Her real mother's life was cursed by that evil man and her life as well. There was no way she would let Lana or her step-mother suffer any more.

Stephanie cried out upon entering the living room. "Jean, Lana, come *quickly*." Jean was surprised to see her come through the front door since her father expressly forbid her from it. But that took a back seat to simply missing her. Jean hadn't realized just how much Stephanie's mere presence mattered.

"Oh, dear Stephanie, we've missed you so." Jean threw her arms around her, exchanging hugs. Then Jean moved out of the way, for she knew what would happen next.

"Stephieeee!" Lana, a blur, raced so fast and hard into her arms that Stephanie almost got knocked over. Picking her up, she twirled her around, squeezing and kissing her, noticing the ache in her arms that had desired for so long to hold Lana.

"Hey, Sprout." But Stephanie turned to Jean, speaking more as a woman than she ever had. "We have to leave, *now*. And not come back!"

Jean looked puzzled. "What? What are you..."

"Father killed all the Appendaho. He's determined to have his way with us or else. I'm afraid he's completely insane."

Jean looked dazed. "But he said he was just..."

But Stephanie had thought out the possibilities and had already prepared her reaction. She cut Jean off in mid-sentence. "Mother, look into my eyes."

She saw more than she could understand, but one thought stood out. "Oh God, where is your dear friend, Arlupo?"

Stephanie looked away, breathing heavily as the pain tore into her again. She could feel Arry's hands sliding out of hers, the bullets striking her. Lana was still in her arms, listening. Stephanie stood silently, biting her lower lip.

Jean didn't want to understand Stephanie's silence, but painfully, horribly, she did. Stephanie was using most of her strength to keep from breaking down. Lana was getting heavy. *Damn, there's no time to be selfishly indulging my feelings. I have lives to save.* Lana, still in her arms, pulled her head back from Stephie's shoulder to look into her eyes. She felt more than she understood, and she had never seen, heard, or felt her sister as she did now.

"Stephie?"

The meaning of Stephanie's words and of the loss finally sunk into Jean. Her voice sounded shell-shocked. "You're telling the truth, but where would we go? We have no money."

Stephanie straightened and squared herself, easing her head around the child. "I have money. Arlupo put enough money away for me and you and Lana."

Again, shock. Kindness in this country was so rare, but the words she now heard were *impossible*. She could only whisper, "You're kidding."

Once again, Stephanie's eyes and her silence spoke more than words. Jean covered her mouth with her hands as she remembered how terribly she'd spoken to Arlupo and how Arlupo had spoken so kindly to her, how she'd told her, her secret and brought Jean back to her real self. *And now she's provided us with money? And now she's dead?* It was too much to hold. Tears blurred her vision.

"You're not kidding. Oh my God. Why?" Jean's tears turned into weeping.

Stephanie hadn't expected this possibility. In fact, it surprised her as tears began to take her over, also. "Damn it!" she cried in anger as Lana began trying to wipe her tears away with her little hands. Stephanie took a deep breath. She scolded herself. *There's no time for this. I have to move this along.* "Arlupo was, is, has been a real person. She loved us." Again a small cry of grief burst out, but now Stephanie viciously scolded herself inside, remembering Arlupo's words, *Would it be more meaningful if you failed?* Stephanie decided she wasn't going to fail. She set Lana down. "We have to go, *now,* Jean, otherwise we will fail Arlupo's kindness. You don't want that, do you?"

Jean asked her, "But, where will we go?"

"Last month, when I was at the store, the owner was grieving because his brother died. His brother had a sister store about two hundred miles up North. He has no one he trusts to run it. I stopped there tonight before coming here. The store is still for sale, and I wrote down the phone number he had posted. I'm going to buy it!"

Jean couldn't believe it. It had to be a dream. "But… but, you have that much?"

"Yes. But we won't buy it from the owner here. We will buy it from the agent up *there*."

"But what if someone else…"

"I've already sent a message to the agent from a different part of this city, where they don't know me, that we'll be up in a day or so. *Listen to me*. I'm no longer a child! From now on, we have to make people believe I'm eighteen. Don't lie, but we can make them believe this by being clever."

Jean's eyes widened with the scope of understanding. "Yes, I understand. You could probably pass for three years older. Lana, help Mommy pack up."

Stephanie patted her head and gave her a love pooch in the backside to get going, but Lana turned with big gray eyes. "What about Puppy?" Her eyes were all concern. Stephanie had completely forgotten. Her heart sunk when she realized her father had killed *everything*.

"Oh Lana, we'll see. Maybe we can pass by and pick him up. Go help Mommy. We have to get away from your Daddy or he'll hurt us bad."

☙

Vaughn took another hour before he reached the cave under the huge overhang. When he glanced over his right shoulder, he could see the village square below.

"Oh my God, they watched," was all he could say to Spot who was inside the cave already, growling. Pictures flooded into Vaughn of the scene unfolding below with Stephanie

SACRIFICIAL WOOD

and her friend watching from above. He couldn't imagine how Stephanie would let her friend return to be killed. But then he realized he would have given his life for her, also. *I bet Stephanie tried to stop her, but she made her let her go.* Then comprehension of just how hard that all would be, made Vaughn lean against the mountainside, because his head swam. Spot growled more intensely and darkness began to creep into Vaughn's eyes. The cave was dark, and he pulled the torch from underneath his pack strap and sparked it.

A shattered stone table in the center of the large, square room looked to have been recently destroyed. At his feet were pieces of something crushed and when Vaughn maneuvered them around a bit they formed a box.

"Spot, I don't think Stephanie would have anything to do with all this destruction. Whoever did this was obviously looking for something, and judging by his anger, he didn't get it, Oh my God, that means Stephanie did! Spot, how could anyone crush this stone box like it was thin wood? That table, Oh God, looks like a huge foot just stepped on it and crushed it."

There were four torches still standing in posts that once were the table's corners and Vaughn went over and lit them. Then he noticed that the walls of the cave were painted all around with people, animals, and something evil looking. But it was the beautiful pictures to the right of the entrance that called to Vaughn, drawing him over. Spot had been growling as he sniffed at different places in the cave, but now he picked his head up and his ears pointed outside. Vaughn saw pieces of the stone table lying at the foot of the paintings. It seemed that they had been hurled against them, but there was no visible damage.

"Spot, how could these paintings not be harmed? And where did Stephanie go? Where did the man go? There were no footprints back. None." Spot walked slowly back towards the cave entrance, not acknowledging his master's words. Vaughn was captivated by the paintings and didn't notice his dog's warning behavior. The paintings were obviously of a king and queen.

"Oh my God, how beautiful." Vaughn's eyes widened and goose bumps crept all over as he recognized the man's painting on the wall, even though it had black hair and was in royal robes. "Spot, do you see that man on the wall? He looks like… No, couldn't be." He looked just like the old man who helped him bury the bodies.

Vaughn's mouth dropped open and tears clouded his eyes. He rubbed them away and shook his head. He didn't believe what he thought he saw, next. Maybe it was his imagination. People were always seeing such things in old photographs. But he had no predisposition to make such a connection. "Spot, that woman, around the eyes, *and their odd brown color,* the shape of her forehead and those cheeks, modestly high…" But Vaughn noticed one thing that allowed him to see all the similarities, drawing it all into a vivid picture. The way she carried herself in the painting, her posture, her presence. She's, my GOD, she looks like Stephanie!"

Then a soft, feminine voice spoke from behind him. "So, you're the young man who's sworn to avenge our blood."

SACRIFICIAL WOOD

Feeling like in a dream when he heard the voice, he turned to see. "Huh? Oh, pardon me, Ma'am, Lady. I didn't, Oh my God, you're, but…"

Though dressed only in a modest, long-sleeved, full red dress, her identity was obvious. She giggled, and her words felt as if love itself were speaking. "You and Stephanie have that word very much in common."

Vaughn's thoughts raced. *That smile, I've never seen such a beautiful smile. I could cry for that smile, so true a smile of acceptance. I feel it all through me.* "Ma'am?"

"The word, *but*."

Vaughn was at a loss for words.

"You're very brave, just like my beloved husband."

Vaughn's eyes widened as he pointed behind him to the man's picture. "Is he your husband?"

"Yes, that's a picture of him. A fair picture."

Vaughn noted the affectionate humor in her voice, but he wanted to see if his thought was right, so he took the chance to question her.

"Ma'am, was that old man…"

She laughed even more deeply. "He kinda disguised himself a little, but he didn't do a very good job. I always told him, I'd know him anywhere, no matter what he did. He's just that kind of person."

Vaughn could feel her powerful love for her husband radiating all through him. Yet, the man deeply troubled him, and Vaughn couldn't refrain from asking. "But the things he was saying."

Her eyes glinted with foresight as soon as she heard the word, *but*. "They were for your benefit, Vaughn, to draw out *your* thoughts and feelings. We know you're true."

Amazement at so many levels Vaughn couldn't keep track. "But, how do you know, and how can we even be…" He couldn't finish.

She stepped closer. In her presence, he felt very much like a little child.

"We are spirit, but we were allowed to come because of *that*, below. The last of our children, except for Stephanie."

Overwhelmed now. Way overwhelmed. Speaking to her in person, rather in spirit, person spirit, he could almost feel Stephanie through her. "Stephanie?" he asked.

"When you find her, she'll explain. And she's a child by faith, as are others, as well. I'll let her tell you. Do you trust her, have faith in her?"

There was no hesitation to his answer. "Oh yes. *Yes.*"

"Then you'll look into her eyes and know she speaks truth."

Vaughn sensed there was more to this answer than just the words, but all he could do was file it away for later. Now he needed to know, "But where is she?"

"Go north. You'll find her."

Joy burst into him at her words. Now curiosity had a chance to reign. "Were you, are you, the picture, a Queen?"

"Yes."

When Vaughn heard it, he fell to his knees. Really, he had the feeling of wanting to bow to her all along just from

❖ SACRIFICIAL WOOD ❖

her mere presence. Learning of her royalty just gave him his excuse to express his heart. "My Lady."

She touched his left shoulder, imploring him, "Oh please, Vaughn, don't bow. We never allowed it. Bow only to Goodness. Look at the picture. Tell me what you see." Her power seemed to lift him and turn him around to the painting.

"I see love, Ma'am, incredible love in both of you, and bravery, strength, peace, holiness, kindness."

She warmly spoke to herself, *I should have realized he would answer like that.* "What about the details of the picture, besides our character?"

Vaughn felt a little dumb for not starting with the basics first. "Oh, you're holding hands, looking into each other's eyes, but somehow… Hmmmm, also outward to those like me standing and beholding. In his other hand, your husband… what's his name?"

"King Mafferan."

"King Mafferan is handing you a book." Then Vaughn remembered his quest that seemed so long ago but was only about six months past. *King Metran. Mafferan. I bet…* "Oh my God, is that the Book of Wisdom? Queen, I don't know your name."

She'd disappeared, but the voice echoed in the cave. "Yinauqua. Touch the book, dear Vaughn!"

"Yes my Lady, Queen Yinauqua." Vaughn went over to the life-like, life-sized paintings, whose vibrant colors seemed to have all been freshly painted, and reached out with his fingers, gingerly touching the painting of the book. "Oh my God!

Its… it's not part of the painting! It's THE BOOK." Vaughn jerked his hand back feeling he shouldn't touch so precious an object. There was a power coming from it.

Queen Yinauqua's queenly voice replied as if bequeathing knighthood. "It's our gift to you! You've earned it!"

"But, but…" So totally embarrassed, because he felt so unworthy, he would've been unworthy to receive something like this from a flesh and blood person, well, even more so from a spirit.

But the Queen met his emotions with more of her loving humor. "There's that favorite word again."

Vaughn protested, feeling very, very small. "I haven't…"

But she wouldn't hear it. "You buried our fallen and risked your life. You swore to avenge their deaths, and most of all," she let out a laugh, "you challenged my husband." Then several more laughs. "And *won the challenge*. We're both proud of you."

But all Vaughn could say was, "But…"

"We respect truth, dear son. You have spoken it with heart and mind as one. There is no other to inherit the book. It was even hidden from all those you put to rest. It was reserved for *you!*"

Vaughn was beyond overwhelmed and into the impossible. "But this is ancient, how?"

"It's a little matter of me having a gift for prophecy. And, you know, rulers are always trying to see to the end of things. I knew of you before I passed away from this Earth. I told my husband what to do, and he created the book for you! We are ever in your debt, also, for saving Stephanie."

Vaughn fell to his knees in tears. All his life he was nobody, less than nobody in everyone's eyes except for Stephanie's and a few old timers'. But he had been thought about even thousands and thousands of years ago. A certain personal value he had never felt before began permeating his being. And this was the book everyone spoke of when they chided people saying, 'Where is *your* Book of Wisdom?' The secret prayers his heart had prayed, but his mind never dared to utter them, but now they were coming true. He stood up and ran his fingers over the fancy cover of the book, trying to figure out the best way to remove it.

He could feel it was a real book, but it so perfectly fit into the painting he couldn't find an edge to take hold of. Placing his hand upon it, he gently began to push. Instantly he jerked back. The book dislodged, the top part falling backwards and the bottom leaning upward.

Vaughn pulled a knife from its holder at his side and he slid it under the book's bottom edge. He took a red handkerchief from his pocket and slipped it over the top edge then he carefully wiggled the book until it was straight again but then he pulled booth the hankie and the knife and the book came out from the wall.

Formed gold edging on the cover prevented the book from being damaged as it rubbed against the rock. Behind where the book was, Vaughn saw a wedge of rock that had prevented the bottom of the book from also being pushed backwards. It had what appeared to be three carved indentations. *Why would they go to the trouble of carving something no one could see except…?* Vaughn reached in his hand and his three longest fingers fit into the recesses.

He pushed. When he felt the stone begin to move on its own he jerked his hand out. The wedge slowly sunk. When it vanished, all of the sudden something from the back of the hole began moving forward and arrived in perfect place! *My God, it looks like the book. I can't tell the original was ever taken!*

"Thank you, kind Lady. But…why me?"

"We'll let your future wife tell you, my son. Now, trouble is almost upon you. Prophecy now begins with Stephanie and you! You must decide what to do. Will you kill again, or run, or be taken prisoner?"

CHAPTER EIGHTEEN
Wisdom

"How did we ever agree to such a lopsided truce?" GrrraGagag asked.

The High Councilor narrowed his eye at the insult, seeing as how the High Council forged it. "Apparently, you missed Claynomore's famous oratory. The benefits of such a truce are long range, not short range. We knew it was inevitable that populations change over long periods of time, and that the parameters of the truce would eventually serve our purpose. The only good reason for a truce is as a tool to conquer. But that is why I am a High Councilor, and you not much more than an underling."

"Oh, I was, in fact, at that oratory. I hit Claynomore in the head with a piece of the Black River." GrrraGagag vanished while having the upper arm.

The shift in extremes boggled his senses. "But, I don't know yet. Queen...?" Spot bristled, and in the back of Vaughn's mind he knew he shouldn't have ignored his dog sense earlier, as he whirled to face the cave entrance.

Spot growled and ruffed his warnings, barking at a large man with the bright light of day behind him, giving him all the appearance of a shade. Vaughn's eyes strained to adjust to the contrast of the bright light from the entrance and the shadowed figure blocking it. But when he spoke, he recognized the voice, and pains of revulsion shot through him. Darkness invaded Vaughn's eyes.

"Well, well, call off your *dog* if you don't want me to *shoot him*." As the man stepped in, the torches flickered upon him, making him seem unearthly. Vaughn grabbed Spot across the neck with his right arm, and pulled him back, sneering, "*Glen.*"

Glen joyously corrected him as he waved his pistol at him. "Officer Glen." He paused for a bit to let it sink in. He was going to savor every moment of this. "Well, what do I do with you, huh? I *could* shoot you now. Did you know I have a license to kill you? Or, I could play with you a while. Oh, what the heck, let's play, shall we?"

Now that he had a little power, he was even more repugnant. But Vaughn set to doing what he did best. Learning. "How…"

More than willing to brag, Glen proudly stated, "Isn't it interesting? Here you are, and me, just boys. But somehow we both live adult lives. It was easy for me. My father simply appointed me. You murdering Tracy was very convenient for the purpose. You went through all that trouble for her for *nothing!*"

The implication tore at Vaughn. Painful images of Tracy and him fighting the blackness together once again flooded him. He could still feel her fighting to live. Vaughn's eyes darkened more. "You mean to tell me that you killed her just so you could get a stinking adult job?"

"No. You did!" he laughed. "The evidence all points to you. But do you have any idea at all what kind of job this is? The government gives me all the money I need to investigate, you understand, to travel. No one dares give me any trouble, not adults, not even *grown* women. I can have whoever I want. It's perfect. Even husbands can't do a damned thing about me if I want their wives." Glen laughed again with what Vaughn could tell were fond memories for him. "They can watch if I so desire."

The darkness in Vaughn's eyes turned into deep, raging blackness, and he recognized that power as the same invasion at the hospital. But this time, the deep desire to kill was unquestionable, and Vaughn knew, if the chance presented itself, this desire would rule him. But he hadn't thoroughly analyzed it yet, to know whether it was good or evil. Since Glen had the gun, Vaughn took advantage of the threat holding his bloodlust in check, and he forced his heart to push it away, and he remained silent. Besides, Glen was doing a good job at teaching him what he wanted to know without even asking.

Glen continued with his spiteful tone. "But to tell you the truth, I killed her for more than that." He stretched out his arms, puffing out his chest like he had the whole world at his hands. "I *owed* you. You embarrassed me. Hell, you even almost got *me* sent to the State Farm instead of you. Hey, how come you didn't *die* in that hospital? I can't figure that one out. Everyone kept saying it would be any day now. There was a big party planned. Then, you just up and disappeared. Do you have any idea how disappointed everyone was?"

The darkness kept fighting to return to Vaughn as his anger rose. "You killed Tracy. You could have found some other way." Spot's continuous muffled growl felt like a rattle snake coiled to strike. Vaughn found it more difficult to restrain him.

Glen cut him off, waving the gun back and forth at them, "You know what she had the nerve to do?"

Vaughn waited.

"She turned me down! After having gone with me so many times before, and just about everyone else, suddenly she got sick in the head and said she wouldn't be with me."

Vaughn smiled as a new image of Tracy came to him. He could feel it as clear as if she were in his arms now. "Thank you for telling. I'm proud of her."

"Yeah? Well, be proud of *this*. Because of *you*, she's dead. If you hadn't messed her up, she'd still be jabbing someone. But since she was no good anymore, I decided to show her how I *really* enjoy women. She screamed and squirmed all night. Oh, since we're on the subject of people you got killed, you know that crusty old farmer with all those *damned dogs*?"

Spot growled ferociously, almost braking loose. Vaughn grabbed him with both his arms, holding tight. Glen was about to shoot him, but Vaughn shielded Spot with his body as he dragged him back further. "SPOT." Spot whined and growled together.

SACRIFICIAL WOOD

Glen shook his head at the sight. He didn't want to shoot Vaughn. He hadn't suffered enough yet. Glen stared into Spot's eyes as he spoke. "Amazing, you put your life in danger for a *damned dog*." Glen began to realize how much fun it would be to bate the dog and watch Vaughn try to protect him. But for some reason, a very un-dog-like reason, Spot just stared back. It surprised Glen as he continued his rant.

"Well, anyway, that old *dog* lover farmer had a little accident. I had to kill him in the line of duty, you know. If only you hadn't bothered him. You know what that old fool did? He led me in the wrong direction! Caused a perfectly innocent man to be killed in the line of duty, too, because I thought he was hiding you. Let's see, that's three people you caused to be dead." Glen paused to look deeply into Vaughn's eyes. "And oh, nice touch, burying all those bodies, but the government *forbade it*. So, I could just hand you over to the local authorities. But I think I can have more fun with you, myself."

Vaughn finally decided to ask a question. He was sick of the direction that the conversation had been taking. "How did you find me?"

"Ha, that was easy. All I had to do was *think*, and poof, there you were."

Vaughn scowled in disbelief. "Right."

Glen smirked, "That red-haired girl. I heard you loved her. I figured you had no better place to go than chase after her."

"But how did you know where she would be?"

Glen put his hands on his hips, puffing his big chest again, "You see, Vaughn, *you* wouldn't understand these things, but women like to talk after it's done. You know, we want to go to sleep, be left alone, but they want to talk for some reason. You know who *really* hates your redhead?"

Vaughn lost control of the darkness, and it came rushing back into his eyes. His words came through his tight mouth. "No, tell me."

"Oh, I'm so glad you asked, because you should really appreciate this. You thought *you* were clever, killing Gary and his gang. Karen's got you beat by miles. Karen hates Stephanie even more than I hate you. You spoiled her plan that night at the party!"

Vaughn was agape. He couldn't believe what he heard. Incredulous, he said, "That was HER plan?"

Glen proudly confirmed. "Yep, all the way! She played my poor cousin like a puppet. The poor fool didn't even know it. Except Stephanie was supposed to be so high she wouldn't have known up from down. There was a double dose of drug in her glass. No one could figure out what held her up. Hell, Karen had the video all set up and already had buyers! The title? *Red Hot Phanie*. Oh, you *really* angered Karen."

Vaughn looked away shaking his head. "I can't believe another woman…"

Glen mocked him, "You're a *fool*. Women are *far* more treacherous than men could ever be. After all, they bring *us* into the world. But this gets so much better! It turns out red-hair's father came for a visit a while back. He happened to bump into Karen first. Well, Karen, being the helpful type, took him to a restaurant and told him all about Stephanie and her Mom. She made a point about how terrible her mother was, always trying to *boss men around*."

Vaughn's mouth dropped open, not wanting to understand what was coming. His voice still at a distance, whispered. "But that's a lie!"

Glen stared at him like he was a complete *idiot*. "That's what makes this so ingenious."

Vaughn was still lost.

"It seems you two are the biggest *fools* and don't watch who you talk to. Red-hair used to tell *everyone* how terrible her father was, and how he hated women to even look the wrong way at a man. So Karen played up to that, and now remember she's telling me the whole story right after an excellent screaming jab, so she's all relaxed and everything. Real relaxed like, she flips her hair back and recounts, 'And oh, that woman should be killed, and it'd be real easy, too.' That's what Karen told Stephanie's father about her mother. He bought it right away! She couldn't believe how easy it was to manipulate a grown man. So she laid out her mother's whole work schedule and everything."

Vaughn still wasn't accepting it. "But they said it was an accident."

Glen frowned at him, wondering at his utter stupidity. "Nope. Stephanie's father bought an old car from another town, gave it to Karen, she ran her over, then drove out into the country and ditched the car. And got paid for her effort! Isn't that unbelievable?"

Vaughn's head swam. He felt nauseous. He was still holding Spot back. The darkness in him was put at bay by his astonishment. He actually felt weak. "But why would she kill Stephanie's mother. Her mother never…"

Glen's pleasure began being invaded by irritation, "You really are an *idiot*. It didn't matter to Karen. She knew the worst thing she could do to Stephanie was to make her live with her father!" Glen's voice became peppy. "Now, doesn't that make you feel just *wonderful?*" Watching Vaughn's reaction produced the kind of heartfelt gloating that Glen had heretofore only imagined, but to be experiencing it for real became pure ecstasy. But he wasn't quite done yet. "You know, sometimes there's just no better way to hurt someone than to just flat out tell them the truth."

It was no lie. The crushing weight in Vaughn's chest bore witness to that fact. *To think that all that suffering was caused for mere spite.* Vaughn couldn't speak.

Ever since Glen discovered the depths of pleasure in Tracy's suffering, a whole new world had opened for him. It was as if his fundamental nature had changed, like the difference between species, or perhaps even between phylum. Besides gloating, Glen basked in Vaughn's pitiful torment like a reptile needs the heat of the sun. It truly warmed Glen's heart. Yet, Glen decided there was still more to squeeze out of him.

"You know, I had wanted to try to use you to kill Jargon, but I realized you're way too stubborn to be leveraged." Vaughn was still dazed. "I can't believe it, the all-wise Vaughn is speechless. Hey, what's in your hand?"

❖ SACRIFICIAL WOOD ❖

Sounding hollow, Vaughn responded. "A book of wisdom."

"Throw it over here. Let's see if it's really wise."

Vaughn, still feeling empty, tossed the book to him, but when Glen looked at it, he seemed confused.

"Huh, no title, one page and it's blank! Well, there's wisdom for you." Glen threw it across the cave. "*You* won't be needing it. You know, I was going to wait until you reached Stephanie, because I wanted to have some fun with her while you watched, but then, when I saw you up here and realized there was no way out, I just figured it better to get you now. Besides, I already know where your whore is. Well, now you know the whole story. *It's pretty bad, huh?*"

Glen was taking exceptional delight in this reality he created. *So much power with innumerable possibilities.* His heart began to drift to Stephanie and how he would tell *her* the truth, too, not only about what happened to her, but about what happened to Vaughn.

Vaughn responded dryly. "Unimaginable!"

Delighted with the power of truth, Glen decided to resort to it yet, again, to describe what he planned to do, in detail. "OH GOOD. Ya know, I figured I couldn't hurt you any worse than to just plain tell you the truth. There's no wisdom, no cleverness that can escape it, like you escaped me before with the Judge.

"I'll tell you another truth. When I'm done with you and done with Red, I'll go to Red's father. Karen told me what to say to him to make him go off on his daughter. Oh, and what the heck, I'll make a *rug* out of your *dog*." He paused just long

485

enough to inspect Vaughn's pain level, to ensure that it reached its peak. Finally deciding he could get no extra pleasure from prolonging Vaughn's life, Glen, in a friendly, self-satisfied matter of fact tone, said, "O.K. Now would be an excellent time for you to die *with absolutely no peace at all!*"

As Glen raised the gun, Vaughn, who was on one knee holding Spot, whispered to Spot to stay. The crushing vile injustice rampaging through Vaughn left him broken. All his hopes and dreams were like a fragile fruit hanging by a broken stem, about to fall far below to the ground. His heart was that fruit.

Impending doom, futility… but yet, even in these last moments, the preciousness of life combined to move Vaughn to calmly and slowly stand up to meet his fate with dignity, even as he imagined the people he buried met theirs. It didn't make sense that just a short time ago he had been blessed with his utmost desire, the Book of Wisdom, only to now lose everything? But Reality is what Reality *is*. His mind no longer knew what to do so he yielded fully his last moments to his heart. Glen waited, the gun still trained at Vaughn's chest, being intrigued by Vaughn's calm reaction. *Hmm, is there yet some bit more pleasure you're going to give me before I kill you?*

Spreading open his arms and raising his head, Vaughn listened to the words that his heart softly began to speak to the beyond. "Oh spirits who yet live, behold mine and your daughter's enemy, and avenge us. *Seal this cave shut!*" As Vaughn spoke, his eyes began to shine brightly with a golden light.

SACRIFICIAL WOOD

"What's he doing?" Queen Yinauqua asked, as they watched through the golden glow of their orb.

King Mafferan shook his head. "I really don't know. That boy's a mystery. But this isn't any of the choices you'd suggested."

She wrapped her arm around his waist, watching with double admiration. "He so reminds me of you, my love."

"You know, I really can't refuse his request! See how he phrased it? He's asked us to avenge *them!* He's already sworn to avenge our murdered children. How much more so should we avenge them being yet alive? He's asked for justice with proper faith. He knows our nature of goodness can't turn him down."

"But we aren't allowed to interfere. The Truce."

"Not directly. But somehow, he's chosen a request we *can* answer. Sealing the cave breaches neither side of the truce because it doesn't favor anyone on Earth, here, or the Ethereal! They'll *both* be trapped! So it's not really interference!"

"But then what good…"

"That's just it. I don't know! Which is why I'm allowed to grant it, and why the Lord isn't rejecting me from doing so!"

Yinauqua tried peering into her husband's depths. She narrowed her eyes at him and…

As Vaughn's last word faded into silence, a palpable calm entered the cave. Glen laughed, shook his head, and then straightened his arm to shoot and… the ground began to shake terribly, knocking them down, and the huge overhang above the cave entrance collapsed, sealing them in.

Glen picked himself off of the cave floor, ran over to Vaughn, who was still down, straddled him, and shoved his gun in Vaughn's face. "What? WHAT DID YOU DO?" he yelled, not believing how suddenly his soon to be greatest pleasure in life had vanished, as if it never existed. Grossly cheated beyond comprehension, Glen's whole being felt… violated.

Vaughn was in no hurry. "You won't be able to hurt Stephanie now. You'll die here, alone, with me. I couldn't think of a better ending for you!"

The words bit at Glen and he smacked Vaughn across his face with the gun. Blood ran from his cheek. Spot obediently stayed, but all his muscles strained to be still. Glen laughed, "You *fool*, I'll just dig myself out."

Vaughn rubbed his face and spit out blood, but he smiled broadly. "Go ahead and try. But those boulders are too heavy for you, and the harder you work, the more oxygen you'll use up, along with the torches." Vaughn pointed at the four torches that still burned.

Glen stood up, looked at them burning, and began to understand his fate. Fear slowly began to creep into his eyes, widening them slowly by degree. He shouted his command to Vaughn with the gun waving, as he stepped aside. "We don't need that many torches, put all but one out."

Vaughn sat up straight. Vibrant blackness began to creep back into his eyes, but he didn't fight it this time. "You put 'em out! Whacha gonna do, kill me?"

Glen rushed over to the torches, smothering them with their torch caps, each giving off a hiss, and then he came back waving his gun again. "You think you're so smart, don't you?"

Vaughn was in no hurry and kept silent.

SACRIFICIAL WOOD

Glen ordered him as he pointed his gun at Vaughn's head. "Tell your spirits or whatever to unblock the cave."

Vaughn softly replied. "No."

Glen's eyes got wider. "DO IT." He shoved the gun against his forehead. Vaughn's yawn angered Glen even more. He wanted so desperately to just pull the trigger, but he couldn't. How would he get out of the cave?

"You know Vaughn, you're really *stupid*, you know that?"

Vaughn scooted all the way back and propped himself against the painting of Queen Yinauqua without saying a word. If anything, he looked quite uninterested.

Glen found himself trying to carry the conversation. "Because if you could get the spirits to obey you, you didn't have to trap yourself, you could have just trapped me."

Vaughn leveled his eyes into Glen's. "All I knew was I couldn't let you escape. My life is *nothing* compared to Stephanie's. Perhaps both of ours deserve to end here, together! Maybe neither of us is so clever. Anyway, the prayer was from my heart, not my mind! It just *felt* right!"

What kind of garbage is he talking about? Just felt *right?* "Come on, say another prayer. Ask them to unblock the cave."

Another calm one word reply, "No."

The calmer Vaughn got, the more upset Glen got. *"DO YOU WANT TO DIE?"* He shoved the gun up under Vaughn's nose, pressing Vaughn's head into the cave wall, but Vaughn offered no resistance.

He spoke with resignation. "I was dead already. You were going to shoot me."

Glen eased back, not knowing what to do, so he sat down. As they sat across from each other in silence, Glen studied him, but Vaughn just leaned his back against the painting with his head bowed. Fear caused Glen to breathe more rapidly, while Vaughn seemed to be in quiet meditation.

Finally, Glen couldn't contain himself. "It's getting hard to breathe. You have to open the cave. PRAY."

But Vaughn gave him the same quiet answer. "No."

"I'll let you live! PRAY."

Vaughn looked up at him, and noted the change in his tone, a humorous combination of concession and command. "Scared of dying Glen?" Vaughn was beginning to enjoy himself, noting he had never had this kind of pleasure before. It was an I've-got-nothing-to-lose pleasure.

A more conciliatory tone gushed forth. "Hey, sure I wanted my fun with you, but I got a great job. I'm in heaven here. I can't lose all that on account of you. You can have your life. PRAY"

"Yeah, right."

Spot got up, no longer worried about Glen, and slowly walked away from them. He began sniffing around. Vaughn remembered how he'd ignored Spot before.

"Look here, take the gun! O.K.? Now pray." The gun was dropped in Vaughn's lap.

He let it rest there without touching it. "This means nothing. When you get out, you'll just do the same damn thing. Maybe I should just kill *you* now, and then pray."

Glen smiled, knowing that he had the upper hand. "I took the bullets. But I don't think you're the type! You see, I know you killed Gary, and I bet you even killed his gang, but they were directly threatening you. They had it coming! But I've decided to leave you alone. I've given you my word. You have no good reason to harm me now. In order for someone like you to kill, you need a good reason. No, you're not the type."

Vaughn thought about Tracy. His eyes darkened again, and Glen could see it. He leveled those eyes into Glen's, piercing his soul with menace. It was Vaughn's turn to speak friendly. "You see, you can't even begin to understand the *type* I am. I'm your worst nightmare."

Vaughn's stare unsettled him. It didn't go along with the do-goodder psyche Glen figured him for. He looked at the gun in Vaughn's lap. Vaughn took it, and put it behind him in his belt. Glen shouted at him. "WHAT DO YOU WANT FROM ME?"

Vaughn went back to his meditation. *I should just kill him. I didn't kill Ralph, and he blocked my escape and almost caused me to die. He'd already deserved to die for dealing drugs, just like Glen does now, only for far more.*

Vaughn roused himself to kill him, moments passed and he envisioned how he would take Glen's life. Blackness began to vibrate around him. Glen saw it. Vaughn remembered Gary convulsing in death, and imagined Glen doing the same thing. He remembered the look in Gary's eyes, that look that said he suddenly, desperately, wanted to live. Vaughn's stomach lurched. *Damn!* He thought about Tracy again, and then about the farmers. His eyes shined with the deepest blackness. He looked at Glen. The blackness wanted him *dead*. More moments passed. *DAMN, he's right! I know he deserves it. I…I just can't be his judge. He's right. Well how 'bout that! He's right! All those I killed were in self-defense. But he's not sincere. HE WAS JUST ABOUT TO KILL ME. He doesn't need a good reason to hurt people, but…damn, I still can't be his judge. JUDGE. What about judges and laws? They sentence people to death all the time. Why not me? But they have a sworn responsibility to uphold the law, a responsibility to protect others from harm. YES! I should kill him NOW.* His muscles tensed. The line between initiative and action blurred as his mind told him to act. *Why can't I? Why can't I be like a judge? O.K., people appointed others to do that. They didn't just appoint themselves. Damn, he's right. But why should that make a difference?*

But the blackness continued to urge him, placing him on the edge again. He could feel it. Revulsion at Glen's evil. *Avenge the innocent!* Any time, any time now he could lose control like he did at the hospital. But this time he would follow through.

Glen began to worry, *Maybe I misjudged him.* "Alright, I'll write out a piece of paper clearing you of all charges and I'll sign it. Where's that book I threw away?"

Vaughn's head snapped up. "Don't even touch it." Vaughn got up and went to the corner of the cave to retrieve the book. He inspected it for damage, but all he saw was a roughened gold corner.

"YOU'RE CRAZY. It's just a blank piece of paper inside a *blank* cover."

SACRIFICIAL WOOD

"Well, then it would be my blank piece of paper, wouldn't it? Find something else to write on." He sat back down in his spot against the Queen's picture.

Glen fished out his wallet. *I know I've got to have a stupid piece of scrap paper in here. Besides, after I kill him, I'll take it back.*

Vaughn hid his amazement. The cover, front to back, now looked like the cave walls. The title, *Wisdom From the Inside-OUT*, was written over the cave pictures. He wanted to open it, but the time didn't feel right. *This is sacred. If I open it, it will be with respect.*

This was becoming a nightmare to Glen, but he had to do whatever it took to save his life. "What do you want from me?"

Vaughn's eyes turned to black daggers. "What's *right!*"

No, it wasn't *becoming* a nightmare, it *was* a nightmare. "WHA…?" The stale air choked Glen. The tightness in his chest alarmed him. "It's getting harder to breathe. Please…. O.K. PLEEASE, I WANT TO LIVE. PLEEASE, PRAY."

Even though Glen was begging now, Vaughn stayed silent, ignoring him.

Glen got down on his knees. "I'm begging you. I'm sorry for what I did."

Vaughn looked into his eyes, questioning. He softened his tone. "You really mean that?"

"Yes, YES, I REALLY MEAN IT." Finally, Glen detected progress.

Vaughn continued to silently stare at him with an almost child-like innocence, and finally spoke with a matching innocent tone. "You wouldn't go back on your word?"

Glen reassured him with *powerful* words. "May I suffer a fate worse than death if I go back on my word."

The blackness in Vaughn's eyes flashed. Vaughn began to explain. "When all that killing was going on down below, someone was up here."

Glen didn't really care. All he wanted was to get out. "So?"

"I know this because that old box lying crushed over there, must have had something important in it. I don't think it was a regular box. I think it was emptied because of the things happening down there. But someone came later and didn't find its contents, and got very angry and crushed it. There's no other good explanation that I can think of."

Glen was growing impatient. "SO?"

Vaughn gave him a hurt look. "You're not sounding very repentant."

Glen forced himself to bow his head. Vaughn paused, waiting.

"I…I…I'm sorry." Glen sounded as if the words choked him.

Vaughn, still calm and looking doubtful, called him on it, "I don't know. I don't think I like your tone."

Glen couldn't stand the humiliation, the helplessness he felt. The pressure burst him into a blubbering fit. "I'M SORRY DAMN IT. WHAT ELSE DO YOU WANT? I'm SORRY." The tears pouring from his eyes weren't fake. He had never felt smaller in his life, having to grovel at the feet of this, this…

"*Tears from you Glen?*"

Now he really did bow his head in shame. He just couldn't believe he had to beg *him* for his life. He couldn't speak.

Vaughn continued as before in a calm, collected way. "Well, whatever was in the box had to be very important. There was no way for someone to escape going back out the way they came in, and they couldn't risk being found in here. Three sets of tracks went up, but only one came down."

Vaughn coughed. The air was getting very stale, and both were coughing and breathing heavily now. Glen was beside himself with frustration, but he knew he couldn't push Vaughn. He was beginning to suspect that all the pain may have driven Vaughn mad, because he didn't seem at all concerned that they were suffocating. *Tracks? What tracks? How could he see any tracks? It's all rock! He's imagining things.*

"SO?"

Vaughn calmly reassured him. "There's someone missing for sure."

Glen tried calming himself and continued to play along. "Who?"

"Stephanie, *the red-haired girl.*" Vaughn flashed his anger purposely, but then calmed as if he never had. "She was befriended by these people. She would have protected whatever was in the box with her life. I'm sure of it. You see, I know her character." He stared again at Glen, but this time very innocently, with the expectation that Glen could now empathize with understanding good character.

He's acting erratic, imagining things. Red-Hair lives a long way from here. Oh God, I'm going to die! "How do you know she wasn't caught? She might not have been killed with the others, because she wasn't of those people."

"The tracks. That means there has to be another way out of here."

Oh, what the hell. That much is possible. Glen sprang up, grabbed the torch, and started madly rushing around feeling the walls.

Vaughn sighed. "Stop running around like that."

After a quick exploration, Glen came back panicking. "There's no way out. You're *crazy*. We're inside a bloody mountain."

Vaughn finally stood up while Spot sat patiently in a corner of the cave.

"Give me the torch." Glen politely handed it over. "Thank you."

Its flame seemed to be shrinking.

Vaughn sat down and studied the cover of the book. Glen watched him, rapidly breathing, trying to get enough oxygen. They were running out of time. *He's crazy. Damn, I've driven him mad.*

The cover to this book is a picture of the inside of this cave. Vaughn thought it odd that the paintings of the king and queen were not in the center of the cover. The whole picture seemed rotated, to put the extreme right corner of their cave painting in the center of the book. *Why do that?* The title was perfectly centered with the single word 'Wisdom' at top center. 'From the Inside' in the center, and the word 'OUT',

◆ SACRIFICIAL WOOD ◆

in all capital letters, was in the center bottom. *Why capitalize it?* Vaughn saw where the word 'OUT' was superimposed.

Spot was sitting in that corner. Vaughn had watched him earlier when he sniffed his way over there. He hadn't growled when he sniffed as he had when sniffing around the box and the crushed table. *Stephanie went to that corner. He followed her trail to there…then stopped!* "Spot." Vaughn stood up pointing to the ground in front of the queen's picture, where he figured Stephanie had stepped. Spot eagerly stood up, came over, and sniffed around. "Find her trail, Spot." Spot arfed with excitement, doing a little dance. He sniffed his way back to the corner. Vaughn followed him, watching carefully. Spot's nose followed on the ground, and then he picked his head up, sniffing a stone several times. Then he turned around, ruffing several times, beckoning his master to the stone as he returned again to sniff the end of the trail.

"Good boy, Spot. Good boy." Vaughn smiled as he patted his faithful dog. Remembering the last time he and Spot went through an unknown passage, Vaughn's hand went to his head. The bump was still there. Spot averted his eyes.

Vaughn patted his head again, anyway, then pushed on the stone near the demon's picture. Part of the wall slid to the side. "Follow me, and watch your step. SPOT, let Glen come then you!"

Vaughn headed into the narrow passage first. It seemed a lot tighter to the much larger Glen, who had to literally squeeze himself between the walls. Vaughn emphasized his next point, "This is a pretty narrow passageway. Sure you can get through? I see light."

Vaughn stepped out onto the outside trail and inhaled deeply. He turned to the emerging Glen who immediately took several gulping breaths. Seeing that Glen was quickly returning to his confident self, Vaughn made sure he understood how he should protect his recent, repentant conversion. "Watch your step going down this mountain. The drop is pretty steep. This trail is ancient, and besides Stephanie and one other, probably hasn't been used for a very long time."

Vaughn scanned the narrow trail again. It was mostly bare rock with fine dirt settled in every depression. Much to his satisfaction, he saw a single set of a woman's tracks. But then, the hairs on the back of his neck stood up as he wondered. *What happened to the man who came later? He didn't go back the way he came, and he didn't come this way. There's something* very *odd going on. How on Earth did he crush that stone table and box?* But Vaughn had no time to contemplate that now.

He directed Glen. "We'll have to go single file, one at a time. I'll go first!" Vaughn turned his back to Glen and started down the trail. Without turning around, he called back to him as he eased down the rocky, steep descent. "So Glen, now that you're sorry for what you did, you do realize you'll have to turn yourself in?"

Vaughn heard no reply, but still didn't turn to look at him, as he had to pay attention to where he was putting his feet. "You gave your word, Glen."

Feeling quite relieved, Glen countered, just for the sake of it, knowing he had plenty of time before they reached the bottom of the trail. "I said I was sorry. I didn't say anything about turning myself in." Then he wondered where Vaughn had put the gun.

"Oh, I see. So just what did *sorry* mean to you?"

Glen had enough of being embarrassed by this...this... "It meant I was sorry for being so stupid as to be caught in a stupid cave with *you*."

Vaughn continued to face forward, speaking calmly. "So, you're going back on your word? You know you don't have your gun any more. As I recall, last time we fought, I knocked you out. Hmm, perhaps you don't recall that, though. Losing consciousness does things to the memory."

Glen had regained his dignity, feeling powerful again. "You got in a lucky shot and I'm ten times more powerful now than I was then. I hadn't *killed* anyone back then, either. I don't need you anymore, so you better watch your step, or you might fall off this cliff."

Glen knew if Vaughn turned around to keep an eye on him, chances were quite high he would misstep and fall because of the unevenness of the steep trail. But, if Vaughn didn't turn around, Glen had every intention of making sure Vaughn took the shortcut before they reached the halfway mark. For now, there was plenty of time to play, again.

Vaughn seemed oblivious to the danger. "No. I'm watching very carefully where I put my feet. It's always important to know where you step in life. To have faith. You know, you were standing in a holy place when you gave your word. You *sure* you don't want to *reconsider* your repentance?" Deep blackness rushed into Vaughn's eyes, and he could feel tingling all through his body. But all he could do was let it take its course.

Glen realized there had always been something about Vaughn that *really* irritated him, that he just couldn't stand, like the odor of vomit. "Oh God, *please* spare me from his foolish prattling. It's just a matter of time before I get you. You know that. Nothing has really changed."

Vaughn felt a flash of power that was much greater than himself surge through him. His thoughts were guided, and he spoke what came to mind. "You never told me how you killed my farmer friend."

Glen decided it would be perfect to tell him, and then kill him. "I caught him in a field and stopped him just short of the farmhouse he was driving to. I forced him to lie down in front of the truck, and I rolled it over him, pinning him there. Then, I punctured the tire to make it look like he was trying to fix a flat and got trapped. You should have heard the *screams*."

Pains stabbed Vaughn in his heart, but then he remembered the old farmer's words, how in his dying breath he wouldn't go back on his wonderful faith and understanding of life. *No, he held tightly to the Tree of Life. You have killed yourself Glen. Now is the time of your judgment.* "This farmer, you mean the one with all those *dogs?*"

Spot's eyes flashed black, and his ears went forward listening, waiting, never taking his eyes off Glen.

"Yeah, those *damned dogs* threatened…" Spot broke into a ferocious roar. He'd long been trained to react against the phrase, *Damned dogs,* because, quite obviously, only those who were trouble would say, *Damned dogs.*

In reflex, Glen flinched, twisting himself around to look at Spot. There was a still moment between the man and the dog. Each stared into the others' eyes with the knowledge that if Glen just had a mere second more, he could regain his balance. Spot could relent or press forward. Spot roared ferociously again, readying himself to spring at Glen.

Glen couldn't help tensing, to try to brace himself against the *damned dog's* forthcoming attack. But in stiffening, he lost the suppleness he needed to regain his balance. The dog never jumped. Glen realized he couldn't have jumped from that position as he lost his footing and began to fall over the edge.

Horror! Shock! To be beaten by a *dog!* The falling through the air matched the sinking in his heart. *My life was so precious…*

Spot peered over the edge satisfied. Vaughn, pressing his back against the cliff wall, watched also. They saw his body bounce off a rock outcropping, and then flail outward. As Glen fell, his screams of disbelief, pleading, and futile rage echoed in the mountains. When he finally landed on the ground, he was lying on his back, blankly staring upward.

After the shock wore off, Glen focused his eyes. The sky was beautiful. A few small, puffy white clouds took their time drifting by. *I'm alive!* He went to move, but nothing happened. *My legs! My arms! Oh GOD! I can't feel them!* A voice.

"Tisk, tisk, tisk, what has happened to you?" Jargono happened to be in The Forest at the time, and saw a tree flare with glow, even though it was only for an instant. Immediately, he went to it and popped to Earth beside Glen. *I see, they always make a call to God right before they think they're dying.*

Glen recognized him. This was the man he one day hoped to kill for being such trouble. He didn't like bowing to anyone, even if he was only a figurehead. Glen's eyes widened, and Jargono read his mind.

"Yes, I am sorry your plans haven't worked out. You know, I don't hold it against you that you wanted to kill me. Heck, if I was you, I'd want to kill me, too!" Jargono's pleasantness only served to anger Glen more. "Well, if you don't want my help…"

"NO! Wait. How? I'm paralyzed."

"Hmm, so you are. Well, that's too bad. You won't have much of a life, now. But I'm not evil like some say of me. I'll get you the best care. You can live a long life like this."

"NO! Kill me!"

"*Kill you?* Oh, I don't know if I could." Jargono paused long enough to let Glen's torment multiply. "There is a small possibility I could restore…"

"DO IT."

"But, you have to understand, know all the risks. There's even a chance you could die or possibly become worse."

"Nothing is worse. DO IT."

"You have to understand, what I do, you have to accept totally. No matter what comes, what you see or feel, you have to not only accept, but you have to embrace it, *love it.*"

SACRIFICIAL WOOD

"DO IT, *DAMN YOU!*"

Jargono pulled a black bottle from under the baggy, long sleeve of his brown Appendaho robe. He raised his hands to the sky, and immediately deep black swirls came from all directions toward him. A brightly glowing, blue netting appeared out of nowhere surrounding him and Glen, and the blackness pushed against it. Glen's eyes widened in horror.

"I see you're not very good at keeping your word. This won't work."

Glen looked at the swirling blackness. He could feel it. He could sense it hungering for him. *It's not that much different than me. It wants to be alive here. TO RULE, I WANT TO RULE. It wants me to help it. WE'LL BECOME ONE! I'll have more power than I ever dreamed.*

The blackness sensed Glen's compatibility. It pressed ever harder at the blue netting. It wanted Jargono even more, but he wasn't willing. Glen felt the logic of the Black Essence. It was pure. His heart agreed with its principles, its desires. *I do love you. I don't have to convince myself.* "COME FOR ME!"

The blackness surged. Jargono was losing the nettings' restraint. He knelt down. "If you want to survive the joining, you must drink this and *love* it. It won't taste good now, but it will later."

He uncorked the bottle and put it to Glen's mouth. Glen gagged at first, but held onto the bottle with his lips. He wouldn't let go, and forced himself to drink it all down. As the blue netting collapsed, Jargono dove away from Glen, surrounding himself with yet another blue netting, which he

503

wrapped tightly around himself. The Black Essence stormed them both. When it couldn't get through to Jargono, the essence stormed Glen with its full force.

Jargono watched closely, as the blackness swirled in and out of every fiber of Glen's being. It seemed to be fighting itself. *Damn, just as I thought, there's too much of it for just one body.* Finally, all the Black Essence that could enter and stay inside Glen settled into him. The rest fled in anger, searching, searching…

Glen roared as the transformation began. His hands and feet began to lengthen, his chest puffed out even more. Claws! His face lengthened, his eyes turned red, his nose stretched longer, and his ears pointed. When the transformation was complete, he began to shimmer with a gray glow.

Jargono studied him the whole time. *Yes, it's working. And he's not* deforming *like all the others, he's* transforming. *I told you,* Mafferan, *that I had a solution. One more soul should do it. I don't have to experiment any more.*

Glen, *Demon* Glen, stood up! Jargono smiled at him. "I told you I could help."

Demon Glen laughed, "You *fool*. I don't need you."

Jargono threw a brightly glowing golden netting around Demon Glen. He shrieked in pain. "Tisk, tisk tisk, now that's gratitude for you. First of all, if you want me to reverse the process, I shall!"

Both the demon's essence and Glen howled together in rage. "I thought so. You're well suited for each other. One might even say destined. Not only can I reverse the process,

SACRIFICIAL WOOD

but since you have a fully integrated physical form, there's a good chance I can destroy both parts of you." Demon Glen howled in rage again.

Jargono warned Demon Glen, staring directly into his Earth-demon eyes. "We'll work together, but don't think I'll ever make the mistake of trusting you. You'll do *exactly* as I say every time, no more, and no less, or else I *will* end this lovely union." He increased the power of the netting's glow. The Earth Demon screamed in torment. Jargono smiled, then touched the netting with his hand, and they all vanished together.

Vaughn and Spot carefully made their way down the trail, and then came around to where Glen had fallen. Vaughn shook his head and his eyes retraced his steps several times, looking back and forth from up to the mountain and down to the ground. Spot sniffed around at someone's short trail, growling again, as he did back in the cave. But when he got to where Glen had landed, he whined and jumped back in fear! Spot, now with his tail between his legs, delicately approached again, but this time, nowhere near as close as before, and he backed away again, and wouldn't re-approach. He sat staring at his master as if trying to tell Vaughn something. It was the strangest expression one could ever see on a dog. A look of deep trouble, fear, bewilderment and some kind of knowledge. It was the knowledge part that made it so strange.

Spot's reaction sent goose bumps all over Vaughn. Suddenly, deep blackness funneled into Vaughn so powerfully that he felt he might faint. His eyes teared. Life itself seemed to be trying to tell him something, but his mind couldn't understand it… but his heart did. And his heart's reaction terrified him, as it was just like in his visions. *Oh God, MY VISIONS!*

He looked at Spot. "You know, don't you Spot?" Spot's eyes shot up to his master, and just stared.

CHAPTER NINETEEN
Little Rest For The Weary

"The Truce has wrapped itself around their necks, and by it, the star of the Tree shall be pulled to Earth and beyond. And by it, the desire of the Great Eye shall be forced into the Ethereal, where he had never been and no one thought to go. Only the wise one knows that the Truce they have fought to preserve, has never been so for all. It is for the Alpha, their greatest weapon to achieve their long awaited purpose." So prophesied Master GrrraGagag at the banks of the Sacred Black River unto the wisps, waiting in hope of the Earth.

Stephanie balanced herself on a ladder while putting up advertisements for onions and potatoes in the store's front window.

"STEPHIE-E-E-E, WHERE DO YOU WANT THIS?"

Lana precariously held up a heavy can as high as she could, straining with all her effort.

"Sprout, just put it on the counter over there." Stephanie tilted her head in the right direction. The counter was a good foot over Lana's little head.

Hugging the can tightly, she rushed over, and leaning it against the side of the counter for support, then pushed it up and over the edge. Half on and half off the edge of the counter, she gently eased it further. Then, she ran back to Stephanie skipping and singing. "O.K. I like being your helper…I like it, I like it, I like it…I..I..I…like IT."

Stephanie's joy at such a sight bubbled through her. "And I like your singing, Sprout."

Jean's happiness seemed surreal, as she never had imagined it possible. "I can't believe we own a real store. You know, for the first time in my life, I feel free."

Stephanie looked down from the ladder. "Arlupo told me you were married to a good man before."

Jean didn't give her a chance to say it. "He was good compared to *him*. But I was young and, well, all I thought about was being his wife. But now, I'm going to think about being me."

Stephanie decided to tell her. "I put the store in your name."

Shocked, she couldn't bear the thought of being sole owner of the store. She protested. "But it should be in both…"

Stephanie cut her off. "No. I'm not sure how long I'll be here. I opened an account for you, and placed enough money in it to last for a good year. But way before that, you should be living off your profits. I placed your bankbook in your center desk drawer."

Jean walked over to the ladder, peering up with concern. "But Stephanie, what do you mean? Why would you leave?"

Finished with hanging the last poster and smiling at her effort, she climbed down to face her. "I don't know. I just feel that my destiny isn't here, that's all. I'm not sure what to do about Vaughn. When he arrives at the place I told him, he won't find me there."

Jean reflected. "What if he arrives now, or very soon?"

The thought greatly disturbed Stephanie. "Oh God, then he would find… no, he's so far away. I don't see how he could make it any time soon. I just don't know what to do. It's not like I can leave word with anyone as to where I am."

Stephanie went to take care of the cans Lana pushed up on the counter. As she did, her mind traveled deep in thought. *The Tree of Life is gone. I only faithwalked with the Tree's help. I have its Seed. Oh dear God. How am I to protect such an invaluable thing? Does evil know I have this? Oh God, I need Vaughn with me. Pleeeease guide him to me.*

"Stephie. Stephie." Lana kept tugging harder on her sister's green peasant dress.

Stephanie smiled. "Lana, you're about to tug my dress completely off."

"I put all those away." She pointed to a row of cans sitting on a small, low table Stephie had set up for her. They would have to be moved to a higher place, but that wasn't important now. What was important was that Lana felt important for helping.

"Come here you, it's big hug time." Stephanie wrapped her up in her arms, giving her a bear hug.

The little girl squealed. Stephie kissed her many times on the head and cheek. Jean came over with her head hung.

"Stephanie, I'm so sorry for the way I've treated you." Stephanie looked up with soft eyes. "Mother…"

Jean didn't want her to call her that, so she interrupted. "You don't have to call me that anymore."

"I know, Mom. I understand how hard it was. You know I do. You have a new life now. Be true to it."

Jean shook her head, wondering. "So many times, it's funny, but I feel like you're the adult and I'm the child."

Stephanie eased Lana out of her big hug, and the little girl stood watching. "You still have lots of experience over me, Mom. I never gave birth. I can't imagine. Vaughn told me that there are some trees that are very old but don't look large for their age. But they still have the rings. I think you're that kind of tree, but you're looking at your size instead of your rings. I think that as you tend this store and raise Lana, you'll be surprised at just how much you really do know and feel. I'm still a child compared to you, and…" Stephanie began to choke up. Her confession opened a sleeping door. "I would like a hug."

Jean wrapped her arms around her. Stephanie's sobbing seemed to come out of nowhere. Caring for Lana created feeling in her of what she'd missed, what she needed. It all came very much alive in her. 'What about the need,' she had asked Vaughn just after her mother died. He told her there's no way to compensate for true needs except to simply appreciate what she already had, and determine to give all the love she could to others to better their lives. In giving that love to Lana, she found herself suddenly, in some way, very much on the same level. " *'Cause I really am just still a child. It's been...*" she sobbed.

Jean hushed her and kept patting her as Stephie pulled long seated, deep sobs from her gut, suddenly feeling very weak. She ached for her real mother. She ached for the Appendaho. She ached for the normal childhood she never had. It took her completely off guard. Jean suddenly could feel her down to her very core. "There, there, child, there, there. Let it out. Let it all out and you'll feel better."

Suddenly, Jean seemed to come to her senses in a way like waking from a dead sleep. *I feel like a mother, again! When did I stop feeling it? Oh God. Thank you. Thank you for this child.* Her arms tightened even more around Stephanie, stroking her with even deeper emotion. And as the two held each other, a special healing took its natural course. "There, there, child… there, there…"

Lana grew very concerned. "Stephie, Mommy, why is Stephie crying?" Lana began to have tears in her eyes, too, at seeing her beloved sister cry so hard, and her mother took Lana in one of her arms, and drew her in with them.

"Because she's a child, too, and she's been very hurt for a long, long time. Because, well, when you're older, I'll explain it to you. Right now, let's just hug her and hold her."

Vaughn rested on a thick, low tree branch on the side of the northern trail, and Spot disappeared behind the large tree. The sound of some small animal whining broke his concentration. Then, he heard Spot Arf, followed by several little arfs, followed by Spot's bigger ARF and louder whine. Vaughn picked his head up, wondering if his ears were playing tricks on him. Spot's voice seemed to have oddly changed.

"Hey, what's goin' on, Spot?"

There was more of the same doggy conversation. Then, the cutest golden-haired puppy with floppy ears bounded around the tree. He ran smack into Vaughn's leg and bounced off. A bit confused, he sat looking up at him.

"Well, well, what do we have here? Have you found a new friend?" Vaughn reached down and picked up the ball of fur, setting him on his lap. The puppy squirmed, trying to free himself. "Hey little fella, c'mere." Vaughn rubbed him under the chin. The little golden-brown puppy was all licks in Vaughn's face.

"O.K. O.K., you can come with us. Here, have some dried beef." Vaughn pulled a piece from a package in his shirt pocket.

Obviously hungry, he looked to be only three or four months old. He growled at the piece of beef as he tugged on it, while Vaughn held it firmly. For some reason, the puppy invigorated Vaughn, and he had energy to move on. "Well Spot, let's head north and find my love."

☙

Jean sat down behind the counter with Stephanie.

"Well, we're in business. I just counted this week's profits. Three hundred dol!"

Stephanie's eyes popped. "YOU'RE KIDDING!"

"No, I'm not. I counted it three times and took away for expenses. It seems word of mouth spread that a widowed family of girls took over the store, and people have been coming for miles. Stephie, haven't you noticed how many nice men have come here?"

"I guess not. I've been too busy."

Jean leaned closer to her. "Well, some look at me, but some look at *you*, too."

Stephanie frowned. *"Mom!"*

"I know. You already have your love. You told me."

Stephanie seemed worried. "Mom?"

"What is it, dear?"

"What if *he* finds you, us?"

Jean pulled her stool closer. "I've been thinking hard about that. It would be just like him not to give up. From what you told me, the government is doing some weird thing concerning women down in the province to the South. But I haven't heard any such thing up here. We're rural. No universities. Frankly, these people are different. I don't think they'd hear it. I've already given notice to the government that I divorced him, and that I support myself. Look what I have. I've been saving this to surprise you."

Jean reached under the counter, pulled open a drawer, and pulled out a folder and set in front of Stephie.

Stephanie opened it and could hardly believe her eyes. "Oh MY GOD, Jean, Mom, this is GREAT. But how'd you get the official papers?"

"Apparently, the head official here was best friends with the store owner who passed away. When he saw that we were three girls alone, and that I had money to run the business, he said that his friend could not have asked for anyone better to take the store over. You see, the former owner was once married, but his wife died in childbirth. It broke his heart. He raised his daughter to three years old, and then she died in an accident of some kind. After that, he just ran the store by himself until he died. His best friend said that we were meant to have his store, and that he felt his friend's spirit would watch over us. He gave me the official papers that my store is government certified, and I am the certified owner. No more questions asked. All I had to do was show him the papers you gave me, showing the store was legally in my name."

Stephanie was still concerned about her question. Jean had avoided it. "But what will you do if…?"

Jean reached further under the counter and brought something up quicker than Stephanie could see. She almost fell off her stool trying to get out of the way, as Jean slung it around and slammed it down in front of Stephanie. "*I bought this!*"

Startled, Stephanie couldn't get over the two things she was now looking at. How Jean had changed so quickly, and what she just banged down in front of her. "JEAN, A SHOTGUN?"

"Damn right. I'm not letting that bastard intimidate me anymore."

SACRIFICIAL WOOD

"But, you have to use your head. He's government."

"Yes, of the province to the *South*. I'll send him to *our* official. Fred would be lucky if he didn't get himself thrown in jail… I think *ours* is sweet on me!" Jean blushed a bit, and Stephanie noted it with humor.

The little bell rang at the front which meant someone had opened the gate and was walking up the sidewalk to the store.

Lana excitedly petitioned for the duty. "Oooh, another 'custmer', Stephie. Can I get the dooooor?"

Stephanie was engaged in conversation with Jean, and saw no harm in letting the child answer the door. "Sure Sprout."

Lana went and pulled hard on the door knob, and the door swung slowly open. "Hi, hi, wel…welcome to our store." She threw her little hand open to lead him inside.

"Well, thank you little girl. You've learned your manners well, hasn't she, Stephanie?" A young man dressed in Appendaho modest male garb of faded brown tunic and brown pants stepped inside and stared directly at her.

Stephanie's heart came into her mouth, a chill ran over her body, and her hairs stood up all over her. Stephanie had the silence of death about her that stops a heart in mid-beat.

Jean felt the sudden change in spirit. "Stephanie, what is it? Who is he?"

Stephanie thought to herself, even as Jean persisted in her question. *Oh God, no! Don't put your hand to the Seed, you idiot.*

The man spoke again to her. "Stephanie, have you no greeting for an Appendaho brother?" Her thoughts continued,

❧ DARRYL MARKOWITZ ❧

He wasn't around that much. I don't know how much he knows. But I know he has some kind of darkness and evil power. I remember the black oil he had. I can see the darkness in him. Oh God, he's after the Seed. I just know it! What do I do? Do I have power to fight him? I don't know.

"Hmmmm, lost in thought, I see." The young, handsome man with short, straight black hair, peered into her eyes and then roamed his gaze elsewhere over her.

Stephanie realized she needed to divert his attentions. "Oh, I'm sorry, it's just that I really don't remember you that much."

"Yeah, you were always with my departed sister, Arlupo. I guess you two were pretty close, huh?"

Stephanie could feel his presence trying to penetrate her. The mention of her best friend stung her as she gazed into the eyes of Arlupo's betrayer. Her tone flattened. "What is it you want?" Somehow she felt that her thoughts were too loud, but she couldn't help it. *Oh God, he's walking right up to me. No, too close.*

He dropped his politeness. "O.K., let's drop the games. You have something that belongs to me. *I* am the last Appendaho, and you have *no right* to it."

Jean didn't like what she saw. She began to get angry. She realized she had a very strong, protective feeling for Stephanie. She asked her point blank. "Stephanie, what's going on?"

Stephanie tried to ease her down. "Mom, please…"

Jargono picked up on it right away, and raised his eyebrows.

SACRIFICIAL WOOD

"Hmmmm, Mom? So you're the ones he's been crazy to find." His politeness returned, but only in tone. "Stephanie, if you care about your family here, you'll give me what I want."

Jean reacted. She really didn't know who this man was, and frankly, she didn't care. "You'd better leave, Mister. I don't..."

Stephanie urgently tried to calm her. "Mom, *please*, don't, *Mom* DON'T!"

Jean had reached for her shotgun, but somehow Stephanie knew it was the wrong thing to do. She dropped the weapon as if it burned, screaming in agony. Stephanie cried out, aghast with horror, kneeling over her mother's writhing form fallen behind the counter where they had been talking peacefully just a moment ago.

Lana cried out, "Moooomy!" and ran to her mother.

Jargono spoke calmly. "Your weapons are only as good as the mind that wields them. Apparently, you have a ways to go." He peered at Jean, musing, unfazed by her hideous screams.

Lana felt something come over her. "MOMMMMY! STOP IT YOU BAD MAN!" Lana ran back around the counter and bit him on the hand as hard as she could!

He smacked her hard, knocking her down. She cried as she scampered on the floor back over to her screaming mother. "MOMMY, MOMMY..."

While Stephanie examined Lana's face, fire flared up in her eyes as she scolded Jargono. "Enough Jargono, leave them *alone*. Smacking a little girl, *shame* on you!"

Examining and rubbing his hand, he didn't pay her warning any mind, but defended himself, almost sounding like a spoiled child. "She deserved it."

Jean's screams grew more hideous. Stephanie knew she had to stay calm. She didn't want any signs of her abilities leaking out, like they often did when overcome by strong emotions. But holding Jean's tormented form twisting in her arms connected her even more deeply to her agony.

"What are you doing to my Mother?"

Jargono explained the technical aspects. "It's not me, it's her own mind. I just made her aware of it."

Stephanie's thoughts raced. *Oh God, I feel like I could stop this. I feel Your power in me. But then he'll know I have deeper abilities, or at least he'll suspect I might. No, I have to hide it from him.*

"What do you want?"

He motioned her to come to him. He was standing a few feet in front of the counter, and Jean and Stephanie and Lana were a ways behind it. She eased Jean down to the floor, but Lana grabbed for her sister's dress as Stephanie got up to go to Jargono. Stephanie pulled her little hands off as she walked up to him, but stayed behind the counter. Lana's frightful screams were piercing, interweaving with those of her mother's.

He came closer, and leaned over the counter, placing his face in front of her face. "I told you, it's mine and not yours."

Stephanie pulled back, yelling at him, "I DON'T KNOW WHAT YOU'RE TALKING ABOUT."

It was true. She didn't know that kind of warped thinking. The Seed to the Tree of Life could never belong to the likes of him.

"Alright, I'll play, just this once. I know you saw me that last day."

Jean's screams intensified, her voice beginning to sound strangled. Lana, panicking now, turned bright red with wailing, as her mother's screams grew worse and worse and Lana couldn't get or give comfort. Forcing herself to tune it all out, Stephanie remained silent to learn what she could without giving him any knowledge.

"You were up in the Sacred Cave watching with Arlupo. I know, because after everyone left, I came back and found the sacred box opened. I WANT WHAT YOU TOOK, *NOW*. If you don't give it to me, I'll inform your father about your family and *that doesn't include what I'll do to them myself*"!

He wasn't bragging. He was telling the truth, and Stephanie knew it. She saw in his face, to her surprise, not the face of a crazed man overpowered by evil like her father, but something far more dangerous. He had the eyes of a cold, calculating businessman, with a sharp, perceptive mind.

Vaughn's discussions concerning fighting a superior force flashed in her memory. When Vaughn taught her the *Art of Fighting* during their many ice cream shop rendezvous, she felt she would never have need of such things, and only listened to please him. Now, grateful beyond words that she had something to draw upon, she chose to divert Jargono just a little.

"Even if I had what you're talking about, how would I know that you wouldn't hurt them anyway?"

The man sneered back. "Look into my eyes. I don't care about them. I don't want to waste any more time on them. They're not important to me, nor is your father. JUST GIVE ME WHAT IS MINE."

Now his demand was taking on a feeling closer to maniacal, but still the chains of his reason kept him in check. He had no problem telling her the truth of his thoughts, either. Stephanie instinctually decided to play up his strengths, even as she remembered Rule eleven, *When an enemy has well founded confidence, it cannot be dissuaded, but he often can be encouraged to overrate it.* After peering into his eyes, she stated her assessment in a confident, believing tone, with just a tiny hint of withheld respect to reinforce that part of him.

"You're telling the truth."

Jargono eased back a bit, as if surprised. His tone softened just a bit. "And why should I not be able to? Because you think I'm evil? I don't know how much you learned in your little stay with my former people. I know they put you through their little ceremony. Even that you bonded. I wish I would've been there to see that. All that wasted crying for nothing. Just mind tricks, that's all. And, *I don't care.*"

He paused for a second as if checking himself, then he changed direction. "Are you going to give me what's mine? No? FINE. Your mother can stay in that screaming state for the rest of her short life, and I'll inform your father." He turned around and began to leave.

❖ SACRIFICIAL WOOD ❖

When faced with immanent defeat, seek to postpone the end, time always holds the possibilities of the unknown. "No, wait! If you want it, you'll have to come with me back to your land!"

Jargono whirled in anger on her. She was just a girl. He was a grown man of twenty one. *I don't have time for her little childish tricks.* He bit at her. "WHAT?"

The best time to attack your enemy is right after he has won a major victory. Stephanie bit back with sarcasm. "You don't think I'd be stupid enough to carry it with me, do you?"

He eyed her. That seemed like a dead giveaway that she certainly did! *She's cocky, stubborn, and proud. She's ignored both her mother's continued suffering and her little sister's panic. She thinks too much of herself. If I'm to get what I want from her, I need to break her self-pride. She won't break for the others. Whatever she got from the box must be truly valuable.*

Jargono walked quickly back toward the counter, and motioned her to come out from behind it. Stephanie knew that was not a battle to die over, so she complied, slowly easing herself around the counter, her back pressed up against it.

Jargono regained his calm. This was best done being calm. "There is a saying, Young and dumb. Strip!"

Stephanie's eyes grew wide, and she hesitated before whispering. "What?"

Jargono was pleased to see her weakness. He thought, *The best way to rule an enemy is to make them weak, and then show them even more overpowering force.* He adjusted his tone accordingly acrid. "STRIP! I'm not going all the way back there if you have it with you."

Stephanie's mind went blank. "But...but..."

Jargono saw that now was the time to increase the pressure, so he put forth menace. "Either you do it or I will. Which do you want your family to see?"

Her heart pounded in her ears. Now tears and anger were getting hard to control. But if they weren't controlled, her power would become evident. Somehow, she felt her only chance was to keep it secret for now.

She understood what he was trying to do. She was quite familiar with *this* kind of behavior, and wasn't going to let him have the better of her. She held her head up and lashed out. "FINE." Stephanie pulled her green dress over her head and set it behind the counter, but he wagged his index finger back and forth at her, "Nah, nah, give each piece to me so I can check."

Stephanie was silent. She retrieved her dress and threw it in his face. He noted her breasts bouncing from the throw.

Her mother's screams were *still* intensifying, even though her hoarseness had diminished their actual sound. Stephanie didn't know how long her mother's heart could withstand the intense pain Jargono was inflicting. Lana was close to passing out from fright. Stephanie, standing helpless, in only her undergarments, submissively begged. "Please, stop using your power on her."

Jargono thought, *The best time to show kindness to an enemy is after totally vanquishing them.*

"Done. She's distracting me anyway."

Jean gasped, and it took several moments for her to even be able to gather her breath and thoughts. Finally, she grabbed

SACRIFICIAL WOOD

Lana, holding her tightly, protectively, so that the child could calm down, too. Then she sat up from the floor and propped herself up on the counter, saying, "Oh Stephanie, don't. Please don't…"

She didn't want it to, but her mother's plea brought tears to her eyes. It was the love and sacrifice in her plea that did it. "I have to, Mom. Please, for me, and don't say anything more. Take Lana in your bedroom."

Jargono smiled. "Good. We *need* privacy. Come on, don't be shy, the rest of it!"

Stephanie resigned to herself that she had to do whatever was necessary to save her family. But, she also noted that she had gotten away unchallenged, with having her mother released from torment and sent away to her room. She threw each piece of underclothing in his face in silence.

Jargono couldn't help being taken by her beauty. Stephanie had always been a beautiful girl, but her holiness magnified it tenfold, and she still maintained all her exercises. "My, my, but you *are* something to look at, and *all* red hair. Sit-ups?"

Oh God, PLEASE don't let him touch me. But that is exactly what Jargono did, as her beauty drew him to her, and he roamed his hands freely over her body.

"Mmm, you feel *very* good, soft, smooth, so *very* sensual, such *intense* receptivity. Do you know the power I have over outsiders? Do you know what I could make you do? And I wouldn't be forcing you. Your own mind would force you, *and you would love it!*"

Stephanie shouted her prayer within herself, because she couldn't think any longer. *OH GOD, PLEASE, HOW DO I GET HIM TO STOP WITHOUT BETRAYING MYSELF?*

And then the words coldly came from her mouth. "Is that because you couldn't get a woman to want you with her *whole* mind and heart?" Stephanie was shocked at what she said. It was an attack! It was a *true* attack at his vulnerability! Her eyes widened in that instant of understanding.

He laughed. "What do I care?"

As Stephanie stood naked and unresisting, with his hands exploring her sensitive flesh, she pressed her onslaught. "Oh come on, you mean it wouldn't be pleasing to you to *actually* have a woman appreciate, *truly* appreciate you for what you are?" As Stephanie heard her own words, she realized the power of truth, even over one such as him.

His hands dropped from her body as he considered her words, "I don't think such a woman exists."

Now, I have to make him believe. Oh God, help me do this. His constant probing into her mind was evident from the very beginning, but she had reflexively blocked all entry. *Now, I have to let his mind in, but just a little, to see only what I want him to see.*

Jargono's eyes went distant. *There, finally. O.K. even a little is a start. Hmm, no wonder my people took you in. You have great capacities. Perhaps...* His tone came back reticent. "You know, you're the first to do that to me. No man or woman has *ever* made me think before." He actually looked stunned, almost human in character.

SACRIFICIAL WOOD

Stephanie scoffed the compliment. "I find that hard to believe."

But he leveled his gaze at her, and she knew he was going to speak more truth about himself. "Believe it. My people bored me to death with their empty traditions and meaningless words. I searched all by myself for true knowledge. You wouldn't believe what I found."

Stephanie did her best to bury her thought. *I know what you found, you bastard. I just can't tell you, yet.* Instead, she asked. "What?"

"POWER, TRUE REALITY. There's a much greater world of spirit beyond this physical world. You've made me think. If you give me what I want, I'll give you a choice."

Stephanie sensed an opening that she knew she had to take, but didn't know where it led. But this was an advantage she didn't have moments ago. He wanted something from her besides what was in the box, he wanted her choice. So now would be the time to draw back…just a little. She spoke dryly. "What choice?"

"Either I hand you over to the Ethereal Powers, or I hand you over to your father, or you let me try to win your heart, so you can be my wife!"

Stephanie quickly got control of her thoughts and feelings. *Don't lose your cool now, Stephanie. This is not just your life, but other's lives, too. Make him come to you.* "And why such choices?"

"Oh, sometime ago, one Power wanted you for himself, although I cannot imagine why. But now, another Power wants you placed back with your father. BUT, I WANT YOU FOR MYSELF, because you've done something for me that no one else has!"

This was more than she could have hoped for, or dreaded. "What?"

"I told you. You've made me think of something important to me that I hadn't thought of before. I somehow *feel* you could do this a lot for me. Hmmmm…maybe that has something to do with the Powers wanting you."

Stunned, Stephanie began to realize how deeply she affected him. *He's lonely. He searched for knowledge all by himself. My God, in a way, he's like Vaughn!* Now she needed to learn as much as she could from him. "Aren't you afraid the Powers will be angry with you?"

His laugh playfully, mocking her idea, but his tone became truly friendly. His quickness to scoff at the demons surprised and alarmed her. "First, I've learned a good deal about them. They're limited as to what they can actually do here. I have enough power over the outsiders, so they can't use them against me. The powers are *users*, and so am I. They'd expect nothing else from me. They'll adapt to my new offer."

Stephanie's feelings were growing ever more intense by the second. Her heart was pounding. She had created a little advantage. Vaughn had taught her that when in a battle against a superior force, and you have no escape, but you have a small advantage somewhere, press it with all you have.

She needed knowledge. She was naked. She pressed her tiny advantage. She eased just a wee bit away from him, meeting his eyes with hers in seriousness. "What makes you think you could truly win my heart and mind?"

Surprisingly, he backed up a step! "Hmmmm, again you make me think. I guess like any man, we'll just have to see. But, I have much to offer that's appealing, and very real, and very special. What's that around your neck?"

This was a question Stephanie had already considered and needed no more thought. "Just something my father gave me."

Jargono scrunched up his face in surprise. "Why would you keep anything that *idiot* gave you, especially after what he did to all your friends?"

Stephanie deflected him. She was naked, but she spoke with the strength and dignity of a woman clothed in royal apparel, "I don't think he could have done anything without your help."

He mused over her. "True. But my reasons were totally different than his." He looked at her expecting an answer to satisfy his curiosity. He wasn't one to be deflected easily.

Stephanie knew she had to quickly come up with something, otherwise his curiosity would turn to suspicion. "Because I was taught by your people that the goodness in me had to partly come from my father. So when I wear this, I remember that."

He recoiled from her in disgust. "Oh *please*, you almost make me want to withdraw my proposal. Take it off and throw it away."

As she reached behind her neck fumbling to find the clasp to the necklace, Stephanie pressed harder her advantage, snapping at him. "*Fine.* Is this how you intend to win my heart and mind *freely?*"

His eyes left her breasts and widened, and again he got that distant look. "There you go again, making me *think.* O.K., keep it if you like. I like the blackness of it anyway. Now, take me to your bedroom. Oh, don't look at me like that. If I was going to have you in that way, I could make you do it anywhere. I'm going to search all your stuff, first. *I don't trust you.*"

She yelled at him. "FINE." And she stormed off to her bedroom.

Wow, she's even prettier when she's angry! It gives her a certain shine. Wow, really *nice backside, too.* Jargono licked his lips as his imagination tasted her. No woman had ever drawn his interest this deeply.

Little by little, Stephanie was gaining tenuous freedom from him. He searched everything she had in silence, until, at the bottom of her bottom drawer, he found…

"What's this piece of paper in this drawer? It's very old."

Stephanie's heart leapt, her gut wrenched, as she saw him holding the letter from the sacred box. The fancy writing, so clearly written, faced down, as that is how she had placed it in the drawer after she ironed it flat. Her thoughts convicted her, *Oh GOD, YOU* IDIOT. *I SHOULD HAVE DESTROYED IT. OH NO. I wanted to show it to Vaughn. OH GOD, WHY DID I KEEP THAT STUPID PIECE OF PAPER?*

Jargono was staring at her face, trying to figure her thoughts, but for some reason, he still couldn't get a read. That made him

◈ SACRIFICIAL WOOD ◈

even more interested. Waving the paper around, "Hello, anyone home? Stephanie, you're lost in thought, again. What is this paper? It's very old, this I can see." He turned it over.

Stephanie's emotions at failing overwhelmed her. Tears streamed down her cheeks. *Arlupo said I would fail. All my maneuvering failed, because I kept a stupid piece of paper. I might as well go down fighting. I'll let him read it, and then I'll hit him with everything I've got.* She yelled at him in bitterness. "*Why don't you just READ IT and see for yourself.*" Her eyes were like daggers. She hid her power with all her might, so as not to give him any warning.

His puzzled look searched her for some clue. "Very funny, why are you crying over a blank piece of paper?"

Her thoughts shouted, *BLANK! BLANK! I CAN SEE THE WRITING. OH GOD, HE CAN'T SEE IT! WHY? Oh God, thank you Arlupo, for telling me the secret. Evil can't see Good, but good can see both good and evil for what they are. Is this a possible way that I can beat him?* "I'm crying, *you idiot*, because I'm standing here *NAKED*, being treated worse than a DOG."

He stepped back from her, a bit wide eyed at her ferocity, and then reluctantly pulled his eyes away, turning his back! He very meekly spoke, "Oh, I'm sorry. Get dressed. We're leaving." *Wow! What a woman!* "Where did you say you put what was in the box?"

Stephanie was totally shocked, again. She almost gave the secret away, herself! She actually did tell him the letter was real, but he totally missed her meaning. She felt like throwing up.

She realized, *He doesn't know ANYTHING! He's trying to get me to tell him.* "I didn't. And, I *won't* show you until we're far away from here. You wouldn't find the secret passage, anyway."

Stephanie put on fresh undergarments, her holy dress, and began gathering things to take on the journey back. Ever since she left the cave, she had kept her hair in the same three braids, only undoing it to wash and comb. Then she would tie the ancient ribbon to the middle of the large middle braid.

He nodded with a knowing expression. "I knew it. Of course. How else could you have escaped?"

"Let me say goodbye to my family." The tone Stephanie used was not a request but a statement. *Steady progress,* she noted, because his reply to it did nothing to chastise her for her absconded freedom, except to indicate his desire to be on their way.

"Hurry up."

As battles go, she thought, *somehow I've actually won this one. But the war is obviously lost unless I can learn something useful from him. I need to know the extent of his powers, and then how to turn my little advantages into a total victory. Right now, all I have is the time it will take us to get to the cave.* Stephanie entered the bedroom where Jean and Lana were holding each other on the bed. For all Stephanie's bravery, as soon as she saw them, she ran into their arms crying like a baby.

Jean gathered her up, and Lana added her little hands. too, holding the braid with the ribbon. Finally, between sobs, Stephanie broke the news. "Mother, Lana, I have to go with this man."

Jean's mouth dropped open, and she pulled her daughter away so she could look in her face. Her adamant tone said more than her words. "No, Stephanie, you can't."

Lana grabbed her arm in a little iron grip. "Nooooooo, Stephie, he's baaaaad."

Her crying, and her innocent rendition of the truth cut Stephanie. She put her arm around Lana. "Please don't cry. Please, you just make it harder. I love you all so much. You're the last family I have. I can't let him hurt you."

Jean was dismayed. First Arlupo dies, providing them with a fortune, and now Stephanie was willing to give her life as well, just to protect them. If it wasn't for Lana, she thought, she would rather die first than let this be. But all she could do was say, "Oh dear God, I'm so sorry, Stephanie. I should be able to protect you."

Jean wept. She felt so humiliated, so undeserving that yet another person should die helping her, another person whom she never treated that well.

Stephanie spoke frankly, as she stared into Jean's eyes. "Mom, there's no one on this Earth that can fight *that* man except, maybe… No, I can't."

Jean's eyes widened. She understood. "You're thinking about Vaughn, how he rescued you, how he heard your prayer. I remember how special you told me he is. When he comes, I'll tell him…"

Stephanie grabbed her shoulders in fright. "NO, NO, you *mustn't!* I couldn't bear him being harmed."

"But STEPHIE…!"

Stephie scolded her again with steel eyes. "NO. *Promise me you won't say anything to him when, if he shows up.*"

Jean's face folded into horror. She couldn't believe Stephanie had made her mind up to sacrifice herself to that hideous, evil man. "But what should I say?"

"Just that I left mysteriously, that's still true."

"OH STEPHIE, Vaughn may be able to…"

But Stephanie cut her off in desperation, begging, "MOM, PLEASE, I can't go through with this without your promise!" Stephanie's stare bore into her.

Jean knew it was true. She could tell Stephanie was barely holding on. She understood that Vaughn's safety was a strength she was drawing on, that she needed for very survival's sake. Jean, helpless to resist, said, "OH GOD, I promise."

Stephanie didn't know why Jargono wanted whatever it was he thought was in the box. She couldn't imagine the Seed to the Tree of Life, or the knowledge of the letter being useful to him, except to give him a clue of her potential. But then again, she understood so little of his dark powers. *Perhaps he could do something terrible with the Seed. I don't think he can destroy it. But he could hide it for sure, so it would never, ever sprout for anyone.* Then a worse thought. *Oh God, he could give it to the demons. They have those strange trees already, and the blue orb. They're spirits and…*

Ignorance. Not knowing much was her greatest enemy now, because without knowledge, she had no idea how and when to respond. Vaughn had taught her, *The strongest weapon in any battle is, first knowledge of yourself, and right beside that is knowledge of your enemy.* She wasn't even that self-knowledgeable yet. She had no idea the extent of her own powers, nor whether she could defeat Jargono with them. If she hadn't seen him nullify the burning of her evil father's hand when he grabbed Arlupo's mother, Stephanie would have immediately thrown everything she had at Jargono, whatever throwing everything she had actually meant… Again, she remembered another of Vaughn's lessons, *Only a fool gambles all his strength in a single attack, unless he is, in that moment, going to die.*

CHAPTER TWENTY

Dog Sense

Yana looked at her captor. "Why have you taken me against my will?"

"Because I love you... you shall be my wife."

"You've broken the oath our people have together."

"I've left my people, and we'll go far away."

"You love me. Does it matter to you that I love you back?"

"Your people have a saying, 'That is your choice.'"

Yana held her tied hands out, and he untied them. "I'm alone, and we're already far away. If you truly love me, you'll do whatever I require to prove it."

He looked at her, his eyes widening. "Now I'm not sure who is the prisoner."

"That is your choice."

"Mommyyy." Lana bawled while hanging onto her mother, as Jean sat at the store counter. Jean had come to believe Lana had some extra ability to sense things. Sometimes, Lana understood her or others before they even said a word. As Jean tried to comfort her, she sensed deeply that Lana was experiencing Stephanie's suffering, and feeling the evil of that horrible man. While holding her, and stroking her long light-brown hair, Jean remembered how Lana bit Jargono's hand with all her might, and she wondered greatly about her child. Jean didn't know what to do, because she was so ignorant of these kinds of things.

"Don't cry, Lana."

"But I miss Stephie. I'm *scaaared* for her. That man is bad, and he's…" There it was again. She wasn't just telling her a feeling. She was telling her a knowing, as if she was experiencing it in that very moment.

"I know… me to." Her mother broke down in tears, folding her arms on the counter, and burying her head into them. Sick in heart, she thought about all that she now had in her beautiful life, and she owed it all to that red-haired girl and she never even treated Stephie right. *I don't deserve such a beautiful life. And what life will Stephanie have with that evil man? Oh dear God… What am I even calling? That's just an expression people use. I should stop using it. If there really was a God, He'd be Just. Why do all these terrible things have to happen?*

But Lana tugged on her mother's arm, because she knew her mother didn't know, and she knew little girls were supposed to tell their mommies *everything*. But it was hard to say, but she just had to tell her mommy. So she whispered it. "Mommy, he's going to hurt Stephie *real* bad." But when she saw inside her mommy, that it hurt her mommy so bad,

Lana began to think that maybe little girls shouldn't tell their mommy's everything.

Then there was this strange sound of scratching at the front door. The bell hadn't rung, so it was very odd... then they heard muffled sounds of something whining. Lana's eyes got big. She couldn't believe it. She ran for the door as she called back to her mother. "Mommy, someone's at the door."

Jean's head shot up in fright. "Lana, *wait*, we don't..."

But it was too late, as somehow with one big pull, the five year old opened the front door, and Lana shouted, "PUPPY, MOMMY! PUPPY'S FOUND ME ! OH PUPPY!"

On the floor, rolling over each other, paws, feet, more paws dancing, hands, tongue licking, little girl laughing, little puppy arfing, panting, joy...

Jean wiped her wet face in her hands, beholding a sight. "I don't believe it! How?"

"Puppy, I LOVE YOU."

She squeezed Puppy, and Puppy bounded out of her grasp to lick her face again. Their joy unmatched, Jean just shook her head. She wasn't quite sure why such a small, mundane thing as a pet returning home felt almost like a miracle.

Lana brought Puppy some of last night's dinner. She took a special doggy dish they sold at the store, and filled it with water. Then she plunked down, sitting inches away from the water and food bowl, watching her long lost best friend, besides Stephanie. For the next hour they played, tussled, and rolled, interspersed with renditions of *Sit Puppy*, and *Shake Puppy*, until both were exhausted, finally curling up on the

SACRIFICIAL WOOD

blanket that Jean had laid in the back corner, and designated as Puppy's sleeping area.

Hours later a sound woke Puppy. He bounded up so fast, his paws were moving, but he wasn't going anywhere fast on the smooth wooden floor. Loud, deep ARFs came through the front door. Puppy shot to the door right past Jean's feet, as she watched the commotion unfold. A barrage of little arfs punctuated at the end by a little ruff, escorted the sprint.

"*What is going on?*" Jean called out.

Lana ran right past her mother, following in Puppy's tracks. But this time, she knew better than to open the door right away. She peeked out the front window.

"Mommy, it's another doggy. A *BIG* doggy." "Get away from the door, Lana."

Puppy was scratching, arfing and ruffing. The big dog seemed to reproduce an adult version of the same inflections, but added to it. Puppy reproduced the addition and added to that. Jean wrinkled her brow, because she could swear the variations in the barks and other doggy sounds constituted an actual conversation. A young man's voice could be heard through the door. "Hello?"

The door cracked open. Jean peeked out at a handsome young man with very dark, almost black eyes and hair, and with the beginnings of a finely haired beard upon a well-proportioned face, and dressed in brown work clothes. She thought of the last handsome stranger that entered her store. She spoke in a flat, quick tone. "I'm sorry, we're closed." She went to close the door again, but Puppy pushed his snout into the open crack of the door, and the unusual doggy conversation started up again.

The young man seemed to pretend to understand doggy speak, judging from the expression on his face. He modestly confirmed the notion. "Ahh, I think you've found my puppy, but he's very glad you did."

Lana instantly squeezed her head between her mother and the crack in the door, protesting, while straining to look up at the stranger. "MOMMY, He's MY Puppy!" She then began to stare up at the young man with a terrible brooding expression.

Jean quickly decided to end the conversation. She wanted to slam the door, but Lana's little fingers were tightly clamped around the door's edge. When Jean bent over to pry her fingers loose, a combination of Lana's pressure to open it to get a better look at the Puppy thief, and the sudden pressure of the big doggy trying to squeeze in… "I'M SORRY, YOU'RE MISTAKEN! OOOHHH…" Spot forced his way through the door, pushing past Lana and Jean with a brief comment consisting of a long, deep Ruff.

The young man hollered. "SPOT, COME BACK HERE."

Jean hollered in disgust, "HE'LL RUIN OUR STORE."

The young man, appearing thoroughly embarrassed, scolded his dog, but realized right away he needed to go get him. "SPOT! Please, may I come in to get him?"

His pitifully embarrassed expression, even for Jean, was too irresistible. But she made her tone hard, almost mean. "Yes, *please* get him and GO."

SACRIFICIAL WOOD

Entering with his head hung, and mumbling his apology, he quickly tried to recover his dog. "I'm *very sorry*...SPOT!"

But Jean's dismay grew by the instant, as Puppy led the big dog underneath two tables stocked with store goods. Worse, Jean could swear that Puppy told the big dog to follow and that Spot assented!

Jean cried out in frustration, as the big dog knocked into the two tables, spilling the stacks of cans and boxes across the floor. She eyed a broom in the corner, thinking of grabbing it and chasing the whole lot of them out. Then, Puppy suddenly made a bee-line into the back rooms, seemingly on purpose. So direct an action it was!

Jean was beside herself. Lana stood with her little hands covering her mouth, her eyes wide, and a large part of her wanting to laugh, but knew she didn't dare. Jean cried out beyond frustration, which faded into resignation. "NO, Oh no, they've run into the back rooms." Jean's and the young man's mouths were both agape, and feeling helpless, they tentatively waited for the next development.

With Vaughn's heart in his throat, he assured the woman. "I'll get him."

Then Jean realized he would see what had happened in the back, and began to stop him. "NO, don't go..." *Damn, too late.*

He caught Spot in a back room. Down on one knee, he held him in both his arms, scolding, "SPOT, BAD DOG." Spot held a green piece of clothing in his mouth as he whined.

Vaughn scolded him again, "Don't you give me that sad look. Give me that." He took the green garment and discovered it was a long dress. Then he realized just how terrible the room appeared. "What, what happened in this room? Ahhh, I don't think Spot did all that Ma'am." He was beyond shame, and well into deep guilt.

Jean fumbled for words. For all she knew, this young man was that evil man's accomplice. "My daughter got mad."

Spot grabbed the green dress in his mouth, again, but the young man freed it without speaking. Spot whined, but he ignored him.

"Wow, I'm sorry. Where is she? I'm young. Maybe I could talk some sense into her. You seem like a very nice woman."

Jean couldn't understand how he could say that. She'd been consistently trying to appear mean, and it was frustrating to not be taken seriously. Her conscience convicted her, though. *Damn, why'd he have to say I was nice?* So her tone softened. "Oh, thank you. No... she just runs away… for a while."

He looked into her face and could tell she'd been crying. "But how old is she?"

Jean didn't want him to know *anything*. "You're pretty nosey, aren't you? Who are you?"

Her question alarmed him. Almost no one ever asked such a question. If there was one cultural standout within the country he lived, it was that a person's identity was their own private knowledge and only shared with the closest of people.

"Oh, I'm sorry, again. I'm just a hired hand looking for work. This is Spot, my dog."

Jean noted his desire to avoid telling her who he was.

SACRIFICIAL WOOD

But he couldn't keep from confessing, after witnessing all the canine conversation, and how well the dogs knew each other.

"Ahh, you know Ma'am, I'm sorry to say this, but that is *my*, ahhhh *our*, mine and Spot's puppy. Can't you see how they know each other?"

Lana immediately dove onto Puppy, who was sitting atop a pile of disheveled clothing. Holding Puppy tightly, she sobbed, "MOMMY, NOOO, HE'S MINE!"

His heart pained. He couldn't understand how the little girl could become so strongly attached, so quickly, yet, she was absolutely adorable. He sensed a very good spirit in the child, which made him feel even worse. "I'm sorry, Spot tracked him here. I didn't realize just how much you loved Goldie. But you've only known him for no more than an hour or so."

Lana stared back at him, speaking distinctly, almost as if attempting to educate the young man. "Noooo, his name is PuuuPPPY and I known him for *years*."

Jean broke in, "My daughter is only five. So she…"

He concurred quickly, wanting to put an end to the little girl's hardship. "I understand. I don't know. I guess we could let you have him. Spot here is already a handful…errrr…as you already found out."

Curiosity took hold, because Jean knew that Puppy somehow came from the village. Perhaps this man was one of the murderers, although he just didn't seem the type.

"Why do you say Puppy is yours?"

Alarmed again, he sensed she was trying to find out something about him, and wondered why. He didn't want anyone to know where he'd been, because then they could accuse him of burying the dead. "We found each other a ways back, and have been traveling North ever since, about a week."

By the way he just said he found Puppy a ways back, I'm sure he's hiding something.

Vaughn's thoughts began to trouble him. The hairs on the back of his neck began to prickle, but that kind of sense didn't match up with this woman or her child. *She's hiding a lot. I can feel it. This room wasn't spoiled in anger. Someone was searching for something. I bet she was robbed. That's why she seems so afraid.*

He offered his help. "May I help you straighten up your store from the mess Spot made? You don't have to pay me, of course. And help you clean up this room?" The stranger watched as Jean was too quick to keep him from the room he was in.

"No. These are girl things. All right, you can help with the store for an hour. Have you had anything to eat this morning?"

"Not really Ma'am. Ahh, neither has Spot."

"After you're done cleaning up, you can eat, and then be on your way."

"Thank you Ma'am. I'll pay you of course."

"We'll see."

Lana finally decided the matter was settled, and Puppy wouldn't be taken from her. She squeezed and kissed Puppy, proclaiming her love, and then turned to look deeply into the stranger's eyes. "Mister, Mister…"

The handsome young man looked down on the very cute little girl with straight, long brown hair, and large, drawing

SACRIFICIAL WOOD

gray eyes. "Yes, little one, what is it?" He reached across and patted her on the head, as her eyes captured him.

"I taught Puppy a trick, watch." She got up and Puppy got up with her. "Sit Puppy," she quipped.

And Puppy arfed and sat, looking obediently at her!

Truly astonished, the young man stared back and forth at each of them, which delighted Lana even further. "Wow! You did a good job. How long did it take you to teach him that?"

Throwing her arms out wide, she rolled her eyes and head. "Oh, a *looong* time. Arlupo told me that I should teach her to sit first."

Jean squirmed. She didn't want their association to the Appendaho to be known. "My daughter doesn't have anyone to play with, and so she makes things up."

Lana couldn't believe her Mommy was *lying*. She turned on her mother, scolding her. "MOMMY, *I'm not*. You know…"

Jean spoke sharply. "That will be *enough* Lana."

Lana didn't understand why her mother would say such a thing. She sniffed away a tear, and then looked into the stranger's eyes. She liked his eyes a lot. Then Lana decided to persist, because she knew she was right. She *was* telling the truth. "Arlupo gave me Puppy."

He'd never heard such a strange name. *What's she so scared about? What's this got to do with being robbed? Why be scared of her daughter's make-believe? Maybe, its religious make-believe. That's it. She's afraid of the government.* "Well, anyway, Puppy is *your* Puppy." The young man smiled, looking deeply into the child's eyes.

Puppy squirmed around and began licking Lana's face, barking at her. Spot picked up another piece of clothing in his mouth, making soft growling noises, and Vaughn freed it, and gave it to Jean. Then rapid knocking at the door drew everyone's attention. Jean couldn't believe how utterly frustrating the day kept becoming. *Can't they read? CLOSED! Damn, not now,* she thought as she left. "Excuse me, but I have to get the door. I'll be *right* back."

"Yes Ma'am."

As soon as her mother left the room, Lana focused deeply into this new stranger. She'd made up her heart, as her mind was yet too young, but she needed to tell someone. She liked *this* man's eyes a lot. But he stood up, concerned about who was at the door. *No,* she thought. Lana jumped up and grabbed his arm, stretching her neck upward staring at him. Once again, her eyes captured him. *What's with this little one's eyes? Alright, alright, I won't go.* Sitting back down so he could be at her level, he crossed his legs and bowed his head in humility to the child.

She came close, putting her little hands into his wavy, thick, dark hair. She liked the soft feel of it, squishing it between her fingers. Using his head for support, she leaned close to his ear and whispered. "Can I tell you a secret?"

He smiled, keeping his head bowed. "I don't know. Secrets are special. You should only tell them to very special people. People you truly trust."

Lana put both hands on either side of his head, gently trying to lift. "Can I see your eyes?" The sweetness of her

SACRIFICIAL WOOD

touch seemed to overpower him, as his head straightened. Her little hands held him resolutely as the object of her concentration.

But he couldn't keep from breaking into a broad smile as he asked her. "My eyes?"

Lana nodded, but after only a brief moment, she confirmed quickly, "O.K., I can trust you!"

He laughed. He could tell she really meant it. His brow rose in curiosity as he leaned his head back. "Just like that? All you had to do was look at my eyes, and you can trust me?"

But surprisingly, Lana moved closer to his face, shaking her head, as her little hands moved to his cheeks to hold his attention. "Noooo, I don't look *at* them. I look at *YOU in them!* I knew that was a bad man who came to our store yesterday, even *before* he hurt Mommy *real* bad, and hit me, before he talked mean to my sister and made her take her clothes off!"

Dazed, as if struck in the head, Vaughn's eyes went completely wide. The brutality he so abruptly received into the midst of the tenderness she'd created in him, deluged his senses. But the darkness was kept from his eyes by the sweetness of her hands on his cheeks, which focused him into her. He decided to take it one step at a time, "A man *hit* you?"

Lana nodded seriously, a tear in her eye. Her face was now only inches away from his, but her deep gray eyes still held him in their innocent power.

"So, that's your secret. Hmm…" The stranger stated.

But Lana surprised him again, shaking her head, again, "Noooo! Well, I just wanted to tell you about that, but I have an even *bigger* secret. Come closer." She cupped her hands around his ear and whispered. "I listen to Mommy and sister talking when they think I'm asleep."

He nodded his head. "Oh, I used to do the same thing."

In total surprised glee, she squealed, "*You did?*"

Vaughn stared at her, trying to keep up with her rapid swings of intense honesty. *Little children are so much more real than adults. They feel everything to its fullest.* He reassured her with an honest look and nod, but then they were interrupted. "O.K. you two, what are you whispering about?"

"Oh *nothing.*" he grinned and Lana giggled.

"Oh *nothing* Mommy," she said, copying his inflections.

Jean silently eyed them both.

The stranger redirected, even as he wished he had more time to listen to Lana. "Well, I better start helping clean up."

With the contact now broken between him and that little angel, her words played back to him, *Hurt Mommy* real *bad, hit me, mean to my sister and made her take her clothes off.* Anger swarmed through his heart, his mind, right through to his very fingers and toes, aching to pour justice upon the perpetrator. Yet, he also felt a deeper love, enhanced by the pain of their violation, which competed equally for presence, and seemed to balance him out. *Hmm, now this combination makes sense.*

More than once he brushed a tear away. But he knew he had to be patient and hide it. *This world, will injustice* ever *end?* After a few hours, he sat down at the dining table, really just an old, worn, all-purpose, rectangular wooden table and

◆ SACRIFICIAL WOOD ◆

ate the wonderful eggs, pancakes, and sausages Jean cooked for him. He noticed she was a good looking woman, well kept, and wondered about the pain her thoughtful blue eyes had endured.

Lana decided to eat with Puppy and Spot. She was intent on teaching them manners, as the dogs smacked their mouths too much when they ate. Jean had given her daughter some of the store's extra special doggy food. Spot had recognized the doggy picture on the bag and started dancing. But Lana kept taking their food away every time they ate too loudly. Vaughn was glad Lana was occupied.

"Well, young man, you're a hard worker. You did a lot more than straighten up what your dog knocked over. I'm going to pay you." She slid a small pile of bills towards him.

He had thought it through. He couldn't leave without offering help, even if just for a week. Even though he needed to find Stephanie, he just couldn't leave these people unprotected. Then he remembered the old farmer's words, *I know you young man. You listen, and you listen real good, you're going to want to fight too soon. The hardest thing for you will be to leave those who need help.*

Jean watched him shaking his head, wondering at his internal battle. *I think he's a good young man.*

Vaughn folded his hands on top of the table and leveled his serious eyes into hers. "Ma'am, I may be young, but I'm strong. You're daughter said a man hit her, and I can *still* see the mark on her face. If I can help…"

Instant fright transformed Jean's face. "NO! No, it was just a stranger. He's gone now."

He knew he couldn't press. "Alright. Well, thank you for the food, I haven't had a good meal like that for a very long time."

Jean shook her head, looking ashamed. "Young man, thank *you*. You're very kind and I haven't been very nice at all."

"No, it's alright. That man scared you. I understand."

"If it wasn't for my daughter coming back, I'd offer you a job. She put a lot of this store together."

He now understood why she'd run away. He hated to think what the man did to her, and it angered him to the very depths of his soul. But he knew it wouldn't be appropriate for him to bring it up so he just said, "I understand."

"What will you do after you leave here?"

"I don't know for sure. Probably keep heading north, I guess."

"Ahhh… to be young and free!" She smiled.

The stranger got up to leave. He really didn't want to, but there was nothing he could do if she refused his help. Besides, he knew he had to keep heading north if he was to find Stephanie.

"Well, I best be heading on."

Jean sighed a torn sigh. Even though Lana was engrossed in her pet responsibilities, the child kept one ear peeled to everything the adults said, and she began to be very worried. She felt safe with that man around.

"Alright young man." Jean got up and shook his hand.

But Lana had different ideas. She raced over and grabbed him by the leg, hollering. "NOOO!"

❖ SACRIFICIAL WOOD ❖

He tried to redirect her emotion. "OH MY! You give such very good hugs little one."

Shocked at how strongly attached her daughter seemed to be to the young man, Jean seemed frozen. But it only made good sense to Lana. Spot and Puppy seemed *meant* to be together. She felt the same way about this stranger and them. Actually, it was quite obvious to her. It was all the same feeling of togetherness.

"She seems to have really taken to you. I've never seen her do that before." Just then, there came a very insistent knocking at the front door. Jean couldn't understand why the bell didn't work, because if it had, she would have at least had warning, but now she had to rush away again to answer it. "Oh, the door, *again*. They're not used to me being closed, and I think they're worried. Please excuse me for a second."

Lana took the stranger's hand and tugged, and he bent over. Lana whispered. "I have to tell you my secret."

So he sat down on the floor and leaned over, whispering back, "You already did."

But she shook her head, so he gave in, "O.K. You tell me a secret, and I'll tell you one."

Lana couldn't believe it. No stranger had ever told her a secret before. "*Reeeealy?*" Instant delight spread through her.

"Look at me in my eyes." He smiled, speaking it as Lana had described what she did earlier

She rubbed her little hands. "Oh goodie." But then she hesitated. "But my secret is sad." And just as quickly, her expression changed to grief that overwhelmed her, and she began sniffling.

549

DARRYL MARKOWITZ

He swallowed, remembering the impact her last confidence had on him. He comforted her. "It's O.K., I'll listen to yours first."

She cupped her hands over his ear again and whispered, "Arlupo, she was my friend, too, and her Mommy, and her Daddy… and all them." She tried to get the words out, but began to cry in his ear. He gathered her up in his strong arms, sitting her down on his lap. She sobbed against his chest, and he stroked her hair. "Dear little one, you don't have to tell."

But instead, she picked her head up, and with her tearful, deep gray eyes she looked squarely into his with a strength that surprised him. "They're all dead! My mean Daddy and that bad man that came to the store did it. I wasn't asleep when I heard Sister tell Mommy what happened. Isn't that what killed means? It means they're deaded, right? They shot them with guns. But Mommy has a gun, now…I won't see them…*ever anymore.*" She fell back into his chest, fully releasing her sobs now, having shared her secret. He wrapped his arms tightly around her, rocking her back and forth, but rocking himself, too. Suddenly her preciousness meant the whole world to him.

Knowledge . . . it poured over him, entering into his depths. *Oh GOD!* He choked back his own sobs. *Lana was with them, they were her friends. Her sister was with them, and she saw what happened!* He lifted his head up while his heart pounded. He couldn't see how it was possible that these people were… He whispered, "Little one, what do you call your sister, her *name?*"

She looked him straight in the eye, again. "Stephie."

He stared at her as if in a never ending moment, as tears ran from his eyes. Pains shot through him, but also joy at being so close, but also terror, not knowing what state Stephanie was in. It was Stephanie who had run away, who had been treated so badly by the mean man. He hugged Lana even tighter. *This little girl's like family to me!*

Being hugged so tightly, Lana felt him crying. And she knew by that look in his eye when she told him her sister's name that he *knew* her sister. She pushed back from his embrace, and held his face in her little hands again, her face only inches from his, and asked, "Do you know Stephie?"

The stranger smiled and whispered in her ear. "Want to know my secret?" Lana nodded. "Not only do I know Stephie, but I love her, *and*…I kissed her!"

Lana gasped in excitement. "Ahhh! Oh, that's a *secret!* I won't tell. You know Stephie, and you love her, and you *kissed?*" Her eyes were big. Her whisper was a loud whisper, and she pronounced that she wanted to hear it again to be sure.

"Yep! Before she came to live with you, we fell in love and helped each other a whole lot."

Lana grabbed both of his cheeks tightly, again only inches from his face, and she shouted, knowing for sure now that, "YOU'RE *VAUGHN*. STEPHIE TALKS ABOUT YOU *ALL* THE TIME. AND SHE LOVES YOU TOO!"

Jean had just walked up when Lana made her proclamation. "You're Vaughn? But…" Thousands of thoughts hung Jean in indecision. "How did you get here so quickly?"

Vaughn looked up and smiled. "I found work with a train master. He's even offered me a steady job going cross-country, back and forth. Gee, just about everyone has offered me a job."

"*Oh my God!*" She put her hands to her mouth, as if in prayer and sat down on a dining chair to keep from falling over. She was so overwhelmed, she thought she might faint. Instead, Jean folded her arms on the dining table, burying her head weeping. She knew God *had* to have sent him, and she knew the promise she had made, and she knew that whatever way this turned out, it couldn't turn out well.

It upset Lana to see her mother so. "Mommy, why are you crying? This is Vaughn. He saved Stephie from the other bad man."

Vaughn lifted Lana to the side, and stood up and took Jean by the shoulders, straightening her up, looking straight into her eyes. "Ma'am, please tell me the truth. Tell me what happened. Lana said that Stephanie's father and some bad man killed everyone? Why?"

Jean looked into his intense eyes, and could see the love in them, the stern uprightness of the young man. She knew there would be no denying him, and that the best and only way was to tell him everything. "I think I better start from the beginning."

She started from the day Arlupo walked into the house, and left out very little, telling the story in chronological order. When she was done, she begged, "Vaughn, she made me promise not to tell you, because she couldn't live with herself if you were harmed. Please Vaughn, I only told you because Lana had already told you, and I know you're too smart for me to try to hide the truth."

Vaughn spoke calmly. "But it's not for Stephanie to decide for me what to do. If I want to risk my life for her, that's *my* choice. Even in this, no one has a right to restrain a person's will."

But Jean begged him, shivering at remembering what Jargono had done to her. "What good would it do Stephie if you're *killed*? *He will kill you.* You have no idea what he did to me, *none*. And I was totally powerless."

Vaughn, thinking deeply, sensed something. "Did he do that to Lana?"

Jean looked at him surprised. "No."

"Why bother to hit her when he's much quicker with his mind? Maybe he couldn't do it to Lana."

She shook her head with growing confusion. "I don't know. What's your point?"

"I don't know, except that I think his power is stoppable. Jean, what was he searching for?"

"Vaughn, I don't know. I honest to God don't know. But he didn't find it. Stephanie said she hid it back at the cave."

Vaughn scrutinized her. Something didn't feel right. Vaughn interrogated her. "Was that her *exact* words? *Think Jean, it's important.*"

Jean started crying because, "No, I don't think so, but I can't remember her words really, only what I thought she meant…"

Vaughn rubbed the beginnings of a youthful beard. "Did she have anything unusual, different?"

"When she came to me that night, she had a beautiful blue ribbon in her hair, that was all. That's all I know." Tears streamed down her face, because she could see she wasn't being much help, and she wanted to be.

Vaughn sighed, beginning to understand what Stephanie had done. She had done as he had taught her. He shook his head at the implications. "I doubt we'll find anything, but let's clean up Stephie's room."

Suddenly, it occurred to him how Spot had been acting. "I'm a complete IDIOT! Spot!" Spot came over to his master. "Next time I ignore you, tell me to pay attention! You knew Stephanie was here way before I did!" He remembered how Spot kept handing him her clothing. Spot picked his head up and got his pat.

They took all the clothes that had been strewn across the room, and folded them up, and put them back in drawers or closets, along with various girl things. An hour later…

"There Vaughn, that's the last of it."

Vaughn sat on her bed and put the green dress she had worn last to his cheek. Spot sat in front of him and ruffed out what sounded like, *I told you so!* Vaughn realized this was the garment Spot kept taking. He looked at his dog. "I've *got* to pay closer attention to you." Spot just stared at his master.

Vaughn's heart ached beyond measure. Lana sat in front of him, watching his every move and every expression. Since she found out who he was, she never took her eyes from him.

SACRIFICIAL WOOD

"Oh God, touching her things, I can almost feel her here with me. Did they leave on foot?"

"Yes, Vaughn."

"Let me have this dress of hers. It'll help Spot to track her."

Jean shook all over as she remembered how she suffered from that evil man. She started weeping again. "Vaughn, I'm begging you, pleeeease..."

Vaughn tried to ease her fear. "I'll just follow them, that's all. But if it looks as if he'll hurt her, Jean, I have to try to stop him. I couldn't live with myself if I didn't."

Muffled growling and little arfing sounds came from the corner behind the door.

Spot was doing a big dog version of the same thing directed at Puppy.

Vaughn paused, rolling his eyes at Jean because of the dogs, and he pulled the door away. "What are you two doing Spot?"

Jean scolded Puppy, as he had perched his paws up against the rim of the trash can that was wedged into a small cubby, "Puppy, stay out of the trash! Oh my! Ha! He's jumped into the trash can!" Amused, it was a welcomed break from her grief. Lana was laughing, too. Spot was trying to pull the upside down Puppy out of the can, but Spot dislodged it, tipping it over instead. Puppy wriggled out, dragging half the trash with him.

Vaughn looked helplessly at Jean and sighed. He went over and picked Puppy up, brushing off some dusty dirt clinging to his shaggy, golden fur, and handed him to a giggling

Lana. Then he turned to Jean. "I'll clean it up." He began scooping up tissues, an older edition of *Teen Fourteen*, pieces of leftover snacks, and other trashy stuff, and dumping them back into the can, but then his fingers touched something in the pile that sent a powerful surge of feeling through him. He fished out a balled up paper that had golden threads running through it, and began uncrumpling it, saying, "What's this?"

Jean shook her head. "I don't know. It just looks like an old piece of blank paper. Wow, it's got the most beautiful gold edging. Vaughn, I've never seen it before. Why would it be in the trash?"

It was the kind of question that Vaughn felt might be important, especially because of the way the paper felt. He went over to Stephanie's small, wooden desk and sat in its chair, then placed the wrinkled paper down, trying to smooth out the creases. His hands felt as if they were absorbing power. *Such a strange feeling.* Suddenly, the creases vanished. The paper was as if it never had been squashed. *It's not blank anymore!* He looked at Jean and then back at the printing. Her face looked quizzical, but there was no sign of surprise. He eased back a bit to be sure she could see, but still no change to her expression. *She can't see what just happened! She must figure I somehow got all the wrinkles out. But...*

Vaughn decided to inspect it before saying anything. It was a letter, and he scanned the address, *Stephanie!* And signature, *Mafferan!* He could feel the powerful spirit with the letter. He knew he was holding something sacred, and so he read it carefully. Then he whispered, "My God!"

❖ SACRIFICIAL WOOD ❖

Jean, standing over his shoulder became concerned at his expression. Puppy and Spot looked back and forth at each other, and at Vaughn. Lana never took her eyes from him. Vaughn couldn't take his eyes off the letter and reread it again.

Dear Stephanie,

Long ago I came upon the two most precious things in this world; besides the Light from which I was born, The Tree of Life and my true mate who became my Queen. I found the Tree alone on top of a dead mountain. The Tree of Life, standing asleep on top of a poison mountain, like a prisoner, as I and my future wife were. As I wept upon the Tree, it sprouted, as did your Tree for you, as you wept the true tears of true grief. The day I married my Queen, we went to the top of the mountain, and the Tree had born a single fruit that glowed to us. We ate from the fruit, and as we ate, the Tree died, and crumbled to ash.

Inside the fruit was a single, beautiful seed, shiny like a black pearl. That same day, we took the seed, and with the whole town, constructed the inner basin of the sacred brass receptacle where the current Tree resides now. That same day we were married, we planted that seed together. On our first night, we slept together in the sacred room you are now in. It was the first time we had been together that way. When we awoke in the morning, the Tree of Life had spouted. Nine months to the day, our first of many children was born to the Tree of Life.

On the day of my beloved's passing away, I wept before the Tree, and it bore another fruit. As I looked upon the Tree, the leaves began to fall off, and the Tree began to sleep, even as my heart felt from my beloved's passing. But we were just the tiniest twig on that Tree, and I did not know the meaning of these things that were happening to the Tree, even though I had been taught a long time and deeply by it. I was again as a helpless child, not knowing, not understanding. Then the fruit began to glow, and the Tree became a vision. The vision I saw was you, dear Stephanie; red hair, true tears, scars not a few, and true love and faith, my daughter, and I understood that this fruit was to be put away for you. But I knew the fruit would perish. So, knowing through wisdom that the spirit of feminine goodness passes from mother to daughter, I took all the fruit and placed it with my wife's body with a prayer that the spirit of goodness would be passed down to you.

One of our children, a red haired girl, the only one to be born such, had long ago disappeared from us when she was just thirteen. We never knew what happened to her. We were stricken with grief, as we felt for each child as if each was our only child. But I know that you are her descendent.

When the Tree showed me your vision, I understood that this was the way the Tree of Life was to return to us that which was lost, so I wept again to the Tree, to God, and to my departed wife, that all had been put at peace, and that our child's life had not been in vain. Then I understood that I should place this seed in the box, and tell you of your ancient history. But as to *what* you are, that will always be your choice, my beloved daughter.

You must guard this seed with all your being. I have fastened it to a gold chain, which my wife assures me will be

SACRIFICIAL WOOD

fashionable in your time. Wear it my daughter, next to your heart, where also your beloved mate rests. At the time that you both know is right, do what you know is right with the seed. My daughter, there is no other seed like the one that you now protect. Protect it with your faith. This is not the time of the end for you, my daughter, it is your beginning. Queen Yinauqua, your mother, used the ribbon I tied the scroll with, to tie our lost child's hair. You and your mate shall always be with us through our prayers.

Your beloved father for eternity, *King Mafferan*

Weeping. He couldn't help it. Jean didn't understand. Lana didn't know how to read, so she just held his arm, staring at the words. Spot and Puppy laid their heads down on their paws, but their eyes were continuously watching Vaughn. *She's so much more than I ever realized... so much more. Oh, God, I have to protect her.*

With his new knowledge, he could feel the great depths inside Stephanie, and the enormous potential she had yet to mature into. A huge piece of their life's puzzle suddenly dropped into his understanding, and he saw everything about Stephanie within this greater perspective. A new kind of love, respect, and understanding for her was added to that which he already knew. Then, he thought of her stripping naked, something he knew she purely hated, just to protect Jean and Lana.

"Oh my God," Vaughn wept. So much knowledge, so much love, so much pain . . . all at once.

Jean finally couldn't restrain herself. "Vaughn, why are you staring at that blank piece of paper for so long and weeping so?"

Vaughn looked up. "Jean, you have to trust me on this, but the paper is full of words, but apparently, not everyone can see them."

"He's right Mommy, see?" Her little finger ran along some of the words. "They're right here."

Jean leaned on the desk, staring, "What does it say?"

Vaughn hesitated and then spoke gently, apologetically. "I'm sorry, but I don't think I'm supposed to tell you. If it was for you to know, I think you could have read it, yourself, and I think Stephanie would have told you. It's really not my place to tell anyone."

Jean bowed her head in humility. "I understand. But if it was in the trash?"

Vaughn straightened. He understood. "Then that means that the man couldn't read it either. I just don't think he would have thrown such a thing in the trash if he could have read it. He either would have kept it or destroyed it, so no one would ever possess its knowledge. No, it was just an old blank piece of paper to him. Who was he Jean?"

"You know, that's odd, because I thought for sure I recognized him, but somehow, I just can't figure it out. How do you know Stephanie could read it?"

Vaughn looked deeply into her eyes. "Because it's addressed to her!"

Jean's scalp tingled, as some kind of picture was trying to reveal itself to her mind, but she just couldn't bring it into focus. "But, but . . . that's a *very* old…"

Vaughn politely cut her off. "Please Jean, don't. I'm betting that when Stephanie realized he couldn't see the writing, she decided to hide as much as she could from him. Oh God, Jean. She's taking him to the cave, but what he's looking for is *not* there!"

Jean's eyes welled up with tears, as her hands went to her mouth. Lana's eyes got wide. She felt something. Jean asked Vaughn the obvious. "But how do you know?"

"All I can tell you is that I know from *this*." He held out the paper.

Fright painted Jean all over. "Vaughn, that means that when they get there..." she couldn't finish.

Their hearts seemed to join in that instant, as he whispered what they both knew. "Her time is up."

Lana was trying to figure out what 'time is up' meant, but she knew it was very bad. She went over to sit between Puppy and Spot, and put a hand on each doggy. They, in turn, each gave her a lick in the face, and then all three sat staring at Vaughn.

Jean continued. "Why would she do that, knowing...?" again she couldn't finish.

The answer to that question came to him as soon as he read about the Seed. *He had to have seen it, because he made her strip. But he doesn't know what he's looking at, otherwise, why head off to the cave?* "She did it to buy time, to think. Possibilities exist as long as you have time. *Look, I have go.*"

As Vaughn rose, Jean firmly put her hand on his shoulder. "*Wait* a minute. I want to talk to you, *seriously*. I may not have the sight to read that, and I certainly don't understand the things you and Stephanie do, but she's told me a lot, and I've seen her change a lot. Vaughn, the Appendaho helped her achieve something within herself. She said something about letting go and getting a new will. I know she's been different ever since."

"I know what you speak of. She came to me in," he paused, realizing how strange it would sound, but decided to continue anyway, "a dream, or vision, but it was *more* than a vision."

The look of understanding lit up her face. She asked to confirm her hunch. "AHA, when you were in the hospital?"

Vaughn was surprised. "Yes, how'd you know?"

Jean looked into his eyes, remembering, again, that horrible night Stephanie received the letter about Vaughn dying. She wanted Vaughn to feel, to see what she remembered, and somehow she knew this could be passed to him if she opened her eyes, so to speak, wide enough. So she reminded him of what she had already told him, but now it was seen by them in a different light.

"I only knew back then that she was grief stricken. Oh God, I thought she might die on the spot when she read your friend's letter, telling her that you were about to die. Then, about a week later when she came to visit, she was full of life. Somehow, I just knew by the confidence she had, that she did *something* for you. I couldn't explain her change any other way. But there was a whole change in herself, as well. Her father recognized it, too, and kept, unsuccessfully, trying

SACRIFICIAL WOOD

to dig at her, like when a foolish child finds a bug and tries to understand it by pulling it all apart. As a last resort, he kept Lana from returning with her." Lana nodded and squeezed and kissed her puppy.

Vaughn opened his eyes so she could see. "She came in spirit somehow. I owe her my life." But his words clearly meant more than the words he had just spoken.

That worried Jean. "And she owes you hers as well, Vaughn. She told us how you rescued her."

Lana burst in now, nodding profusely, remembering the images of the tremendous story. "Yeah, she did." Her look into Vaughn intensified. She was seeing something in his eyes she hadn't seen before.

Jean continued. "But Vaughn, please listen closely, I think there's good reason why Stephanie doesn't want you to confront this man. She told me at some point that he has evil power. God, I can't remember when she told me. I think he did something to my mind! I think, I think he's kind of like the opposite of what Stephanie is! She gave her will completely to God, but him to the devil. And I think only someone who has gotten that new will can fight this evil. But even she acted like she couldn't fight him. Although, he couldn't seem to directly force her to give him what he wanted. But if *you* try to fight him, *you'll lose*. He'll be able to turn your mind against you somehow, I *know* it. He did it to *me*."

Vaughn sighed a long, drawn out sigh, because the understanding she transferred to him made good sense. "You don't know what I've been through, Jean. I understand what you're saying, and you may be right. I don't know. But, that still doesn't change what I must do."

Jean was becoming increasingly more disturbed. If anything happened to Vaughn, Stephanie would never forgive her. Worse, she wouldn't forgive herself if she caused this very last important person in Stephanie's life to be destroyed. But, she didn't know what to say. "But Vaughn, maybe you should first try to do what Stephanie did before she saved you from death. I think she first had to gain that new will."

Vaughn hung his head, sure that she was right. "Jean, first of all, she had all those people helping her to understand. I don't know how to do it. I was supposed to come here and get the same help. But, besides that, I just don't have the time. Stephanie doesn't have that time, I feel it Jean. I'm being pulled like I've never been pulled before, even stronger than when I had to go save her the first time. But this time…" Vaughn looked down and folded his hands, as he couldn't finish the words. Then he took a very deep breath, and let it out slowly.

Lana suddenly understood what 'time is up' meant, because Vaughn needed to go save Stephie again from the bad man. It meant she was going to die. Tears started to cloud her little eyes, but she brushed them away, because she wanted to watch and listen. There was something growing in Vaughn's eyes that seemed important, and she could feel it.

Jean looked deeply at him. "What Vaughn? This time, what?"

He sighed deeply, trying to find strength to speak through the crushing weight. "I feel that my life, her life, our life…" Jean came up, grabbed his shoulders and squeezed, losing control and raising her voice. "VAUGHN, WHAT?"

He sighed, yet again, and took another deep breath so he could speak. "It's the type of feeling one has when they know they're facing death, and they can't avoid it. But they know they must fight with all their might, even though they know it won't be enough! We're just too young, Jean, and we don't know enough yet."

If Stephanie was able to win, she would have stopped him before he hurt anyone. She had told Vaughn of her powers when they were together in his dream. He remembered how awed he was. *I can't imagine what* greater *powers this man can have!* That ignorance alone, according to fighting theory, would cause him to lose.

Jean placed her fingers under his chin and lifted his head up, because she knew his mind was made up. "Oh Vaughn, I'll pray for both you and Stephanie. Please, you have to win, you just *have* to."

He opened his gaze into her eyes to transmit the understanding. "Wanting does not change reality."

Lana had been silently watching everything for some time, studying them closely. "Vaughn?"

He looked over into the sweet child's face that seemed much more serious than a five-year-old's abilities would allow. He noted she definitely had a powerful effect on him. "Yes, little one?"

She sniffed a tear back. "Can I pray for you, too?"

He opened his arms, and she got up and climbed into his lap, facing him. She liked his lap almost as much as his eyes. He hugged her, and she hugged him, and he felt the power of life in the little girl. He imagined Stephanie must have been the same way when she was little. Then she took his face in her little hands as before. She wanted to look more closely at what she saw, but she still didn't understand what was in his eyes.

"Yes my dear, you can pray for me, oh yes, *especially* you."

Lana grabbed him by the arm and tugged him to the floor. Then she tugged her Mother down beside him, as well. Then she went over and picked up Puppy and sat him down next to her Mother, then she took Spot by the neck and made him sit by Vaughn. She then sat down on her knees between the dogs, folded her small hands, and bowed her head. The dogs went down to their bellies, and put their heads on their paws, their eyes darting back and forth between the people, but they remained still.

Lana prayed, "Oh dear God, I love all my people; my mommy, my sister, Puppy, and I love Vaughn and Spot, too, because they are all good people. I can just see them in their eyes. Sister always helps Mommy and me, and she's *real kind*, and, and Vaughn, he always helps too, and we share secrets together, because I know I can trust him, because he's a good man. But the bad man, he's *real bad*, REAL BAD, and *please* don't let him be more bad than Vaughn and Stephie are good. Amen."

❖ SACRIFICIAL WOOD ❖

Vaughn and Jean whispered *Amen* through their tears, and even the dogs gave a muffled whine. A special peace settled into the little circle, as each of their hearts filled with feeling, and their minds laid back to watch.

The Art of Fighting

Author unknown
Publication date: 2075
Previous publication: Unknown—antiquity
or earlier. Origin: unknown
This book is a non-religious text in accordance
with government ordinance 3123.b and
is classified as an historical text.
Not to be used for instructional purposes.
MAY REQUIRE PERMISSION BEFORE PURCHASE.
CHECK GOVERNMENT I.D. OF PURCHASER

Rules:

1. Better to die fighting being what you are, than loose the battle from within.

2. With time, there are always possibilities, so never throw it away or rush to battle when time is open.

3. Procrastination is a choice.

4. Never let an angry enemy tackle you. You have two enemies: him and his anger.

5. Determine your outcome, then your enemy's.

6. Accept the consequences; better to know them beforehand.

7. It is better to strike first, when your enemy has already decided to do so, but be prepared for accusations.

8. When declaring formal war: plan; then think about your plan; then reason about it; then imagine it until you are sure you have fought the battle ten times.

9. A quick retreat often saves a miserable defeat.

10. When gaining a slight advantage over a superior force, quickness is your best ally. Press the attack now! But in a way not to lose.

11. When an enemy has well founded confidence, it cannot be dissuaded, but he often can be encouraged to overrate it.

12. When faced with immanent defeat, seek to postpone the end; time always holds the possibilities of the unknown.

13. Only a fool gambles all his strength in a single attack, unless he is in that moment going to die.

14. Never make a battle plan against overwhelming odds that you will change while fighting.

15. Better to hunt the hunter, than to be his rabbit.

16. A spider is well prepared for battle.

17. A wasp is better equipped for battle than a spider.

SACRIFICIAL WOOD

18. When you cannot be a wasp or a spider, be a mite on their backs. If they don't eventually die, you'll irritate the hell out of them, but they won't be able to touch you.

19. Moles never see the light of day. If you can take pleasure in their life, you may be able to survive. Yet, when they multiply, the gardener hunts them—so is the fight between good and evil-which can be the mole and which can be the gardener.

20. The best time to attack your enemy is right after he has won a major victory.

21. Better to die fighting honorably, than to die a coward and in disgrace.

www.TheFaithwalkerSeries.com

CPSIA information can be obtained
at www.ICGtesting.com
Printed in the USA
LVHW020541201021
700907LV00001B/2